ARIAH

B R Sanders

ARIAH

Cover art by C. Bedford.

SECOND EDITION published September 2016.
First Edition published April 2015 by Zharmae Publishing Press.

Published in Print and Digital formats in the United States of America.

This book is dedicated to the lovers I have and will have, to those I had and lost, and to those who, in my stubbornness, I didn't name as lovers in time.

Table of Contents

PART ONE:

RABATHA

CHAPTER 1

THERE ARE TIMES I still have nightmares about that first day in Rabatha. I'd come from Ardijan, which is a small place built around the river and the factories. It's a town that is mostly inhabited by the elves who work the factories with a smattering of Qin foremen and administrators. We outnumber them there. We're still poor and overworked, we still get hassled, but there is a comfort in numbers. It was a comfort so deeply bred in me that stepping off the train in Rabatha was a harrowing experience. The train, a loud, violent thing that cloaked half the city in steam, plowed right into the center of the city and dropped me off only three streets away from the palace. Even with all the steam, I could see its spires and domes. Even with all the commotion, I could hear the barked orders and vicious slurs of the Qin enforcement agents.

I was searched. My single bag of clothes and books was searched. Everything I had brought with me except my citizenship papers was confiscated, including what little money I had. I was one of exactly seven elves on that train, and all of us were detained, and all of us were robbed. On the train, the seven of us had shared a single compartment. I knew, intellectually, that the train was full of Qin people, but I was with my own, like I had always been, and the nearness of that truth was lost on me. The train station was a sea of brown skin and fangs. I came to Rabatha for training, and as is traditional I came to my mentor on my thirtieth birthday. Thirty is when we consider a child to be grown. Before I got on that train, I felt grown. I felt adult. I felt ready. But when I looked around and saw no one who looked like me, it scared the thoughts right out of my mind. I was thirty, but I felt like a child.

So it was that I arrived alone in Rabatha, penniless and empty-handed. I arrived and had the securities of my youth brutally ripped away. I also arrived in the mid-afternoon, with only a few hours before curfew to find the man who would be my mentor. My parents had made me commit his address to memory, which had been good foresight, but the shock of the train station drowned the memory of it. All I knew was that he lived in the Semadran borough, and the Semadran boroughs inevitably sprang up on west side of town. That's where the Qin like us to be. They know that magic in the westlands is stronger than in the east, and so they prefer to live east of anything and everything. I went west. I got to the borough without incident, though the walk took three hours. I was born in the summer, so it was a miserably hot day. I thought I'd die of thirst, but I wasn't brave enough to ask anyone for water, not even other elves.

I never found his place. No matter how hard I wracked my brain, I couldn't remember the address. He found me. The borough in Rabatha is cramped—it houses twice as many elves as Ardijan in half the space—but Semadran boroughs are alike all over. The center had a schoolhouse. Elvish homes were planted around it in ever-widening circles, all facing outward, like sentries. When you are Semadran and you are lost or hurt or in need, you find the schoolhouse, and eventually what you need finds you there.

I made it to the schoolhouse a little before dusk fell, just when the streets were beginning to empty. I sat on the steps, cowering in the schoolhouse's shadow. It was a stately building, two floors tall with real glass windowpanes. I don't know how long I sat there. My mind was numb, my body was sore; I was tired inside and out. I hated everything about everyone. I was well entrenched in these thoughts, the arrogant and bitter thoughts very young men think, when my mentor found me. "Are you Ariah?" he asked.

I looked up. I didn't know whether or not to answer him. I didn't know before then that Dirva was not fully Semadran. I am certain my parents didn't know. My father likely would not have cared, but it would have been a deal breaker for my mother. It would have been hypocritical of her, but she had her standards, and she stuck to them.

I have always felt conspicuous. I have always been conspicuous. There is red blood in my family, and red blood rises to the surface. Both my mother and I have her mother's green eyes. My mother even has freckles. I just have the green eyes; everything else about me is appropriately silver. My green eyes had always been an ambivalent thing for me. My father loves them, loves difference. My mother thinks them a curse. It is true that she and I got strange looks, that there were children growing up who were encouraged to play with boys other than me. And it's true that some sought me out, curious and fascinated. As I said, I was very young then, and I had not yet lived enough or grown enough to know really how I felt about my diluted blood.

When you're very young and you're different, you begin to believe that no one has ever been as different as you and that no one has ever felt that difference as keenly as you. But there was Dirva. He was a tall man and broad-shouldered, a big man. He was a dark man, with skin a deep, deep gray, nearly black. And his hair was the same color—inky black. His eyes were green, like mine, but they were green in a vibrant and forceful way, the pupils a hair too small and the irises a hair too wide. He had whites in the corners of his eyes. He was a man with blood a far sight more muddled than my own, a man who looked like he had at least a dash of mundanity in him. His blood was so muddled that my mother's suspicions took root. I didn't answer. It was the strangest thing, but I felt when I saw him that I'd seen him before. I knew I hadn't, but I felt it anyway. It made me trust him less.

He frowned and glanced out at the street. The shaper in him had cut its teeth on noticing the fear and disgust of those around him. He held out a hand to me anyway. "I am sure you are Ariah. I am Dirva. We have corresponded."

There was nothing to do but take his hand. I was there in that unknown city, alone, with no money. I could not have gotten back to Ardijan. I knew no one else in Rabatha. All I had was him. "I am glad to meet you," I said.

He laughed. Like most people, he has many laughs. This one was sharp and cold. He looked me over and sighed. "Oh, you came on the train."

"Yes."

"You have had a long day."

Suddenly the weight of it all bore down on me. I felt tears well up. Oh, it was awful; the shame of it was a force to drown in. I wrapped my arms around myself and stared at the ground. I nodded and somehow managed not to cry. I felt I would die if he saw me cry, if that was the first thing about me he saw.

He took me gently by the elbow and led me down the street. "I have had long days, too," he said. "Tomorrow will be kinder."

* * *

The next morning, I woke facing *The Reader*. The actual painting, the original. At first I thought it was a dream. When he is not working the assembly line, my father is an artist who specializes in portraits. He is something of an expert on the Nahsiyya Movement. He has copied *The Reader* himself for at least a dozen dignitaries. He invented a press to print paintings with a high level of fidelity. He prints books of art, and his books end up in Qin libraries all over. Every one of those books has a print of *The Reader* in it. In short, I was extremely familiar with this particular painting, this monstrously famous painting, which inexplicably hung on the wall in a cramped set of rooms in an elvish ghetto.

Food sizzled in the kitchen, and it smelled slightly strange. I crept out of bed, barefoot and timid, and studied the painting, which my father himself had seen only once. It had hung in a gallery in Tarquintia for a fortnight many years ago, and my father spent all of his money to get there and see it. He wanted to drink it in, absorb it, let it burn into his mind so he could replicate it again and again. No one was entirely sure what had happened to it after that. No one besides me, Dirva, and the artist.

My father's copies are excellent copies, but they are still copies. The copies couldn't quite show the way the bold lines captured movement and obscured it at the same time. The palette was brighter than in the copies—the blues and the greens burned bright and ice cold at once. I think it might have been a matter of the medium, of my father's use of ink instead of the original artist's use of oil paints. The paint gave it a dimensionality lacking in the prints. The artist slapped it on thick in ridges that cast subtle, shifting shadows. The shadows made the subject look like he was breathing, like he was just about to turn the page. I studied the figure: a black-skinned boy with black hair and green eyes. He wore a subtle smirk. He had broad shoulders and long, graceful fingers. It was a face I'd seen a thousand times before, and it dawned on me as I stood there that it was a face I had seen the day before.

Curiosity got the better of me. I crept around the corner and peered into the kitchen. Dirva was at the stove. I watched him for some time, star-struck, before he noticed me there. "You survived the night," he said. "Are you hungry?"

"I...yes?" I said, though it came out closer to a question. He glanced at me quickly. His eyes were overly expressive; you could tell precisely where he looked. He is a reserved man, but his eyes give him an air of penetrating intensity.

"Did you sleep well? Will the cot suffice?"

"Yes?" Again it came out like a question.

He turned towards me. It was then I learned he is not a patient man, that he has a brusqueness rooted to the core of him. "You seem to have some question for me. It would make sense for you to have questions, considering the circumstances. You should ask it."

"What?"

"You should ask your question."

I blinked. I likely blushed. "I don't have any questions."

Dirva stirred the food but kept his gaze pinned on me. "If you have no questions then there is little I can do for you as a mentor. Curiosity is a virtue, so say the wise."

"The wise say curiosity, in moderation and used with tact, is a virtue."

He frowned slightly. "Just ask it. Whatever it is, just ask it."

"There's nothing to..." He looked at me again. I laughed erratically, nervously, and he frowned a little more. "I have...I have just a little question for you. I guess. You don't have to answer it. I didn't ask because...I don't know...it struck me that the answer might be personal? I didn't want to pry. There's no reason for me to even know the answer, whatever it is, and..."

"Ariah. Please, just ask it," he said, turning his attention back to the stove.

So I asked it. "Is that…is that the actual *Reader*? The original?"

"Yes."

My mouth fell open. *"How?"*

"How what?"

"How is it here?"

"Where there are borders and guards, there are also smugglers, Ariah," said Dirva. "It was smuggled to me."

"It must have cost a fortune."

"I am sure it cost quite a lot to smuggle it, yes, but it cost me nothing. It was a gift." He turned away from me. He opened his mouth to change the topic.

And I couldn't let him do it. My heart thudded against my ribs. I had to know. "Is that you? Are you *The Reader?"*

He froze. His eyebrows knit together, then he sighed and looked over. "Your father is an artist. He mentioned that. You know about art. Yes. It's me." He pulled the skillet off the stove and emptied the contents into a bowl. He gestured at the table and laid out flatbread for each of us. I sat across from him and scooped up some of the potatoes and peppers in a bit of flatbread. They had been spiced with something uncommon in the Empire, which was not bad but unfamiliar. I couldn't help but stare at him. It was him, undeniably him, but he had none of the magnetism or quiet enthusiasm of the figure in the painting. The sharpness was there, the quickness, but in the painting, as a boy not much older than myself, he looked happy. Across the table, as a man approaching middle age, he seemed mostly irritable. How did one grow into the other?

"Please don't stare," he said. His eyes flicked up at me when he said it. I tried to stop, but I couldn't quite do it. I resorted to staring at him from the corner of my eye while pretending to be very much interested in the floor. He let out a short, impatient noise. "It is me. Yes, I know the painter. I trained in the City of Mages, and I knew Liro when I was young. He sent me this painting some years ago. Please don't ask me why he did such a fool thing. He was always prone to grand gestures. I do not follow art closely, but I know enough to know that, if word got out it was here, I would be very quickly robbed. Please don't say anything to anyone about it. Do not write of it in your letters to your father, for example. I do not want to be robbed. Do you have any other questions?"

I stopped chewing. I swallowed. I felt vaguely sheepish. I cut a quick glance at the painting, just visible through the doorway, then back at him. "Just one."

He flicked one hand at me, dismissively, irritably, and rested his forehead in the palm of his other hand. "Ask."

"I've always wondered. What are you reading? In the painting, what book is it that you're reading?"

Dirva looked up at me. "That's your question?"

"Yes?"

"That is an odd question."

"Well, it's, uh…it's my question."

Dirva smiled. He stood up from the table and went into the other room. I followed closely at his heels. He studied the painting and began to laugh. "I've never looked. You know in all these years, I never looked. It could have been anything. It's not really a book." He covered his mouth with his hand and looked over at me. His eyes were bright; they crinkled happily at the edges. It brought out a warmth in him that I had not thought he had. When he looked at me like that, conspiratorial, surprised, that was when I began to trust him. That's when he became my mentor, and I became his student. He laughed again. "I am not proud of this. I can't believe he painted me like this. That's not a book. That's my brother's diary. I'd stolen it. I used everything I read in there to get under his skin. He never knew I read it."

CHAPTER 2

DIRVA DID NOT have the patience to mentor me conventionally. I had expected to do the cooking and the cleaning during the day, to run his errands and do his shopping while he worked. I had expected to have some time to myself. My expectations were not met.

Dirva was employed as a translator to the Rabathan Office of Foreign Relations. He worked closely with the Qin bureaucrats who developed suggestions about foreign policy, which eventually filtered up to the Emperor. The Qin did not quite trust Dirva—no one quite trusted Dirva, not even the Semadrans—but they valued his skills with something that approached respect. He transcribed foreign documents. He worked as an interpreter for diplomats. He was conscripted with regularity to teach language classes at Ralah College for the sons and daughters of well-to-do Qin families who were interested in foreign politics or foreign trade.

To the Qin, he was his work: a cultural and linguistic resource. To the Semadrans, he was his magic: an auditory mimic and a man who had once been considered for training by a shaper. Exactly like me. He wasn't there to teach me his trade, exactly. That's not what we do. We had been paired because his mind worked the way mine did, and he could show me how to live with a mind like mine. That he was a linguist was not really important. He was supposed to help me hone my gifts, understand them, grow comfortable with them. I very much needed training. Mimicry nagged at me, surfaced at inopportune times and in odd places. When I grew nervous, I sometimes repeated what was said to me in the same voice in which it was said. More than once I'd been thrown out of places, assumed to be mocking someone. Before my training, it had already gotten me arrested twice by particularly bad-tempered Qin policemen. Shaping was even worse. I had no control over it. It was a needling curiosity, a need to know, and it was unearned knowledge that got me in trouble. I didn't always know when I'd read something, and when I was reading someone, I didn't know how to stop. This particular set of gifts I have is not common. It took my parents some time to find a match.

Dirva was supposed to train me in the skills that let me control how the magic expressed itself. I'd gotten some training in school, but school was primarily to teach literacy and math and mechanics and our history. The five years of mentorship is how we dealt with magic. Dirva was supposed to sit with me at night and drill me through established exercises. He was supposed to talk me through what scared me and what didn't. I was supposed to have the time during the day to reflect on what I'd learned, and to make myself useful around his house. That's what was supposed to happen. What happened instead was

Dirva and I had one short conversation about my gifts. I told him I picked up languages easily, both if I heard them and if I read them, and I was extremely insightful when it came to other people. He asked me if I was a shaper, and I told him emphatically that I wasn't. The Ardijan shapers had met with me, felt me out, but decided the gift was not present enough to benefit from training. He decided I would make a good linguist. He decided to mentor me in action instead of through abstract evening exercises and heartfelt conversations. I have wondered in the years since if he decided that because he had so little patience.

I became his right hand. He took me everywhere with him, and he was valuable enough to get away with it. I served as his secretary, his attaché, his note taker, and his teaching assistant. Whenever my gifts got the better of me, he stopped whatever he was doing—a meeting with diplomats, a class, shopping in the market, it didn't matter—and he had me tell him how it felt. He coached me through and told me what he did when he felt like that. The entire world waited for me to grasp his techniques. It was quite a lot of pressure, but in time it began to work.

The thing that was strange about this was that he and I grew quite close. Well, that's not so strange. A man is usually quite close to his mentor; it's a pity when a mentor and a student don't bond. What's strange is that we grew quite close, we bonded, and he wove me into the fabric of his life—but that as well as I knew him, I knew virtually nothing about his past. It never occurred to me to ask. He was a single man, just him and me in his apartment. He kept me as busy as he kept himself, so I had little time to ponder him. I got used to him, and I forgot to wonder about his blood and black hair and foreign spices. He was just Dirva. That's just who he was. I think part of me didn't want to ask. To him I was just Ariah, just myself. He never asked me about my green eyes. It didn't matter to him. I wanted the strangeness of him to not matter to me in turn.

I spent four years in Rabatha with Dirva. By my last year of training, I was happy and comfortable and making good progress. He groomed me to become a linguist like him, perhaps to be placed in an important city when my time with him was up. I felt very potentially important. I think he was happy and comfortable, too. But then his past came knocking, and life grew much more complicated.

His sister did not tell him she was coming to see him. We found her asleep on his doorstep. His apartment then was a bachelor's apartment: he had no family to insulate from the Qin, so he lived in a set of three rooms carved out of the attic of a building which housed a smuggler fronted by an ink-and-stationery shop on the first floor, the smuggler herself on the second, and Dirva on the third. The building sat on the outer edge of the district where the Semadran shopkeepers congregated. It was not an obvious place or one that was particularly easy to find, and in fact it did not even have his address listed outside. The only sign that the third floor had an apartment was a set of narrow, iron stairs discreetly bolted to the back of the building, which led to a small landing at Dirva's door. He had his mail addressed to the ink shop. His sister must have known where he lived. She must have had more than an address, because it would have taken a measure of familiarity with the district in Rabatha to know where to look. More likely, she had to have been there before to have found it.

We didn't see her until we came around the back of the building. It was deep winter the day she arrived and getting on towards dusk. The days in Rabatha never get properly cold, but at night the temperature drops like a stone. "We have a vagrant," I said.

Dirva looked up. She was wrapped in a patched coat up to her ears. Her white hair was the only thing visible. I could tell by the way her clothes hung on her that she was not a large person. The white hair and her size made me think she was a half-grown runaway seeking shelter in the district. Possibly a nahsiyya. Possibly an escaped slave from the Qin parts of town. In any case, I had assumed she was at least mostly Semadran. Dirva knew better. He cursed, which was exceedingly rare for him. "It's not a vagrant," he said. "It's my sister."

He started up the stairs before I could ask him about it. I scrambled up the stairs after him, and between the two of us, we made a bit of a racket. The figure in the doorway stirred. She pulled her head up and blinked. Her skin was very pale, a milky white. Her cheeks had a smattering of freckles across them. Her eyes were elvish—flat, broad pupils, no whites—but the pupils were ringed in a steely gray. Where Dirva's face was narrow and angular, his sister's was round and wide. His eyes were almond-shaped, one of the few decidedly Semadran things about him, but hers were ovals with deep folds. His nose was thin, hooked, and hers was flat. They looked nothing alike. I saw absolutely no family resemblance. She grinned. Her face lit up when she grinned, her emotions so raw and uninhibited that it embarrassed me. She had a grin that made me feel like I'd eavesdropped. "Lor! Was wondering when you'd get home."

She spoke in City Lothic, which I'd never heard spoken before. Dirva spoke City Lothic back. He pinched his forehead with one hand and rested the other on his hip. "Abbie, what are you doing here?"

She pulled herself upright. She was short. She had a roundness to her, frankly outlined by her close-cut City-style clothes, which embarrassed me further. She shrugged on her coat and ruffled her short, white hair. "Came to see you, you daft bastard. What else would I be doing here? What, not happy to see me? Been ages."

Dirva's eyebrows drew together, then apart, then together again. The corners of his eyes crinkled. I could feel a ripple of contradictory emotions flicker through him. He frowned at me and I marshaled my rough skills to pull the shaping back. "I am happy to see you. Of course I am happy to see you. But there's a catch, I know there is." His sister's grin turned canny. He sighed and hugged her, and then he unlocked the door.

She stared at me as he unlocked the door. It was different than the stares I usually get, something more penetrating. More overtly judgmental. It made me extremely uncomfortable.

"Hey, Lor?"

"Yes, Abbie?"

"Who's this little copper shit you got following you about?"

Dirva sighed and held the door open for her. "He speaks Lothic. He can hear you. Please stop insulting him."

She hovered in the doorway, still looking me over as she gathered her things. "So what's your story, kid?"

I blinked. I opened my mouth, and then closed it again. Dirva pulled her into his apartment by her elbow. She half-stumbled through the doorway, head cocked to one side, watching me too closely, like I was a potential threat. Dirva's sister, who had the improbably Semadran name of Abira, declared herself hungry as soon as she stepped inside. She found Dirva's armchair, the single comfortable piece of furniture in the apartment, and curled up in it. She was dusty from travel and left a trail of sand wherever she went. She seemed bored and playful, and I was left at her mercy when Dirva went to go start dinner. I took a seat at the table and made a pretense of sorting through Dirva's correspondence. There was nothing to sort through, just a handful of already-opened envelopes, and I could feel her watching me. The shaper in me fought to the forefront of my mind, reaching out to her, as curious about her as she was about me. I kept my eyes pinned to the envelopes. They passed through my hands, one after another after another in a steady, unending, and pointless march. I could feel her canniness, her curiosity. I hated the way she studied me; it made me feel meek and trapped. Periodically, she shouted something to Dirva, questions and quips for which I had no context, but her voice was distracted, and I knew I was what she really wanted to ask about.

I had hoped that when Dirva laid out the food that she would turn her attentions to him. After all, they hadn't seen each other in at least four years and likely much longer. I thought, perhaps, that her interest in me was a placeholder until he came back again. He sat down next to me and pulled the mail from my hands. He waved her over, and Abira sat on his other side, right across the table from me. I very much wanted to slink into the other room. I paid far more attention to my food than was strictly necessary.

Abira leaned across the table, her head cocked to one side. Her hair was fine and straight; it slid in lazy waves across her forehead, this way and that as she moved. She had hair like mine, but her brother's was coarse and tightly curled. "Kid, you are a copper, yeah?"

I glanced up and back down again, blinking fast. "I'm sorry, miss—"

"Miss?" she said, cocking an eyebrow. She turned to Dirva. "He's a proper one, eh?"

"...a copper what?" I stammered.

"It's City slang for someone with mixed parentage. Someone with Athenorkos and Semadran blood," Dirva said. He waved at both of us. "Eat."

I couldn't eat. My stomach was in knots. I took a piece of bread and tore it slowly to pieces. Abira dove into to the food, eating with a passion that precluded table manners. She kept talking to me and about me regardless of how full her mouth happened to be. "Still odd as all hell. What's your name, kid?"

"Ariah," I said quietly.

"That mean anything in tink-speak?" she asked.

Dirva frowned at her. "It means wild. Don't say it like that."

Abira snorted. "Gah, you're a quarter, tops."

"I'll throw you out. I know it's hard for you to show respect to anything, Abbie, but you'll have to find a way to do it."

Abira started to say something, thought the better of it, and went back to her food. "Don't seem wild to me," she said after a second. I hated that I was once again the topic of conversation. I had hoped that she would continue to press Dirva on whatever old nerve she had just pressed so that they would fight, and I could slip away.

"He isn't. Ariah's very, very well-mannered. Unlike you," Dirva said, grinning at her.

"Manners are overrated," she said. "Like education."

Dirva's grin evaporated. He tapped the fingers of his left hand on the table, a gesture I had come to notice—after four years at his side—meant he was holding his tongue. "Abbie, please."

"Rest of us turned out just fine," she said. Dirva's jaw clenched tight. He went to the faucet for a glass of water. Abira once again turned her attentions to me. "How old are you?"

"Thirty-four."

"And he's just got you stuck up here day and night with your nose in a damn book, eh? What a waste of youth. Gah, when Lor there was your age, he was…"

"He doesn't need to know, Abbie," Dirva said sharply from the other side of the kitchen.

Abira raised her eyebrows. "Oh, someone's a might protective. Guess he's red enough after all."

Dirva's head whipped around. "He is my student." His voice was a touch too even, too controlled. It made me uneasy.

"Bet you're giving him all sorts of lessons, eh?"

"Don't," he said.

I looked over at him. It happened by itself, thoughtlessly. We made eye contact, and I could feel it: shame and fear and a hot, visceral anger. I'd read him before when he'd been upset, but I'd never picked up anything like that from him. I sat up a little taller. My eyebrows shot up of their own accord, a hundred questions leapt to my tongue, and then I grew protective. Tentatively, very slowly, I reached out and tapped Abira's arm. "I'm a quarter Athenorkos," I said. I spoke Lothic, but Coastal Lothic. It's a flat language with none of the colloquial flair of City Lothic. I have never particularly liked speaking it. "My mother's mother was Athenorkos. My mother's father was a cartographer with a caravan. He met her in Susselfen and brought her to the Empire."

She turned to me, surprised that I'd spoken. "Yeah? I know a fella back in the City whose folks were like that. Must've been a grand romance, them. Can't imagine coming here to all these rules you lot lay down for yourselves were it not grand."

Dirva leaned against the counter with his eyes closed. I felt that he was grateful, but I couldn't have told you why I got that impression. I don't think it had to do with the gifts. I think I just knew him well by then, and sometimes, when you know someone well enough, you can tell how they feel without magic. I pushed on. "I don't know. My mother's father was killed before I was born. She didn't talk about him much. But she did say she'd take the constraints of the silver over the war in the South."

Abira nodded and ran a hand through her hair. "Well, hell. No arguing with that. My pa ran from that war. Always seemed a smart move to me. Hey, want to split a pipe?"

She was not talking about tobacco. "Oh. No, thank you."

"Gah, just silver through and through, green eyes or not, eh? Hey, Lor, smoke with me for old times' sake, yeah?"

"No, Abbie."

Abira sighed and leaned back in her chair, craning her neck to look at him. She was a small person, but she was the kind to take up as much space as possible. "Why not? Long trip. Could stand to take the edge off. And you should loosen up."

"It's illegal here."

"I know."

"You could have been thrown in jail."

"I wasn't though, was I? Be a shame to take all that risk and not savor it. Would make sense to smoke it all up here before I risk crossing the border with it in tow a second time, eh?"

"There is a child in the house; it's irresponsible," Dirva said.

Abira looked me over, a quick flick of her eyes that

measured me and summed me up. I'd seen Dirva do the same thing when meeting new Qin bureaucrats or Lothic dignitaries. "Hell, he's mostly grown, and it's not like that stopped our folks back in the day anyway. C'mon. It's City-grown, can't get any better."

Dirva looked over. "City-grown? Really?" Abira nodded, and to my great surprise, my mentor seriously considered consuming drugs right in front of me. He caught me staring and shook his head. "No, no, I shouldn't."

"Yeah, you should. Used to right along with the rest of us back in the City, it's not like the herb's changed any just 'cause you did," she said.

"I did not change!"

"Guess you're right. Guess you were always a selfish ass." There was a moment of heavy, sharp silence. Dirva left the room. He gave no pretense at all, just left. Abira shook it off like a dog shakes off water. She pulled a small wooden pipe and a pouch out of her sleeve. She packed herself a bowl, watching me watching her do it with a sly smile. Her fingers were quick and deft; in a few seconds the pipe was packed, and she fished a match out of her other sleeve. She shoved the pipe and the match at me. "Quick, kid, before he comes back."

I took it. I admit I was intrigued. My grandmother smoked pipeherb right up until her death. It has a rich smell, one I still associate with her and all her stories of the war in the South and her life before her silver husband swept her away up into the Empire. Thinking back on it, I'm not entirely sure how she supplied herself with it way out there in Ardijan. She was resourceful; she may have grown it herself. Still, though, she never let me have any. My parents very much disapproved of her smoking it, and she said it wasn't worth the trouble getting me into to trouble with her.

I must confess I was also intrigued by Abira. She was unlike anyone I'd ever met. She struck me as someone totally unfettered, a person with no comprehension of law. That she was Dirva's sister fascinated me. They had been raised together yet were so different. Part of me had always wanted to be wild and lawless, and that part of me had been handily seduced by Abira. I struck the match. Abira grinned and nudged me with her elbow. My heart pounded against my ribs. She elbowed me again, harder this time, and I sucked in a huge, billowing lungful of smoke. It was heavy smoke, dry smoke, which felt like it was strangling me from the inside. It sent me into a violent coughing fit. I doubled over, gripping the edge of the table for dear life. My eyes watered. I felt I was going to vomit any second. The pipe clattered to the floor.

Dirva rushed around the corner asking questions I couldn't quite hear and couldn't answer. He shoved Abira out of her chair and ordered her to get me a glass of water. He pulled me back into my seat and patted my back until the coughing subsided. I felt safer when he was next to me. Once I felt safe again, the situation struck me as impossibly absurd, and I began to laugh. It was a painful sort of laugh, one of those laughs where it seems like there's a muscle trying to launch itself out of you, and the more you try to stop, the harder you seem to laugh. Dirva snatched the glass out of her hand. "Drink this, it'll help," he said. I took the glass in both hands and drank as much of the water as quickly as I could. The pipeherb had taken hold by then. I remember having some strange epiphany about the pureness of water, which I fully believed was quite profound. "Abbie, what the hell is wrong with you?" Dirva hissed.

"Hell, I didn't know he was going for half the bowl," she said.

Dirva plucked the empty glass out of my hands. "Ariah, are you all right?"

I let out a couple of weak-sounding coughs and nodded.

"He's fine! Look at him, happy as a clam," Abira said.

I grinned and gave Dirva's sister a playful shove. She no longer seemed so threatening. "Did you bring drums? Did I see drums?"

Abira sat next to me. "Oh, sure. I'm a drummer."

"Let's play the drums."

"Do you play?"

Dirva sighed. "No, he doesn't play. Ariah, I think you should lie down."

I let him lead me to my bed. Sometime soon after that, I fell asleep.

My life before Abira's arrival had been a very stable thing and comfortably slow-paced. By that I mean that very few things happened to me suddenly. Even moving to Rabatha had not been a sudden thing. I had known for months beforehand. The train ticket had been bought five weeks before I left. My single bag had been packed a week and a half in advance. I didn't know that life could change direction so sharply so quickly. I was young enough to think there was ample time to consider any major decision, and I was inexperienced enough to think that life gave you ample time to make the right one.

I fell into a deep, black sleep that first night of Abira's arrival. When Dirva woke me the next morning, her things were still piled in his armchair, but she herself was nowhere to be found. I could feel the change in the air as soon as I woke. There was a certainty of difference, intangible but inescapable. Dirva carried in him a steely darkness that day. He was closed and hard, whatever he felt secreted away from the rest of the world. There was no warmth to him. He asked me if I was hungry. I said I wasn't. He looked at me closely. "How's your mind? Can you think straight? Have you slept it off?" he asked.

"I don't know. I think so."

He leaned against the wall and peered out the window down into the narrow alley below, his arms crossed against his chest. "There are things I need to explain to you, Ariah, and then you will have to make a choice, and you will have to make it today. Do you understand?"

"Yes?" I said, but I didn't, and he knew I didn't.

"Your mother's mother was red. Tell me, did she tell you much about the way the reds live? Families and marriage, things like that?"

"Not terribly much, no."

"You are unfamiliar with the term 'da,' then?"

"I am. I'm sorry."

Dirva shot me an impatient frown. "Why should you be

sorry?"

"I…because, well, I…"

He waved at me. "I'm going to tell you the situation, and then you can ask me for clarification if you need it. You'll get tonight to think it over, but you'll have to make a decision by morning." The fingers of his left hand drummed against his right forearm. As he spoke, as he explained himself and where he came from, he watched me closely. He wasn't reading me; I would have felt it if he were. Instead he regarded me with a deep and yearning curiosity. I knew him well enough to know that however I reacted mattered and would have consequences. I was still very Semadran then—as Abira said, Semadran through and through, green eyes be damned—so I pulled out all my silver reserve and showed him nothing at all. My face remained a perfect silver mask while he spoke. Looking back, I wish I hadn't. I wish I'd shown him something. Compassion, understanding, something. I didn't realize how vulnerable he was forcing himself to be.

"As you may have guessed by now, I grew up in the City. As anyone who has seen me can tell, I'm nahsiyya. I tell you this to say I had a different sort of family than yours, though now that you've met Abbie I'm sure that's another thing you've guessed. My mother is nahsiyya. City-bred. My father is a red elf from the mountains. My da is Semadran. You have two parents; I have three. My father's married to both of them. Ma and Da are not married to each other, but it works out somehow anyway." Dirva's dark eyebrows pulled together, and he turned towards the window a little more, a little further away from me.

"My da is not well. Abbie is here to bring me back. She's been here before to bring me back, but she says if ever there was a time to return it's now. I believe her. I'm leaving for the City tomorrow. You are welcome to come with me. The timing is not ideal for your training, I know. You are welcome to come with me, but I will understand if you choose not to. Sleep on it tonight. Think it over." He looked at me over his shoulder. "Do you have any questions?"

"Yes, I do."

He frowned. "Well, ask them."

His annoyance with me made me flustered. I ran a hand through my hair, stalling. "About your father. He is married to both?"

"Yes." His answer was short, curt. The way he said it was a closed door, but I ignored it and pushed on anyway.

"He has two wives?" This was a thing I'd heard implied in the stories my mother's mother told, a thing which had fascinated me, but a thing which I had always believed could not really be true. The truth was actually stranger.

Dirva stood minutely taller. A hardness settled on him like armor. "No, Ariah. My father has one wife and one husband. Da is a term for a male co-parent."

The words sunk in very slowly, but my mask was impenetrable, and he was not reading me, so I don't know if he could tell how much the facts of his life caught me off guard. I took a quiet second to recover. "You are close to him? Your da?"

"Very close."

"And he is not well?" Dirva frowned at me. "Yes, you

said that. Well, I...it is not a fast trip to the City, is it?"

"No, it isn't."

"So, this will take some time. The travel, and then you'll want to stay with your family, and then there's travel back."

Dirva stood still, calm and composed, but his fingers beat a twitchy rhythm against his elbows. "There's half a year left in your training, and this trip would take you out of the country for most, if not all of it. I welcome you to come, but I should say that you're quite bright, quite disciplined, and I am not convinced you actually need these last few months of training."

I swelled with pride when he said it. There was a kindness to Dirva, but he was a man who was not generous with praise. I was, and still am, a man who laps up praise like a cat laps up cream. "Oh, I need the training."

"I don't know that you do. And I don't know that I'll be in a state to teach you much of anything in the City."

"I have tonight to think it over?"

Dirva nodded and stared back out at the alley. "You have tonight."

The rest of the day was a blur. Dirva was in and out of the apartment sporadically as he and his sister tied up loose ends and made arrangements. Looking back, I think he might have been planning to return for some time. Perhaps planning is too strong a word—he may have suspected he'd have to go back. It only took him a day and a half to tie up his loose ends in Rabatha. He already had everything in place, ready to go in case he got called back. He was, after all, nothing if not practical. For my part, I stayed out of sight and tucked out of the way and agonized over the decision of whether or not to go. It was a huge decision to make, a heavy one, which changed the course of things. I felt so torn: I wanted to be there for him in a time of need, but I wasn't sure if he wanted me there. I wanted to know more about him, where he came from, but it struck me as invasive to find it all out. I wanted to travel, to see the City, to see more exotic and fascinating people like his sister, but I was afraid of the effect they might have on me. After all, in less than an hour his sister had turned me to drugs. I knew I was impressionable. My mother said it had to do with shaping, and perhaps that's true. I had the feeling that if I went with him, the City would leave indelible marks on me, and I wasn't sure I would still fit in the Empire if I let it mark me. I knew by then I was not like Dirva. He had a will of iron. He was a man that changed the world around him instead of it changing him. I was, and still am, the opposite.

More than anything, I kept thinking I needed more time to think. I wanted to talk it through with someone, but the only people to talk it through with were Dirva and his sister. Everyone else I knew in Rabatha knew him, too, and to explain my quandary meant sharing personal information about him I knew he wouldn't want shared. I mulled my choices over well into the night. I lay awake on my cot going over it and over it. I didn't sleep, and I was still thinking about it when Dirva woke at dawn. He raised his eyebrows at me. The unvoiced question demanded an answer, and I couldn't give him one. I just stared at him, terrified and paralyzed. Helpless. "I can't tell you what to do, Ariah."

"Yes, you can."

"No, I can't. I have preferences about this, strong preferences, and they are not rooted in what's best for you or your training. My preferences are personal. I don't...I don't want to influence your decision, and I know I will if I give you advice." He smiled slightly. For the first time since he laid the choices out to me, some of his warmth resurfaced. "You ought to trust your instincts more. You have a sound mind."

I dropped my head into my hands. I had spent hours thinking about the choice as it related to me. I spent seconds thinking about the choice as it related to him. I'd seen him with his sister, and I'd seen how the bond between them was a thing that brought him both deep comfort and a wealth of pain. My own future was a vague, unformed, looming thing. My future was something too fraught with unnamed failures to make sense of. I didn't know how this decision would impact it. But I did know how it would impact him. "I'll go with you."

He didn't ask me if I was sure. He didn't ask me why I made the choice I did. All he did was give my shoulder a quick pat as he passed by. That was enough to convince us both, I think, that I'd made the right decision.

CHAPTER 3

DIRVA, ABIRA, AND I took the train from Rabatha to Tarquintia. In those early days of the railroad, Tarquintia was the furthest out the rails went. We made the rest of the trip on camelback. It was a slow trek. The desert out there is flat and empty; the days of travel were monotonous. My camel and I did not get along very well, and I spent most of the time keeping my feet tucked under me so he couldn't bite them. It took us a week to reach the walls of the western border. We came to it in one of the empty places, where there was just us, the sand, and the wall. Dirva rode next to me when we got there. "Have you ever crossed the border?" he asked.

"No. I've only ever been in Ardijan and Rabatha."

"Crossing the border is something you should go into with open eyes. They will separate us and interrogate us in different rooms. They will search our things and confiscate whatever they happen to like or whatever seems valuable."

"We don't have anything valuable left!" I said. We'd been searched at the train station. They'd taken some books and whatever cash they could find. They had tried to take Abira's drums, but she managed to bribe a guard to let her keep them by trading most of her remaining City herb. It was, it turned out, one reason she'd brought it. Dirva lectured her about how stupid it was to use illegal drugs to bribe Imperial officials, but Abira pointed out it had worked more than once, and he grew silent and frustrated.

"They will find something to take," Dirva said. "They will ask us why we are leaving the Empire, if we plan to return, when we plan to return, and they will ask each of us questions about the people with whom we are traveling. To prevent you from getting detained, you should look through Abira's and my papers." He pulled the papers out of his pocket and handed them to me. "Don't lose them."

"I won't lose them," I said, frowning at him.

"It bears mentioning," Dirva said. "Remember: I am going to the City for personal reasons. Abira is returning home. You are with us because of your training." He nudged his camel forward and trotted away from me before I looked at the papers.

I had thought I would have trouble keeping everything straight. When I get nervous, when I am put on the spot, often my mind abandons me. I held the papers and wished that Dirva had not said anything. I thought it would have been easier on me. Sometimes when demands surprise me, I fare better than when I know answers will be demanded in advance. Abira's papers were on top. They were stained and creased, just a sheaf of documents unprotected. Dirva's, like mine, were protectively encased in a leather sheath, but hers were impractically naked to the whims of the world. Her name was listed simply as

Abira, with no patronymic or matronymic attached. It seemed fitting for her, this name that suggested she sprung fully-formed from the ether. She had listed her race as "mostly elf" and had left the ethnicity field blank. She had listed herself as a drummer for both her occupation and her primary magical ability. Her papers, like Abira herself, were flippant and bold and terribly unhelpful.

Dirva's papers were not what I had expected. He had always struck me as a thoroughly honest man, but his papers were full of peculiar lies. I had, by then, suspicions about the verity of his name, which would be borne out later. His address and his occupation were accurate, but very little else was. He had listed himself as half-Semadran and half-Qin and claimed he'd grown up in Mahlez, a small city in the Empire's northwest territory. He had listed no siblings and claimed his Qin father was dead. His travel history suggested he'd served as a translator for a Qin caravan, and thus had spent some time in Vilahna and the City for professional reasons. The strangest thing, though, was that he lied about his gifts. He had listed auditory mimicry as his primary ability and listed no secondary abilities at all. His gift for shaping was conspicuously absent.

I gingerly urged my camel to speed up. When I caught up to him, I handed back the papers. He caught the look on my face when I did it and let out a short, sharp sigh. "Yes, the things in my papers are not accurate," he said.

"May I ask why?"

"May I ask you why yours are so truthful?"

I blinked at him. "I...false papers are a criminal offense. I could be jailed."

"You could be jailed for anything. There are things in your papers, Ariah, which are not criminal, but could lead to detainment. You will remember what's in my papers?"

"Yes."

"Then we should make it through the border without difficulty." He gave his camel a sharp swat and sped up to his sister.

I realized what he meant when we reached the border guards. We followed the wall north until we hit a gate out of the Empire. The border guards had a different character than the Qin policemen in the cities: they were rough-hewn men, dusty and unkempt. There was a rawness, a frankness, to them which made me uneasy. I couldn't help but wonder what drew them all the way out to the edge and what about the edge kept them there. We were the only travelers there that day: it was just the three of us elves and the fifteen Qin border guards. That alone was enough to set me on edge. They separated us, five guards to one elf, and took us into separate rooms while our camels were fed and watered.

The first thing they did was search me and my bag. They had me strip to my underclothes, and one especially large guard patted me down. I was bright red the entire time, frozen and terrified. I felt exposed and vulnerable. One of the other guards poured out my belongings on the table and sifted through them. The other three guards just watched. Two of them smoked long, hand-rolled tobacco cigarettes; the air in the room was thick and hazy. The guard searching me finally finished after what felt like an eternity. "He's clear."

"His bag is clear, too," the other guard said. As he said it, I watched him slip all of my ink pens into his pocket. They were not even very good pens.

One of the smokers came forward and pointed first at me and then the table. I pulled my clothes on in frantic, jerking movements and sat down. My heart beat wildly in my chest, and the pulse of blood in my ears made it hard to hear what was said to me. Panicky sweat tickled the back of my neck. The Qin border guard sat across from me. He sat with an unruffled ease, his cigarette sleepily draped in his fingers. He took a draw on it and blew the smoke at me, then gestured at my scattered things. "You can put them away now." I threw my things haphazardly into my pack. "Tell me why you're here."

"To cross the border."

"No love for our Exalted Emperor?"

My head jerked up. "I...no, of course I...I am grateful for the life he grants me." The words were a struggle to get out. There was a smattering of rough laughter. The blood drained from my face. I was scared, hopelessly scared. I was scared enough that my fingers went numb and clumsy. "I am here with my mentor, who is traveling to the City of Mages on personal business. I am traveling with him because my training is not yet complete," I said very fast.

"What kind of personal business?" The guard spoke slowly, and his words ran together in a slight slur. At first I thought he was drunk. When I screwed up the courage to look directly at him, to face the terrible piercing sharpness of his Qin eyes, I saw that the left side of his face was viciously scarred. The scars pulled the corner of his mouth up in a perpetual grisly grin. They made it hard for him to speak clearly. They were desert scars, not battle scars. I ripped my eyes away quickly, partly out of shame for having seen the scars, and partly to keep the gifts at bay. An accidental reading would lead to nothing good for me.

"It's personal."

"Yes, you said. What kind of personal business?"

"It is not my business."

There was a slight pause. He tapped the ashes from his cigarette. "I will not ask you again."

I tried to remember the details of Dirva's papers and could not dredge them up. I knew he'd lied about his parents, and that he'd said one of them was dead, but I couldn't remember which one. "A relative is not well," I said.

"Best thoughts to the relative. You know the relative?"

"No."

"And yet you go beyond borders with him?"

"Yes."

"Hmm." The guard waved two of the others out of the room. I could not help but wonder why. He thumbed through my papers again. "There is a woman with you."

"Yes."

"Who is she? Why are you traveling together?"

"Her name is Abira. She is a drummer. She is returning home. The City is her home." I hesitated. "We are traveling with her because she's made the trip before."

"Do you plan to return?"

"Yes."

"When?"

"I don't know. It depends on my mentor's relative."

The guard smoked his cigarette in silence. I don't know how long the silence lasted, but by the time he spoke again I was drenched in sweat. He tapped my papers with a large, blunt finger. "A shaper at my gate."

I forgot to breathe. There was danger in his voice. I could hear it. Or maybe I could feel it; I'm not sure. "It is not my primary ability."

"It never is." The guard leaned forward. I stared at the table. "Tell me, Mr. Lirat'Mochai, how can I trust the things you tell me? How can I know that you have not picked what is best for you to say from my mind? I do not like to be tricked, Mr. Lirat'Mochai."

I closed my eyes, as much to keep me from reading him as to keep him from being read. I, like most of us with this gift, have a terrible tendency to lapse into magic when threatened. It's involuntary, I think—a pure reaction. Much of the training for a shaper deals with this, that when we grow scared or anxious or threatened we eavesdrop whether we want to or not. "It's not mind reading," I said quietly. "That is a misconception."

"Ah, so you admit to it." There was a rustle of cloth, and I believe just then he was performing a warding against the impurity of my magic.

"No! No, I just...no, I have not used the gift at all since I arrived at the gate. You would have felt it if I had. You've been read before, yes? It burns. You would have felt it!"

"So you say. I am pure. Me and mine are pure. We only know as much about your so-called gifts as you tell us. Yes, sometimes the intrusion burns. But what if sometimes it doesn't? How would I know? I wouldn't. You and yours keep secrets from me and mine. I understand why. If I was like you, I would too. But, Mr. Lirat'Mochai, you must understand the position this puts me in. How can I trust you?"

"If you're that worried I am dishonest, why not employ a shaper here?"

The guard laughed. "And trust that shaper to tell us the truth about you? Elves will stick together. No, that would be even more dangerous for us. But there are ways to ensure loyalty. I could, for instance, detain you, get you reassigned here, and work you under threat of prison if you don't tell us the truth. It's not perfect, such a thing. It does not prevent you from keeping things secret. And it certainly does not make my life or the lives of my men easier. All the time we'd lose just warding you off; think of all the lost time. But I could do it. Should I do that, Mr. Lirat'Mochai?"

"I do not believe so, sir," I said. My eyes were still screwed shut. My voice was soft and trembling. "It is my secondary ability. I am not a strong shaper. I would be of little use to you."

"You are of little use to me now."

I dropped my face into my hands. "Are you going to detain me?"

"I haven't decided." Without another word, he left the room. I was alone but for a disinterested border guard posted at the door, one who I understood without having to be told would kill me if I tried to escape. I don't know how long I was left there alone. There was nothing in me but the wordless panic, a visceral terrible thing that just kept on and on. I felt like I was being strangled from within, that my heart would explode at any moment, and time ceased to really matter. Eventually, the door opened, and the scarred guardsman told the man at the door I was free to go.

It was approaching dusk when I left the building. The sun sat low on the horizon, bloody and wounded. Dirva was waiting for me, flanked on either side by guards. I was a wreck, and I'm sure everything could be seen on my face, but his was meticulously impenetrable. He showed nothing at our reunion.

"Ariah, come with me," he said. He thanked the guards for their time and their protection of the Empire's borders and wished them pleasant days ahead in flawless Border Qin. His voice was strong but deferent. His carriage was tall but compliant. As he led me to our camels, I could feel the guards watching me. I wanted desperately to turn and see them, to feel them out. Dirva kept an iron hand on the back of my neck and forced me to look forward. I am grateful for that still.

Abira stood with our camels. She helped me secure my pack to the saddle and coaxed the camel down so I could mount it before she mounted her own. She held the reins of my camel in her hand and led him along beside hers. We passed through the gate into the narrow strip of badlands, which separated the

Empire from the City. We rode in silence for an hour or two—long enough for night to fall and the gate to turn into nothing more than a dark spot in the distance.

We spoke again as we made camp. Dirva set up our tent, and Abira built a fire to stave off the night's chill. I beat a stake into the ground and tied the camels' reins to it. She waved me over to sit next to her. She looked grim. "You all right? Lor said you had a time back there."

"I'm all right."

Abira looked me over. She smiled slightly and patted my shoulder. "You're a good kid. You owe me big, you know."

"Why?"

"I traded my drums to get you out of there."

PART TWO:

THE CITY OF MAGES

CHAPTER 4

IT TOOK US two days of travel through the Inalan badlands before we reached the City walls. We sold the camels to an Inalan man lingering just outside the city. I steeled myself for another round of suspicious Qin searches as we were ushered into the City. The City of Mages is a Qin protectorate and had always been discussed as thoroughly Qin by those in the Empire. I assumed it functioned as a bastion of Qin culture and governance even if it was not technically part of the Empire. I was both right and wrong.

We entered through the City's East Gate. On one side of the walls was the emptiness of the badlands; on the other side was a loud and bustling city. Peacekeepers lazily walked the tops of the walls, peering out at the desert for nothing in particular. Dirva, Abira, and I were waved through. We came to a narrow corridor of stately stone buildings. Awnings had been hung against the sides of the buildings, and tables were laid out in neat rows in the shade. A handful of peacekeepers stood here and there, each with a crossbow strapped to his back. Each was Qin.

We were waved over to one of the shaded tables by

fox-faced red elf with ink-stained hands. She wore the same uniform as the peacekeepers—a set of official Qin robes, which were slightly out of date compared to those in the Empire—though she lacked a crossbow. "You all speak Qin?" she asked. She spoke perfect High Qin. She had the ease of a native speaker with it. I found it disorienting, hearing that language come out of her face.

"Yes," said Dirva. He slid his papers across the table to her, and Abira and I followed suit. She flipped through our papers. She smiled and glanced up at Abira. "Welcome home." She said this in City Lothic.

"Glad to be back," Abira said.

The red elvish border guard raised her eyebrow. "No love for the Empire?"

"Not a bit."

The improbable border guard laughed. "Well, it's got no love for us either, eh? You traveling with Imperials?"

Abira shrugged. "They're elves, right? Long story anyway."

"Fair enough." The border guard picked up a large, well-worn stamp, smashed it onto a pad of black ink, and stamped Abira's papers. She turned to me and Dirva. When she spoke to us, it was in Qin again. "Reasons for entry?"

"Personal," Dirva said. "Ariah is my student."

She stamped out papers and handed them back. "Enjoy your visit." As I started to stand, the border guard caught my eye. "Don't you and yours have a saying? Something about keeping your gifts secret?" she asked in Semadran.

I blinked at her. "I'm sorry, what?"

Dirva leaned across the table. "I know a man." She waved us off and beckoned over a new immigrant.

"Dirva, what was that? Was she an official?" I asked as we stepped into the crowd.

"She is, yes. This is not the Empire. The Qin control the government, but there aren't that many Qin here. They need bodies to fill the positions. They'll take anyone who is not nahsiyya as long as they are either Qin or they were born here in the City." He pulled me out of the path of a fruit cart. "She was trying to tell you to get your papers forged. She was trying to tell you to keep your shaping undeclared."

"It's illegal."

"Perhaps, but if you'd done it, Abira would not have lost her drums," he said. He left it at that.

We walked deeper and deeper into the City. The East Gate spits you out into the Qin Quarter. It is a strange place for someone born and bred in the Empire. The City is a populous place built on a small square of land; the buildings are solid stone and built tall, story upon story upon story. The streets are narrow. In the Empire, cities sprawl. The buildings are predominantly adobe and rarely more than one story. Only the most important and official buildings are made of stone. The streets are wide with plenty of space for carts and rickshaws. The Qin are a people who like open space. We Semadrans in our ghettos pile on top of each other, struggle through thin alleyways, but the Qin take up as much room as they can. But there in the City, they are penned in like a herd of livestock.

We walked fast, heads down. If it makes sense, the Qin in the City are somehow more Qin than those in the Empire. I think it's to do with them being outnumbered and not quite as in charge of things as they'd like to be. They are more religious and more vocal about it. Every third building had an Eye of the Exalted, intricately worked in silver, bolted above the doorway. Everyone's hair reached their elbows. The hoods of their robes were universally pulled up. As we passed through, whispers crowded us. Nahsiyya, impure, ghalio, tinker—whatever they had to say was said. Abira's face grew redder and redder as we walked on. Dirva had her by the elbow in a grip tight as a vice. I think he was reading her, because every time she started to turn or open her mouth, he told her under his breath to keep walking.

All quarters of the City open into the Main Square. The Magi who supposedly built this city had a reverence for stark geometry. The streets are precise, grid-like, the width proportional to the density of buildings. Each quarter is a perfect square with hundreds of squared blocks embedded within it. At the heart of the City is the Main Square, an open plaza paved with long slabs of stones intricately fitted in a dazzling fractal. Seen from above it is something almost religious in nature. Seen from the ground, especially when the Square is somewhat empty, it can be disorienting and dizzying, the way going down a very long, unbroken flight of stairs can be. The Square is the seat of City government: the courthouse takes up much of one side, and Sanctuary takes up another. Next to Sanctuary is a Qin temple. The City Library—a building of stark and incomparable beauty—overshadows the entire city on the Square's northern edge. The City Library has a timelessness woven into its stonework. It is a building that I found overwhelming in its size and perfection. Every angle is exactly 90 degrees. Every face of stone is exactly smooth, down to the last infinitesimal speck.

All the grandeur of the Square is undone by the shambling building struggling to stay upright on the south side. It is a patched thing, with walls made of hunks of wood, sheets coated in dried mud, anything that could be nailed to the failing bones of the building. Parts of the structure were still stone, but much of the original walls now lie around the house in crumbled boulders of varying sizes. The roof sagged heavily on one side. A set of platforms had been secured with some bare competence to the outside of one of the sturdier walls. A pair of very thin youths sat on it, smoking and peering out at the falling night. I could feel them watching us as we crossed the Square. This building had a defiance to it, a willful sense of survival, like it dared the stately institutions in the rest of the Square to knock it down. Abira grinned wide when she saw it, and I knew this had been her home. She and the shambling, careless building had the same spirit.

When we were halfway across the Square, one of the youths on the makeshift balcony stood up. The way the light fell cast him as a silhouette, an empty spot of black. He whistled. The sound was piercing, sharp, and carried through the Square, which grew steadily emptier as the sun set. Abira laughed and waved her arms. Beside me, Dirva sighed. There was an electric tension in him. He took Abira's elbow and drew her over. "I'm going to Da. Can you get Ariah settled?"

"C'mon, you're not going to see them?"

"I'll see them," he said. "Just not tonight. Can you get him settled?"

Abira pulled her arm out of his grasp with a sharp, sure jerk. The violence of her movement surprised me. She was quiet for a long second. "Yeah. All right. I'm bringing everyone by tomorrow. We're a family, right, you can't be here for Da without being here for the rest of us, too."

Dirva was, to my practiced eye, visibly relieved. He turned to me. "Abira will get you settled. I will come by tomorrow morning and make sure you are all right." I nodded. "Ariah, thank you for coming here."

I smiled and looked away to hide it. I may have blushed. "We are cut from the same cloth."

"Still," he said, "thank you for coming with me. I will see you tomorrow morning."

Abira and I watched him walk the Square. He disappeared into the crowds on one of the eastern streets. "He likes you," Abira said. There was a roughness in her voice, which made me wary.

"He's my mentor. We're cut from the same cloth."

"Yeah, that must be a tink thing. I don't know why you keep saying it," she said, shouldering her pack. "At least he likes somebody. C'mon. It's a long walk from here to my place and I'd like to crash before dawn breaks. Let's get you settled, kid."

I had hoped in vain that wherever I was to be settled for the night was a safe distance away from the decrepit monstrosity in the Square. I was wrong. As we walked steadily towards it, on a course of inevitable collision, dread sat heavier and heavier in the pit of my stomach. I began to suspect—for the first time since I'd agreed to travel with Dirva—that perhaps I should have stayed put in the Empire, training be damned.

A bright burst of laughter rang through the air when Abira and I drew close. One of the people perched on the balcony swung himself down to the ground, agile as a monkey. He was fast, and he ran to Abira and hugged her before I had a clear sense of what was going on or who he was. He was a blur of dark skin and red hair.

"Oh, Abbie, you're back!" he said. By virtue of the gift of mimicry, I suppose, I pay a lot of attention to people's voices. His voice was an odd blend of quiet and forceful, deep and soft. His was a baritone voice that was surprising given that he was not a large man. He pulled back away from her just enough to see her face. They held each other close and spoke like no one else was around. "He stayed behind, didn't he?"

"No, he came," Abira said. Her voice held surprise in it, and triumph. She stepped back and pulled me over. "And he brought this with him. Ariah, that's my kid brother, Sorcha. Sorcha, Ariah. Ariah's gonna crash at the squat house."

Sorcha noticed me for the first time then. He looked me over, up and down, measuring and final like Abira when I first met her. He has an extraordinarily expressive face, and I could read his mind without help from any gift; anyone could have.

He looked me over, he smirked at my Semadran clothes, the stiffness of my posture, and then he grinned a silent proposition. I burst into nervous laughter. His eyebrows flicked up, and his grin grew that much more canny. Abira shoved me towards him. I landed about two inches away from him. We saw exactly eye to eye; Sorcha and I were exactly the same height. "You get him settled in, would you?" she said. "I just want to get back to the Refuge and crash already."

"You could crash here for the night," Sorcha said. I had long since dropped my gaze and was peering idly out at the Square on no pretense at all, but I could feel him staring at me as he said it.

"No, I'm all right," she said. "Fond memories and all, but my roof don't leak. It's all yours."

She left me there with her younger brother. He ran a hand through his hair—a bright, shocking red—and nodded towards the dilapidated house. "Well, let's get you in, get you settled. Your name's Ariah?"

"Yes," I said tentatively.

"Well, is it or isn't it?"

"It is. Ariah. Ariah Lirat'Mochai. A pleasure to meet you," I said, holding out my hand. We were still standing too close together, and it was awkward, holding my hand out in the thin thread of space between us.

He took my hand. "Yeah, sure. Same. You hungry? Thirsty?"

I stole a quick glance at the disheveled house. "No. Just tired, I think."

He ushered me inside with an arm draped around my shoulders. I didn't know how to react to that, so I chose not to react at all. Somehow, the interior of the building was worse off than the exterior. He made no apologies for it. Inside, a dozen or so scrawny, hard-eyed youths milled around, all of them obviously of mixed heritage. "This is the gang," he said. "The Natives. Nahsiyya to a man, and all City-born. With your eyes you'll fit right in." He whistled the same piercing, sharp whistle as he had out in the Square. "Hey! This is Ariah. He's bunking with us."

A woman with creamy skin and wild, woolly black hair poked her head around a door frame. I felt my throat close up at the sight of her. I was terribly attracted to her. "You vouching, Sorcha?"

"Yeah. You'll never guess where I found him."

"We can all guess where you found him," said a lanky girl with Qin eyes. She sat in the broken shell of what had once been a window, one leg trailing to the street.

"No, you really can't. I'd lay a bet on it, but I'm not so heartless that I'd take everything you got. Caddie, hey, you got to hear this." The attractive woman with the wild hair came back into view. She leaned in the doorframe, her chin held high and her face stony, expressionless. "Found him with Abbie," Sorcha said. He was savoring it, the delivery of all this news. "Lor came back, and he brought this fella with him. Caddie, he *came back*."

"What? Really?"

"Yeah."

"Then where the fuck is he?"

Sorcha shrugged. "Think he's with the folks already. Abbie said he bolted. Left this one with us." Sorcha leaned back, angling his body to face the Qin-ish girl in the window. "You guess that? Eh?"

The girl scoffed in feigned disinterest.

"I'm gonna get him settled," he said. He took my hand in his and started towards a set of stairs I did not trust in the least.

Cadlah whistled. "No one settles here unless they're with us."

"Aw, c'mon."

"My house, my rules," she said.

"He's on loan!" Sorcha said.

"No one settles here on loan," she said. "He wants to sleep here, he's got to abide the rules. Got to join up."

I was tempted to say that I did not actually want to sleep there, that I was being forced to sleep there, but I held my tongue. Sorcha sighed. He let go of my hand and pushed me towards Cadlah. "Fine. Whatever. I know you; you're just doing this 'cause you like stabbing folks."

My head whipped around to face him. "What?"

He pointed to his ear. The top of his ear was pierced and threaded with a thick gold ring. "Mark of the Natives, right, and now you're getting one, too."

Cadlah pierced my left ear. Oh, it was terrible. She sat me down in the kitchen—easily the best-maintained room in the squat house—and pulled a bottle of whiskey and a set of tools wrapped in leather from a cabinet. The tools were medical in nature: a clamp and a long, vicious needle. It also held a set of gold rings. The needle was sharp, but harrowingly thick. She poured a glass of whiskey and dropped in the needle. "What's your name again?"

"His name's Ariah," said Sorcha.

"Right. Ariah, we got rules, yeah? You want to stay here, you got to abide by them." She looked me directly in the eye as she laid them out, counting them on her fingers as she went. I stared right back, bloodless and on the verge of panic. I, like most with a tendency towards shaping, do very badly with pain. The fact that she was about to hurt me very much undermined that nascent attraction I'd harbored moments before. "One: cause no problems in the house. Don't pick fights with the rest. Two: bring no problems to the house. Last thing we need is a peacekeeper sniffing around. The courts are always a heartbeat away from demolishing us and then we're on the street. Keep your nose clean out there. Three: stay clean. Addicts always end up breaking those first two rules. Give the poppy dens a wide berth. Got it?"

"Yes." It came out half-whispered, strangled.

She narrowed her eyes at me. "You agree?"

"Yes."

"Good." She made me shake on it, narrowed her eyes once more to make sure I knew she was serious about it, and reached for the needle. She grabbed my ear with the clamp, which had narrow holes worked into its feet. I had a moment of panic and tried to stand up, but she held me in place with that damned clamp. I squealed in pain. She scoffed at me. "I've not even pricked you yet," she said. And then, with a sure and steady hand, she shoved the needle through my ear. I howled, but still she wouldn't let me go. She told me to keep it down, but I couldn't. The faces of the other gang members crept around corners and watched me weep. It stung worse when she fed the ring through. She clamped the ring shut, patted me on the shoulder, and told me it was official. Now that I was appropriately wounded, I was allowed to sleep in that awful place.

Sorcha frowned at her and shooed the other Natives away. None of them ever let me live that undignified moment down, by the way. He wrapped his arm around my shoulders again and led me up the stairs. His room was private by virtue of the length of his tenure with the Natives and the amount of money he contributed weekly to their communal pantry. Room, though, was a very generous term. Space, as I have mentioned, is notoriously tight in the City of Mages, and it's even tighter someplace like the Natives' squat house, where half the space is not structurally sound. His room was really more a closet. It had exactly enough space to hold a narrow mattress and a single chair. Planks of wood had been nailed to the wall in one corner, and the shelves held Sorcha's clothes and other sundries. A tall, heavy mirror with clouded glass leaned against the far wall. Tacked above it were a series of sketches of someone who was unmistakably Sorcha, done in an oddly familiar hand. A Semadran lamp—a well-constructed one, which operated by windup clockworks—hung on a peg nailed above his bed. It was the single source of light. All in all, it was a cell, but one which was well kept and inviting. "Right, drop your bag wherever. You want something to take the edge off your ear?"

"I'm all right," I said, but I wasn't. I could feel the blood oozing out of the wound, and it made me lightheaded and nauseous.

"The hell you are. 'Bout to swoon, you are." Sorcha rummaged among his shelves and pulled out a pipe and a satchel of pipeherb.

"No, no, I'm all right!" I said.

"Not yet, but you will be. Come with me." He stuck his pipe and the drugs in his vest pocket, threaded an arm through my elbow, and led me out of the room. Down the hall was another set of stairs, ancient stairs of crumbling stone which had once led to a third floor, but which now led to the makeshift roof. He led me out, guided me across the "safe spots," and goaded me until I jumped down onto the platform he'd been on when I'd first arrived in the Square. Night had fallen properly by then. The only people in the Square were the Natives. It felt private. The night, like all desert nights, carried in it a crisp coldness. My coat had been confiscated at one checkpoint or another, and I sat in the dark with my ear aching and my teeth chattering. Sorcha laughed and told me to stay where I was. I told him I wasn't going anywhere. He scaled the wall and hopped back down a few minutes later with his clockwork lamp, a spare jacket, and a violin. "Here. Wear this." He turned the lamp on and inspected me once I'd pulled on the jacket. "You'd cut a figure in City clothes. You're built like me. That fits you right well." He plucked a string of the violin as if to tune it.

"So, you run with Lor, do you?"

"I'm Mr. Villai'Muladah's student," I said.

"His name's Lorcani." He said it with a resigned disgust, like it was an argument with me he was already sick of having. "What's he teaching you exactly?"

"How to manage the gifts."

"Tink stuff."

"Yes."

He plucked a string. He glanced at me out of the corner of his eye. "You know he's like me, yeah? Nahsiyya. Mongrel through and through. He's not Semadran proper."

"I think he is," I said. "He's in the boroughs. He has a student. We're picky; we turn people out. Maybe blood doesn't matter as much as everyone thinks it does."

Sorcha frowned and turned back to this violin. "I'm telling you, he's not Semadran. So, what's your story?"

"I don't have a story."

"Everyone's got loads of stories. Why'd you come all the way out here? With Lor, I mean. Considering why he's here."

"It seemed the right thing to do." I poked gently at my ear. Sorcha clucked his tongue at me and batted my hand away, citing the threat of infection. I drew my knees into my chest and stared out at the falling night. From the edge of my vision, I saw the orange flash of a lit match. Sorcha drew on his pipe and handed it to me. I was alone, in a strange place. My ear stung fearfully. I was bone tired. And there was something about Sorcha I trusted. He was one of those people where right from the start there was a bond. A friendship sprung up fast, easily, all on its own, without any effort on either of our parts. There was a simple consonance between us. I knew he and I were different from one another. I knew what the grins meant, what they signaled. And it should have given me pause. It should have made me uneasy. But honestly it didn't seem to matter much. I took the pipe with little hesitance. I smoked a little and fell into a coughing fit. Sorcha patted me on the back, laughing quietly, until it subsided. And by then the herb had taken hold, and I didn't care as much about the pain. No one talks about this, but it's an open secret among shapers: drugs dull the gift. Herb slows things down, closes you off, and lets you relax into a bit of privacy. It made me less aware how evident my pain was to Sorcha, which made it matter less to me.

Sorcha played the violin. He sang a little. His voice did not change much between speech and song; it was situated somewhere between the two naturally. I settled against the wall of the squat house, wrapped in his jacket, letting the music wash over me. It didn't take very long for the fatigue to get the better of me. I think I may have fallen asleep; I'm not sure. Eventually, though, Sorcha tired of the violin or the outdoors or both. He elbowed me, and I started. "Want to crash proper? You look frightful tired."

"Yes, I think so." He laughed, and I looked at him in confusion. "What?"

"The way you talk," he said. He shook his head. "It's all proper. And you sound human, you sound mundane the way you talk. It's just odd." He laughed again.

I laughed with him. "If I stay here long enough, I'll end

up sounding like you."

"Yeah?"

I nodded.

"How long would it take you?"

"I'm not sure. A week, maybe two." He scoffed. I considered not telling him, but then it came to me that he was not Semadran and did not hold Semadran standards of politeness. "I'm a mimic."

"You are not."

I glanced over at him. I grinned. The herb may have still been idling in my blood. "Want to crash proper? You look frightful tired." It came out in his voice.

He blinked at me. His eyebrows flicked up. "Well, shit. Guess you are at that. How do you do that?"

"Oh, well, mimicry is one of the forms of magical expression which…"

"No, I mean what does it feel like?"

"Oh." I reached up to poke at my ear. He swatted my hand away. I'd never been asked that. It's not the way Semadrans discuss magic. We teach it, we theorize, but we don't discuss it in any personal way with anyone besides our mentors. "It feels easy, I guess. Sometimes…sometimes it's a simpler thing to mimic. Sometimes it feels strange to speak in my own voice. Sometimes it feels like my voice is a pretense, so it's easy to slip into someone else's. But it's not always easy to slip back out. And if I don't, things get…sometimes they get confused. Does that make sense?"

"No, not really," he said, but he smiled as he said it.

"You're an odd bird."

"I know."

"Good on you."

I had a strange urge to thank him. I stood up instead and kicked idly at the wall. Sorcha walked to the edge of the platform, took a running start, and scrambled up the wall. He leaned over and offered me his hand, dragging me bodily up and over the edge. He was a good deal stronger than he looked.

I followed him back into the squat house. "Where am I sleeping?" I asked.

"With me."

"What?"

He glanced over his shoulder. "What do you mean 'what?' It's either with me or with someone else. Not much floor space available. You got the ring, fella, you're a beggar now. No room to choose, eh? C'mon, I don't bite. Got no bedbugs. Got a wall and a door away from the rest, which is a good deal round here."

"What about privacy?"

"Privacy is overrated. C'mon. I got to get up early. Prynn makes me play at the crack of dawn, and you're so tired you can't hardly see straight."

I underestimated what he meant when he said that. I followed him in and untied the bedroll I'd used on the trip out. Sorcha hung his lamp on its peg. I heard the rustle of cloth and thought it was a blanket. I sat back on my heels to find a good spot to roll out my bedding.

"Oh, for fuck's sake, you're not sleeping on the floor."

I looked over my shoulder to tell him it only seemed polite, that I was already an imposition, but I couldn't get the words out. He was naked. Unabashedly so. I blinked once or twice and whipped my head away. I swallowed and found I still could not conjure up any words. It was, in fact, the first time I'd been in a room with a naked person since, perhaps, my birth. Certainly I had not been in the same room as someone in that state in my conscious life.

"Look, you want the inside or the outside?"

I hastily rolled up my bedding and made for the door, my chin tucked down and my eyes pinned to the floor. I was almost there when Sorcha caught me by the wrist. "This is improper," I croaked.

"What's improper is you being such a dainty priss. Come on, man, let's just get some sleep. I'm the youngest, yeah? I'm used to sharing."

"I'm not. We don't. I...you're naked!"

"Well, yeah."

"I can't."

Sorcha sat on the bed. He leaned against the wall with his arms resting idly on his knees. He'd chosen a place in the small pool of light from his lantern. From the corner of my eye I could see the smooth, unbroken lines of his body. "Can't what?" he asked.

"I can't share a bed. It's not done."

"Really? Not even with your brothers and sisters?"

"I'm an only child."

"Oh."

"Yes, so I should really just…"

"So, what, you just up and bolt whenever you're done fucking?" he asked. I glanced over. He was stretching, his arms snaked up the wall and his chest pulled tight and tall. He caught me looking and grinned.

I turned a deep red and stared at my feet. "That's not done, either."

Sorcha laughed. "Oh, sure, me neither. Certainly wouldn't ever, no. Sure, Ariah. Look, just curl up and get some rest, eh? You can have my spare blanket all to yourself. We'll have to share a pillow, though."

Now, I have always been impressionable. It has always seemed to me that to go with the flow of a situation is more prudent than to hold steadfast to arbitrary rules. And I was very tired, and perhaps still a little stoned. The mattress didn't look like much, but I'd just spent weeks sleeping on bedrolls so thin they might as well have not existed, or trying to sleep sitting upright in the train since the elves' cars never have bunks. As impressionable as I was, there was yet one thing that held me back. "You're naked," I said. I just blurted it out, my voice horrified and slightly shrill.

Sorcha laughed. "Fucking hell, that's what's keeping you on the floor?"

"Well, I…yes?"

"I'm not sleeping in trousers. Gets too hot keeping them on. C'mon, you've got your own blanket. I'll keep myself to myself. Inside or outside?"

I opted for the outside. I waited until Sorcha slid in and

cut the light. He gave me plenty of room and fell asleep quickly. I lay on my back and stared up at the ceiling. I had his spare blanket tucked tightly around myself. I started the night fully clothed down to my socks. I listened to the formidable creak of the squat house, the patter of feet outside the door. It was a loud place. The night was cool, but his room was small and had no window. Sorcha alone was enough to warm it up. The blanket he'd given me was a Lothic wool thing, thickly spun and tightly woven. Between his body heat and the effectiveness of the borrowed blanket, I grew first comfortably warm, then uncomfortably hot, and then I began to sweat and could not fall asleep. I took off my socks. A little while later I took off my shirt. Halfway through the night, blushing furiously in the dark, I slid off my pants. So it was I spent my first night in the City of Mages: ear freshly pierced, the smell of pipeherb still lingering in my hair, sharing a bed with a naked stranger, with my Semadran clothes in a pile on the floor.

CHAPTER 5

SORCHA WOKE ME only a few hours after I'd managed to fall asleep. He sat up and shook me awake by the elbow. I have never woken easily, and left to my own devices would have slept fully half the day away. But, as he had mentioned the night before, Sorcha had a standing appointment in the early hours of the morning, and apparently he'd decided that I was to make said appointment with him. "Hey, wake up. Prynn's isn't close and I don't want to have to run there, yeah?"

I pulled his borrowed blanket over my head. I was not awake enough to really understand where I was. I was not awake enough to remember I'd met him the night before. Sorcha climbed over me. "Gah, you snore," he said. "You could've mentioned that. Wake up, dammit!" He kicked me in the back. I responded by shuffling over onto his side of the bed. It was warm, and it smelled like honey. It was really very pleasant.

There was a burst of cold air as he ripped the blanket off of me. I was mercilessly thrown into consciousness. Sorcha grinned down at me. He was bare-chested, and his pants slouched lazily around his hips. They were, as yet, unbuttoned. He looked wicked and brilliant and predatory. He poked my pile of clothes with his foot. "What's all this then, Captain Modesty?"

I pulled the blankets up around my chest. I felt exposed. "I got hot."

"I told you." He held out a hand. "C'mon, we got to get out of here. We're gonna be late."

I let him pull me up. "Late for what?"

"Got a set with Prynn and Tayvi. Can't miss it. If I missed it, he'd...look, I just can't miss it, yeah?" He pulled a shirt on and tucked it into his pants.

I sat back down on the mattress. "You should go without me. I wouldn't want you to be late."

"What're you going to do? Hide in this room?" That was exactly what I'd hoped to do. "Nah, you're coming with me. Get dressed!"

"Fine, fine."

I reached for my clothes, but Sorcha's hand closed around my wrist. "For fuck's sake, not in those. Here." He dropped a pile of his own clothes into my lap.

"What's wrong with my clothes?"

"I have standards is what's wrong with them. Just wear mine." He handed me a razor. "And shave off that scraggly mess you're trying to pass off as a beard, yeah?"

"What? No!"

He shrugged on a high-collared vest and looked at me over his shoulder. He fixed me with a stern look, one that bore no questioning. One that I'd seen on Dirva's face countless times. The sudden resemblance between them made me laugh. "What?" he asked.

"You look like your brother when you make that face."

He laughed with me. "Oh, I don't look nothing like Falynn."

"Who?"

"Falynn. My brother, Falynn. We don't look nothing alike."

"No, I meant Dirva," I said. I was reading him a little as I spoke. "I meant your brother, Dirva."

"Oh," he said. "Hey, stop it with the prying eyes, would you? Shave and get dressed."

Caught, abashed, I followed his directions. I shaved haphazardly in the dark and pulled on his clothes. I couldn't help but think about what I'd eavesdropped: at the mention of Dirva he had turned hard, irritable, and confused. I followed him out of the squat house. We were the only ones awake. When we were outside, Sorcha dawdled by the door. "Aren't we late?" I asked.

"Yeah, but..." He peered out into the Square. He whistled, and someone else whistled back. "Yeah, just had to wait for Caddie to get back. Can't leave the little ones on their own, right?" He started off, towards the south end of the Square.

I walked with him, but craned my neck to catch a glimpse of his sister. I saw nothing but the soft yellow glow of the streetlights. "She's just getting back?"

"Tables run all night."

"What tables?"

"Card tables."

"Sorcha, she's not…is she a gambler?" I ducked close to him when I asked it, very much scandalized.

He laughed. He wrapped his arm around my shoulders, charmed, I think, by my naiveté. "I don't know that I'd call her a gambler. Gambling makes it sound like she might lose. Ariah, she's a card sharp. Keeps the squat house afloat practically single-handed. Gets it from Pa."

We walked deep into the musicians' district of the South Quarter. It was populated predominately by red elves who ran from the war in the South and blue elves who'd run from whatever it is in the forest they run from. The South Quarter had no order to it—it was all chaos, with some streets already alive and bustling before dawn and some that did not wake until noon. The edge of the quarter, which bordered the Qin quarter, was home to card and drug dens. Brothels were sprinkled throughout. On the other end, where the South Quarter met the West Quarter, which the locals called the Tinker's Borough, blue elves felled Magi buildings and grew gardens in their place. In the heart of the South Quarter was the musicians' district. It was there that I saw my first satyr. I saw several of them on that first morning's walk to Prynn's apartment. My mother's mother had spoken of them when I was young, but I had thought them legends. The first one I saw leaned against a building, impossibly tall, hoofed and horned. I slipped close to Sorcha, eyes wide, too surprised to know whether or not to be afraid. The satyr grinned at me. "Off to see the Lover's Lover, Sorcha?"

"Yeah. Morning, Violet," he said.

I could not help but stare at her as we passed by. I tried not to, and I failed miserably. "You know the satyrs?" I asked Sorcha when we turned the corner.

"Huh? Oh, sure. Can't be a musician and not know at least some of the bards." He caught sight of my face and stopped. "Hey, you all right? Look like you've had a fright."

"Are they safe?" They didn't look safe to me. The satyrs looked feral.

"Who, Violet? Yeah. Well, I mean, I guess it depends, but yeah, they're safe to us. They can get brutal with their own kind. Hey, they're just canny bastards who mess with you, that's all. You all right?"

"I've never seen one."

"They don't go into the Empire?"

"I guess not."

Sorcha raised his eyebrows. He motioned for me to stay where I was. He jogged around the corner, calling the satyr girl's name. A second later he was back in front of me. "Violet says you Imperials don't drop coins for them. They stay out of your way. Huh. Didn't know that. Hey, you a runner at all?"

"What?"

"We're late. Gonna have to run the last bit. We're not far."

"All right."

Sorcha shouldered his violin case and took off. It turned

out he was a runner. He ran for pleasure most days, just for the hell of it. I have never been prone to such a masochistic thing. He had said it wasn't far, but that was a lie. I could only barely keep up with him. I was drenched in sweat, bleary-eyed and lightheaded by the time we got to where we were going. It was an apartment building a few blocks away from an already-bustling opera house called the Barlan. A pair of men sat at the foot of the building's steps. One was an old red elf, a man with a face more weathered than lined. He had heavy steely eyebrows that furrowed over a pair of bottomless black eyes, eyes so black they seemed not to have irises at all. Next to him, sitting with a matronly, protective hand on the old man's back, was a middle-aged man with elvish ears and short, black hair. The old man looked up as we approached. "You're late, Sorcha."

"Sorry, sorry."

The old elf pointed at me with a violin bow. "Who's that? You got a shadow."

Sorcha grabbed my hand and pulled me forward. I was a disheveled mess, the sweat seeping through my borrowed clothes, my hair going every which way. I'd cut myself shaving, and a trickle of blood wound its way down my neck. I had hoped Sorcha would let me slink behind him, tuck myself out of sight, but I had no luck with it. "This is Ariah. He's with me."

"Aye, a blind man could see that. I've a set, boy. Music's a discipline, right, you can't pop in and out with your conquests. It's work."

Sorcha laughed. "No, he's not...Prynn, it's a long story.

C'mon. Let's go play."

The man with the black hair stood up and offered a hand to the old man, Prynn. Prynn refused it. "If he's not a conquest, why's he in your clothes, Sorcha?" the black-haired man called.

Sorcha laughed again. He glanced down at his boots. There was an odd tension in him, one threaded with gentleness. When he looked back up, there was a curious half-smile on his face. "I'll tell you later, Tayvi. I promise I'll tell you everything after we play, yeah?"

They went to the Barlan with me in tow. They played a set of traditionals, none of which I was familiar with—most were Lothic and dated back to the war in the South. Both Prynn and Sorcha played violin; Tayvi sang. They were extraordinary. Even I, with little exposure to music, could tell they were extraordinary. It was very early, but the Barlan was packed. When Tayvi bowed after the last song, the crowd surged forward, bearing me along with it, and coins poured forth from their pockets. Sorcha pulled me on stage. He sat me next to Prynn, who thanked everyone who gave them money. He was warm with his audience, easy with them, an altogether different sort than the cantankerous old man who'd glowered at me at his building. Prynn seemed profoundly uninterested in me. I was glad for it.

Sorcha pulled Tayvi off to the side. They had a whispered conversation I couldn't hear, but the talents are what they are, and I saw more than I should have. There was no amount of gentleness that would have adequately softened the blow he delivered to Tayvi. The loss, the bitterness, was palpable. I knew with some odd certainty—a certainty, which may not have been magical—that it had something to do with Dirva. I knew it, and the curiosity burned me alive, but I could not bring myself to ask Sorcha about it. We went directly back to the squat house after his set. We walked slow, and he told me about how he'd started playing the violin. How Prynn had taught it to him since he was young, how Prynn was from the Lothic coast and had trained formally with human musicians, but then turned rebel and fought in the war. He told me about a man named Ezra who'd been married to Prynn, who'd died a violent and pointless death, and who had a place in satyrs' songs. Sorcha spoke in an unbroken monologue, and at most a quarter of what he said made any kind of sense to me. I didn't try very hard to make sense of it. I didn't even listen very closely. This happens sometimes, even now, even after years of marshaling my gifts. There are times when someone speaks to me at length and I listen to the tenor of their voice, the cadence of their words rather than the content. It gives a window into their frame of mind, but it has also given me a reputation for a wandering attention.

Back at the squat house, Sorcha handed me a plum and asked me if I was properly awake yet. I said I wasn't. He grinned. "Yeah, me either. I'm gonna crash for an hour or two. You're lucky I'm a heavy sleeper. You're lucky I don't kick you out of my room for the snoring."

It took me a second to realize it was an invitation. An invitation to what, I was not completely sure, but the way he watched me, measuring my reaction, made it clear that he was waiting for me to respond. I had no idea what the proper response was, so I didn't respond at all. Sorcha plucked the plum out of my hand, took a bite, and gave it back. He left me in the kitchen. I listened to him walk the stairs as I idly ate the rest of the plum. When I was done with it, when there was nothing else to do, I went up the stairs myself. Sorcha was already asleep. He was curled up on the inside, facing the wall, still clothed. I lay down next to him and was asleep myself soon after.

It was Dirva who woke me next. He shook me gently by the shoulder, whispering my name. He loomed over me when I opened my eyes.

"Dirva. Good morning." I was relieved to see him. He was a fixed point of familiarity, a remnant of the Empire. I noticed he was still dressed in Semadran clothes even if I wasn't.

Dirva held a hand to his lips. He pointed at the door. I nodded and pulled myself up. Dirva was already at the door, his left hand on the knob. It was already half-turned. And then Sorcha rolled over. "What time is it?" he murmured. "Where you off to?"

"Oh, I...Dirva's come to get me."

Two things happened at exactly the same instant. Dirva opened the door, his back still turned, and Sorcha shot across the room and grabbed Dirva by the back of the shirt. "No you don't, you bastard," Sorcha said. "You're not sneaking out of my room without even a word to me."

Slowly, deliberately, Dirva turned around. The way he

looked at Sorcha was so strange. His face was tender and suspicious at the same time. He slowly rested his hands on Sorcha's shoulders. Carefully, he smiled. "I didn't want to wake you."

The harshness in Sorcha's face evaporated, just like that. He wrapped his arms around Dirva and buried his face in Dirva's chest. "Holy shit, Lor, you're really here."

"You're grown," Dirva said.

Sorcha laughed. "You're old."

"I am," Dirva said. "I am at that. I need to speak to Ariah."

Sorcha pulled away. He crossed his arms against his chest. "You been speaking to him for four years. I've not seen you in twenty-five."

"I need to speak to Ariah," he said again. He said it simply, easily, and I watched as he pointedly ignored the hurt it caused in his brother. He caught my eye and nodded to the door. Guilt gnawed at me as I edged past Sorcha and left the room with Dirva. We did not speak until we were out in the Main Square. "What happened to your face?"

I rubbed a hand against my jaw. "Your brother made me shave in the dark."

Dirva raised an eyebrow just the slightest bit. "He made you?"

"He insisted. It seemed polite to acquiesce. He insisted on the clothes, too."

"Ma told me he lived with Falynn for a few years. The vanity must have rubbed off on him. Have you eaten?" I told him I'd had exactly one plum since I'd seen him last. "Let's get something to eat. There are things we should discuss."

He took me to a cafe in the Tinker's Borough. It was strange, because the place was so thoroughly Semadran, but no one in it so much as raised an eyebrow at the two of us. It was strange to be in a place among my own where I was no longer notable. Over familiar food, Dirva tried to speak to me. He couldn't for a very long time. He was as emotional as I had ever seen him, and emotional in a quiet, tightly-controlled way. A Semadran way. I gave him the space to marshal himself. "Will the squat house suffice?" he asked.

"As long as it doesn't collapse, I suppose so," I said. He laughed, and I felt a wave of relief wash over me.

He wrote two addresses down one a slip of paper and handed them to me. "The top one is my parents' place. The bottom is where I am staying. Should you need me, I will be at one or the other."

"You're not staying with your parents?"

"No, I'm not." He said it with a finality, which precluded further conversation. Dirva sighed. He had not eaten much more than a few bites, but he pushed his plate away. "We won't be here very long."

I heard what he wanted me to hear. I heard what he could not bring himself to say. "I am sorry."

"It is what it is." He was quiet for some time. The counter-minder came and cleared away the plates. She returned with a glass of water for me. "You've met my sisters and my younger brother. You don't have to meet anyone else if you'd rather not. But if you would not be opposed to it, I would welcome you to meet the rest of my family."

"Yes, of course."

He nodded. Then, he caught my eye. "I bid you remember they are not Semadran. I know you know that. Between Abira and Sorcha and Cadlah I am certain you know that, but remember it. My family is not like yours."

"I will remember."

* * *

Dirva's family was bound together by their traditions. The children orbited wildly, swinging out away from and back again to their parents again in settled rhythms. It was tradition for the children to strike out and join the Natives when they grew testy and adolescent. It was tradition for them to scrape a living in some half-illegal or wholly illegal way. They were a defiant, willful group: smart and crafty, street-seasoned, full to the brim of tempered bravado. It was tradition for them to have dinner with their parents once a week. These traditions were sacred: they were the glue that held the family together. Dirva methodically, intentionally, broke every single tradition he could. He was the only one to avoid the squat house. He sought out a formal education in the Semadran schools of the West Quarter. He left the family, left the City, and didn't return for twenty-five years.

The family dinners were deeply private; to be brought to one meant you were adopted into the family. My closeness with

Dirva and my growing friendship with Sorcha granted me entrance. It was there I met the rest of them: Dirva's parents, his da, his older brother Falynn, and Amran, a man who I can only describe as Falynn's other half though they were not married. Dirva's father was a full red elf, old yet spry. He was a tender man, a man who doted on his children, but there was a coolness, an uneasiness between him and Dirva. They circled each other like wary animals, both afraid the other was about to strike. There was love between them, but it was a broken thing, something shattered long ago and never fully repaired. Dirva's mother was the unquestioned head of the household. She was an improbable scientist — street-born, abandoned, illiterate until nearly adulthood, but she'd been taken under the wing of an academically minded half-Magi man in the City and had produced volumes of work on the mathematics of time. She could not seem to utter a sentence without a curse word in it. She had a total lack of patience with everyone around her. Dirva resembled her inside and out. They understood each other, I think, and it smoothed things between them when he came back after so long.

Falynn, Dirva's older brother, was a healer, trained in three different elvish traditions and mundane Qin doctoring by a close family friend. Sorcha had told the truth when he'd said he looked nothing like Falynn: like Cadlah, Falynn had his father's pale red elvish skin and his mother's black hair. Like Dirva, he was tall. His eyes had the same startling brightness as Dirva's. They may not have looked alike, but there was a lot of Falynn in Sorcha. Falynn was the beauty of the family, and he knew it. He was someone who was used to being looked at, used to being fawned over. The first thing that came to mind when I met him was my father's lectures about the golden ratio, how beauty is beautiful only in the right proportions. Falynn was a study in perfect proportions. He was distinctly androgynous, a wild sort of beauty that flickered between masculinity and femininity moment to moment. Beyond the beauty was an effortless charisma, a natural charm. It was strange, then, that Falynn was always shadowed by Amran. Amran is a well-known poet both inside and outside of the Empire—like Liro, he is part of the Nahsiyya Movement. But his gentle poems do not give you a sense of the man. He is a force. A dark thing, a man with an icy cruelty right at the center of him. Amran and Falynn together are a study in contrast and balance. One thing they had in common is that neither ever forgave Dirva for leaving.

Dirva's return was something that threw this family out of balance. It was unexpected, and it was unsettling. I think they thought they knew him better than they did. They had an idea of who he was which calcified into family lore over the years of his absence, and his return did not fit neatly into the mold they had cast for him. It brought out buried hatchets. It raised ghosts of half-remembered childhood rivalries. The family dinners I attended were storms with Dirva at the center, but Dirva himself seemed peculiarly unaffected. He paid very little attention to anyone but his da, and his da paid little attention to anyone but Dirva.

His da was Semadran, but only skin deep. He wore his

hair long and unbound like a red elf. Even very old and very weak, he shaved daily. Like the rest of Dirva's siblings, he was a man who made his way through shady dealings. He was a forger. He sat on the left of Dirva's father; their hands stayed clasped as they ate. They were old men who had loved each other much of their lives, and the love was a thing so deeply woven into both that I could not find a way to understand who either of them were apart from it. Believe me, I tried. I was, as I have said, very young then. It was a relationship I could not yet understand, one that did not make any sense to me. I studied them—fascinated, disgusted, fascinated by my own disgust. Dirva sat at the left of his da, their chairs pulled close and conspiratorial. They spoke Semadran with each other, and his da was the only one of the family to call him Dirva instead of Lorcani. When they were together, Dirva's face broke open, relief painted across it, comfort etched in every line. He looked young with his da. He looked sweet and full of life. He looked like the boy in the painting. And his da responded to him with an equal fervor, a matched love. Dirva was his favorite: it was unequivocally, unabashedly a fact of the family, and perhaps one that the other members of the family had tried to forget while Dirva was gone.

But Dirva had come back. This old man was dying, the life leaking out of him second by second no matter what Falynn did, and in Nuri's final days all that seemed to matter to him was Dirva. He was dying, leaving many children behind, but Dirva was the one who had his attention. The pair of them cloistered themselves together, living those missing twenty-five years together in the space of weeks while Dirva's brothers and sisters looked on.

Those family dinners were extremely hard on me. The shaping has always been harder for me to handle than the mimicry, though neither has ever been easy, and those dinners were a thicket of traps and thorns I could not navigate on my own. I drowned in the jealousies, the tensions, the bright spots of laughter. I felt too much at those dinners: those dinners were the meeting place of too many people living full, complex lives, and they were the site of grief and mourning. There is a reason why known shapers notoriously avoid funerals. The reason is that a place like that, with all the weight and the woven emotions, is a place where the gift threatens to swallow its host whole. I felt the emotions of Dirva's family so much, so deeply, that at times a sigh of disappointment caused me literal physical pain. But I kept going because, except in very rare circumstances, I only saw Dirva during those dinners. I needed to see him. I needed to see he had not fallen apart.

I had thought, before I went to the first one and saw his entire family assembled with all their tangled histories and threaded presents in that tiny, cramped apartment deep in the South Quarter, that I knew what I was getting into. I remember some years ago a mundane friend of mine told me that those of us with magical gifts are arrogant. We know slightly more than the mundane, she said, so we think we know everything about everyone. And she's right. I knew Athenorkos. I knew by then that Athenorkos and Semadran, as languages, are peculiar mirror images: Semadran is a language of fastidious precision;

when you say something in Semadran, you're trying to communicate the objective truth about a concept as specifically as possible. We are known for the complexity of our sentence structure and the breadth of our vocabularies. But sometimes truths are simple and can be best expressed simply. For a Semadran, the family is one such simple thing: mother, father, sister, brother, son, daughter. That's all. There's no word for cousin, for example, just a qualification that whoever it is you're speaking about is your mother's brother's son. Instead of grandfathers, we have our mother's father. We have small families. Factory assignments cause us to settle in areas far away from our natal homes, so you don't find many dense familial networks among my people. We have no need for nuance in such relationships because we keep them as simple as possible. Divorce and remarriage is unheard of. Children are not born out of wedlock. Your father is always your mother's husband; it's as simple as that. That is the world I was born to.

But I knew that Athenorkos was different, and I thought that by knowing the language I understood the people. Holistically speaking, Athenorkos is a fascinatingly simple language, one with few descriptors. Speakers of Athenorkos rely almost exclusively on nouns and verbs. I find the clarity of it somewhat intoxicating. The purity of the language, its simplicity, evaporates with the family. A Semadran is faced with a mind-boggling number of names for the complex, reflective, shifting relationships the red elves have to each other. Siblings can be full (meaning you share both biological parents) or half (meaning you share your mother) or split (meaning you share your father) or linked (meaning you bear no actual biological relation, but you regard this person as a sibling because of his or her relation to your biological parents; for example, if your half sibling's father has a child with another woman and the two of you are raised in the same household). There are close-links and far-links. There is an elaborate typology of relationship structures: romps (fleeting physical relationships with little emotional interaction), flings (short-lived relationships with a highly emotional component that end amicably), tosses (short-lived relationships with a highly emotional component that end badly), joinings (the Athenorkos equivalent of marriage), broken bonds (essentially a divorce), knots (several individuals all married to each other), and tangles (a messy sort of arrangement of those engaged in joinings and broken bonds). I was fluent in Athenorkos. I thought that meant I understood what these terms meant. I thought, as I stood outside the door that first evening with Sorcha, that my fluency with the language meant little would surprise me. But everything about these people surprised me. The depth of the relationships they had with one another—even when they weren't related by blood—shocked me. The bareness with which they expressed themselves with one another overwhelmed me. The palpable trust they had with each other was a thing that felt like it would swallow me whole.

Dirva came back, and I came with him, and at those dinners I bore witness to the trail of carnage he had caused by both leaving and returning. It sunk into me, through my pores and into my blood. It rooted itself in me. And then I would see

Dirva and his da, this ghalio criminal who had made him the man I knew, the only one in the room who saw Dirva for himself, and it took every ounce of strength I had not to weep.

CHAPTER 6

IT TOOK ME three days to forget all about my Semadran clothes. I lived in Sorcha's cast-offs without complaint because he was right—they suited me better than the clothes I'd brought with me. It took a week for our sleeping arrangements to lose their forbidding strangeness. It took a week and a half for my drab Coastal Lothic to blossom into florid City Lothic. It took three weeks for my ear to fully heal, and a few more days for me to forget it had ever been pierced. By then, I looked and sounded like I belonged at the squat house. I lost a little weight and gained the hungry look of the rest of them. I had been hassled by peacekeepers while minding my own business in the Square and had picked up their defiance. Sorcha and I were inseparable. We woke together, I followed him around while he conducted his musical business, we ate together, and then we fell asleep together. We were rarely apart for longer than an hour. Three weeks was all it took for me to grow closer to him than anyone else I'd ever met. I fell into the rhythms of his life, which were smoother and simpler than the rhythms of my own.

Three weeks in, though, I still could not shave to Sorcha's satisfaction. I had never had to learn; Semadrans don't shave.

My beard was a mark of manhood back home. Granted, it was patchier than I would have liked, but it was mine, and it had its worth. Sorcha would have none of it. He himself had enough red blood in him that he grew little facial hair, so his razors left much to be desired. Even when he scraped together enough to present me with my own—a Qin razor bought in the Qin markets—I still was not very good with it. I was unused to its sharpness and nearly slit my own throat at least twice. And then, out of fear that I would hurt myself further, I took to scraping very gently, so gently I was hardly shaving at all.

One morning, just shy of a month after my arrival, Sorcha woke me after my morning nap and told me he couldn't stand it anymore. If I couldn't shave myself properly he guessed he'd have to do it himself. I laughed and burrowed under the blankets. I didn't think he was serious. And, looking back I don't think he actually was; I think it was a pretense for what followed, but he claimed he was serious. He dragged a chair over. He went outside and brought back a basin of water from the pump outside. He slung a tattered towel over one shoulder and told me to pull my shirt off and sit down.

"Why do I have to take off my shirt?" I asked.

"Fine, you want to run about all day in a damp shirt, be my guest," he said.

I sighed, but I pulled off my shirt and sat down. "This is pointless," I said.

"Is not."

"What're you going to do? Shave me every day?"

He grinned. "Well, hell, Ariah, someone's got to do it.

Mark of my generosity that I'd take care of you so."

"Mark of your vanity, more like."

He laughed. "Lean back." I did as he asked. He came over and set the basin on the floor. I heard him sharpen the razor on a whetstone. I sat with my head titled back, resting against the wall, with my eyes closed. I was still half-asleep. I felt his hand on my bare shoulder and thought nothing of it. The actual shave itself was relaxing in an odd way. I didn't have to do anything. The water was pleasantly warm. Despite the fact that Sorcha himself never needed to shave, I had absolute trust that he knew what he was doing. After a few minutes, he cleared his throat. I opened my eyes. "Hey, you mind if I take a seat? Looming over you like this is a bit awkward."

"Yeah, that's fine." I settled back in my chair.

He laughed, and I opened one eye. "We only got the one chair, yeah? Mind if I take a seat on you?" he asked.

I blinked at him. It was such an odd request. He stood there, waiting for a response, his head cocked to the side. "Uh...all right." One corner of his mouth hitched up. He straddled me and finished the shave with his chest pressed against mine. The physicality of our relationship was, by then, something I accepted without much question. At first it had shaken me, but it was always so innocuous and so gentle that I could never find a good reason why it should shake me. I would wake with Sorcha's arm thrown over me. There were times when he'd decided I need to try whatever he was eating and he'd pop it into my mouth. Sorcha had no reserve, no sense of privacy, and as I lived with him, he steadily chipped away at mine. When he curled up against me that day I thought nothing of it.

He washed and dried my face when he finished the shave. He ran a hand down the right side of my jaw. "There, that's better. Hey, Ariah."

"Hmm?"

He poked me in the ribs until I opened my eyes and looked at him. He was smiling, but it was a rare smile: hopeful and soft and utterly without guile. "Ariah." And the way he said my name just...it was like a lullaby. Like a private siren song. My name in his voice echoed around the emptied reaches of my mind.

"Yeah?"

He put his hands on my chest and leaned forward. "Ariah."

A warmth spread through me. Everything outside of that room fell away. I felt something welcome and wanted wrap around me, tying me in place. I felt like a fly trapped in a spider's web, but it was a very pleasant web to be stuck in, and I was a fly who really didn't mind the spider. I noticed things about him I never had before: the thickness of his eyelashes, long and lush and dark, and the way his lips were thin and full at the same time. It is all a haze now, but I think I might have touched him, reached for him. It was all very surreal. He was himself and not himself at the same time. "Sorcha?"

"Yeah." He wrapped his arms around my bare neck and came so close I could taste his breath. He ran a hand through my hair. "Yeah, it's me," he said. And then he kissed me. It was a deep kiss, a slow and unhurried kiss. If I am being honest, and I might as well be honest, it was likely a series of kisses. I have no idea how long he kissed me. Or how long I kissed him back. Eventually, Sorcha dropped the razor. It fell with a heavy thud to the floor, and the noise of it was enough to wake me from the haze. Whatever the case, when I snapped back into my right mind, he was shirtless, and I had a hand on his thigh. I let out some terrible wordless noise. I tumbled out of the chair and skittered back to the opposite wall, putting as much distance between us as I could.

Sorcha stood next to the chair. He looked confused, adrift, a little lost. "Hey, you all right?"

"What just happened?" The words came out hoarse, coated in fear.

"Well, I thought...hell, Ariah, I thought we were making it finally."

"What?"

Sorcha sat heavily in the chair. A bitterness settled over him. "Ah, shit. Ah, for fuck's sake. Look, we been circling each other for weeks, right, I figured you as shy. Look, if you didn't want to you could've broke the charms."

"You charmed me?" It came out horrified, but actually I was relieved. *It wasn't me*, I kept thinking. *I wouldn't have done it if there hadn't been magic involved. It was all him.*

"Yeah. Don't be like that. You're a quarter. Could've broke them easy."

"I don't know anything about charms!"

"What? You're a quarter!"

"I'm Semadran!"

He stared at me for a long moment. He softened slightly. "I guess that explains why you didn't charm me back."

"Yeah, it explains it! You charmed me? What the fuck, Sorcha?"

He turned away from me. He drew his knees up to his chest and sat there in the chair curled up and taut. "Fuck you, Ariah, it was an honest mistake. Stop playing like you're all spooked."

What I had not told anyone then, not even Dirva, was that I was more shaper than mimic. One of the shapers in Ardijan plucked me from my classroom when I was young and felt me out. She told me I had it, the gift, but that training would be hard for me. There is not enough of me in me, she said. I didn't know what she meant, and frankly I was glad for it because it meant I wouldn't have to live a shaper's life, so I pretended I only had streaks of it. I'd used what she said as a way to avoid the training, which let me pretend I was something I wasn't even as the gift took advantage of me. The years have shown me what she meant, and I believe what she meant was that the way that gift works for me is that I am in danger of obliteration. Much of Semadran shaping is bound up in the walls, developing strategies to know what someone else is feeling without really feeling it yourself. And I can't build those walls.

I tell you this because it explains what happened next. It explains a lot about me and Sorcha, I think, but specifically what happened next. Every fiber of my body was heightened. I was in a panic—I'd just broken a whole host of rules with him, and I think some stupid part of my mind fully believed my parents were about to run in and disown me. I panicked, and the gift leapt out of me, thirsty for knowledge, dying to understand the situation.

Sorcha was not looking at me, but I could tell. I could feel it, what he wanted, how I'd hurt him. I felt it with a clarity that I doubt he even had. And I cared about him enough to want to bring him some peace. The memories of what happened next are discrete, jagged things in no real order. I must have crossed the room, but I don't remember doing it. I remember kissing him and knowing exactly how he wanted to be kissed. I remember letting him push me down to the floor, and then onto the mattress because that's where he wanted to go. The next thing I remember is hesitance. Sorcha's hesitance. "Are you sure you want to?" he asked. Pulled along by him, caught in his current, I said the last four words of his question precisely at the same time and in his voice.

He pushed me back gently and held me by the shoulders at arm's length. His fervor cooled and mine along with it, but it was still there, and I knew he wanted me to kiss him again, and I tried to do it. He held me in place. "Hey. Hey. You still in there? Ariah, you in there?"

Slowly, I came back to myself. He was naked, and I was down to my underclothes.

"This don't seem right," he said. "You were about to bolt. Maybe we should talk this through?"

I was myself again, and I was confused and scared. I

couldn't talk about it; I had no words for it besides slurs. I bolted. I pulled on my pants and boots, grabbed his shirt instead of mine because it was closer, and ran out the door without a word. I was drenched in anxious, clammy sweat. I felt like everyone on the street who saw me could read everything, knew everything, and I was drowning in shame. In my pocket, mercifully, was the slip of paper Dirva had given me. I could not face his family, but the second address listed seemed promising, and I headed into the West Quarter.

The address took me to the West Quarter's edge where the blue elves lived. I thought I was lost, but a street vendor confirmed I was going in the right direction. Really, the only thing I knew about the blue elves was that many of them were pirates. The men in their gardens looked forbidding, dangerous, to me. The City is a loud place, but the neighborhood of the blue elves has a thick quietness in it. It feels very separate from everything else there. The browns of sand and stone give way to green. The air is different. The blue elves watched me from their gardens, curious about the outsider. The house I came to was the only one on the street with an empty garden. The small house sat on a plot of empty land. I knocked on the front door, and Dirva answered. I had never been so happy to see anyone. "What's wrong? What happened?" he asked.

"May I come in?"

"Yes, of course." He ushered me inside. Speaking Semadran stabilized me somewhat. He pointed at a threadbare couch on the other side of the room. "Take a seat; I will get you a glass of water."

I didn't make it to the couch. The room was covered in paintings. They hung on the walls; they were stacked on the floor four and five canvasses deep. One wall held a collection of paintings from several different artists. One was even done by my father. All of the rest were by Liro, and many of them were his more famous works. Folded easels were crowded into one corner of the room. Sketchbooks were strewn on tables and chairs. A set of shelves held brushes and paints. "Dirva, where are we?"

"West Quarter," he called back from the kitchen. "Ariah, what happened?"

"An artist lives here," I said.

Dirva came around the corner. He looked slightly embarrassed. "Yes. An artist lives here. Liro lives here."

My eyes grew wide. "Liro lives here?"

"I mentioned when you first came to live with me that we were friends when I was young. I am staying with him." He brushed sketchbooks off a couch cushion and told me to sit. He sat next to me and handed me a glass of water. "You are in a state."

On the Market, a portrait of a nahsiyya boy whore courting Qin men, which is widely considered to be Liro's first masterpiece, stared at me from across the room. I found it unnerving. I also found it, considering the situation that had driven me to that room, oddly fitting.

"Yes, I am." I drank some of the water. I wanted so badly to tell him what had happened, but I knew I couldn't have stood it if he disapproved. I couldn't see how he wouldn't disapprove. "I need guidance. I need guidance on shaping. I can't build walls."

He knew. He was part shaper, too, after all. "You're not hurt, are you?"

"No. No, I'm not hurt."

"Good." He sighed and watched me for a long moment. I was still shaky; my hand trembled slightly as I drank the water. "You must show yourself compassion, Ariah. There are allowances made for ones like us."

"I am not a shaper."

"You are close to it. Ariah, I know we don't talk about it, but these things happen to everyone, shaper or not. You have…there is a vulnerability in you, which I sometimes find worrisome. You want direction. I think what you need is confidence. For me, it was easy to build the walls when I decided who I was. A sense of self gave me an anchor."

Well, I thought to myself, *I am not a ghalio. I am not nahsiyya. I don't belong here, and I'm not like Sorcha. I am Semadran,* I told myself, *and I am everything that entails.* But still, I sat there in Sorcha's clothes, freshly shaved by his hand. I sat there and could not help but wonder how I'd hurt him when I'd run. "Dirva, can I stay here with you? Tonight, at least, can I stay here with you?"

"I…we'll have to ask Liro. But, yes, I think so."

I drank the rest of the water. I felt better, more like myself. I needed more guidance. I needed a sympathetic ear. I looked over at Dirva, shocked at what I was about to tell him. I couldn't do it while looking him in the eye. I was afraid that if I did I'd read him, and I was afraid of what I would read. I dropped my face into my hands. "It was Sorcha. It was your brother. I didn't—it didn't get far, I don't think, but I—Dirva, it was with him. I'm not...I'm no deviant. I can't understand...he charmed me, but then he stopped, and the gift pushed me to it anyway. I don't understand. I can't stay with someone like that. I can't."

I waited for a protective hand on my back. I waited for gentle words. All I got was silence. The couch moved slightly as he pulled himself up. He stepped away from me. "Given what you've said, Ariah, this is not the place for you." His voice was cold and opaque.

I thought it was judgment. It was judgment, but not for what I thought. I looked up at him. "No, no, it wasn't me. It was him! He's the ghalio, not me."

"Ariah, you should go," Dirva said.

"Go where?"

He turned to face me. "You should go back to the Empire. It seems I have overestimated you."

The words cut deeply. His voice, his face, everything about him told me he knew exactly what he'd said, that he knew exactly how it would affect me. He had considered it, this choice of words, and he had made the conscious decision to wield them as weapons. I felt nauseous. I felt desperate. I was on the verge of tears. "I have no money. I don't know the way back," I said feebly.

He held the door open for me. The street outside was desolate and frightening. "We are not cut from the same cloth."

"No, we are. We are! I've upset you. I've offended you, but I don't know why," I said quickly. I had stood, taken two steps, and couldn't make myself go further. I burned with shame. "I told you, I'm not a ghalio," I said very, very quietly.

Dirva's face was hard as stone. He was a mountain of steadfast, brutal reserve. The surface of him was sheer, and stark, without any ledges or handholds. "You are too free with your words. You have no sense of the man to whom you speak, Ariah. Get the money from Cadlah. Tell her I will repay her."

I left. My heart broke as I crossed the threshold. I felt very alone, indescribably empty. I had nowhere to go. My only real choice was to return to the squat house, to wake Cadlah, and hope she gave me money and directions back to Rabatha. I walked slowly. I was wounded and unguarded, and the feelings and voices of the passers-by on the street sunk into me. I was only half-myself. It is a very strange way to be.

I had hoped, of course, that I would not have to face Sorcha. Certainly he would have business to attend elsewhere, I told myself. At the very least he would be out somewhere complaining about me to one of his friends who had never much seen the point of having me around in the first place. I had convinced myself that he would be gone by the time I reached the Square, but he wasn't: he sat on the platform playing his violin. A Qin peacekeeper yelled at him to stop under threat of arrest for disturbing the peace. He yelled that the racket was disrespectful to the courts. Sorcha played anyway. And the thing he played cut me to ribbons. Sorcha, like most musicians, communicates best through song. It's his language. His violin spoke of hurt and confusion and resignation. Of loss. It told me that he, too, thought he'd overestimated me.

He spotted me. I felt it when he spotted me; it was like a crashing wave. I wanted to hide, but where could I have hidden? There was nothing to do but face him. At least it was on the street, where certainly my gifts would not get the better of me. He dropped the violin and jumped off the platform. He fell twelve feet and landed graceful as a cat. The Qin peacekeeper ordered him over, but Sorcha spat at his feet. "The racket's over. Only one disturbing the peace now is you." He darted away when the peacekeeper lunged at him and disappeared into the crowd. A handful of seconds later, he reappeared right in front of me. It was around noon, and the Square was a crush of people moving from one side of the City to the other. The flow of people parted around us like we were stones in a river. "So," he said. "Rough morning."

"I'm not like you," I said.

He frowned and crossed his arms. He stared down at his feet, and then peered up at me from the corner of his eye. "Thought you said you were only a little bit shaper?"

"I'm not a shaper."

"Yeah, all right. Take your word for it. You'd know better than I."

"Sorcha, I have to go."

"Go where?"

"Go home."

"You are home."

"No, I have to go back."

He stared at me in disbelief. I don't think it was clear to me until that moment that the depth of our friendship was shared. I had thought his interest in me was a thing of circumstance, a passing fancy. "What, cause of that? Look, I'll keep my hands to myself. I'll not ever charm you again. Word of honor. You can't just run off."

"It might happen again."

He glanced away. He tried to stifle a smile and couldn't. "Ah, that would be so bad, eh?"

"It would, yeah. Sorcha, it would. I can't...I'm not...I'm Semadran. *Semadran*, Sorcha."

"So's Da."

"No, he isn't. I am."

Sorcha's jaw twitched. "Look, can't we talk this through? Let's go in, yeah?"

"I can't go in there with you!"

"You want to have this out on the street?" he asked.

"It might happen again."

He threw his hands up. "Ariah, fuck, give a man some credit, would you? I am not so hard up that I'm about to try and trap you. I have my dignity. Trees and streams. You're not the only one in this, you selfish ass."

He was right to call me out. I nodded and followed him into the squat house. We went up to his room, which had been our room. He sat on the bed, and I sat against the opposite wall. I refused to make eye contact with him. "I guess you've not been with a fella, then?" he asked.

"No. Mercy, no. Of course not," I said quickly, the words falling out over each other. "Sorcha, I'm Semadran, and I'm not married. I've not been with anyone."

"Come off it. Just be straight with me," he said.

"I am! This is not me! I don't do things like this!"

"Really?"

"Yes!"

He was quiet for a long time. "Shit. Ah, shit. I thought…ah, shit, this is a mess. I mean, I knew you were tink. I did. So I just thought you needed time to ease into it. I mean, you knew, right? I been all over you for weeks."

I had known. I had known right from the start. "I thought you knew I couldn't."

"You could. You were about to. I didn't know you wouldn't."

I burned a deep red. I hid my face in my hands. It was true. It was horribly, inescapably true.

"Look, all I'm saying is this isn't the Empire. I don't see why the way you live there has to be how you live here. I don't see why you got to be so Semadran when you're crashing with a nahsiyya gang."

"I am here with my mentor."

Sorcha raised his eyebrows. "Yeah. I know. You're here with Lor, right? So why hold back? I'm not trying to pressure you, I'm not, I just don't understand."

Something about the way he said it struck me as very odd. I looked over at him. "Why would it matter that I'm here with Dirva?"

Sorcha looked back at me with impatience. "Because! C'mon, he plays at it, sure, but he's not so silver deep down. He had Ro. Like he'd hold me against you. He's a lot of things, but he's not a hypocrite. I don't think. Hell, I don't know. Maybe he is."

"Ro?"

"Liro. C'mon! Ariah, this is you and me. Can't we leave him out of it? Can't we ever not talk about him?"

My mind ground to a halt. I had idolized Dirva for four years, which felt to me a lifetime at that age. I had struggled so hard to grow into him, with his brusqueness and his ineradicable will. Four years I had lived with him, studied him, mimicked him, and suddenly it seemed I had no idea who the man was. At that moment, he wasn't Semadran, he wasn't who I thought he was, and suddenly I didn't really know who I was either. It was terrifying.

Sorcha let out a noise of frustration. "Ariah, look. I like you, I do, but I don't need this shit right now. My da's dying, yeah? Lor's not the only one feeling it. So, just hurry up and decide. Stay or don't. I don't have the patience these days to sit around while you sort it out. Just pick one or the other and go with it."

He had not spoken with me about his da's death until then. I had been, shortsightedly, keeping my life with Sorcha and the heavy weight of Nuri's death separate. They felt separate. In some meaningful way, I had forgotten Sorcha was part of that family and one of those children about to be left behind. "Sorcha, I'm sorry."

He leaned back against the wall and stared up at the ceiling. "Just go, then."

"No, I'm sorry about your da. I'm sorry about this. This is stupid. I'm being stupid."

He looked at me, surprised, unguarded. He had a bravado that made me think he was older than I was, but actually we were the same age, only months apart. In that moment, he looked terribly vulnerable and terribly young. "I could use a friend these days. Could stay the way it's been, that'd be fine with me. But I could use you around."

I didn't feel that there was much choice. Yes, perhaps he was a bad influence. He was not the sort I should have been around. But he needed me, and it didn't seem right to leave. I agreed to stay. In unspoken compromise, Sorcha slept clothed that night.

CHAPTER 7

CURIOSITY IS WOVEN deeply into Semadran culture. There is a tension, a fine line we walk, where we are compelled to know what we don't know, understand what we don't understand, without giving anything of ourselves away. It is a thing of survival bred from generations of living under the thumb of the Qin. In any case, there was suddenly much about my mentor that I did not understand in the least. I was desperate for answers. I pumped Sorcha for all that he knew—all of which he told me, but it was not much. Dirva had left when Sorcha was very young, only about ten years old, so everything he knew were secondhand stories from his siblings. And Sorcha was the youngest—young enough that he was only a bare handful of years older than Falynn's first child—so he had grown up with his siblings like they were his parents, and his siblings' friends like they were aunts and uncles. He knew Liro, but not in a terribly personal way. All I could really get from Sorcha was that in their youth, Dirva and Liro had been inseparable. The family expected them to marry. But then, Dirva left for Vilahna with no notice, no warning. His da arranged travel and forged papers to get him to Vilahna, but no one else in the City knew he was planning to leave. Dirva, apparently, had not told Liro he was leaving. He, family lore claimed, had not even said goodbye. He was simply there one day and gone the next.

The man I knew was one who, in spite of his impatience and brusqueness, was unfailingly respectful. Dirva checked and double-checked appointments he had. He was compulsively punctual. But then again, he was a man with a great capacity for secrets, and the notion of him preparing for a new life in a foreign country while living his old one as if nothing was about to change did not seem so far-fetched. I pushed Sorcha for more than this rough sketch of Dirva's youth. What had drawn them together? How long had they been together? Was it the shaping? There are stories of that, tales of a shaper so thoroughly caught in the thrall of an admirer that they cannot extricate themselves for weeks, months, even years. How had they met? What happened to each of them after Dirva left? But Sorcha didn't know. He said no one talked about it. Dirva's exit was a sore spot for his parents, and whatever happened to Liro in the weeks after was a sore spot with siblings.

I had to see Dirva. I needed to see him. I fought the urge for two or three days because I knew coping with his dying da was sapping all his strength, but there are times when the things you need are so immediate that you can't help but demand them, even when you hate yourself for being so selfish. I went alone. Sorcha asked me where I was off to, and when I told him, he rolled his eyes. On the long walk to Liro's house, I rehearsed my questions and my statements over and over. Seeing Dirva again was a thing for which I needed to prepare.

It was late afternoon when I got there. The world was painted in primary colors: a red sky served as a backdrop to the blue houses, and the sandy street burned a glowing yellow. I knocked on the door and stared down at my feet, running through my prepared statements one final time in my mind. I heard the creak of the door and launched in. "Mr. Villai'Muladah, sir, it is not disrespect that brings me to this door today but instead a deep wish to..."

"You must be the student." He spoke Semadran, but the voice was not Dirva's. I looked up and saw instead a nahsiyya man with blue skin and black hair. He was razor-thin and narrow, all long lines and sharp angles, and stood about inch or so taller than me. His eyes were large and black, ringed with Semadran violet. He was dressed simply, in a loose linen shirt and wool pants, barefoot, and covered with bright streaks of paint.

I did not need to be told who he was. I blinked at him, wide-eyed, star-struck. I looked away quickly when I remembered what I knew about him and blushed a terrible red when I remembered the things I had said in this man's own house. I could not find any words to say to him. I tried to; my mouth opened and closed. My brows furrowed together, but I could not get a single word out. My mind had gone blank.

"He's with his da," Liro said. The formality of Semadran when he spoke it seemed an odd fit. I managed a nod. I stood there, rooted in place, but I couldn't have said why. After a second, Liro invited me in. I managed to decline in some approximation of politeness. I had half-turned when he invited me in a second time. "Come in. Get your bearings back," he said. "It might make some sense for you and I to talk."

He held the door open for me. He seemed exhausted, a little withdrawn, but he hardly seemed angry. I felt it would be rude not to go in. I kept my eyes pinned to the floor and followed him inside. He asked me if I wanted anything, tea or food or water. I shook my head. Then, he asked me if I wanted any pipeherb. My face jerked up. He laughed at my expression. He had a warm, slightly caustic laugh. "I don't mean to lead you astray, but sometimes it helps me gather myself when I'm nervous. You seem nervous."

I was nervous, but it struck me as irresponsible. "No, thank you."

"Suit yourself." He sat down on a couch and watched me expectantly until I sat down on the couch across from him. On the wall behind him hung portraits of Dirva as a young man. In the portraits, he read and wrote, lost in a private world. The questions about their shared past, and all that it entailed, came back to me unbidden. I pulled my eyes away from them and glanced at the table between us, but it was no safer. A sketchbook was open to a rough portrait of a shirtless man who could only have been my mentor. I resorted to staring at my hands. "Given what you said when you were here last, and given the way you're acting now, I am going to guess you know about him and me."

"I...yes. Sorcha told me."

"The two of you are on speaking terms?"

"Yes."

"Huh. Well, Sorcha's always been quick to forgive. You know, I'm not a leper. It's not contagious." I looked up at him, trying and failing to find a way to tell him that in my case, with my gifts, it could be contagious. "Dirva thinks you've gone. I told him it's a rare one that up and leaves just like that." He snapped his fingers. "I told him most people, when they get attached, tend to linger at least a little bit. And here you are. Why have you lingered?"

"I...I want to make amends."

Liro raised his eyebrows. "You think you can after that?"

"I don't know. I want to. I can try. It seems worth trying."

Liro sighed. "You know life is hard for him right now. You know that, and you're adding to it."

A wave of shame swept over me. I nodded. I could not bring myself to speak.

"I could wring your neck for doing that to him. But it's done. And he's very fond of you. Did you know that? He hasn't stopped talking about you since he got here. Well, until you came by the other day, but he's not one to voice his sufferings." Liro sighed again. He pinched his forehead with the thumb and forefinger of his left hand. "He says you know about art. My art."

"I do, sir."

He waved at me. "Don't call me sir. I grew up on the streets. He says you're Mochai Tzotel'Mosol's boy."

"I am."

"It's hard to hate a kid born and bred to good taste. Look,

I'll talk to him when he gets here. You should go. There's no telling how things are with Nuri; it's touch-and-go day to day, and I don't think he'd take it well if Nuri had a rough day and you were here lying in wait for him. I'll talk to him, and I'll tell him you're at the squat house. He'll come find you if he wants to find you."

"Thank you," I said. Liro nodded at me, distracted. He looked like he was carrying a weight far too great for him. There was a deep bittersweetness about him, and there was a fierce privacy to him, and I felt I'd trespassed even though he'd invited me in and done most of the talking. I saw myself out without having to be asked to do it.

* * *

When Dirva arrived at the squat house, I finally felt I could breathe again. Sorcha and I were smoking pipeherb on the platform at the time. I grew more stoned by the second, and when I am in that state, I am not terribly observant. Sorcha could do virtually anything through the haze of the herb and had an unwavering awareness of his surroundings built from a life constantly skirting the edge of the law. He saw Dirva first. He elbowed me in the ribs. "Hey, Lor's here."

I sat up taller. "He is? How does he look?"

"Hell, I don't know. You're the one that lived with him, not me. Look for yourself."

Dirva walked across the Square with the same kind of contained purpose I'd seen him use when meeting with Qin dignitaries. It did not bode well, but I was stoned, and I have always had a hopeful streak a mile wide. I scrambled clumsily up to the roof and ran down the stairs of the squat house. I took a second to catch my breath, smoothed the front of my shirt, and stepped outside. He must have seen me, but he did not acknowledge me. He walked past me to the platform. He shielded his eyes and called up to Sorcha. "Can we talk?" he asked.

Sorcha leaned over the side. "You and me?"

"Yes," Dirva said. "You and me."

"Oh. Uh, yeah, I don't see why not." He jumped from the platform and landed in a plume of dust.

"I would've waited for you to use the stairs," Dirva said.

Sorcha shrugged. "No harm."

"You're going to break something one day."

"Well, when I do, Falynn'll patch me back up. What's up, Lor?"

Dirva may not have acknowledged me, but he took pains to keep me from eavesdropping. He led Sorcha across the Square, far out of my earshot, and angled himself so that he could see me in his peripheral vision. He would have caught me if I had dared to sneak over. I very much wanted to sneak over. Instead, I stayed where I was and watched them.

They spoke for some time. I confess, I thought it would be over and done quickly. Neither of them had had much to say to the other since our arrival. They spoke with warmth that was obvious to me all the way across the Square. There was laughter; there were smiles. There was an obvious comfort with each other in the way they stood. And at the end of it, there was a hug. When Sorcha started across the Square back towards me, Dirva made a move to turn away. Sorcha plucked at his sleeve until he nodded and followed Sorcha over. "Your turn to talk," Sorcha said when he got to me. He slipped past me into the squat house.

The Square was bustling then, but it felt empty. It felt like it was just me and my wounded mentor. He stared me down, his face hard, the hardness masking a wary vulnerability. "I've been told you want to make amends," he said.

"I do. I'm sorry. I didn't know. I never guessed." The words tumbled out in fits and spurts. I tried to remember the things I had decided to say to him, but the pipeherb had gotten the better of me. "It's been very confusing here. Seeing you with them. Sorcha. It's been strange."

Dirva sighed. "You're stoned."

I let out a strangled laugh. "I am. I'm sorry. But it helps. It's helped me from falling into it—him—all of that again. It is a…preventive measure? I guess that doesn't matter. I shouldn't be smoking it, I know, but I can't build the walls. I'm sorry I keep doing everything wrong."

Dirva studied me for a moment and sighed again. His hands were on his hips, and his head was bowed slightly. He looked to be at a loss with me. Something about the way he stood there propelled another incoherent stream of words from my mouth. "I didn't know. And I-I thought…it's strange here because sometimes you're still Semadran and sometimes you aren't. And if it had happened in the Empire, I thought you'd, uh, that you'd disapprove. Or worse. You'd send me back to Ardijan, and people would know, and I'd be pushed out. Because that's what we do, and that's how we think."

He looked at me. The brightness of his eyes in that moment was harsh, forbidding. "No, Ariah, that's how *you* think."

"No! No, I mean to say that's how Semadrans think."

"No, that's how *you* think. You never stopped to wonder. You never questioned. You took what they told you, and you drank it in. You stand there, you who will never know, and you tell me that's just how Semadrans think. Not all Semadrans are the same, Ariah. You are...were...my student, and I welcomed you into my home and my life, and this is what you think of me and my brother."

"You never told me!"

His eyebrows shot up. "I never told you?" he said. His voice was steely. There was an edge of dark, dark humor in it: a mockery, a condemnation. "I owed you this? You had some right to know private things about me, my past, which had no bearing at all on your life? Things that disgust you, that make you shrink away from me? I can feel it, you know. I am a shaper, too. I have spent a lot of time feeling that. No, Ariah, I never told you, because you are truly Semadran, right to the heart, and you carry in you all that's good and bad about our people. No, I never told you. And you never asked. And why would you? It has never been relevant."

I had thought him a simple man in Rabatha. Brilliant and determined, but at heart a man who made easy sense to those around him. He never seemed to doubt his place in our community, even when others did. He never seemed to struggle with it. That he housed within him such contradictions was a shock. That I housed such contradictions within myself was a greater shock. I understood him in that moment because I had tried to do what he had done in the Empire so effortlessly. There is much about me, which is classically, irrefutably Semadran, and there is much that has never been Semadran. I had always thought there was only one viable path, but seeing him then, it became suddenly clear that there were thousands of ways to live, and all of them were valid. There were consequences for choosing one over another, to be sure, but consequences did not mean they were the wrong choice. This had never been relevant. He was right about that, and it chastened me. But I could not help but see that he had chosen a life, constructed a life, where it would never be relevant. And I could not help but wonder why he had chosen that.

The truth was that I was still perplexed by his relationship to a man. I still could not shake this deeply bred feeling that it was wrong. But there was nothing in the world that could turn me away from him. He could have murdered babies and laughed gleefully while he did it, and I would still have killed myself trying to impress him. The Semadran word for mentor is closely linked to the Semadran word for parent. I loved him more than I loved the tenets of my culture. I loved him enough to want to unlearn everything, to start the arduous and fearsome process of questioning these beliefs I held. I gathered my thoughts, and I spoke very, very carefully. "Sir, I believe it's relevant now. It perhaps shouldn't be, but I know it and you know I know it, and we both know how badly I have reacted to it. I would very much like to make amends. I cannot see a way to make amends with you, if you are willing, other than to acknowledge that this is now relevant. The things I have said are relevant. I am sorry I said them, but being sorry doesn't mean they weren't said, and doesn't mean they caused no damage. The only way to repair damage is to acknowledge it exists." I took a breath. "If you want me to leave, I'll leave."

Dirva did not answer me for a very long time. "I will think on it," he said.

CHAPTER 8

AT THE END, some silver shreds left in Nuri rose to the surface. The red elves have a sanctity for life bred into their bones. We Semadrans are more careful about life: there are times, it is generally agreed, that a child should not be born. There are times when it is, perhaps, better to die than live. I am not sure why this difference between us and them exists. It may have something to do with the red elves losing so many in the war in the south: two lost generations to the Lothic Civil War. Semadrans, on the other hand...we have so little time, so few resources, and it behooves us to allocate them thoughtfully.

There came days where Nuri could no longer get out of bed, could no longer feed himself. His breath became ragged and uneven. There came days where the struggle of living and the indignity of the life in which he was trapped were more than he wanted. There was a family dinner two months into my stay in the City where Dirva and Falynn practically carried him out to the table. He was given a pretense of strength, a suggestion that all they did was aid him, but we all knew he could not have walked on his own. Like always, Nuri sat at the left of Dirva's father, their bony, spotted hands clasped tight.

Like always, Dirva sat on Nuri's other side, but this time a little closer than usual, and this time he kept a hand protectively on his da's back. We had not spoken since he'd come to the squat house, but I watched my mentor closely anyway. I felt the sadness radiating off of him in waves, pouring into me. I believe that Dirva knew what Nuri wanted before any other member of the family.

Nuri waited until we'd finished eating. He ate very little himself. His hands shook and his bones ached. He was given bread and a cup of broth, which he drank very slowly and very carefully. The bread sat untouched on a plate before him. He gave Dirva's father's hand a squeeze and released it. He cleared his throat softly, and conversation around the table died. "I am done living," he said.

There was a heavy beat of silence. Falynn was the first to speak. "No, Da, I can help. What is it? The headaches again? You're dehydrated. Are you not sleeping? I can..."

"I am done," he said.

The blood drained from Dirva's father's face. His mother's mouth turned to a hard line. "What the fuck does that mean?" she asked.

"You know what it means," he said.

Dirva's father left the room. Cadlah and Sorcha followed him out.

Falynn went to follow, too, but Nuri caught his wrist as he passed. "No, Da," Falynn said.

"Falynn, sit," said Nuri. Falynn sat in his father's chair. He stared hard at Nuri, willing him to change his mind, but it was no use. Nuri took Falynn's hands in his. "I love you. You are my son. I hate that this will hurt you, but I am asking for your help. Give me this last gift: let me choose when and where."

Falynn ripped his hands away. "No. No! I'm a healer!"

"There is no more healing to be done."

"No! I won't have your blood on my hands."

"If you do it right, Falynn, there won't be blood," Nuri said. A peculiar smile flashed and disappeared across his face and Dirva's face at the exact same time. No one else was amused. Abira let out wordless noise, a primal thing of loss and frustration, and went after her father. Amran and Dirva's mother drifted to the back of the room. The pair of them stood together, arms crossed, eyes watchful and wary. I alone sat on my side of the table.

Falynn dropped his face into his hands. "No."

Dirva took Falynn by the elbow and pulled him aside. They spoke in low whispers, but the room was small, and I couldn't help but hear what was said.

"He wants to die, Fal," Dirva said. "Letting nature choke the life from him in the dead of night when none of us are there, that would be better?"

"You haven't been here for years," Falynn spat back.

"This is not about me."

"No, it isn't. It never has been. You think you can waltz in here, you think you still know anything when you've been gone so long? You don't!"

Dirva took a breath. "He wants this. He raised us."

"You sure it's not you who wants this?" Falynn said. "Moment he's gone cold you'll be gone again." In the back of the room, Amran let out a low whistle. Dirva's mother smacked Amran's shoulder and told Falynn to stop being an ass.

"I would do it," Dirva said, "but I know nothing about medicine. You were taught all of Semadran medicine; you must have been taught this."

"Just because I was taught something don't mean I'll use it. Pa sure as hell taught you loyalty, and it don't seem to me that ever stuck."

"This is not about me!"

"All I know is you're the only one who's not been here, and you're the only one saying this is the way it should happen."

Dirva was as angry as I have ever seen him, before or since. He opened his mouth to respond, but Nuri reached back and took his hand. "Falynn," Nuri said, "I am saying this is the way it should happen, too."

"His life, his choice," Dirva's mother said from the back of the room.

Falynn's face swung around to her. "What?"

"You heard me. You do it, Fal, or I will." Her voice was iron; her voice had within it a deep and fiery protectiveness for this old man who was her husband's husband. "Go tell your pa this is what's happening. Tell him to make his peace with it. Nuri, let's you and I have a chat about logistics, yeah?"

Nuri smiled. "Oh, Switch," he said, "I do so love your pragmatism."

"Oh, Nuri," she said sitting next to him, "I do so love it when you make these announcements of yours." When Sorcha and I left, Dirva and his mother were discussing funeral plans and wills with Nuri. It was, somehow, sweet and macabre at the same time.

* * *

Nuri died in the early afternoon on the 13th of Fourthmonth-Last, 6572 IC. Spring had settled over the City, and that time of day was hot, but not yet blistering. The time of day had been chosen for its warmth and the golden light in which the City basks then. The day itself was chosen because the Pet was full and close; the moon the previous evening had been a thin white ring. The days after a ring night—a night where the Pet is closest to Aerdh, hovering between us and the dusty craters of the Moon—those days are known to heighten magic.

I was there that day, but I was not present for the death. I walked Sorcha to the door and sat outside on the stoop. Nuri was not my family. Bearing witness to his death felt an intrusion. Not long after I sat down, Liro arrived. "You're still here?" he asked.

"Yes."

Liro sat next to me. "You're here for Sorcha, aren't you?"

"I am."

He patted my shoulder. "Good. Good. You mind if I sketch you? It's a heavy day. I need something to take my mind off it."

"You want to sketch me?"

"I do."

"It would be an honor."

"It'll be a sketch," he said, pulling a pad of paper and a pencil from his shirt. We sat there for hours. I watched the golden light turn pink, then red, then lilac. The air cooled. The streets were as loud as they always were, but the day felt quiet anyway. And Liro sketched; the whole time, he sketched. He produced a dozen or more drawings of me on that stoop, my back bowed, my chin resting on my knees. You can see the depth of my worry in those sketches.

Just before dusk, Sorcha burst through the door. His face was streaked with tears. He ran for the street and caught me by the hand as he passed by, dragging me with him. He said nothing the entire walk back. The others in the squat house knew what the day would bring, and they had enough respect to have cleared out when we got there. He led me up the stairs, his hand clasping mine so tight it hurt, and pulled me into the bed. He wept for hours. He said nothing, but he didn't need to. I felt everything, every shard of loss. He wept for hours, and I held him while he wept.

* * *

Sorcha told me much later how it happened. Falynn refused. Nothing could move him. The already-bad blood between him and Dirva grew poisonous after that. It was Dirva's mother who brought Nuri the peace he'd asked for. She consulted with Falynn's teacher, who gave her herbs and instructions. They were Semadran herbs culled from magical plants grown by the City's blue elves, and their properties had been heightened by the proximity of the Pet. The instructions were for her to brew the old man two cups of tea: one to soothe him and ease him into sleep, and the other to gently stop his heart.

Sorcha told me Nuri asked to speak with each family member alone. They went into his room one after another, and Dirva went in last and had the most time with him. Then, Nuri asked the family to come in. He wanted to see them together. Dirva's father, weeping, crawled into the bed with him. Dirva's mother brewed the tea, and Dirva held the cup steady to help his da drink it. And then they waited. Sorcha said it didn't take long, and that it was quiet and peaceful, but that it was still hard anyway. Falynn was the first to speak the red elvish mourning words. Sorcha repeated them and left immediately after.

I don't know how long Liro had to wait before Dirva came out of that apartment. I don't know what he was like in the days to follow. Dirva never spoke of it to me. I knew him well, though, and there were times in the years after where the unfathomable well of loss he carried from this threatened to drag me under. All I know was that Dirva stayed with Liro in the days immediately after, and that it was Liro who slowly coaxed him back from the jaws of grief. Dirva had Liro, he had no one else, and it was then that I began to understand that the things we need from others make their own kind of sense, have their own logic, create their own legitimacy regardless of what we've been taught. If he hadn't had Liro, I am not sure Dirva would have been able to patch himself back together.

I am grateful for this, but in the years since, I cannot help but wonder at the sacrifice it required of Liro. It is not easy to hold someone through their grief. It is hard to see someone you love in pain, in irreparable pain. It takes an extraordinary type of kindness, a rare patience, to let the loss run its course. We always want to help, but there are times when there is no help, and the pressure to take help only makes things harder on the ones trapped in mourning. I don't know what transpired between them. I don't. But I do know that Dirva left him without explanation, reappeared without warning, and that there was nothing for Liro to do but offer himself up. I never knew Liro well, but he seemed to me a very bright man. Like anyone who scraped a childhood by on the street and survived to adulthood, he had a watchfulness about him and an uncannily honed feel for other people. Liro knew the moment Dirva set foot in the City what he would need, and what he would take, and Liro let him take it anyway.

CHAPTER 9

THE WEEKS AFTER Nuri's death were steeped in uncertainty. Nuri's death was an orderly thing, but for those of us left behind it had in its wake a terrible chaos. It is a hard thing for a family to grieve together. Grief marks itself on a person in unique ways, and it grows so total that a person can't always see past it. One can't always remember that your mother, your spouse, your sister are grieving the same loss in a different way. Sorcha spent little time with his family in the two or three weeks immediately subsequent to his da's death. He clung to me like a life raft. I think it was because with me, Sorcha was able to fall into it. He was able to feel the loss. It was not shared with me, and because it wasn't shared, he could begin to understand what it meant for him. At Prynn's insistence, he kept playing the morning sets, but he spent the rest of the day in his room with his head on my shoulder telling me stories about Nuri. Anything he could remember about him—things he'd seen himself, things the rest had told him about, the small private moments and the big, grand ones. I have never seen him smoke more pipeherb before or since. I have never smoked more before or since.

The physicality of our relationship had diminished since the fateful day he kissed me, but it came back. There were moments where Sorcha wanted to forget, wanted the ache of loss gone, and wanted me to banish it. There are times I wish I could have given him what he wanted, but I couldn't, and I was kept stoned enough that the gifts were at bay. Sorcha was not shy about it. "Kiss me," he'd say. We often sat on the bed with our backs to the wall, side by side, our bodies balanced against each other from shoulder to knee, but there were times when Sorcha would sling himself across me, crouched and ready. And then he'd ask.

"I can't."

"You could."

"Sorcha, I can't." It hurt to turn him down, but probably not as much as it hurt him to be turned down. He'd sigh, and then he'd settle against me, curled up in my lap like a child, determined to get something out of me. It struck me more than once that the intimacy we had then—with his face tucked into my bare neck and my arms wrapped tight around him—was something deeper and more telling than sex would have been. I knew I was toeing the line, that this was something no one back home would have approved of, but I still wouldn't kiss him. I held him and stroked his hair instead. We took to sleeping mostly naked under the same blanket. We'd start the night apart, but by morning he was curled against me, and I had an arm around him. It began to feel natural.

I knew the physical comfort I gave him helped, but if I am honest, there came a point where it helped me, too. By that time, I was no longer sure why I was in the City. I suspected that Dirva would never forgive me, and if he didn't, there seemed no real reason to stay there. I felt, then, that I perhaps should have been trying to scrape together the cash to get back to Rabatha on my own. More than once I resolved to do it, to find some form of gainful employment, but Sorcha was there, and Sorcha was broken, and after the day's first pipe I had no motivation anyway.

If I am honest, there was more than one moment where I wondered what held me back from him. I seemed trapped there in the City for good, and if I was trapped there, and I was part of this nahsiyya gang where there were so few rules and no one batted an eye, perhaps Sorcha was right, and I could. But I couldn't. Maybe if I had been told with some finality that Dirva would have no more dealings with me I could have crossed that line, but until he said it, there was still a sliver of a chance I'd return to a place where I needed to be Semadran again, and it seemed prudent not to get ahead of myself.

What I mean to say is that I had no idea where I would be, or who I would be, day to day. I waited for Dirva, and I grew bitter about the waiting. I planned to get back to Rabatha with Dirva, and at the same time made plans for a lifetime in the City with his brother. It was maddening. Sometimes at night Sorcha would wake me while he rolled over. He slept fitfully then. When I woke at night, I was sober, and all of this came crashing down on me. I lay there, drawing in panicked, shallow breaths, so frozen by the choices ahead that I could not think. Sorcha and his insistent grief served to anchor me in the present. He was an escape.

* * *

While we were cloistered in his room, the days began to run together. Time slid by; spring turned to summer, and then it was my birthday. I was thirty-five, and I was faced with the cold realization that even if Dirva relented, the training was over. He no longer had any obligation to me. The day of my thirty-fifth birthday occurred nearly three months after Nuri's death. When I turned thirty-five, I had not worn Semadran clothes in over half a year. I had not spoken my mother tongue in at least three months. I felt thoroughly nahsiyya, like a true member of the Natives. Every member is expected to make a contribution, and by then, I was making mine: I taught the Natives how to read. I sharpened their Qin and Inalan so they could get better rates in the markets. These skills were sorely needed; even Sorcha was illiterate. Certainly, the ability to sign their own names made navigating the Qin court system much simpler for Cadlah. She was able to get them out twice as fast, usually before they'd been beaten. I had, in fact, earned the highest level of praise one can aspire to in a community of vagrants: I was considered useful. I had begun to feel I belonged there. A nagging need to return to the Empire remained, but mostly because I missed my parents and worried about them. Little else about my life before seemed to matter.

Two days after my thirty-fifth birthday, Dirva came to the squat house. Sorcha had not recovered from the loss of Nuri, but three months was enough time for him to begin breaking out of his shell. We had been out. He had dragged me to see some sets in the musicians' district played by satyrs recently arrived in town. The entire musicians' district in the City swarms these—word gets out, and the musicians flock. They take bets on the songs the satyr will play, and whether or not what they sing actually resembles language. I still found the satyrs deeply unsettling, but I went with him because he wanted me there. Dirva was in the squat house when we came through the door. He and Cadlah sat next to each other on the floor, each with a cup or red elvish tea in hand. When I saw him, I swear my heart stopped beating. I could not breathe. I felt at once a tremendous burst of happiness and a deep shock. I realized when I saw him there that I had fully believed I would never see him again. Sorcha saw the effect he had on me, and he took my hand.

Dirva was thin. His face when he looked up at me was gaunt: all cheekbones and hollow eyes. His beard was slightly unkempt, and his hair was longer than I'd ever seen it. The weeks had been rough for him, but he retained his steely dignity. He looked anything but frail. "Ariah, may I speak with you?"

Sorcha darted close. "You can tell him no."

I couldn't tell him no. I let go of Sorcha's hand. "Of course, sir."

Dirva stood and pointed to the door. Sorcha told me again I didn't have to speak with him, but I tucked my chin into my chest and followed Dirva out the door. He walked us to the shadow of Sanctuary. The window was open, and I could hear the shouts of the prisoners and the prayers of the desperate. "I have only just realized what day it is," he said. "Your training has ended."

"It's strange, the way things can end before they've finished," I said. Sorcha had rubbed away a good deal of my meekness.

Dirva looked at me, surprised, somewhat amused. "Yes, it is strange the way that happens. Cadlah tells me you've done well by the squat house."

"It's done well by me."

He studied me for a moment. "You are not the same as you were."

I looked away. It was both a compliment and a condemnation. It stirred in me a thousand feelings, none of which I knew what to do with. "May I ask why you're here?"

"I don't know," he said quietly. He sighed. "This is not a good place for me. There is little left for me here. I will return to Rabatha soon. I suppose I...I am here to see if you want to return with me."

And then what? my heart screamed at him. *Return for what? Return to what?* My training was over. My few promising contacts were lost, and I saw no way out of the factories. If I even made it far enough into the Empire to get conscripted into the factories. There was a good chance I would be detained at the border this time. I had nothing to bribe the Qin with. My voice locked in my throat. I stared at him for a long time. I felt a hard-edged, wild anger in me; the kind of anger that only comes from a well of urgent love.

"I will think on it," I said. I said it in his voice, exactly the way he'd said it to me weeks before.

Dirva raised his eyebrows. Again, he studied me like he'd never seen me before. I had a moment of uncertainty then—was I really that different now? What did it mean to be different? What did it mean that I felt largely the same? If I couldn't tell, maybe I'd lost my footing. Maybe I still needed him. Maybe I still needed the Empire.

"Yes," he said. "You should think on it. I will be at Liro's until the end of the month. I will be there if you need to speak again," he said.

CHAPTER 10

WHEN I CAME back inside, Sorcha wanted to know everything that had happened. I told him. Sorcha is a very canny man, a man who has an instinctive knack for other people. He has always asked me probing questions, ones to which I have no answers. And I know he had a host of them, and because I felt very raw just then, I decided to head them off. "Let's smoke," I said. "Let's smoke a lot." And we did.

We smoked on the platform for hours. It was high summer then, and the only relief from the terrible heat is the dry, sandy summer winds. The height of the buildings and the way they're placed one on top of another serves to funnel these scratching winds through the streets. They move with a ferocious velocity. We sat on the platform wrapped in high-collared quilted vests in the sweltering heat, remnants of a fashion the refugee Athenorkos had brought with them from the cooler, wetter climes of the land south of the mountains. When Sorcha dragged me inside, my face and hands were covered in a film of dust. The sand coated my hair. I had smoked enough by then that I had grown passive and insensate. He had me strip off my sandy clothes, wash my face and hands and hair, and then piled me into the bed. I assumed he was going to pile in after me. I think I imagined he had. But the truth was that he lingered until I fell asleep, which likely only took a bare handful of seconds, and then he struck out on his own.

He woke me well after night had fallen. I had slept the majority of the day and woke bleary-eyed and disoriented. "Ariah! Ariah, damn it, wake up!" he hissed in my ear. He was crouched over me, shaking my shoulder to and fro. When I opened my eyes, he pulled me upright. "You awake?"

"Yeah."

He squinted at me. Light from the clockwork lamp flooded the room. I blinked at the unwanted brightness.

"You sober?"

"Uh, yeah. I think so. What time is it?"

"Late," he said. "Or early. I don't know. Look, that don't matter none. Look, I got something to ask you. You awake?"

I broke free of his grasp and rubbed my eyes. "Yeah. I'm awake. What's going on?"

"I got something to ask you."

"Well, ask it."

He bit his lip. Nervousness poured out of him. "Right. So. I'll, uh…I'll just come out with it. I don't think you should go with him. I don't want you to go with him. You know you got a place here. In case you don't, I talked to Caddie and she says you've got a place here as long as you follow the rules, and she said she can't imagine you not following them. I can't either. And in case that's not what you want, I've got other options. I mean, I know this place is no palace, right? So if you're thinking of heading out with him 'cause of that—'cause this place is in shambles—you've got another option. I know folks going to Vilahna. A crew, and every crew could use another good violinist, yeah? So there's Alamadour. You and I, we could go to Alamadour if you didn't want to stay here. You don't have to go with him. What do you think?"

"I don't know," I said.

Sorcha frowned. He leaned away from me. "You don't know?"

"I don't know."

"What don't you know?"

"It's a lot to think on," I said. "I can't decide just like that."

"Why not?"

"Because it's a lot to think on."

Sorcha let out a frustrated noise and fell back against the wall.

"Why are you mad at me?"

"I'm not mad. I just…really? You really got to think on it? He's a leaver, Ariah. Up and left us and Liro, and he up and left you for months. I been here. I'm the one you called a ghalio, not him, and I'm still here. What, loyalty counts for nothing with you?"

Loyalty actually counts for very much with me. But loyalty is not a one-sided thing, and it's rarely an even thing between two people, and despite all that had transpired I was still quite loyal to Dirva. It was the fact that I was loyal to Sorcha, too, that complicated things. "I'm not saying no! I'm saying I need time to think. That's all. A day or two to think about it. I wouldn't need that time if I didn't want to go with you."

He cut his eyes at me, petulant, like a half-grown boy. "You wouldn't need time to think if you didn't want to go with him, too, eh?"

"It's complicated. It's not just him. My parents are still there. I owe them…I don't know what I owe them, but if I went with you I'd be throwing something away. It's not just you or him. It's all of it. Just let me think, yeah?"

Emotions flickered across his face: anger, resignation, a stray burst of happiness, resignation again. "Yeah, all right. Yeah, think on it long as you want."

And I did. I left him there in the room and went to the platform. The summer night was warm. I needed space from Sorcha to make the decision; I think we both knew that instinctively, and I think it's one reason he pushed me so hard for an answer as soon as he asked. But, to his credit, when I took the space, he didn't intrude.

My mind is indecisive, wretchedly so, but my heart is not so patient. I approached the problem from a hundred different angles, but over and over the same thought came to me unbidden. Dirva thought on it and opened the door again. The possibility of redemption, I think, is embarrassingly seductive to me. I worried about what would happen to him if he returned to his life in Rabatha alone, with no one there to ground him. Just after dawn I struck out for Liro's house. It was early yet and the streets were empty. The day was already hot. I was sweating when I knocked on the door.

Liro answered. He was dressed severely, in a loose Semadran tunic and loose Semadran trousers. He looked like a living mockery dressed like that. It struck me as brave for him to have dressed like that. Liro himself seemed unfazed by his choice of clothing. He grinned at me. "I called it," he said, mostly to himself. "Dirva, I called it," he yelled over his shoulder. He opened the door for me and ushered me inside.

Dirva was on the couch, drinking tea. He stared at me for a second, caught and frozen. He shot an acid look at Liro, which made Liro laugh. "There is no need to gloat."

"The hell there isn't." Liro patted me on the shoulder as he let himself out.

Dirva and I stared at each other for a moment, then simultaneously looked anywhere but at each other. I was the first to break the silence. "I haven't decided." My voice shook, half with bravado and half with nerves. "I have some questions."

"That's fair," Dirva said. "Do you want to sit?"

I shifted my weight from one foot to the other. The questions came out in a steady stream. "Are you going back alone? You're going back without Liro? What about your family? Aren't things still tense between you and Falynn? Why did you need so much time to think? Why ask me to go back with you? The training's over. What is back there for me with you?"

"If you choose not to come with me, I'll go to Rabatha alone," he said.

"Are you sure that's wise?" I asked.

He stared into his teacup. "I am sure that is what I will do."

"Why did you come and find me after so long?"

"I meant to speak to you before your birthday," he said, "but I have been distracted. It is not easy for me to forgive. It's a failing of mine, and it always has been. When you spoke to me that day, I knew you'd never see me the same way. Liro says that is the nature of things; he says we are all constantly evolving. But he doesn't live the way I do, and the life I've chosen requires discretion. And now you know." He sighed. "I came and found you after so long because I am the one who brought you here. And because I didn't finish your training. I came and found you because we have both wronged each other, and because after all those years of feeding you and teaching you, it seems a waste to go on wronging each other. I am not a young man. I am too old to be this self-righteous. One of us had to offer peace, and it needed to be me."

* * *

Sorcha took the news better than I thought he would. He was stoic about it, and he wrapped himself up in a carefully constructed nonchalance. I had prepared myself for the worst and had approached him with a gentle caution one typically reserves for injured animals or the sick and elderly. I sat across from him on the bed we shared and took his hands. "I don't know if I'll stay there," I said slowly, "but I have to go back."

He pulled his hands from mine. "Yeah, all right. How long 'til you go?"

"Two weeks, I think."

He nodded. Sorcha leaned back against the wall, his head tilted up in some slight cocky defiance. He smirked. "You know you're walking yourself into a trap, yeah?"

"He doesn't have anyone else, Sorcha."

He raised his eyebrows at me. "Well, who's at fault for that? And it's not like he's the only one who needs you."

"I know. I'm sorry. But I'm the only one he needs right now."

Sorcha smiled, but it was a private smile, one that was unreadable to me. It surprised me to see he still had hidden corners, that there were parts of him I didn't know. "Two weeks, you said?" I nodded. "Well, let's not waste them. Kiss me."

"Sorcha, no."

He rested his head on my shoulder. "Hell, it was worth a shot."

The day I left, Sorcha pulled that deliberate nonchalance back on like a coat of armor. He skipped his morning set with Prynn to stay with me. We checked and double-checked my things against lists I had made. He made me take an extra set of his clothes. Dirva and I had agreed to meet at the East Gate, and I'd said my goodbyes to the Natives and various members of Sorcha's family the day before, so Sorcha had my last morning in the City all to himself. We smoked a final bowl together. We talked about how I'd miss pipeherb back in Rabatha. He asked to see my papers and scolded me for being honest enough to list myself as a shaper. I told him I hadn't known better until I'd tried to leave the Empire.

"You didn't know shit about anything before you got here," he said, and I admitted it was true.

The seconds piled on top of each other, and the minutes flew by hideously fast, and then it was time to go.

I stood up, and Sorcha stood up with me. He handed me my pack. I studied the room, trying with some desperation to memorize what it looked and felt like, how it smelled, and the shape of our shared pillow. I looked at anything and everything but him. I took a step towards the door, and Sorcha slammed into me. He fell into me with enough force to send us both stumbling back against the far wall. He was raw, and he made me raw, too. He held me tight and planted a long, lingering kiss on my cheek. "Gonna miss you, Ariah. Damn it, I'll miss you."

"Sorcha, I…yeah. Same." I held him back and took a deep breath. The smell of him—herb, and honey, and resin from his violin bow—flooded me. I was drunk with it, the smell of him. "Same."

"You take care, yeah? Don't go all silver again."

"I won't."

"And, you know, don't stay there if you don't have to."

"I won't."

He held me just a little tighter. He sighed into my neck. "Lor's lucky to have you," he said, and then he pushed me out the door.

PART THREE:

RABATHA: A RETREAT

CHAPTER 11

THE SCARRED MAN at the border did not recognize me at first. He stood against the wall and directed his men through curt gestures: Dirva was to go with one group, and I was to be brought to him. He separated us before he had even seen our papers. His green eyes shown with suspicion, wariness, when he saw me. The border guards shoved me into a cell; my papers were ripped from my hand. This treatment, which would have left me cowed and pliant before, hardened me. When the man with the desert scars came in, I stood leaning against the back wall. My arms were crossed against my chest, and this time, I looked at him. The guard sat at the table. He gestured for me to sit across from him, but I refused.

"I saw you," he said, "and I thought to myself what a bother it is when the City-born try to cross this border. No good ever comes from a City-born nahsiyya coming into the Exalted's lands." He fished my papers out of his pocket. "But you are not City-born. A man from Ardijan dressed like that. A ring in your ear. A jaw as naked as my own." He pulled the hood of his robe back. I pretended not to notice, but it intrigued me that he did it. I had made him for a religious man. With his fingers, with slow deliberateness, he snuffed the flame of the lantern, which lit that windowless room. In the dark, he could see, and I could not. I swear I could hear him smile. "I remember you, Mr. Lirat'Mochai. I am kept awake some nights by the drums that brought you freedom."

"I have nothing to buy my freedom with this time," I said.

"You had nothing to buy it with last time, either. They weren't your drums. Just a few months and you come out of that place looking like that."

I suspected I was to be detained. Dirva had warned me to change into Semadran clothes before we got there, but I, bitter about nameless things, obstinate, and willfully careless, stayed in Sorcha's hand-me-downs. Looking back, I think I know why I did it. Ambivalence tends to drive me to self-sabotage. I do not do well with internal conflict; I do not do well when I am unmoored. I suspected I was to be detained, and I was. Dirva tried to buy my passage, but the scarred captain of the guard could not be bought.

When you are detained and pressed into the Exalted's service, your papers are marked that you have been arrested, but truly it's closer to slavery. You are not sent to prison, but instead to a cell where you sleep. I will say this much for the captain: he was a clever man. He knew enough about magic to think of devious ways to use my talents. If a group of emigrants came to the border, sometimes when one was deemed suspicious they would extract information by standing me outside the window and having me plead with the guards in the voice of the emigrant's companions. I begged for my life as a man's wife. I shouted vicious threats in retribution for violence done to a brother in a father's voice. It was cruel, and I hated it, but the captain knew enough about the gifts to know how to trigger mine. There are times where the gifts come out unbidden. Their preferred tactic was to choke me until I'd nearly blacked out. Just before I blacked out, more often than not, the magic came out just the way they wanted. Sometimes it didn't. Sometimes I woke some minutes later on the ground.

My tenure there seems like it lasted years, but in fact it was only about six weeks. Six weeks after I stupidly, defiantly, got myself detained, Dirva appeared back at the gate. He came with a Qin dignitary from the Rabathan courts. Their camels trotted up side by side, Dirva keeping pace, at ease, with little regard for the status to which his nahsiyya birth relegated him. For a brief moment, I thought him a mirage. When it sank in that he was really there, it took a lot of effort to hold back the tears.

Dirva and the razehm rode into the border station. He rode right up to the captain. "Let him go," Dirva said. He held his hand out to the razehm, who handed him a sheaf of official documents requiring my release. Dirva threw them down at the captain's feet. "His detainment is relinquished."

The captain did not move to pick them up. He said nothing. All he did was look at the razehm. The razehm nodded. The captain let out a noise that was half-growl and half-laugh. He gave me a dismissive wave, and then he walked away. I was free.

"Return his papers," Dirva shouted after him. His voice

was sharpened steel. The captain pulled them out of his robe and threw them on top of the release orders without a backward glance. I scooped them up and scrambled onto Dirva's camel. I left everything else behind me.

"Thank you," I whispered.

"I am sorry it took so long," he said. "Read the orders."

Dirva had pulled strings. I found out later he pulled as many strings as he could find, as hard as he could. It was not a simple thing to get me out of the border captain's clutches: I was a young elf of no reputation whom no one particularly cared about. There was no reason to ruffle feathers to get me freed. The razehm who'd come with him, who had issued this order, did so knowing there would be raised eyebrows, gossip, and possibly an investigation. He was not friends with Dirva. They did not speak, not once, the entire trip to the Tarquintia train station. There was no warmth between them. I can only surmise that this Qin judge owed Dirva something, but whatever his motivations, they were never revealed to me.

The orders issued by that silent razehm on the camel next to me, a man who never so much as looked in my direction, were reassignment orders. He had, for undisclosed reasons, had the concerns of disloyalty stricken from my papers, and he had assigned me to a teaching position at Ralah College in Rabatha. I was to take over Dirva's linguistic instruction classes.

* * *

There is no such thing as a private car for elves on the Imperial trains, but there is such a thing as private conversation in a language just you and another speak. Early in my training, Dirva taught me a dialect of Vinkenti—Vahnan—specifically for this purpose. We elves were packed into our car tight—you couldn't breathe without brushing against a foreign body. Dirva and I whispered to each other in Vahnan, our voices low and drowned out by the sounds of bodies shuffling, vying for space, the sighs, the cracking knuckles. "Thank you, Dirva," I said. My voice held within it reverence and devotion. All the bitterness from before had drained away.

"You got yourself detained, Ariah. Why did you do that?"

"I don't know."

"Where is your sense, Ariah?"

"I don't know. But I...I don't regret it. I wish I hadn't been detained, but I don't regret it."

He sighed. He squeezed my shoulder. "There are ways to resist where you keep yourself safe. You can't barrel in like that. You have to have leverage. The Empire is not the City." He paused. "The City isn't what you think it is. It is no haven."

"I know that."

"I hope so. I don't mean to lecture you. I have no right to; I'm not your mentor anymore. But be more careful from now on. If you must court attention, make sure you've got a way out of trouble." He pulled a stack of letters from his bag. "These are from your parents."

I read the letters slowly. I read and reread them the entire way to the capital: four days by train. It was right that I had come back. They worried. They were concerned. They reminded me that I was not so adrift as I'd thought, that I had roots, and that I did indeed have obligations. I was someone's son, which is not always an easy thing to be. All of us exist in a web of other people, tethered to them and pulled by them this way and that. Mine was a life that mattered, at least to some people, and perhaps shouldn't be thrown away so carelessly. Mine was a life not entirely my own. The letters were not actually addressed to me but were in fact correspondence with Dirva. I only saw their responses, but I could catch glimpses of the things he'd told them in the letters. The training had ended, but he was my mentor still. In many cases the end of training is little but a formality, and such was the case with me and Dirva. In the letters, he took responsibility for my detainment. He made promises to get me back, and he wrote them as soon as he'd figured out a way to make good on those promises. The tone of the first letters from my parents to Dirva were livid. That is not so surprising, given that I followed him across borders without informing them of my departure, and given that I'd managed to get myself trapped in Qin clutches in my failed attempt at reentry. But as the letters went on, the tone softened. Respect tempered the anger, and gratitude finally eclipsed it. I was lucky to have him, my mother wrote, and she only hoped I was bright enough to learn from Dirva his clear-headedness in times of trouble and his impressive sense of loyalty. My mother had phrased it exactly that way: "impressive sense of loyalty."

When we neared Rabatha, I asked Dirva for a pencil. I wrote to my parents that I was safe, that I had been assigned to teach at the college, and that I loved them. I thanked them for pairing me with Dirva. I told them nothing about the City, and I told them nothing about the border. I told them I'd learned my lesson, and when I wrote it, I certainly believed it was true, but it turned out to be an unintentional lie. We arrived in Rabatha, spat out of the train into the heart of the Qin district. The station was crawling with police. Dirva took pains to embed the pair of us deep in the heart of the herd of elves rushing through the station. All of us walked with our heads down, but it was no use: the police spotted us anyway. Dirva's black hair and my odd clothing drew attention no matter how we tried to hide from it. A policeman whistled. We kept moving. "You there, you in City clothes, come here."

Dirva kept a hand on my arm and kept going.

The policeman whistled again. "We've got two nahsiyya here," he called out. Enforcement men broke through the wary elves. We were shoved to the side, our hands were bound, and we were taken into a room for questioning. One policeman looked through our papers, while another pawed through Dirva's things. "Where's your luggage?" he asked me.

"At the border," I said. Dirva shot me a warning look, which I pretended not to notice.

"They took everything but your papers?"

"Yes," I said. "And they tried to take those, too."

The policemen traded rough laughs. "What were you trying to bring in? Had to have been something for all of it to be confiscated."

"Probably drugs," said the one flipping through our

papers.

I was about to answer that I'd tried to bring in some dignity, but Dirva spoke first. "Spices," he said. "Ariah was traveling with spices, and the guards felt they were best allocated to those who protect the Exalted's borders. Ariah relinquished them willingly; they were not confiscated. May I ask why we've been detained?"

"Well, this one's papers say he has the gift. Maybe he can read us and tell you," said one of the policemen.

"As you can see from my papers, I work in the foreign office. There are those expecting my return. Further detainment will lead to questions," Dirva said. He smiled. "I ask only to help you prepare to answer those questions."

The policemen stared at him for a long moment. The one with our papers showed the other something in Dirva's documents. "We'll have an eye on you, nahsiyya," said one as he unlocked the manacles. "Tinkers strange as the pair of you warrant watching."

"I welcome you to do it," Dirva said. He pulled our papers from the policeman's hand, shouldered his bag, and led me out the door. We did not speak until we were safely back in his apartment with the door locked and the curtains closed. Once we were assured of privacy, he read me. He had never done it before, and the force of it shocked me. I had underestimated how much he had in him, I think, though looking back it should have been obvious. I was horrified at the intrusion, and at the same moment, I was impressed at the level of control with which he wielded it. It was masterfully done, his reading: penetrating, but subtle, with little of the burn one usually feels.

"Ariah, I cannot keep snatching you from the law like this," he said. "This anger you have, you should think on it. You should think on whom you're really angry at," he said. He left me there by my old cot, but his words hung heavy in the air. I hadn't admitted the anger to myself. I certainly had not admitted that I was angry at him, or that I was angry at him because I had left Sorcha. He read me, but more than that, he shaped me: he pulled it to the surface, this bitterness, this confusion, and forced me to face it. I had been read before, but I'd never been shaped. I'd never had someone reach deep into my soul and show me its inner workings. It is a profoundly unsettling thing. When he did it, I understood a little why the Qin were so uneasy with magic. I think, until then, I had taken the power of it for granted.

There are parts of ourselves that, once seen, can never be unseen. Things that, once thought, will exist in every thought after. He made me acknowledge it had been a sacrifice to return, and he made me face the guilt I felt at leaving Sorcha behind. Guilt that I'd tried to pin on him, but which I couldn't blame him for once he'd rescued me, and then rescued me again. As I made my bed, I had to reconcile myself to the fact that Dirva had only offered me a place with him, he had not demanded I take it, and he was not responsible for the fact that I took it. Leaving the City had been my own choice made for my own reasons, and he had shaped me into being just grown enough to own it.

CHAPTER 12

I WAS TO teach classes in Coastal Lothic and Athenorkos to potential traders venturing south. I had two days in Rabatha before the classes began, which was no time at all. I spent the first day sleeping. I spent the second day buried under anxieties about the start of my new position. It did not occur to me to do such things as find new clothing, or even wash the one set of clothing I had. It did not occur to me to let my beard grow back or to take out my earring. Dirva, likely, would have suggested such practical things, but I spent the day plaguing him with a thousand questions about where to go and what to do and when to do it. "You've seen me teach," he said. "You attended school. You'll know what to do."

But I didn't. For once, Dirva was wrong. My schedule dictated I was to teach two three-hour sessions a day: Athenorkos in the morning, and Lothic in the afternoon. I had no idea what to bring to that first class, so I brought everything which possibly could have been useful—the requisite pads of paper and pens, but in egregious numbers; some of Dirva's notes from his own days teaching; and any book in Athenorkos or Lothic I could find, including at least three cookbooks. I missed breakfast. Every time I started to step out the door, I thought of something else I might need. When I finally got to Ralah College, only a handful of minutes before class was supposed to begin, I realized I had no roster and did not know where to get one. The notification of which classroom I was to teach in was buried in the heavy sack of documents I'd dragged with me. I made a desperate stop at the college's registrar on the other side of campus, got the information I needed from a Qin clerk who could not be truly convinced I had a legitimate work assignment there even after I produced my papers, and got to the lecture room after all the students had already arrived.

Now, I had known that the class would be full of Qin students. Technically the college is open to all Imperial citizens, but given how work assignments function for Semadrans, and given the paltry pay those work assignments award us, it is rare for us to attend college. I knew this, but it was still a shock when I looked up from the podium and saw three hundred pairs of Qin eyes staring into me. In the wake of my time at the border, the Qin made me hostile and skittish. The anxieties I'd carried within me hardened into something stupidly caustic. I grew willful. I became what the Qin refer to as "uppity" in an elf: there was a decided lack of simpering graciousness in my carriage. I dropped my things and wiped the sweat off my forehead with the sleeve of Sorcha's old shirt. I scanned the room and saw three hundred Qin faces utterly disinterested in me and what I had to say. I saw three hundred Qin faces who saw me as an inconvenience. And far in the back, I saw a single Semadran face. In the back row sat a young Semadran woman, her chin held up just enough to betray an intriguing level of defiance. The only empty chairs in the entire hall happened to be located on either side of her. Dirva had advised me to find one or two students who seemed genuinely interested, who were taking avid notes, who nodded along when I spoke, and to teach to them. I decided to teach to her.

The roster was still in my hand. The brewing resentment within me would not let me waste an hour reciting three hundred Qin names. "I assume everyone is here," I said. The halls had been built by elvish mimic engineers, and the acoustics were perfect. My voice carried well without needing to be raised. I dropped the roster on a table next to the podium. "Feel free to mark your presence, if you wish, after class has ended. Since this is a beginner's course in Athenorkos..."

A Qin man in the third row let out a sharp, derisive laugh. "You can't just ignore formalities. Read the roster."

"No. Since this is a beginner's course..."

"My position requires a record of attendance!" a Qin woman a few rows over said.

"Then mark your attendance at the end of class. Does anyone else have a question?" A dozen or so raised their hands. "Questions will wait until the end of class," I said. In the shocked silence which followed, I taught them Athenorkos. I taught it the way it made sense to me: outlining the patterns of grammar first, how verbs formed corridors for nouns, how word order shaped the flow of ideas from one sentence to the next. For three hours I spoke, diagramming sentences on a chalkboard behind me, lost in the surprising richness of red elvish language. When I turned to address the students directly, I always spoke to the Semadran woman in the back. She took copious notes, her eyes trained on the board behind me.

At the end of the session, I reiterated again that the roster was there for those who wanted to record that they'd sat through the lesson. A line of Qin students queued up to mark themselves present. I noted that a handful of them were students who had, at one point or another, fallen asleep during the lesson. They had no questions for me, no questions about the content of the lesson, simply a concern that policies should be followed. The Semadran woman in the back of the room gathered her papers. She came down the center aisle and made for the door, but halfway to it she turned and came to me. My vicious armor from the moment before abandoned me. A glance at the line of Qin students still waiting to sign their names assured me I was trapped, and that whatever it was she was about to ask I would have to answer.

When she drew near, it became increasingly clear to me that she was more than a match for me. She was older than me and carried an unassailable self-possession I could not help but envy. She was tall for an elf and towered over me by a good three inches. Defiance was marked into every inch of her: she wore Qin robes, but wore them with her hair uncovered. She took up as much space as she pleased. There was, in her, a refusal to be diminutive. She reminded me of Dirva. When we were face to face, she raised her eyebrows. "How old are you?"

I let out a nervous laugh. "I'm...I'm old enough. How old are you?"

"Forty-six. How old are you?" she asked again. She peered at me, her head cocked to one side. She spoke Semadran, which turned a number of Qin heads our way. When she noticed them, she smirked.

I lied. "Thirty-nine."

"You're a boy."

"I am old enough," I said. It came out petulant, adolescent. I blushed. She smirked wider. I began to hate her. "Do you have a question?"

"How did you get this assignment? Who would assign you to this?"

"What?"

"You're very green."

I considered showing her my papers and grew irritated with myself for considering it. I leaned against the chalkboard and crossed my arms against my chest. "Do you have a question for me?"

"You're getting chalk all over your back." I leapt away from the board like it had electrocuted me. I frowned at her. Her smirk turned highly amused and slightly cruel. "Are you teaching the afternoon session on Lothic, too?"

"Yes."

"That would be my luck," she said, and then she sailed out the door without so much as a backward glance. Two hours later, she and I were once again in that same lecture hall. This time, she sat in the very center of the front row. The bravado with which I had taught that session of Athenorkos abandoned me. I stumbled through the class on Lothic. My points were punctuated with shrill giggles. My nerves got the better of me and led to several dropped and shattered pieces of chalk. As the class wore on, her face grew more amused and more disgusted with me. When I dismissed the class, the Qin students glared at me and lined up to sign the roster. She stayed where she was. She leaned on to the arm of the chair and studied me. "Where are you from?"

I pretended not to hear her. It was no use.

"Professor, where are you from?" This time she asked it in Qin. A dozen pairs eyes turned toward me.

"Ardijan," I said. My voice cracked halfway through.

She laughed—a quick, authoritative *ha!*—and leaned back in her seat. "I don't believe you," she said.

Once again I considered showing her my papers. "I'm not showing you my papers. You'll have to take my word for it."

"You're from the City," she said. She gestured at me. "Look at you. How did you get this assignment?"

"I'm from Ardijan," I said again. I left the lecture hall without taking the roster. Her laughter taunted me all the way down the hall. At home, I recounted my failures to Dirva. He told me I was making too much of it, but I wasn't. When I arrived the next day, a Qin official was lying in wait for me. He led me to the hall, handed me my abandoned roster, and said there had been complaints. Ralah College, he said, is not a place students complain about. My assignment was granted in the graciousness of the Exalted's example, he said, and it would be a shame for such graciousness to be misplaced, or worse, for it to go unrecognized.

I held my tongue admirably well. I had no option but to hold my tongue. If I was reassigned due to complaints, I knew it would be to somewhere unsavory. The best I could hope for was a factory. The worse—and probably more likely—scenario was reassignment back to the border. I went into the lecture hall cowed and defeated. I was there early that day, so I had a chance to look through the roster. The only Semadran name on it was Shayat Bachel'Parvi. Shayat herself came in shortly after I'd discovered her name, some minutes before the arrival of any of the other students. "Good morning, professor," she said. The way she said it was a mockery. I gave her a curt nod and refused to look up at her.

"Is this all the classes are to be?" she asked. "Just lectures?"

"That is how the Qin conduct them, yes." At least, that is how Dirva conducted his classes, and he had had no complaints as far as I knew.

"What a stupid way to do it. How will you know we've learned anything? How can we learn a language if all you do is explain it to us in Qin?" It was a good point. I looked up at her and told her as much. She smiled. "I'm not just here for the attendance records," she said. "I do want to come out of this farce actually able to speak it."

I smiled back. I was on the verge of asking her how she thought that would work, what she thought would make the class useful, and then she splintered what little ease I had with her. She pointed at me and raised her eyebrows. "Weren't you wearing this yesterday?"

I blushed. I frowned at her and went back to studying the roster. I told her it was none of her business.

"You still have chalk on your shirt," she said.

"Perhaps I have more than one chalk-covered shirt," I snapped.

"Perhaps, but I doubt you have more than one chalk-covered City shirt with the same exact badly-sewn patch on the left elbow." She wrote something down on a slip of paper and handed it out to me. "My father is a tailor. I'll get you a good price."

She was right about me: I was still very young, and very green, and because of that I took offense instead of seeing it as the offering of help it was. I petulantly ignored her. At the end of the class, she dropped the address of her father's shop on my podium as she walked by.

Late that afternoon, Dirva and I discussed how the day had gone. We sat on the floor of his apartment facing *The Reader*, each armed with a steaming cup of tea. "You should go see that tailor," he said.

"I will not give that woman the satisfaction," I said.

"Why not give her the satisfaction? What would it matter? You would get a good price for the clothes."

"I have my pride."

"You have too much pride," he said. He studied the painting and drank his tea. The mood in the room changed, became settled and sad. He opened his mouth to speak, looked over at me, and closed it again. I asked him if he was all right.

He nodded. "I think...I believe it may be time for me to see a matchmaker." He sat staring at Liro's painting. He didn't look at me while he said it, and he didn't look at me afterward to gauge my reaction.

I was stunned. "Why?"

"Solitude wears on a man."

"But Liro..."

"Liro is in the City."

It felt wrong to me. I had no right to feel any way about it, certainly, as it was his life and not mine, but it felt wrong to me nonetheless. It seemed unfair to Liro. It seemed unfair to whatever match was made for him. "You would be happy with a Semadran match?" I asked carefully.

He glanced over at me. Surprise lit his face. "Ariah, what a forward question."

I stared into my teacup, red and flustered. "I'm sorry."

"If it's a good match," he said, "it's a good match." Dirva studied *The Reader* for a long time. He sighed and took our emptied cups to the sink. When I returned to the apartment after my classes the next day, *The Reader* was gone. The wall was empty. All that remained was a pale square on the wall, an impression that it had once been there. In its wake, Dirva's apartment felt drab and lifeless.

* * *

The vanity that drove me into Sorcha's clothes in the first place drove me to Parvi Doshah'Vanya's tailor shop. It was located on the fringes of the Semadran borough, as far out as a Semadran could reasonably set up shop and still stay safe. The streets there were wide enough to accommodate rickshaws. Qin and Semadrans walked the street in equal numbers. Shayat looked like her father. The man who answered the door was tall and taut, and he had the same deep black skin. He wore Qin robes in a peculiarly Semadran way, just like his daughter.

"Can I help you?" he asked.

"I don't have an appointment," I said.

"I know. Is there something I can help you with?"

"I have need of a tailor."

His eyebrow raised slightly. "Yes. Yes, it would seem so." He glanced over his shoulder. "Shayat!"

I could have died. I began to giggle instead. The door creaked open a little wider, and Shayat Bachel'Parvi stuck her head through the door. "Yes, Papa, that's him. Evening, professor."

"Hmm. I see what you mean," said the tailor. I looked up, horrified, offended.

Shayat laughed at me. In that moment, it was very hard to believe Dirva when he said it didn't matter if I gave her the satisfaction. "He says he's from Ardijan, Papa."

"Well, people say many things."

"Give him a good price, Papa."

The tailor nodded and opened the door for me. I considered not going in, I considered walking away and wearing those clothes until they fell off of me seam by disintegrated seam, but I caught the way Shayat looked at me.

She looked like she expected me to leave, tail between my legs, my pride wounded. I shot her what I hoped was a defiant look and followed her father across the threshold. "Well, professor," the tailor said, "what style do you want?"

"This style."

"All the rage in Ardijan, I take it," he said. He gestured to a bench in the main room of the shop and slipped behind a curtain.

Shayat lingered in the doorway. The robe she had worn earlier that day had been replaced by loose-cut Semadran clothes, which suited her. She was broad-hipped, and the clothes drew attention to her waist where Qin robes hid it. Her hair was long and fell in loose waves down to her elbows, and she was barefoot. My face grew hot. My pride shattered into a thousand pieces. I was undeniably attracted to her, but I would have killed myself before letting her know that. "You're forty-six, and you live with your father?" I asked. Venom dripped from my voice.

"I am forty-six, and I have rented the attic apartment while I take courses at Ralah University. You're thirty-nine and have one pair of pants?"

"I don't have to explain myself to you."

She laughed and held up her hands. "You certainly don't. May I ask you a question about the classes?" She smirked and leaned forward slightly, haughty and conspiratorial. "You don't have to answer."

"Yes, ask." I did my best to sound uninterested, but I'm sure it came out strangled and shrill.

"It might help me learn if you taught vocabulary along with grammar."

I looked over. "But you won't know what to do with the vocabulary until you understand the grammar."

"But I won't be able to work with the grammar until I have some words to use it with."

"But you won't get the words right if you don't understand the grammatical structures."

"But building sentences in foreign grammar using Qin words makes no sense to me."

I blinked at her. "That's what you're doing?"

"Yes."

"But I'm just lecturing."

"There's no way I can learn a language just by listening to you lecture. I've been trying to practice it. But how do you practice speaking a language when you don't know the words?"

You will remember what I said before about how talents make one arrogant. Until that moment, it had never occurred to me that those who were not auditory mimics learned languages in a different way. To be clear, I could not have cared less whether the Qin students in my classes learned anything at all. They didn't seem particularly worried about it themselves. But I felt I was doing Shayat a disservice. "I'm afraid I can't change much in the class. There were complaints."

"I am shocked," she said.

I frowned at her. "I was about to make an offer to you, you know. I could do without the mockery."

She grinned at me. "You're very sensitive."

"I am not."

"Yes, professor. If you say so. What's this offer?"

"I would be willing to tutor you if you'd like. Once or twice a week. To teach you Athenorkos and Lothic in a way that works for you."

She stared at me for a long moment, then she smiled, and the smile was pleased and genuine. I am certain I blushed. "Papa?"

"Yes?" The tailor emerged from his storeroom with his arms full of City wools.

"The professor and I have struck a deal. His clothes are on the house."

Shayat's father shot her a curious look. "You bargain my services, Shayat?"

It was a joy to see her knocked off-kilter. "Papa, it is a good deal."

"For you."

"I will pay you back."

"When?"

"When I get the routes going."

Her father laid out the cloth. "I am marking it in the ledger. Give us some privacy, Shayat. I need to take the professor's measurements."

CHAPTER 13

DIRVA WOKE ME on Saturday morning. The single pleasant thing about teaching at Ralah College had been that the classes were scheduled according to Qin rhythms, and not to Semadran rhythms. We work every day, every single day without exception. The Qin get time for reflection and spiritual growth. Apparently our spirits don't have all that much growing to do. In any case, I was on a Qin schedule, but I was paid a pittance because an elf on a Qin schedule is really an elf working only two-thirds of the time. I had been permitted to sleep as late as my body demanded on Saturday morning, a thing I relished, until I agreed to tutor Shayat Bachel'Parvi. She ripped the simple pleasure of sleep on those Saturday mornings from me as easily as she ripped away my dignity every time I spoke to her.

"Ariah, you have an appointment," Dirva said. He stood over my cot, his hands on his hips. He looked somewhat perplexed, but mostly he looked annoyed.

He was already dressed. This was not surprising; he was an early riser, and he was usually dressed before I woke up, but he was dressed nicely, and that struck me as odd. I propped myself up on my elbows and peered at him. "Do you have an appointment?"

He frowned at me and left the room. "Not one I'm about to be late for," he said as he passed by.

I stumbled out of bed. My one set of clothing sat in a rumpled heap next to my bed. I noticed a stain on the knee of my pants as I put them on, which I knew with unwavering certainty would draw a caustic comment from Shayat. I grew bitter about the deal I'd struck with her, and in my bitterness I took my time. She could wait, I told myself. She should be grateful if I showed at all. I tried to prolong my dawdling by asking Dirva impertinent and personal questions. "You have somewhere to be?" I asked.

"Not so urgently as you do," he said. He was reading the local Semadran paper, his eyes trained to the page. I could glean nothing from him.

"Who is it with? Not with a Qin."

"It is not with you, Ariah."

I lingered in the doorway, my sleepy mind grasping at possibilities. There weren't terribly many things he kept secret from me by then. There wasn't much he felt was in need of hiding or discretion. It didn't take long before I realized where he was going. "Oh."

Involuntarily, his eyes flicked to where the painting had once hung. "You will be late, Ariah."

"Yes, I should go." I slipped out the door a second later. I hadn't wanted to know, not really. Dirva's personal life was not a thing either of us were really equipped well to handle. I walked to the tailor's shop ruminating on this—that I was the one person who knew him well enough to know that he hadn't let anyone in, and may not let anyone in ever again. I wondered at his motives. Was it a bid to gain legitimacy in the borough? He'd been a bachelor noticeably long, and gossip is a cheap and abundant distraction in a ghetto. Was it an anchor to this life he'd chosen? It's harder to up and leave when you're married. I had no answers. I only had the worry and the questions, and a nagging notion that I had already caused too much damage in the City to offer any comfort here in Rabatha.

I was disheveled and introspective when I arrived at the tailor's shop. The bitterness of having my precious lingering sleep snatched away still hung heavy on me. I was late. I knocked on the door, and Shayat answered it. She raised her eyebrows at me. "You're a mess. Is that a new stain on your pants?"

"I can go if you'd rather."

"Don't be an ass. You're getting free clothes out of this, which you obviously need," she said, waving me inside. She led me to a narrow corridor and up two flights of stairs. The attic was small, with one large, bright window, and low ceilings. A sleeping mat took up most of the available space. The room was spotless: the bed was impeccably made, the books on the shelves were meticulously straightened, and not a single stray sock was to be found. A low table against the far well held a camp stove. A kettle whistled to a boil just after we came in. "Do you want some tea?"

"Yes, thank you."

"You do look like you need help staying awake," she said as she poured the boiling water over the tea leaves. It was fragrant, good-quality tea, I could tell by the smell alone. I was still mired in thoughts of Dirva, which by then had turned into thoughts of myself and the reasons why I'd returned to the Empire. I barely registered her jab. My apparent lack of reaction irked her. "If you have something more pressing to attend to, professor, don't let me keep you."

"What?"

"You seem distracted."

"Oh." I let out a nervous laugh. She sat on the floor, and I sat down across from her. "Oh, it's nothing. So. Would you like to start with Athenorkos or Lothic?"

She narrowed her eyes at me and handed me my cup of tea. "You don't even look thirty-nine. You look like you just finished school."

"I finished my training!"

"You can't even grow a beard, professor."

"I can. I shave."

"Why?" She said it with disgust and impatience. She leaned forward slightly. "Are you about to grow your hair long and wear a hood? Do you think they'll take you in?"

"You are very judgmental, you know."

She smirked. "Yes, I know. That's not an answer."

"I'm not here to answer personal questions. I'm here to teach you Athenorkos and Lothic. Let's start with Athenorkos," I said quickly. She smirked wider. It was maddening. "Why are you learning these languages?"

"Oh, who's asking personal questions now?"

"It's not a personal question! It would help to know what kind of vocabulary to teach you."

"Mercantile reasons. Caravaner reasons," she said.

"Fine. Good. We'll start with that."

Even in that first session, I could see how bright she was. Languages did not come easily to her. She struggled with pronunciation, and she had no patience with her own mind. She grew more and more frustrated with herself. In one sentence, she had the grammar right but not the vocabulary. In another attempt, the tenses were wrong. There was always something wrong with the phonemes. That she got anything right at all, frankly, was impressive, but she quickly became as disgusted with her own limitations as she was with anything and everything about me. And since languages came so easily to me, and since I was still a little distracted, I found it easy to be patient with her. About an hour in, she growled halfway through a sentence when I reminded her about word order. "Stop correcting me!"

"I'm teaching you."

"Just stop." She sighed and leaned back on her hands. Her shoulders arced up toward her ears, and her mouth formed a hard, bitter line. She looked over at me. "It must be strange, teaching them."

"Strange how?"

"A whole room of Qin, and you're in charge."

I laughed. "In charge of what? I'm in charge of the roster, that's all. The class is a formality."

"Still," she said. "They're there to listen. To listen to an elf." She leaned forward again. "Can I ask you something?"

I didn't want her to. Whatever it was, I knew instinctively it was something I wouldn't want to answer. Still, it seemed rude to refuse. "Yes?"

She grinned. I had hoped that she would notice my resistance and think twice. The fact of it was she had noticed my resistance, and it likely sparked a hundred more invasive questions. "Just how red are you, professor?"

"What?" It came out a croak. The blood rushed to my face.

"Don't be like that," she said. "You're begging the question, the way you dress. You probably don't even need to shave."

"Just say it."

"Say what?"

"Really? You're going to mention everything but my eyes?"

She glanced away; she carried in her a sullen, irritable incrimination.

"Just say it. Ask me if I'm nahsiyya."

She was quiet for a second. "Professor, I..."

"Am I even really Semadran? What am I even doing here? Who in the district would rent a man like me a room, anyway?"

"Professor..."

"And you're here alone with me. The neighborhood will talk."

She held up her hands. "All right! All right. I was rude. I'm sorry."

"The hell you are," I said, pulling myself up. "From now on keep your questions to yourself or the lessons are off."

Two days later, she sat in the center of the first row. She started the first class half-conciliatory, but by the time the second class rolled around, it had hardened into a mocking irritation. She continued to sit right there, right in front of me, and the crackling tension between us made me remote and cold during the classes. I took no questions from students. I lectured until I was hoarse, wrote endless lines of text, and took refuge in the patterns of foreign languages. I didn't even bother coming up with notes; I simply showed up and started talking. The lectures were elaborate academic cold shoulders. The Saturday tutoring sessions were strained, awkward affairs. She met me downstairs in her father's shop, though occasionally he would have a customer and we'd be forced out. She always took us outside rather than back up to the privacy of her room. I took a vindictive pleasure in knowing I'd struck a nerve with her. She was not young, after all. I wondered if she'd seen a matchmaker. There was probably gossip about it, which more than once I resolved to ferret out but somehow never got around to.

One Saturday, about two months into the class, Parvi forced us out. He had, by then, finished one set of clothes for me, which I was wearing that day. He was then working on a second set of impeccable City-style clothes for me, on the house—I suspect to make up for the inherent rudeness of his daughter. Shayat and I stood on the stoop of her father's shop, glaring at each other. "Well?" I asked. "Are we done for the day?"

"No. We're not. I need more work on counting in Lothic," she said. I could have wrung her neck. "Are you hungry?" she asked. I looked at her like it was a trick. "I am hungry, professor. I can't deal with this on an empty stomach. Let's go to the markets."

"Deal with what?"

"With you!" she said. "With this stupid language! With any of it." She sighed and dropped her hands to her hips. "Look, can we call a truce? I don't care where you're from or who you are or whatever it is you think you're hiding. I don't. I'm curious, but who isn't? I just want you to teach me these awful languages so I can get out of this place. All right? I'll buy you something to eat."

And I laughed. I laughed so hard, delirious in it, drunk in it. Gales of laughter shook me so hard I was sore the next day. Tears squeezed out of my eyes and blurred my vision. Distantly, I heard Shayat badgering me.

"What? *What?*" she demanded.

"I just realized," I said when the spasms finally subsided. I wiped the tears from my eyes, staring at her like I'd never seen her before. And she was beautiful then, truly beautiful. Wild hair kicked every which way by the winter wind. Black skin that drank in the light. "I just realized you're to be a caravaner. A merchant! You! You know if you're going to make a go of it, Shayat, people will have to like you enough to buy from you."

She grinned a canny, cat-like grin at me. "Maybe if you had two coins to rub together, professor, I'd turn the charm on for you."

"What charm?"

"Oh, who's the rude one now?"

I laughed again. "Let's get something to eat."

* * *

It was an ungainly, unlikely friendship that developed between Shayat and me. I think the truth of it was that neither of us was particularly adept at building a friendship. It was a clumsy thing, a blunt thing, that stumbled more often than not, but somehow the stumbles became amusing instead of offensive. She stopped asking me personal questions. I could not bring myself to ask her personal questions. We muddled through a weird and welcome friendship that was, in retrospect, anchored to nothing in particular.

The weeks passed, and the classes ended, and the Qin students retreated for a month of reflection. Shayat lingered in Rabatha. She was not as proficient in the southern languages as she wanted to be. She had ambitions, and she was a careful, thorough person, and her pride was such that she could not bear to start a route when she was not yet fluent. Her ambitions intrigued me: an elf-run, elf-led caravan. Maybe even elf-only. She had separatist leanings. She flirted with divulging them, dropping a reference here or a dig at the Qin there, then gauging my reaction.

It was because of Shayat that I learned Droma. She favored the Qin markets. I rarely ventured out of the borough on my own. The sting of the border still lingered, and any time there were more of them than there were of us, a panic rose in my chest. Shayat, peculiarly, managed to keep that panic at bay when I was with her. Shayat dragged me to the Qin markets week after week. She practiced her Athenorkos and Lothic by conversing with me about prices of this and that, and marking those prices down in small notebooks. She tracked anything and everything but the live goods. And it was the live goods that drew my interest.

She was there the first time I saw a slave auction. It was a lively thing, voices cresting like waves. What drew my attention was the tone of it: it had a crazed character; it sounded malevolent and broken, like the screech of a train felled by a loose wheel. "What is that?" I asked.

"Oh, professor, that's a slave stage. Come on, I know a man who'll give us good pomegranates for cheap." She started off, east, I think, and only noticed I hadn't followed when she was some distance away. "It's a slave stage!" she called out.

But I couldn't turn away. The first one I saw was nahsiyya, probably whore-born, and probably sold back into a brothel while I watched. The next was a gold elf. Now, I'd heard of them, but I had never seen one. We don't have enough gentry Qin in Ardijan to warrant exotic house slaves; that's a game for the urbanite wealthy to play. The gold elf had skin the color of mahogany and a thick mane of yellow hair. The gold elf sang as the slavers led him up to the stage. And I felt it. By virtue of the gift I felt the fatalism, the loss, the bleakness of it. Shayat appeared next to me. She sighed. "I hate it when they sing."

"Do they usually sing?"

"I don't know. I swear it feels like they sing every time. Come on."

I followed her away, but two days later I wound up in the Qin markets again after my classes ended. It was a strange detour, one that took me an hour's walk out of the way, but the song had lodged itself in me and refused to leave. The gift nagged me, needled me, whipped me into a frenzy to seek it out to understand it all the way. There were no slavers that day. I wandered the markets, aimless, listening. Auditory gifts can be demanding. And then I heard it. It wasn't a song, it was speech this time. A soft patter of words, and more words in a different voice. It led me around a corner, and there I found a clutch of three gold elvish house girls congregated around a public water pump. One filled a jar that held orchids. The other two conversed.

They didn't seem to notice me, and for that I am glad, because I would have looked a deranged fool or worse standing there like that. The language hooked into me; there was a richness in it that I could feel before I even understood it. Premonitions crept through my bones. It was one of those horrifying moments where your life changes, where suddenly the course you've tendered veers in a new and dangerous direction.

It was after curfew when I got home. When I slipped in the door, Dirva let out a sigh of relief and hugged me. It caught me off guard. "Do not tempt fate, Ariah," he said, and his voice was hard and tender at the same time.

"It was the gift."

"What was?"

"I have to learn Droma."

And then he understood. "I'll help," he said, even though he was no longer my mentor. "Meet me here after your class tomorrow."

Dirva is more mimic than I am, or at least a slightly different variant, because he picked up Droma in half the time it took me. He came with me to the markets, always close, protective, shepherding me away when curfew drew close. He spoke to me in Droma and helped me hone it. We took to speaking it at home. He told me he had been compelled by Vahnan Vinkenti the same way. He told me there are languages, sometimes, that feel like home. Some languages that have a siren's call, and that Droma must be mine. He learned Droma, with its peculiarities, and he knew it was my home, and he did so without question or judgment. And it was a peculiar language: it was so very communal, with few pronouns and ways of speaking of the discrete, individualized self. There was little sense of "I" in Droma; much more focus was spent on an intoxicating and obliterating "we." And there was the question of gender, too. It took me some time to parse it, but it became increasingly clear that the Droma did not understand themselves as men or women, but simply as people. The slaves in the city, likely as a means of survival, acknowledged that we divided ourselves as such, and they must have understood that we divided them that way, too, but in the conversations I overheard they only ever used variations on the word *voe*—the Droma word for "person"—to refer to other Droma and themselves. It fascinated me—how could something so fundamental and so obvious as gender go unseen among them? And what did it mean? How could I be myself without being a man? I wanted very much to understand it, but it was elusive and exotic and always just out of my reach. I couldn't help but gender them while listening: that one is a male person who is speaking to a female person, went my thoughts.

It took me a month to absorb Droma, and another two weeks to regain my balance. After that I once again ventured to the Qin markets alone. I tracked the gold elves through the streets; I knew their rhythms, and I listened. And at first I was content to listen. Like elves everywhere, they traded gossip. This family broke Sabbath. This family's Exalted Eye was not actually silver: it had been hocked to get a wayward son out of debt.

But on Saturday afternoons, when the markets teemed with Qin fresh from their devotions, many of the Droma found ways to get to the slave stages. You would not know they were there unless you knew where to look. They perched on roofs and awnings. They wedged themselves on window ledges. They slipped into the shadowed hollows under the stages themselves.

The stranded Droma soaked the songs up, these pieces of home. I haunted the slave stages, and I took down every Droma song I heard. The way they were sung gave credit to those who first composed them. They start with "Yalivva said to me" or "Vrisini told me that" — that sort of thing. As I collected more and more of them, I developed favorites. The things Shithilat said were quiet and full of stoic courage. The things Binnira said were simple but grandiose in the telling. And the things Halaavi said made me homesick for a world I'd never actually seen.

CHAPTER 14

"DO YOU LIKE poetry, Shayat?"

She propped her chin in her hand and smirked at me. Semadran passersby on the streets cut their eyes at us, and I blushed. She laughed. "Why, professor? Do you have a love poem for me?"

"No." I sighed at her and stared out at the street. She laughed again. "I just thought...I have heard that poetry and songs help you learn languages quicker."

"You heard that about me?"

"No. You, like a general you."

"I know what you meant, professor."

I sighed again. "You're so juvenile."

"Well, you're prissy. You think poems will work?"

"I think they might work. I can't say for sure. They might not. But they might work." I pulled a small volume of Lothic poetry from my pocket and handed it to her. I had searched Dirva's library specifically for a book that had few love poems in it. She flipped through it and found one anyway. She knew enough Lothic to read the incriminating title. She grinned at me, and I blushed. It was a typical thing between us. She knew, and

I knew she knew, and the teasing, somehow, took the sting out of it. "This is purely educational."

"Oh, is it? You think you can teach me a thing or two?"

"Oh, wouldn't you like to know."

She laughed. She had a brash, loud laugh, the kind that jerked attention to her. I grinned stupidly beside her. "My, my," she said. She glanced over at me. "My, my. In front of my father's house."

"Oh, I-I meant no disrespect, and honestly, Shayat, I...it was a joke, a badly told and ill-timed joke, and..."

She shook her head at me and laughed again, quieter and softer this time. "So, what am I supposed to do with these poems?"

"Well, you read them. And you translate them. And you may want to recite them, because your pronunciation needs work."

"It's a stupid language," she said, but she tucked the book in the pocket of her robe.

"City Lothic is better," I said. She looked over at me, eyebrows raised, and I wished I hadn't said anything. I couldn't exactly articulate why, but the fervency of her curiosity about me scared me. "If this helps you, I'll try to sneak an Athenorkos volume out of the Library."

"You wouldn't dare."

I had dared already. I had cased it, and I had learned which of the guards paid little attention to elves in workman's clothes and which stopped everyone. I had, during my tenure as a lecturer at Ralah College, stolen some thirty books. Dirva had told me that I shouldn't tempt fate, but he also read everything I brought back, and I was fairly certain he would pay the fees if I got caught with one. But I didn't plan on getting caught. A smile flashed across my face. I think she saw it, and I think it confused her, but I couldn't be sure. "Are you taking classes this term?"

"No," she said. She pulled the book of poems back out and flipped through the pages.

"Why not?"

"I can't afford it. Besides, it's just these two languages I want to learn, and I've got you teaching them to me for free."

"Free for you. Parvi's losing time and labor and wool to me."

"He likes you. And he likes making your peculiar clothes. He gets bored of robes."

This was, clearly, her way of asking me to remain on as her tutor. I knew her well enough, by then, to know she never asked for things directly and rarely even suggested. Mostly, she did what she did, and she left it up to the rest of us to decide whether or not to acquiesce. I left soon after that, but I left quite pleased that there was yet an excuse to see her week after week. And then the day got strange.

I had meant to go to the markets to steal more Droma songs, but I wound up at Dirva's apartment instead. This was not a matter of veering slightly off course; Dirva's apartment was embedded in the borough. It was in the opposite direction from the markets. I didn't know then what had led me there, but I knew when I looked up and saw our building that whatever waited inside was not going to be pleasant. I felt it in my bones. And I was right.

I heard voices from the landing. I heard Dirva's voice, muted by walls, quiet, and I heard Liro's voice pierce through those walls, clear as a bell. "No, I don't know why you sent it back!" he yelled. "It don't make no sense! It must have cost you an arm and a leg to smuggle it back to the City. Why not just send a letter, Dirva? If you just wanted to say it was over, why not write me a cheap, easy letter?"

"It belongs with you," said Dirva.

"It taunts me!" shouted Liro. "It dredges it all up, every single moment! I don't want to face it every day!"

"Then sell it! Sell it and make back what you spent smuggling it and yourself all the way here."

I told myself it was best to give them space, but my body didn't listen. Before I knew what I was doing, I was through the door. Against the wall was *The Reader*. It lay on its side, upended. Dirva and Liro stood close together in the middle of the room. There was a charge in the air, a yearning. I could feel it, how much both of them wanted the other, and I could feel the steely walls Dirva had thrown up. It all happened in an instant, and it overwhelmed me. I stumbled back against the door, disoriented, and Dirva rushed to my side. The tension in the room broke. He'd called me there to give himself a distraction, an escape.

"He's more than a bit shaper," Liro said.

"Please get some water," Dirva said. Liro stepped into the kitchen. Dirva took my face in his hands. "Ariah. Ariah."

The smoothness of his voice, the palpable relief he felt at seeing me, pulled me back. I took hold of his forearms. "Build a wall."

"I can't."

"Take a breath, take a moment, and build a wall," he said. He said it without urgency, without pressure. My heart slowed. I felt my mind draw into itself, the curiosity pulling back in like a turtle to its shell. The trick is to feel yourself. I tracked my own heartbeat, let it grow loud and booming in my ears, a steady, doubled rhythm of me-ness.

Liro appeared next to Dirva, glass in hand. "He's past training, and he's like this still?"

Dirva said nothing. He took the glass and handed it to me. I slid down the wall and sat on the floor, drinking it, intently focused on the way the water felt sliding down my throat. I listened to their conversation distantly. Dirva said he and I were cut from the same cloth.

"You're not. Untrained shapers don't fare well," Liro said.

"He's no more than I am."

"The hell he isn't."

"I'm more than you think." This is what began to catch my attention. That he'd say this to Liro, that he'd speak so openly about himself and his gifts...it was a shock to me. "You don't always notice," he said. I drank more of the water, but I watched them now. Contained and separate, but only barely so, and still under the threat of a broken wall, I watched them.

"Dirva, you got trained," Liro said. There was a gentleness in his voice. "You've not trained him deep enough."

Dirva said nothing. He sighed. Liro took him by the arm and turned him slightly away from me. "You can't keep pretending you're not yourself. I know you never liked it, and hell, I wished you'd not left, but Vathorem was good for you. The way you came back...Dirva, you needed it. You were right to go. Give this kid what you got," he said. He said it quickly, it a tight, low voice.

Dirva gently pulled his arm away. "You have never been good at taking your own advice."

"This is not about me."

"And it's not about Ariah, either."

A taut, cold anger lashed through Liro. It filled him up and spilled out into the room. I winced. "Yeah, all right, well, let's talk on what this is about then."

"He has problems with walls, Liro."

Liro swallowed. The muscles of his jaw twitched. He fought it back down. I drank more water. "We have to do this in front of your boy? Really, we do?"

"I can't send him out in this state."

"Did you bring him here, Dirva?"

Dirva didn't answer. The silence was damning. Liro crossed his arms against his chest. There was a bottled bitterness in him that had me half-undone again. "This kid, you're using him as a shield. This kid, he waited for you, and he broke himself down for you, and you are toying with him. It ain't right, Dirva. You know it's not right."

The wall burst. I felt everything. I felt the loss, and I felt the guilt, and I felt the love and the hope and the tenderness and the wounds. I felt it all, and I felt it as a broken mess, and I couldn't tell what belonged to whom or where I began and they ended. I lost a sense of time.

The next thing I remember is waking up late in the night. I was on my cot, still dressed, but I smelled of pipeherb. I had slept heavily; my limbs had the stiff soreness of a too-deep sleep. The gifts were at bay. The herb lingered in my blood just the slightest bit, but even a slight bit has its benefits. I heard them talking in the next room. The walls in the borough are thin, the buildings are cheaply made, and voices carry. I couldn't help but listen. I hated myself for it, I tried to marshal the strength to leave the apartment, but I couldn't do it. I heard every word.

Liro offered him everything, anything. Liro offered to come to Rabatha. He offered Dirva a place in the City. He offered to go south, to Vilahna, to Elothnin, anywhere. The Pirate Isles. The archipelago. Money was no object; he'd sell some paintings, all the paintings. Liro said he'd stop painting. Liro said he'd paint all the time if Dirva didn't want to work. They could hide it, if Dirva wanted, Liro said, but there must be some way to be together. And Dirva told him no.

"But you love me," Liro said. Ah, and the herb was in me still, but I felt it, and it broke my heart. I think that moment was when I finally unlearned it, when the tapestry of old rules finally unraveled all the way. "I know it. I know you do."

"I do," Dirva said. "I have, I will. It's part of me."

"I don't understand."

"There is more to me than you. It's part of me, but this is

part of me, too."

"But why? Why would you choose this?"

Silence lingered for a long time. I am not proud of it, but I strained to hear something, anything. I crept out of bed, ear flat against the wall. I heard nothing: no movement, no rustle of cloth, nothing. Nothing for so long. I have always wondered what happened in that time. Did they look at each other, or did they avoid each other's gaze? Did they sit side by side, hands joined, or was there a distance between them neither could bring himself to bridge? I have no way of knowing. I hope there was tenderness in that moment, but I have no way of knowing.

Finally Dirva spoke, and his voice when he spoke was utterly vulnerable. He was a man who built walls at every turn, who did so as instinctually as I tore them down. It was conscious, this decision to stay so open. "There were only ever two things back there that kept me sane, and it was you, and it was him. And he's gone. And you know I love you, but you can't be the only thing. You can't be all of it, my entire life. I can't just be yours. I'm sorry. It's a weakness, and I'm sorry for it. I would have written when I sent it back, but Liro, how does a man say that in a letter?"

"I knew," Liro said.

"I thought you would."

"When I saw the damn thing, I knew." There was a caught breath. There was the ghost of a sob. "Damn it, Dirva. Fucking hell, Dirva. Damn it."

"You'll be all right."

"I know. We'll both be fine. I don't know, that...fuck, I

don't know, that makes it worse somehow, you know what I mean?"

Dirva laughed, and Liro laughed with him. The bed within creaked. "Yeah. Yeah, I know what you mean, Ro. I'm sorry. I'm sorry for before, I'm sorry for coming back, I'm sorry for all of it. I am sorry for all of it, and I am grateful for all of it."

"But you're still sending me packing, eh?"

"You'll be all right."

"Will you?"

"I'll be all right."

* * *

He wasn't all right. Not for a long time, but he pretended to be. I wasn't all right, either. Our relationship was still fragile, and there was something about that day that splintered it a little more. I waited until Liro left. I gave Dirva a few hours to himself. I went to the markets and listened to the gossip traded by the gold slaves. When I came back, I came back burdened. Dirva sat by the window, near my cot, in the shadow of where *The Reader* once hung. He asked me if I was hungry.

"You shaped me," I said. He could not meet my gaze. "You pulled me all the way here. You knew I couldn't handle that."

He said nothing to me. His frame seemed diminished. He seemed not so much larger than myself, like really the breadth of his shoulders was half shadow. He looked to be slipping away.

"Did you know you did it when you did it? Or did it just happen?"

"I knew," he said. "I was well trained."

"Then why haven't you trained me? Why?

The anger surprised him. The force of it—my voice raised, my posture—caught him off guard. "I...Ariah, you...I can't train a thing you won't admit to having."

"I came to you! In the City, I came to you!"

"In the City, I was useless."

"But you knew! You've known for years. You are this well trained? I thought you studied with a linguist! I thought Vathorem was a linguist!"

Dirva stood up. He took half a step towards me. He was bewildered. It bothered me; I wanted him shamed, and I wanted him frightened. I wanted him shaken to his core. But the most I dredged out of him was concern and confusion. "Vathorem is a linguist. And he is a shaper. I never lied to you."

"You didn't tell me the truth, either!"

"I..." He raised his eyebrows. "Yes. Yes. I do that. I'm sorry for that. Let me tell you about him," he said. He took another careful step forward. I felt a slight pull from him, which abruptly stopped, like he'd thought the better of it. His fluency with his gifts raised my hackles. "Ariah, please. I would like to explain something, something that may be relevant to you."

I shook my head. It was a violent thing, a rapid, whipping movement back and forth, back and forth. He stopped mid-step. "Liro was right. That was improper, what you did. You used me, and you used him. And you're seeing a matchmaker, and you'll use whatever woman the matchmaker pairs you with. There is a code, Dirva. You taught me little about this, but even I know that much."

"Ariah, I'm sorry."

I left. I left before he could say anything else, or do anything else. I left before he could explain himself. I left because I didn't trust him, and I didn't trust myself with him. I had very few places to go, and I ended up at Parvi's shop. On the walk there I thought about Sorcha, and the night he'd caught me in his thrall. I remembered how it felt a violation, but how I knew it hadn't been. What Dirva had done was a violation, made worse because it hadn't felt like it. Parvi opened the door. "Professor? It's close to curfew. We don't have an appointment."

I laughed. It was a cracked, broken laugh. I pinched my eyes shut and laughed that awful laugh again. "Would it be at all possible, sir, for me to sleep in your parlor tonight?"

"Sleep in my...Ariah, are you all right?"

"I have had better days."

He sighed. He glanced over his shoulder, then out at the street, up one side then down the other. He sighed again. We both knew there would be talk. But he opened the door and ushered me inside. We stood just inside the doorway; he stared at me, and I stared at my feet. I felt very numb. I felt very hollow. Life seemed strung together, second by empty second. He cleared his voice. "May I ask?"

"I would rather you not."

"You will not bring the law here, I hope."

"No, sir. It is just personal."

"Ah," he said. "Ah." Gently, tentatively, he squeezed my shoulder. "I will get you a blanket."

I sat in his shop with my head in my hands and listened to the rhythm of my heart. I heard him walk up the stairs, and I knew it was inevitable that Shayat would come down. He must have told her I was not well, but she was not the type to be told much of anything, and in her infinite wisdom decided to evaluate the situation for herself. She sat next to me on the floor. "What happened?"

"I would rather you not ask."

"It had to be something."

"It was something. I would rather not discuss it."

"You could, though," she said. "Discuss it, I mean. If it would help. You don't have to. I'm not going to make you. But if it would help, I'd listen."

I peeked over, my hands still covering half my face. She smiled. I smiled back. I very much wanted to talk to her, just then, but how could I? It was all bound up in my gifts—gifts I ran from, had run from my entire life—and Dirva's gifts. I couldn't. Even if I'd decided to flout the rules, I wouldn't have known where to begin. But her offer helped, and her smile helped more. "I would rather not. I'll be all right."

CHAPTER 15

THE NEXT MORNING, Dirva appeared at Parvi's shop. Parvi opened the door, and I heard him ask to see me. Parvi told him to wait. I was already out of bed and dressed when he came into the shop, already folding the blanket. "I'll see him. Thank you. Thank you for your hospitality."

"You don't have to see him, professor."

"Thank you for that, too. I'll see him." I slipped out before Shayat woke. Dirva stood on the street, large and dark. "How did you know I was here?"

"I checked the jails first. You have a history," he said. "If you weren't there, you must have been here."

"It's Monday. It's eight. You have..."

"I canceled it. Personal reasons. I felt we should talk. If you are willing, I think we should talk."

I nodded. I stared down at my boots—old, beaten boots that had once belonged to Sorcha but before that had likely belonged to several others, boots that had traveled a long, long way. I tried to think of something to say.

"Ariah, I am sorry."

I looked up. "You are?"

"Of course I am." He closed his eyes and sighed. "I am very sorry. I owe you some explanation. And there are things I have needed to tell you for some time. Things I've wanted to tell you for some time, but as you know, I sometimes lack bravery."

"Let's go home," I said. "Let's talk." I walked past him, leading him back, and as I passed by, I reached out and squeezed his hand. I shouldn't have, and certainly not right there in front of Parvi's house, because it spurred gossip, but it felt right to do it. We walked side by side, in perfect rhythm, and in silence. I'd had the night to think on it, and the night to sleep on it, and much of my terrified anger had leaked out. The distance calmed me. I was ready to listen.

When we reached the apartment, Dirva had me sit. He prepared us food and tea. We warmed to each other again while we ate. When we finished, he took the plates, rinsed them, and sat down at the table across from me. "I am sorry," he said.

"I think I know why you did it."

"It doesn't make it right."

"No," I said, "but it makes it make sense. Don't do it again."

"There is no danger of that." Dirva scratched at his beard. He glanced out the window. He was composing himself; when he looked at me again, he was contained and quiet and patient. "There are two things I need to tell you. They are both about me and about you. I have a request of you, and I have an offer for you, and you can do with each of them what you will." He began to speak and stopped himself. He leaned towards me slightly. "You owe me nothing, Ariah. You know this, yes?"

"Yes." But the truth was I owed him everything. He had taught me who I was. He was deeply ingrained in me. He had trained me, and he had rescued me more than once, and he found me a job and let me live in his apartment without financial contribution. Without him, I'd be an untrained mess, homeless, trapped at the border.

He sighed and rested his chin in his hand. He drummed his fingers along his jaw. "I will say it again: you owe me nothing. Nothing. I want you to remember that when I tell you what I'm about to tell you."

"All right. I will."

He laughed. "It's true."

"It isn't true. I owe you nothing? What does that even mean? It makes no sense. But I'll remember you said it."

He laughed again. "Your student has rubbed off on you."

"What?"

"From what you've said, you've picked up some of her brashness."

"I have not. You don't know her."

"Well, no," he said, "but it is a truth that a student marks a teacher as much as the teacher marks the student." There was a kindness in the way he said it, which cut right to the heart of me, and made it that much more difficult to believe I owed him nothing. He laughed. He smiled. He looked on the verge of speech, grew consternated, and laughed again. "A match has been made for me," he said very slowly, each word parceled out carefully, fastidiously, each said with a tiny bit of awe like he himself did not quite believe it was true. "A match has been made, and...and I'd like your approval."

"Your family approves a match." I blurted it out, mostly out of shock. He smiled at me. "Oh! Ah, I...Oh, Dirva, I..." I laughed. I grinned like an idiot. "Are you sure?"

"I am."

"Your mother or Abira or Cadlah, they would..."

"Maybe. Maybe they wouldn't. But I am asking you." I drew in a breath. He reached across the table. "Remember what I said!"

"You're sure about this?"

"Yes. I said I was. You always ask so many questions. Ariah, you can think it over. You don't have to answer now."

"Of course. Of course I will!"

"You can think it over," he said, but he grinned as he said it. His eyebrows knit together. "Considering these past few days, you didn't even sleep here last night, if you need time..."

"I don't need time. Of course I will. Of course." He hid his grin behind his hand. He nodded to me in thanks. I wanted very much in that moment to ask about Liro, to ask why he'd sought a match in the first place. I didn't understand it. But he was happy then, happier than I had ever seen him. He looked, in that moment, like he'd shaken off the weight of his da's death, and like he had no regrets and just a promising future. "It's a good match?" I asked.

"It is," he said. There was a trace of surprise in his voice. "I truly think it is."

"When? When do I meet her? What is she like?" *And why?* I wanted to ask. *Why seek a match in the first place when you've had once since you were younger than me?* But those questions went unasked.

"Soon. You'll see when you meet her." He hid another grin behind his hand and peered at me. "Thank you, Ariah."

"It's an honor."

"The honor is mine."

I beamed. I sputtered something incoherent. I think I repeated that it was an honor. I managed, after a few stilted seconds, to ask him if he had something else to talk about.

"Ah, yes. Yes, there is," he said. Some of his brightness dimmed. "It's about your training. I thought about it. You're right; Liro was right. I didn't give you all the training you needed. I don't know that I can give you all the training you need. And the other day, with Liro, when he said you were past your training, I saw your face, and you believed him." He waited for me to say something, but there was a ringing in my ears. It was a thought, which had haunted me well before Liro had voiced it. I hadn't wanted the shaper training, I'd sidestepped it, and over and over again the thought came to me that maybe the shaper in Ardijan had been wrong, that I should have had a different path, and that the window had closed on me. "Ariah, that's not true. I don't know where Semadrans got this idea, but it isn't true."

"Magical theory says…"

"Magical theory," he said, "is just a theory. I never explained any of this because it's complicated. And because I'm not very good at explaining things about myself. There had been little reason to until I took you in. Ariah, back in the City,

Da found me a mimic to train with. I was like you: the shapers knew, but I hid it. They said they'd leave me alone if I wanted them to, and I wanted them to. Da knew, probably because he'd been raised here, but everyone else just thought I was smart, observant. Well, everyone except Liro. He...he knew, too."

I had a guess as to how Liro found out, and I blushed. I couldn't help it, and the embarrassment I felt at blushing in the first place made me burn a brighter red.

"Yes. Well. They knew," Dirva said quickly. "They knew, but no one else. My parents still don't know. Falynn doesn't know. Abira and Amran have suspicions, I think, but they've never asked. Cadlah only asked because you mentioned it as a secondary ability to Sorcha. In any case, what I'm trying to say is I was trained purely as a mimic at your age, solely as a mimic. I know I haven't trained you well with the other gift, but I've given you something. I didn't even have that. I refused it. It got to be too much. I couldn't...I couldn't stand to be around my family. You've been around them. They were too much. I couldn't stand to leave the borough. I was a raw nerve around Qin, around Inalans. The musicians' district was overwhelming, especially if I heard a bard playing. All the bards are is loss. I couldn't stand to be with Liro anywhere but his place. There were looks, slurs, and I felt it all. I ran from it, Ariah, and it isolated me. I got through the days stoned, but I've never liked herb, I don't like the way it feels. It was...it was an unpleasant time."

His voice had grown rougher, darker, the longer he spoke. He stood abruptly from the table and put on a second pot of tea. The rest of it he told me with his back to me, pulled inward, walls creeping up. "Da had an interesting life. He'd been many different men before he was my da, and he knew people all over. During the rebellion he'd lived in Susselfen. He had worked with some of the rebels. He knew people who knew people, who knew Vathorem, who he knew to be a shaper outside the City. The queen's right hand. He pulled strings, he got Vathorem interested, and he arranged travel. All in secret. I was not in a state to handle a confrontation. You may understand. What I'm trying to say is that training has no window. Vathorem was older than me when he was trained. I was as old as you are now. As you know, I have mastery of it. If you would like mastery of yours, I would suggest you see Vathorem. It is a way to get the training without the label."

"But he's in Vilahna," I said. I think what I meant was, *he wasn't Dirva.* That I didn't know how to have a second mentor, that I didn't know how to break off from the one I had.

Dirva glanced at me over his shoulder while the water rose to a boil. "Yes. I would understand not wanting to go there alone, to an unknown person. I have a way, I think, for you to make an informed decision. Should you approve the match, there would be a wedding. He is someone I would invite to the wedding. We are close. We write," he said. This was, actually, news to me. Even though I picked up what I thought was all of Dirva's correspondence, it was news to me. "I have mentioned you. What I am saying is that you may need space from me, and you may need training for what you're finally willing to admit you've got, and he may be a solution to both."

"Can I think on it?"

"You will have months to think on it."

* * *

I had, perhaps, two days to dwell on the choices ahead of me before life sprang up. The term at Ralah began, and I was to teach Athenorkos and Lothic again. I was on probation, watched carefully, but they had retained my position. This time around, I had no Semadran students at all. Shayat increased our tutoring schedule to three times a week, citing the fact that she wasn't in classes any longer and that once a week seemed insufficient. I had to agree with her. A week and a half into the term, a few hours before curfew, Dirva and I stood at the door of the matchmaker's house. He carried a bottle of Semadran wine in his hand, and he stood taut, and he stood smiling.

The matchmaker's house was deep in the heart of the borough, only a block away from the schoolhouse. I wondered if she had papers. Many shapers don't; many burn them, go underground, to avoid Qin assignments. We protect them. They are powerful, and they are fragile, and the community rallies for them. I wondered what my life would have been like if the Ardijan shaper had thrust me into this path. I wondered what it must be like to be a matchmaker but yet be closed off from marriage. So many shapers turn matchmaker. I don't know that I would have done well with that, being faced day after day with a thing and a life I wanted but could never have. Dirva could feel the thoughts the matchmaker's house kicked up in me. "Ariah," he whispered. "Shh." I tried to focus on the rhythm of my breath with limited success.

Dirva did not knock on the door; the matchmaker already knew we were there. She was approaching middle age, a thin woman with a sharp nose. Her hair was cut short, and her clothes were threadbare and a size too large. She had a willful carelessness about her own presence that intrigued me. She had that imperious remoteness of a trained and polished shaper, a sense of remove, which permeated the air around her. She was a fortress. She looked at me, and it burned me alive. I gasped. I held onto the door frame for support. "Another like you, Dirva."

"He is not here for that," Dirva said. He stepped slightly in front of me. He had grown steely. He did not like her.

She turned and walked into the house. "Such arrogance," she said.

Dirva followed her, and I followed him. She led us to a back room in the house and pointed to a couch. "She will be here soon," the matchmaker said. She left the room without looking at either of us.

I sat next to Dirva on the couch. "Who is she?"

"A matchmaker."

"Which one?"

"Shayma Hepzah'Brahim."

The name was familiar. She was well known in the community, highly respected. A well-known shaper invariably has two qualities: prodigious talents and a deep sense of discretion. This meant she knew about Dirva, and his secrets, and that he had chosen her because he knew she would keep those secrets from his match. "Why doesn't she like you?"

"The same reason she doesn't like you. The same reason no shaper will ever like you, Ariah," he said gently.

Some minutes later, the door opened again. The matchmaker came in first, her face a perfect, empty mask. She carried four wineglasses in her hands. My heart beat a fast rhythm when I saw them. Just behind her was a young woman dressed in factory coveralls. There was grease on the elbows of her suit, and her hair was wrapped in a Semadran headscarf. She lit up when she saw Dirva. She and the matchmaker sat on the couch across from us. The matchmaker opened Dirva's bottle of wine and poured it. All eyes turned to me.

I did not really know what I was supposed to do. Typically it's your parents that bless the match, and if they are your parents, it means they've already been matched themselves and seen the blessing done. I only knew of the process secondhand, through hearsay. I looked at the matchmaker, helpless, frozen. She blinked, but it was a blink that communicated a good deal of impatience and frustration. "There will be introductions," she said, "and you will ask your questions. You and Dirva may speak in private. You make a decision. The courtship either proceeds, or it ends. If it proceeds, we drink the wine." Her voice was soft and clipped and as expressionless as her face.

"Right. Thank you. I have never done this."

"I know."

"Of course you know. I just...I don't want to get it

wrong. I don't..." Dirva laid a hand on my arm. I calmed a little. I looked over at his match, and she looked back. Even in the factory clothes, she had an elegance to her. She had regal features. She held out a hand to me. "Nisa. Nisa Sidera'Chadan. You're Ariah?"

She had a strong handshake. "Yes."

"He speaks of you often."

"Oh, well." I laughed nervously. "We're cut from the same cloth. You do know why I'm here, yes?"

She gave me a strange look. "Yes, I do. The date has been set for weeks."

"Right! Yes! I, uh, I mean that...it doesn't matter what I meant. It doesn't matter. So, I..." I cut a glance at Dirva. I lost my train of thought and found it again. "Questions! I'm to ask you questions. Let's see. You have a factory assignment?"

"I do," she said. "Prototypes. Engineering. I'm in the workshops, not the assembly line. Train work. Engine work." She leaned forward slightly, conspiratorial, sly. "Chasing the dream, you know. Perpetual motion."

"Are you getting very close?"

She laughed. "And work myself out of this placement? No."

There was an odd silence. I remembered suddenly that I was the one asking the questions. "Where are you from?"

"Here. Rabatha. I've never been anywhere else."

I struggled for more questions. Everything I wanted to ask seemed rude or was rude. I wanted to know what gifts she had. I wanted to know what her politics were, and if she had ever been arrested, and what she had been arrested for. I wanted to ask her what she was like, but it seemed a strange question to ask. Failing that, I wanted to read her. It was hard not to. Frankly, I was a bit useless. I turned to Dirva. "May we speak in private?"

"Ariah, already?"

"Yes?"

Dirva sighed. A hint of nervousness crossed Nisa's face. The matchmaker pointed to the door, and Dirva and I slipped out to the hallway. "I don't know what I'm doing," I said.

"I can see that."

"I don't know what I'm supposed to ask. What am I supposed to ask?"

Dirva shrugged. "I don't know."

"What do you mean, you don't know?"

"I've never been matched before. My parents weren't matched." He leaned against the wall. "She knows I am unconventional. She did not run away screaming. I think you should just ask what you want to ask. Within reason."

"Oh. All right."

Dirva leaned forward suddenly. "What do you think of her?"

"She is...Dirva, I don't know. I've only spent five minutes with her. But she seems smart. And she seems to have a sense of humor. And she seems warm. Anyway, it doesn't matter what I think. What do you think of her?"

He smiled. "I think she's a good match."

"But...why?" Dirva shot me a look that told me to drop

the subject, but I didn't. "You said I should ask what I want to ask."

"I also said to do that within reason."

"I am trying, Dirva."

He sighed. He cut a glance at the closed door. "Well, when I am with her, I...I find I don't think so much about things before. People before. She pulls my focus. She is a fresh start."

That made sense to me. It seemed to answer my question. I nodded and went back inside where the match and the matchmaker waited for us. It did not occur to me until hours later that Dirva had never actually said he liked her, or that he loved her. Later, it troubled me greatly. But at the time, I felt his happiness, his hopefulness, and I found I really just had the one question for her. "Nisa," I asked when I sat down across from her, "do you know what you're getting into?"

She looked at Dirva. "Yes," she said. A second later, she smiled. "No. Probably not. It's a risk, but it seems one worth taking."

It was a good answer. I liked her. I liked her ease; I liked the measured way she spoke. Cleverness just poured out of her, and I knew Dirva well enough to know he needed someone who could keep pace with him, the type to now and again outsmart him and leave him perplexed. I knew he gravitated to talent, and she had it. She had the unspoken confidence of someone with proven talent. I liked her enough that I could see us as friends. It wasn't just him she was marrying, after all, but his family, and I was his family. "All right," I said. "You have my blessing."

Her eyes went wide. "Really?"

"Yes?"

"That was so fast!"

"Should it have taken longer?"

"No, I guess not," she said. She laughed. "My parents grilled Dirva for hours, until past curfew. You must be very decisive."

Dirva laughed. "He isn't. Stop questioning him, or he'll reconsider. It's done," he said, taking the glass of wine in front of him. The shaper reached out to stop him, but he ignored her. He drank the wine in one go. "It's done. It's official," he said. The rest of us drank our wine while he watched.

CHAPTER 16

I WAS NO longer Dirva's student in any official capacity, but we lived as if he was still my mentor. The old rhythms were still there. The old habits remained. I still picked up his mail from the shop below our apartment. On my way back from a long day of classes, I stopped into the ink shop below our apartment. The boy at the counter grinned at me. He was fascinated by both Dirva and I, curious about us, but curious in an open, unfettered way that I found a little flattering. He was the type to be seduced by danger and intrigue. His mother was the smuggler who lived below us, after all. I think he saw me in my City clothes and assumed I was up to no good. In that neighborhood, the City clothes made me look like a potentially bad influence.

"Afternoon, sir."

"Afternoon, Mosol. Mail?" I felt peculiarly adult when I interacted with him.

He nodded. "Oh, yes. More than that, sir: a package."

I looked up. "What kind of package?"

The boy winked. "Very special delivery. If you catch my meaning. Very hush-hush."

"Oh." The clothes made me look like I flouted the law, but actually flouting it made my stomach turn. "I'll take it."

The boy hauled a large, flat package wrapped in brown paper onto the counter. The brown paper stretched tight and clean, unmarked by official transport stamps. Wisps of hay clung to the twine that held the brown paper in place. "It came in a hay bale. What is it, do you think?"

"It's a painting," I said.

"Really? How do you know?"

"My father's an artist. I've seen works wrapped for transport before." It struck me as odd, this painting appearing there with no warning. I felt I shouldn't pry, but I pried anyway. I tore the corner of the paper. The boy at the counter gasped, half in shock and half in anticipation. I peered inside, and I recognized the painting. It was by Liro, and it was one of Dirva as a young man. It was *The Reader Unbound*, a portrait of Dirva with mussed hair, shirtless, grinning. It was a moment of flushed youth, a frozen second of Dirva in a state of profound contentment. It was a dagger, this painting. I ripped the rest of the paper away. Tucked into the bottom of the frame was a note written in spiky, lean handwriting. It read as follows:

Liro says you're getting married. Consider this a wedding gift. I hear there's a blank spot on your wall these days.

Amran

"What is it, sir?" Mosol asked.

"It's not wanted." I looked at him across the painting. His eyes were wide; he vibrated with excitement. "Can I ask you a favor?"

"Yes, of course," he said.

"Send this back where it came from. Wrap it up and send it back, and never mention to Mr. Villai'Muladah that it was ever sent here in the first place. Will you do that?"

He blinked. "There's no return address, sir."

But I knew the address. Amran lived in a converted bar named The Refuge on Rivai Street. I asked Mosol for a piece of paper. On one side I wrote the address; on the other side, I wrote a reply. I wrote that Dirva did not need Amran's help filling that blank spot.

"Send it here. Make sure this note makes it into the package. I very much appreciate this," I said.

Mosol chewed his cheek. "It won't be cheap."

I tabulated all of my savings. "How much?"

"Probably more than you have."

I cursed under my breath. "I have...uh...around seventy-five marks saved up. How much?"

The boy sighed. He gave me a sympathetic look. "Close to three hundred."

"Can you...can you keep it here? I'll pay you as I get the money. Can you hold it down here and send it back when I'm paid up? Just so long as Mr. Villai'Muladah never knows it's here."

Mosol took the painting. "I'll talk my mother into it. He won't know."

"Thank you, Mosol. Thank you."

It took me nearly six months to pay up the smugglers.

When I went up to the apartment, Dirva could tell

immediately that something had happened. He didn't ask anything; he just stuck his head around the corner, eyebrows raised. Nisa sat curled in his armchair, still in her coveralls, fiddling with a small clockwork mechanism. "I'm fine," I said.

"Are you?"

Nisa glanced at me over her mechanism.

"Yes, yes, I'm fine. Shayat, you know, she gets under my skin. That's all."

Dirva watched me for a second longer. He went back to whatever he was doing in the kitchen. I sat on my cot across from Nisa. "What is that?"

"It's nothing yet," she said. "Just clacking gears right now. I should make a bird from it or something, but I never get that far. I always end up leaving them naked. Who's Shayat?"

"My student. I tutor her in languages."

"She gets under your skin?"

"Oh, she's awful."

"Then why tutor her?"

"Because Ariah is vain," Dirva yelled from the other room.

Nisa laughed and cast me a curious look.

"Well, her father's a tailor," I said, blushing. "We have a deal. I get clothes made for free if I tutor her."

Nisa smiled and went back to her mechanism. "I read that set of poems you translated for me. The ones from the gold elves." She pulled the notebook out of her pocket and handed it to me. I flipped through it and saw copious notes in the margins. "I think your translations are getting better."

"They are?"

"I think so. Without speaking Droma it's hard to tell, but they read better." She sighed. "I wish you'd give me something less depressing to read."

"What? They're not depressing."

She looked at me, one eyebrow raised. "Slave songs, Ariah. There's nothing not depressing about them."

"I think they're beautiful."

"They are. In a depressing way."

"I know what this is about. Nisa, we're all just elves to them. Slave status, how is that anything more than a technicality? How are we not slaves, too?"

"We are not slaves."

"How much choice did you get in your assignment?"

"I," she said with audible pride, "was recruited."

And I couldn't help it; I grinned at her. "You didn't pick it, then. It was handed to you."

"Oh, it wasn't like that."

"You know I'm right."

"You don't know what you're talking about. You're so dramatic. We have rights. We have papers. The slaves..."

I laughed. She sighed at me.

"Those rights are a mirage! I was detained, Nisa!"

"I know, I know, you never stop going on about it. 'Nisa, they held me at the border! Nisa, Dirva rescued me!' I know. But the papers got you out."

"It was a technicality. I was lucky."

"You were." She leaned forward, a sly smile on her face.

"But here's the thing, Ariah: we have technicalities to exploit. The slaves don't. How are those not rights?"

I admit, she stumped me. She did that often. Once the courtship became a betrothal, Nisa came to our apartment nearly every day after her shift at the prototype lab ended. We spoke often, disagreed nearly every time, but it was playful and it was warm. I waved at her, dismissive, still full of righteous ire, and went into the kitchen. She laughed at me as I walked away.

Dirva was waiting for me in the kitchen. He sat at the table, reading the borough's newspaper, drinking tea. "So," he said. He spoke Vahnan. "This is not a day you usually tutor your student."

"All right, it wasn't her."

He looked up at me over his cup. "It was not the law, I hope."

"No, it wasn't." I took a seat next to him at the table. "Can we declare it personal? It's fine; it's done. I'm fine. I promise."

He nodded. "Yes, of course. We can leave it. Have you thought about Vilahna?"

"Dirva, I don't know."

"Just consider it."

I wanted him to decide for me, to tell me what to do. He'd made his suggestion, but I wanted him to lay it out for me. I was not brave enough to take responsibility for my own life. I changed the subject. "Can you believe the things she says sometimes?"

"Who says?"

"Your betrothed."

"I don't listen when you two talk politics."

"She's never even been arrested. Not once! Ever! How does that even happen?"

"She's lucky, I guess."

"I guess." I picked at my fingernails. "What do you two talk about, if not politics?"

"Ariah."

"You do talk to her, don't you?"

He frowned at me. "Ariah."

I dropped my face into my hands. "I'm sorry."

He was quiet for a long moment. "We talk about her work. We talk about you. We talk about the future. We do talk. I am very fond of her."

He was fond of her—very fond of her—but she loved him. It came bursting out of her whenever they were in the same room, whenever she looked at him. All he could give her was fondness. It was uneven. I couldn't shake that it was unfair. But it was none of my business. I tried to remember that.

* * *

Shayat bought me a plum and watched me eat it while we walked through the market. "You're so messy. You'll stain your shirt."

"Then Parvi will make me another."

She clucked her tongue at me. "He probably would. I

don't know what he sees in you."

I laughed. "Shayat, can I ask you something?"

"Yes, professor."

"It's personal, this thing I want to ask." She looked at me, apologetic, eyebrows raised. I rolled my eyes. "It's not about you."

"Sure it isn't."

"It isn't! Look. What if...what if you thought someone was making a mistake, maybe a very big mistake, but it was personal. And you felt you couldn't say anything. Or, rather, you knew you couldn't without betraying someone else's trust. What would you do?"

She looked over at me. "How can I give you advice without specifics?"

"I can't tell you specifics!"

"Then I can't give you advice."

"Fine." I took another bite of the plum. "We make life so complicated. It doesn't have to be so complicated."

"Complicated how?"

"I told you I can't give you specifics."

She took my plum. She took three bites, and gave the remainder back to me. I frowned at her. "I bought it," she said.

"That was so rude."

"Well, it's done now. Look, professor, your company is not so enthralling that I want to stand next to you while you mutter to yourself. Let's talk about something else."

"All right. I think you've got Lothic down pretty well, though the irregular verbs still..."

She took the plum again. "Ugh, not languages. I'll talk to you about anything but languages."

"Why didn't you just buy it for yourself?"

"I don't know. I didn't really want it until I saw you eat it, I guess." She grinned at me and wiped the juice away with her sleeve. "Do me a favor, will you?"

"Yes? No! Tell me what it is first."

"Visit with my father when I strike out. I worry about him being alone."

I stopped walking. I felt a shift in the terrain of our friendship, a deepening of it. What did it mean? Where had we shifted? Shayat glanced at me over her shoulder. I read her. I didn't mean to; it just happened. Our relationship shifted again.

She dropped the plum. "Did you just...are you..."

"No! No, it's not like that!"

"Then what is it like?"

I swallowed nervously. I held my hands out to her. "Please, not out here."

She narrowed her eyes at me. "What?"

"I'll...I'll tell you, just...please, not out here."

She frowned at me, steely and wary. Mistrustful. Shayat was nobody's fool, and she did not like surprises. But I had banked on her curiosity, and her curiosity won out. "All right. Fine. We'll go back to the shop, but you have to tell me what's going on."

"I will. I promise."

"You remember that you promised," she said as she brushed past me.

When we reached Parvi's shop, she led me up the stairs to her room. She closed the curtains and shut the door behind us. She leaned against the wall with her arms crossed against her chest. "You're a shaper?"

She asked it without any hint of embarrassment or hesitation. I knew it was coming, but I was shocked at the breach. "No! Yes? It's complicated."

"You read me on the street."

"I...yes. I did. I'm sorry. I didn't mean to." I regained my footing just the slightest bit. I stood up the slightest bit taller. "Shayat, that was rude, but I have no obligation to tell you my gifts."

"You do if you can't control them."

It hit me like a slap. "Look, I...I have it. The gift. But I wasn't trained for it. I hid it? Sort of. I'm trained as a mimic, and this, it just slips out sometimes."

Her eyes widened. She crossed halfway to me. Her voice dropped to a whisper. "Ariah, shapers need training more than anyone else. You know that."

"But a shaper's life? The cost is so high!"

"What? Don't be stupid! So you can't get married. So people know your gift. If you don't get training, you'll drive everyone away."

"But if I get the training, I'm isolated anyway."

She stood there silent, chewing her lip. She glanced down at her feet. "I never thought of it that way."

And a decision was made. Just like that, that fast. "I am going to get training. I am. Outside the Empire. I am going to get training, and then I'll just live my life, and things like this won't happen anymore."

Shayat looked up at me. "You're going to come back a trained shaper and keep it secret? That doesn't seem right."

"If we owe no explanation of the gifts to the Qin, I don't see why I owe an explanation to us either."

"We should know! I should've known!"

"Why?"

"So I could...you know why! I have secrets, my father has secrets. I thought they were safe!"

I crumpled to the floor. I was a gangly pile of jutting limbs. "That is why I want to keep it to myself. People know, and they won't let themselves get close. People know, and all they can think about are their secrets, the things they wouldn't want me to find out, and then I'll find them out, and all that's left is distance. Shayat, I don't know anything about you or Parvi that you haven't told me. I swear. I don't want to know anything about you that you haven't told me."

"That's not true! You read me on the street!"

"It just happened! What, your gifts have never slipped out?"

She sighed. She made uninterpretable gestures with her hand. She sighed again. "You are maddening."

"I'm sorry."

"Every time I think I understand you, you pull the rug out from underneath me."

"I'm sorry."

She sighed again. "Well, at least you're not boring.

You're serious about getting training?"

"I am."

"Good," she said. "Good. Your secret's safe with me. I hope mine are safe with you."

CHAPTER 17

DIRVA AND NISA were ready to marry the second we drank the wine. The only thing that stood in the way was logistics. A razehm willing to officiate an elvish wedding needed to be found and negotiated with. Legal documents had to be drawn up. Nisa and Dirva each had to find the time to write their genealogies. Dirva and Nisa had to find adequate housing for a joint life.

All these things take time, but not as much time as you would think. Dirva pulled strings and called in favors for the legalities quite quickly. Nisa leveraged the goodwill of the borough to find a suitable apartment without much trouble. It took them no more than three weeks to get things in place. And then it was a matter of waiting, because ultimately the marriage happened on Vathorem's schedule and not theirs.

Vathorem was the only part of the wedding Dirva could not rush, the only element out of his control. Dirva had written Vathorem the night Nisa's parents gave approval, some weeks before I gave approval myself. He had sent the news in a clockwork bird, which, though expensive, was both faster and more reliable than the post. Vathorem sent the bird back with congratulations and a promise to attend. He sent a promise, but politics were politics, he said, and the red queen was the red queen. He would send word when he was able to get away.

Three and a half months after all the preparations had been nailed down, a battered clockwork bird clattered against the kitchen window. Dirva and Nisa sat in the other room; he was reading a book I'd pilfered from the Library, and she was drawing schematics for something that made no sense to me. I, as luck would have it, happened to be in the kitchen. The bird landed heavily on the windowsill. It skidded off the ledge and reappeared a few seconds later. It ruffled its copper feathers. Its sightless ball-bearing eyes blinked. It tapped the windowpane with its beak. When I let it in, it hopped into my hand. It was docile. Its mainspring had little tension left; it had made a long journey on a single winding. "Dirva!"

"Yes?"

"Dirva, a bird came!"

He was around the corner in a heartbeat. He took it from me, cradling it gently as if it were a bird of flesh and bone. The pressure panel, which made up the bird's belly popped open with just a little coaxing. The mechanical life went out of the creature, and Dirva fished out the note. "He left about a month ago," Dirva said. "He'll be here in two weeks." He laughed; a bright smile spread across his face. "Ha! Two weeks. Nisa, two weeks!"

I was happy for him, I was, but the news filled me with dread. Two weeks and my life would be uprooted.

Nisa came into the kitchen. The air in the room was thick with happiness. Her laughter and his anticipation drowned out my own feelings. Dirva pulled her into a tight embrace. She clung to him, her head in the crook of his neck. They stayed like that for a handful of seconds, and then she remembered that I was there. She pulled away, laughing, unable to look me in the eye. "I'll tell my parents," she said. "I'll tell the landlord."

When Nisa left an hour or so later, my confused feelings crept back up. I hated that I felt that way. I couldn't think of a time I'd seen Dirva so happy or so hopeful. I didn't understand it, where all this happiness and hopefulness came from, but it was there, and I couldn't stand to dilute it with my own worries. I slipped out of the apartment, and I stayed at Parvi's shop until the approach of curfew.

Dirva was waiting for me when I returned. He sat at the kitchen table trying to bring the messenger bird back to life.

"You need a key to wind it," I said.

"I know that, Ariah," he said, irritated. I smiled in spite of myself. "I am trying to determine what size key I need to wind it." He set the bird down. "Sit. Let's talk."

"Oh, no, that's all right. I'm tired. I think I'll turn in."

He caught me by the wrist when I tried to escape. "We don't have to talk if you would rather not, but you do not need to hide it for my sake."

I laughed. It was a pitiful thing, weak and helpless. I sat down in the chair next to him. "I am happy for you."

"I know."

I stared at him for a long time. I looked down at my hands and swallowed. "I am terrified."

"I was, too."

"What do I tell my parents?"

"I will write them."

"I should see them before I go."

Very gently, Dirva rested a hand on my shoulder. "There isn't time. You won't get detained again."

"I might." My voice was a harsh croak. My eyes screwed tight of their own accord.

He went into the next room and rifled through a cabinet. He returned a second later and handed me a leather-wrapped sheaf of documents. "These will make that less likely."

The forgeries were more or less identical to my real papers with two exceptions: I was no longer a shaper, and I had never been detained at the western border. "Where did you get these?"

"Cadlah knows a man."

"You got these from Cadlah?"

His walls were already up. "She did it for you, Ariah, not for me. Da trained this forger. This is quality work."

"Thank you." I tried to say more, but more would not come. "Thank you."

He smiled. "It's not just the border."

"No." I sighed. "No, it's everything. All of it. I don't know him. I don't know Vilahna. I don't know...I don't know what it means to get this training. Or what to do after. Or what it will take. I don't...Dirva, I don't know who I'll be when I come back. I barely fit now. Vilahna? I won't fit after."

Dirva laughed. It was a gentle, deeply kind laugh. "Ariah, for some of us, the places we come from are not the places we belong, and never were, and never will be."

* * *

Three hours before curfew there was a knock at the door of Dirva's apartment. He answered it, but I had a clear view of the door. It was a Qin agent, dressed in dark blue robes with brocade panels. I panicked. I was certain he was there for me, possibly about the books I'd stolen, or maybe about the forgeries. As silently and unobtrusively as I could, I slipped out of my chair and snuck into Dirva's bedroom. I leaned against the door as if to keep the agent out.

A few seconds later, Dirva whispered my name through the door. "Ariah. It's all right. We are needed at the train station."

"For what?"

"For Vathorem."

I stuck my head through the door. "Why is an agent here?"

"Vathorem is a diplomat. It's for his protection." He switched from Qin to Vahnan. "They're keeping an eye on him. The agent is going to escort us there, and then we'll bring him back. You don't have to go."

"No, I'll go," I said. I smoothed out the front of my shirt. I took a breath. "I'll go."

The agent took us to the station house. The walk there was tense, and my heart scrabbled against my ribs like a trapped mouse. It was getting towards summer, and I sweated straight through my shirt. The agent led us into the upper reaches of the station house—a building a full four stories tall—into the office of the stationmaster. She was an old, hard-edged Qin woman. Her office was all polished wood and framed maps. An Eye was nailed above the west-facing window, and it glowed red in the failing light.

Across the desk from her sat two red elves. Vathorem was ancient, hardened and weathered like petrified wood. The other was as young as myself. They were both dressed plainly, in City-style clothes tailored less well than those I wore and constructed of wools and linens Parvi never would have touched. Vathorem cradled a teacup, peering into the Semadran black like he was looking for answers. As far as I could tell, he had no intention of drinking it. The young elf beside him watched everything around him. His black eyes drank in the furniture, the weave of Dirva's shirt, the movement of the breeze through the window.

The agent held the door for Dirva and me as we walked in. The politeness of the gesture set me on edge. "They've come to collect the envoy, Stationmaster."

Vathorem smiled into his teacup. The young one leaned forward in his chair, half-upright, waiting uncertainly for some sign of what to do next. The stationmaster waved her hand at us. "Blessings with you," she said.

Vathorem stood, placed the still-full teacup on the stationmaster's desk, right on a stack of papers she was reaching for. She scowled. He grinned. "Thank you for the hospitality," he said. His High Qin was absolutely, startlingly perfect, but the way he spoke was purely Athenorkos. His voice had an underlying music to it that the Qin lack. "Come, Dor," he said to the younger elf. "One last walk and we can rest our weary legs."

He led the way out. The young elf trailed after him, then Dirva, then myself. I could not help but peek over my shoulder two, three times. Deep in the pit of my stomach I expected the agent to come back and arrest me. But he didn't, and soon enough the four of us were in the station. The rank-and-file policemen patrolling the station had been briefed; they gave Vathorem respectful nods and let us pass without incident. The younger elf carried two very full packs, neither of which looked like they'd been ransacked.

Dirva and Vathorem walked in perfect rhythm through the Qin streets. There was a current between them, a conversation they seemed to have without speaking. The young elf and I eyed each other, both curious, both a little wary. When the streets narrowed and the houses began to cluster tight together, Vathorem looped his arm through Dirva's. "Ah," he said. "Ah, you're all grown, now."

Dirva grinned. "And you! You just keep refusing to die, eh?"

Dor stared at Dirva. Vathorem patted his arm. "Marriage," Vathorem said.

"Yes."

"A nice Semadran girl, I take it?"

"Yes."

"Look at that. My lad. My lad a grown man."

"I was grown when you got to me, Vathorem."

"The hell you were."

Dirva laughed.

There was a pause, and then: "Oh, I'm fine. I'm fine. Battle wounds, you know."

"Vathorem."

"I'm fine." Vathorem glanced over at me. "So, this is your boy?"

"He is, yes."

Vathorem held out his hand to me. When I took it, he looked right in my eyes. He read me through and through. I felt like I'd been turned inside out. Dirva laughed gently on Vathorem's other side. "Well met, Ariah Lirat'Mochai. Well met."

"A pleasure."

"A pleasure?" Vathorem's eyebrows jumped up. He glanced at Dirva over his shoulder. "He's polite."

"He is losing that particular virtue."

Vathorem turned back to me. "We'll talk later, you and I, feel each other out." He reached for Dor. Vathorem caught his hand and pulled him close, grinning, affectionate, parental. "Dor, do you remember that one at all?" he asked, pointing to Dirva. The boy shook his head. His face was carefully composed, a mask as silver as my own. It made me curious. "You fawned over him when you were little. You did. Followed him from room to room."

"I'm sure I did." Dor spoke very good Semadran, and he glanced at me while he did it. "It's a pleasure to see you again,

Dirva da Alama." Dirva nodded at him, a smile half-hid behind a hand. He and Vathorem laughed the same laugh at the same time.

When we reached Dirva's apartment, Vathorem kicked Dor and I out. He cited privacy, questions for Dirva, a desire to catch up. I am sure that's the case, but I think he also wanted to discuss me without me there to eavesdrop. In any case, Vathorem took the packs from the young elf and shut the door behind him. We stood awkwardly on the other side of it. The young man held out his hand to me. "Shaliondor da Alama. Call me Dor."

"Ariah Lirat'Mochai."

"Vath says you're a shaper?"

I jerked my hand back. I let out a strangled laugh and glanced around at the street below. No one was there, but that didn't mean no one had heard him.

"Are you all right?"

"Have you spent much time with Semadrans?" I asked him. I switched to Athenorkos.

He shook his head.

"But you speak Semadran?"

"Vath taught me." He pulled his long red hair over one shoulder and looked out at the street. "It's a long story. You were saying?"

"We don't ask that about each other."

"Ask what?"

"About the gifts. About magic. We don't. And I...those here don't know that I am a shaper."

His eyes widened. "Oh. I'm sorry. I didn't realize."

"It's all right." We stared at each other for a moment. He had an intensity, a burning curiosity in him. "Are you a shaper?"

He laughed. It was a bright, unfettered laugh. "I guess it's not rude to ask me, eh? No. No, I'm no shaper. Red ones are rare." I glanced at the closed door. I heard laughter inside. "Falo has been so excited for this trip," he said. "He missed him, your man. They write, but it's not the same."

"Falo?"

"It means godfather," said Dor.

"I know. Vathorem is your godfather?" I asked. Dor grinned; he beamed with pride. He nodded. It struck me as odd, a shaper serving as a parent. Parenting seemed a much more forbidding task for the most sensitive among us. "Would you mind terribly, and I honestly do not mean to be rude, but would you mind terribly if I asked why you were here? Vathorem came for the wedding..."

"And for you."

"And for me. Would you mind if I asked why he brought you with him?"

Shaliondor da Alama leaned against the railing. His auburn hair blew around him. He had a sharp face, neither handsome nor pretty, but striking. His skin was so freckled it looked a shade too dark. He grinned. "Ah, me. I'm an excuse, that's all, a reason to make the trip. He's valuable, Vathorem is, and my ma had to have a reason to send him on a long trip, a dangerous trip, into country that don't like us all that much. He told her my Semadran needs work, that I need to see the Empire firsthand to deal with it proper when the time comes." He watched me as the words sunk in and grinned a hair wider when they did.

"You're a prince."

"One of several. Though having her as a mother don't really mean much. We're not like your Exalted. Or the Lothic kings. She picks an heir; blood don't mean nothing." He shot me a sly smile. "You know what they say about us, though. All us reds are related to each other one way or another."

The light was beginning to turn. I was late. I had more questions for him, but I was late. "You said your Semadran needs work?"

"That's what Vath says."

"I know someone whose Athenorkos and Lothic need work. Would you like to meet a friend of mine?"

He pulled himself off the railing. "Would be a pleasure."

Dor took stock of the neighborhood as we walked through it. He noticed everything, things I myself had never noticed. "No fruit sellers?"

"Not here, no."

"They were all over the Tahrqin streets."

"We go to market for them."

"Why?"

"I'm not sure. They are expensive."

He whistled. "Expensive to you. Not so expensive to the Tahrqin, eh?"

Things like that. Why were the streets narrower in the

borough? When did curfew get established? When we passed the schoolhouse, he had a thousand questions about it—who built it and when, how was it funded, had there been raids, that sort of thing. He asked me insightful, informed questions about Semadran history. As we walked, conversation drifted into Semadran. "Your Semadran is very good," I said. "It's really just slang you're missing."

"I know. Vath knows. It was an excuse. This is useful, though. Walking through like this. Getting answers from you, this is very useful."

"Useful for what, may I ask?"

He looked out at the street. A clutch of children stared at him—hard, careful—and slipped into a back alley. "Things down the line. Decisions down the line."

"May I ask you something personal?"

"Yes," he said. He said it without hesitation, without alarm. I found it charming.

"Why did you lie about remembering Dirva?"

He laughed. He glanced over at me and laughed again. "Hell, I don't know. It's not like there was a point in doing it, not in front of three of you. Just slipped out. I was little, though, when he was at court. If he remembers me at all, it's as a little one. Does that make sense?"

"What was he like, then?"

Dor shrugged. "I was little. To me he was fascinating: a foreigner, a mix, another shaper. He was always with Vath, and I was always with Vath. He was quiet, and smart. I'm quiet. There's not many quiet folks around where I'm from, just me and him and Vath, really. He was nice to me, let me hang around, let me pester him with questions. He was, uh..." and here he paused. He looked me over, careful, uncertain. "He was close with a couple of my brothers. They knew him better than I."

The conversation had slowed the walk. I was very late for my appointment with Shayat. I felt a dread in my bones when I knocked on the door of Parvi's shop, one that was well founded. Parvi opened it, already apologetic. "Ah, professor..."

That was all he got out. Shayat batted the door open wide. "Oh, you made it."

"Shayat..."

"You're an hour and a half late, and I'm the rude one."

"I'm sorry. Shayat..."

She sighed. She glared at me. And then she noticed Dor. "Why is there a red elf with you?"

"I was going to explain that to you, actually."

Parvi slipped away from the door. "I'll just leave you to your lessons," he said.

Beside me, Dor began to laugh. He tried to hide it and failed miserably. Red elves are not used to hiding laughter. Shayat stood in the doorway, haughty, irate, arms crossed. I was unhorsed by her, swept up in her, and I began to laugh, too. She was not pleased. "I'm sorry! I am! May we come in? I'm here now. I'm sorry for the lateness, I am."

She frowned at me. She frowned at Dor. Then, she held the door open for us. "It's late," she said. "Are you hungry? Did you eat?"

"I haven't eaten, no."

She led us into the kitchen, which I'd never been in before. She pointed to the table and a second later dropped a platter of flatbread on the table. It landed with a heavy bang. Then she dropped a bowl of hummus next to it. The bowl tottered, half-spun, threatened to fall over. Shayat glared at it, willed it into obedience. She sat down next to me, eyeing Dor hard. "Who is he, and why did you bring him here?"

Dor began to laugh again, and I couldn't help it, it was contagious. Shayat threw her hands up at me.

"He speaks Semadran! I kept trying to tell you that, but you just keep on and on!" I said.

She looked at Dor. "You speak Semadran?"

"A bit, yes."

The irritation went out of her. She took a piece of flatbread and scooped up some hummus. "Huh. Look at that. Where did you learn it?"

"In Vilahna."

"He came with Vathorem," I said.

"Ah." She looked like she was going to ask, pry about his gifts like I had already done, but she swallowed down her questions. "Why did you learn it?"

"People smarter than myself thought it would be useful for me to know it," he said. He reached across the table. "Shaliondor," he said.

And something came alive in Shayat. She took his hand and did not let it go. "Shaliondor? Shaliondor da Where?"

"Da Alama."

"You came here with the queen's right hand?"

"I did, yes," he said. There was surprise in his voice, a hint of wariness. He tried, and failed, to reclaim his hand.

Shayat held it tight and pulled him slightly farther across the table. "Are you the heir, Shaliondor da Alama? Are you Rethnali's successor?"

His eyebrows shot up. He glanced at me, then back at her. "I...am. Yes, I am."

"You are?" I could not believe I asked it. My hand flew to my mouth.

"He is," Shayat said. She let go of his hand. "If you plan to trade in a country it makes sense to stay informed, yes?" She switched to Athenorkos. "Mr. da Alama, I have many, many questions for you. About trade. About routes. About, uh..." She searched for the word, her fingers dancing in the air as if to pluck it out of the ether. She grinned. "About prices."

* * *

Vathorem and Dor stayed with us a week. I spent as much of that week at Parvi's shop as I could, partly because Shayat demanded final lessons before I left, and partly because with four of us in a bachelor's apartment there was no room to breathe. Dor almost always came with me to Shayat's. When I came home from the classes, I usually found him sitting on the landing, alone, watching the borough. He had an air of remoteness around him, of separateness, that I lacked. There were times when he spoke, when I caught sight of the way he carried himself, that I could not shake the feeling that he belonged there in Rabatha more than I did. Those thoughts drove me into quietness; they whipped my fears into a frenzy. It is not so surprising, then, that Shayat seemed to lose interest in me. The final lessons were really lessons with Dor while I watched and ruminated and chewed my fingernails down to ragged edges.

Dor and I rarely spoke to each other but for questions about this or that. I avoided Vathorem for days, pleading work and then lessons, and then only getting back just before curfew to sleep curled up on the floor of the kitchen. Vathorem took my cot, and Dor took the floor beside the cot. Vathorem gave me space for four full days, right up until the day before the marriage, and then it was Saturday and I had nowhere to go, and he decided I'd had space enough.

I woke early and tried to slip out, but he was already awake and already waiting. "Let's you and I talk, eh?"

"Yes, well, I…I have to go."

"Go where?"

"To, uh, to…"

Vathorem laughed. He stood up. It was a fluid motion, one that betrayed no hint of how old he was. "Dirva tells me you've a fondness for the gold elves."

"Yes. That's true."

"You know, it's been ages since I've seen one. Show me some gold elves, Ariah, and we'll talk on the way."

There was nothing for it but to do as he asked. We walked slowly, mostly in silence. I felt him watch me, I felt his magic gently prod me and probe me. There was little of the burn our shapers have. I remembered how little of the burn there had been with Dirva. And I asked him my first question, and when I did, my training with Vathorem began. "Why doesn't it burn with you?"

"There we are. There we go. That's the way of it. It don't burn because I'm charming you while I do it. It's all bound up in me, the red magic and the silver. Can you charm, Ariah?"

"No." I wondered about Dirva, what talents he had that were not Semadran.

"Dirva can, aye," Vathorem said. I looked over at him. He laughed. "Oh, I've got it in spades, lad. I've got so much of it I can't see past it. Got so much of it seems it's all there really is of me. Lad, have you ever tried to charm?"

"No."

"Then you can't say for sure one way or another. Tell me about the gold elves. Tell me what draws you to them."

"I don't know." And I didn't; it was a draw, a visceral draw, which until then I'd never questioned or examined.

"Sure you do," he said, and he said it with such expectation that I really had no choice but to divine an answer for him.

"There is a...unity to them. It seems. The boundaries of where one starts and another ends are porous. I think."

"That appeals to you, does it?"

It didn't seem to me then to be a matter of preference, but more a matter of truth. I have come to reconsider this, but at the time, it seemed to me that the gold elves were more accurate, more honest, about life than Semadrans are. And maybe that is true—but maybe it's that they are more accurate and more honest about me than Semadrans are.

Vathorem did not wait for me to answer. "You're very different than Dirva."

"I'm not so different."

"You are. He's a world to himself, that one. All contained, a universe in one man. The magic drives him away from the rest of us. And it drives you right into the arms of slaves. Who, Ariah, who do you think in this city has a more urgent life than a slave? What people anywhere live more moment to moment than them? And when you live like that, you live loud. It's all right there on the surface. Dirva and I are alike. You and I are not."

"You won't train me?"

Vathorem smiled at me. "Oh, no, I'll train you. Are you willing to be trained, though, that's the real question. Will you let me, that's the question."

"I'll let you."

* * *

The marriage was absolutely, perfectly Semadran. We arrived at the matchmaker's house just before dusk. Dor and Vathorem were led into the house by the matchmaker and seated in the front room. Dirva and I entered the house through the matchmaker's back door. We stood huddled against the wall, tucked out of sight. Dirva was calm, unruffled, full of certainty.

Just as the sun dipped halfway below the horizon and the moon crept up into view, the door to the parlor opened for us. I went in first, then Dirva. Nisa's parents came in through the other side of the room, followed by Nisa. The matchmaker and a razehm stood on either side of a small table. They stood in front of a west-facing window, and the mingled light of dusk flooded the room. On the table were the documents: licenses, affidavits, and genealogies.

The matchmaker gestured the families forward. Nisa's mother stepped towards me. "It is a gift and an honor," she said.

"It is a gift and an honor," I said. We signed an affidavit of witness for the razehm.

Dirva and Nisa went forward, drawn together like magnets. I'd never seen her in anything but her work clothes. I'd never seen her hair uncovered. She looked different, there in flimsy, soft clothing. Her white hair was long and wavy; it hung loose, freshly washed, gently curled. She looked young like that. She looked girlish. And she looked so obviously, so totally, in love with him. Dirva stood across from her, a well of lies. The genealogy was a fiction, and she would never know it. He had oceans of love for someone else. She stared at him, devoted to who she thought he was, and he stared back, hopeful that he could become that man for her.

"Now, when the sun and moon meet, in this room where you first met, you are married," said the matchmaker. "A bond is forged, a bridge is built, and two lives are now lived in parallel."

Dirva opened Nisa's genealogy. It was a thick book bound in black leather, the spine a full two inches thick. She had spent days copying her parents' genealogies into it, name by name, relationship by relationship. She had written so much that her hands were still stained with ink that day. He wrote his name, the one on his citizenship papers, the one that hid his family from existence, next to hers. "A life together and only together," he said.

She beamed. She took his hand in hers, and he handed her the pen. She opened his genealogy, a slim volume detailing the course of lives, which had never been lived, and wrote her name next to his. "A life together and only together." Together, they signed Qin marriage licenses. The razehm stamped their marriage onto their citizenship papers. I left Rabatha three hours later.

PART FOUR:

ALAMADOUR

CHAPTER 18

VATHOREM'S STATUS AS an envoy awarded us a private car on a state-of-the-art train from Rabatha to Shalakesh. Not a private cabin, mind you: an entire car. It was strange and luxurious. The car was larger than my parents' house, larger than Dirva's apartment. I had a cabin with a bunk completely to myself, and the mattress in the bunk was softer than any I'd slept on before or since. The Qin rail agents brought us three meals daily from the dining car free of charge. It was a week and a half of creature comforts.

Still, the trip was not particularly pleasant for me. Where Dirva had always been a reactive mentor, a man who waited until I stumbled before he went to catch me, Vathorem was an interventionist. He wanted to see what I could do, he said, and when I wasn't sleeping, he had me across the table from Dor trying to learn red magic, trying to learn to build walls or knock them down, trying to do things I'd avoided even thinking about for my entire life. He gave me no time to prepare, no time to adjust. He gave me no time to breathe.

I sat across a small table from Dor, the would-be king of Vilahna. The Qin coffee in our cups sloshed in rhythm with the sway of the train. Vathorem leaned against the wall, peering out the window at the desert sands. "You're not even trying, Ariah."

"I am." I dropped my face into my hands. "I am not Athenorkos. I'm Semadran."

"Tell that to your grandmother."

We had been at it for hours. It was the second day on the train, and the night before I'd dreamt of magic. I had dreamt I drowned in great foreign wells of it, thick and rushing like a terrible river. "With all due respect, sir, I thought you were going to train me in shaping. I don't see what this has to do with that. I don't see how this will help me."

Vathorem looked at me. "Dirva had a copy of *The Art of Shaping*. Did you ever read it?"

"No."

"And you're surprised you have no control?" I opened my mouth to say something—anything—but he waved at me. "Look, never mind that. All right. I know us folks and you folks talk like magic is this distinct thing, that you're either this or that. I know that's how you were taught—that there's red magic and silver magic and blue magic. But I don't think that's true. There's just magic. How can you master just one piece of what you have? You can't. If you want to understand how to rein yourself in, and clearly you do, you got to understand how it fits with the rest of you. You got to understand the limits of your gift, Ariah. You might be a charmer, or you might pull a mirror. You are so quick with spoken language, and they say that's a red thing. Things are rarely ever so clear-cut as theory suggests." The train lurched. Vathorem lost his footing and half-fell into a chair. Dor stood up, but Vathorem waved him down again. "I'm fine. Sit down. Dor, charm him again. Ariah, try to pay attention this time."

"How can I pay attention if I've been charmed?"

"Pay attention to what it feels like to you," Vathorem said. He was frustrated, irritable. The only one who was not miserable was Dor.

"I can't think when I've been charmed!"

"Then I guess you won't get much thinking done in Vilahna."

I glared at him. "You know I'm scared of that. I know you know it."

"Then you'd better get to work," he said. "Charm him, Dor."

I began to protest, but Dor had me in his clutches in half a heartbeat. He didn't need to touch me. He didn't even need to say my name. He just looked at me, caught my eye, and smiled. That was it; that was all it took. It was not like when Sorcha had charmed me at all. There was no pull with him, just a one-sided hazy fascination. "You're so smart," I said, pulling my chair a little closer. Dor laughed. He thanked me. "You are so comfortable with yourself."

"Oh, well, sometimes I am. Sometimes I'm not," he said. "How do you feel?"

"Me? Fine. I feel fine."

"Tell me how you feel."

"I feel...fine? How are you so sure of yourself?"

"I am and I'm not. Depends." He looked over at Vathorem and shrugged.

A flash of scalding magic burned me. It shook me out of the charms. I blinked and drew my knees up to my chest, an instinctive, protective gesture.

"Ariah," Vathorem said. His voice was heavy, tired. There was no anger in it, but there was little patience in it, either. "How do you lose yourself so quick? I read you, and there's hardly any you in there to even read."

The magic left me shaken. I felt exposed and vulnerable. I crossed to the other side of the cabin and wedged myself in the corner, turned away from both of them. "It just happens."

"You know you read Dor, there, when he charmed you. You know that? Those questions, you were parroting back to him the things he was thinking."

I didn't even know I'd asked questions. I had little memory of it at all.

"It didn't burn," Dor said. "I didn't know."

"Well, hell, boy, it was flattery. I'd not expect you to look all that close at it."

Dor laughed.

A heavy silence settled over the cabin. I felt a tension mounting in Vathorem. It was a thing alive, this tension, a thing that grew, a thing with a beating heart of frustration. He left, and I immediately felt better. I sat down again across from Dor. "Don't mind him," said Dor. "He's never been good with folks. Can't take it personal. Try charming me now, without him in the room. Maybe it'll go better when he's not looming, making you all nervous."

"It won't," I said, but the truth was that I hadn't been trying to charm him, not really. The truth was that I was afraid I could, and I was afraid of what might happen if I did.

"You should try. No harm in trying," he said, and I laughed. It was a brutal and loud laugh, disdainful. Dor raised his eyebrows.

"There would be harm in succeeding."

"It's just charms, Ariah."

The train screeched. Switches clicked into place, and the train began to turn. My chair slid a few feet and landed against the window. Dor's face went white; his jaw clenched. "That's normal," I said.

"Nothing about this blasted thing is normal."

"Sure it is. It's steam-run. What's more normal than water?"

He held onto the table, white-knuckled, while the train turned south a little harder. "We're going so fast," he said quietly. "This great hunk of metal we're in, it's going so fast." He stood up and held onto the window frame. "I'm sorry," he said. He let out a shy, embarrassed laugh. "I'm sorry, I just…I'll be glad when we're out of this thing."

"You should sit on the floor," I said.

"What?"

"Sit on the floor. It feels more stable on the floor. You can feel the rail, and you don't swing so much."

"Oh." Carefully, slowly, he moved along the wall until he found a spot clear of any furniture. He slid down the wall.

There was an immediate look of relief on his face. "This is better."

I watched him for a little while. A bowl of fruit slid across the table and into my lap. I ate a plum, soothed by the clatter of the train. "You said it didn't burn?"

"Not then, no," said Dor. "It's burned before when you read me. Like back in Rabatha. But when I charmed you, I didn't feel a thing."

"Strange." I sighed. "He's right. I know nothing about myself. I have no idea what my gifts really are. How do you control something when you have no idea how it works?"

"You don't," Dor said. "And you've got to use it to learn how it works. You sure you don't want to try?"

I put the bowl of fruit on the floor and made my way across the cabin. I sat in front of him. "How do I do this?"

"Vath told you."

"No, how do I really do this?"

"Just feel me out. It'll just click. Wait until there's a tug, and you just coax me over. That's it."

"But how? How do I do it?"

He shrugged. "I don't know the mechanics. I just know how it works for me. I know it's something to do with attention. Whoever it is you're trying to hook, they've got to be focused on you. From there it's just...intuition, I guess."

"Well...you're...you're paying attention to me now," I said.

"Oh, no, it's more like I need to pay attention to *you*. Not the conversation, or what you're saying, but you. You and me. I need to pay attention to you and me together. This moment where we're sitting here, you and me. That's the start of it."

I tried. I did. I took his hands and leaned forward, peering into his face with a peculiar, willful intensity. "Dor? Shaliondor. I, uh..." I narrowed my eyes and leaned towards him a little more, searching for him, trying to fish him out. "Dor. Dor."

He laughed. "Nothing."

"Really?"

He pulled his hands from mine and patted me on the shoulder. "Nothing."

* * *

The farthest the railroad went was Shalakesh; from there we traveled by horse. By the time we reached Shalakesh, I had been charmed at least a hundred times. I'd been mirrored dozens of times. I had failed at both countless times. But I tried, and that was the important thing. As long as I tried, really tried, did not hold back in the least, Vathorem gave me encouragement. He could tell when I slacked, and he could tell when I feigned effort, and he would have none of it.

I found it a little hard to be around Dor. It felt like he'd seen me naked. He'd charmed me over and over again, and I had only the vaguest memories of what I did and said when caught in his thrall. It felt uneven between us. None of it seemed to matter much to him. He seemed on the surface a simple man, but he wasn't and likely never had been. He had a shell of simplicity wrapped tight around him, like armor. There were times I woke in the night, my mind turning, and I knew I'd caught a glimpse of something when I'd read him in a charm, but I rarely knew what. I had no grasp of him. My attempts to read him outright were generally unsuccessful. Vathorem had taught him to wall up from a very young age. I didn't know until then that the skill could be taught to someone without the gift, but it had, and he was much better at it then than I have ever been. Dor was utterly unperturbed by me, or at least he seemed to be, but I was a bundle of nerves around him.

When we got to Alamadour, we sold the horses. Vathorem gave me the money he got for them. "You'll need a place of your own," Vathorem said. "The palace is crowded. I'll need space from you, and you'll need space from me if the training's to take."

"You think so?" I was dubious; remember, Semadrans live with their mentors. I had lived and eaten and slept at Dirva's side for years.

"I know so," Vathorem said. "Especially you. You got to stake out who you are, what your roots are. You'll not be able to do that with me around. I pull your focus. So, look, I've a friend who keeps a place here, but he's retired to the City more or less, so it's just sitting there wide open. You spend your days with me, at court, and your nights are yours to do with what you will."

I looked out at the street. The people were uniformly red. I felt them staring at me, like a thousand pinpricks. I did not want to leave his side. "Are you certain this is the best way?"

"I am."

"Because I..."

He patted my shoulder. "You're a quarter red. Let that quarter rise to the surface," he said. "Dor, I'll meet you back at the palace. Tell your ma I'll be there direct. Ariah, you come with me. I'll get you settled."

He led me four blocks east of the palace. There was a bar, the Pickled Bear, three doors down from the Alamadour Library. It was hardly a library, actually; certainly it was not Magi-made. It was a low building, wide and languid, built with stark right angles in some lazy approximation of Magi architecture. The Pickled Bear was a dark, fragrant place lit by oil lanterns. It seemed quaint until I realized there was no electricity in Vilahna. Vathorem went to the counter and bought a small jar of pipeherb. He handed me a key, told the bartender I was taking the apartment, and pointed to a set of stairs at the far end of the bar. "Isn't there a separate entrance?"

"Why would there be a separate entrance?" the bartender asked.

I blushed. I stammered. Vathorem gave me a gentle push and told me he'd see me in the morning. I mounted the steps slowly, one at a time. I felt so profoundly alone then. The panic was close to overwhelming me. A single thought repeated in my brain—*I've made a mistake. I should've stayed behind, this is a mistake*—circled around and around, cutting a little deeper every time, slicing me to ribbons. I slipped the key in the door and let myself in.

Lamps were already lit in the main room. It was a

spacious room, with a fireplace on one side, and a stove on the other. A couch, its back to me, and a clutch of overstuffed chairs filled half the room. A table against one wall was covered in detritus: shirts, spools of wire, rags, some unwashed teacups. "Hello?"

The apartment stayed silent. I dropped my pack and crept further into the room, exploring it timidly, gingerly. I was swimming in bitterness just then, angry at Vathorem for leaving me there, angry at myself for having let myself be left, angry at whoever was clearly living in this apartment. "Hello?"

A figure stirred on the couch. A moan of forsaken sleep filled the silence. Short red hair came into view. An arm stretched up, up toward the ceiling, the fingers splayed and reaching. The arm was a dark, dark gray. The length of the fingers and the odd dance they performed was inescapably familiar. "Sorcha?" It came out a half-whisper. It came out full of hope and tenderness.

His face whipped around. His eyes went wide, and his jaw dropped. "Fucking hell! Ariah?"

I have never been so happy to see someone. There are times where emotions are so total, so encompassing, that they transcend language. This was one of those times. I leapt over the back of the couch. I slammed into him, clutching him tight, and we tumbled off the couch together. He laughed, and, oh, the familiarity of that laugh was such a comfort. "Fucking hell," he said again, but softer this time, with wonder threaded through his voice. He ran a hand through my hair. I struggled with a strange and unforeseen desire to kiss him.

We were a tangle of limbs. I lay half on top of him, drunk on the smell of him. He was right there, just beneath me, exactly as I remembered him. I felt a thousand things in that moment, all confused, but all good. "What are you doing here?"

Sorcha laughed. He sat up against the couch. "What am I doing here? Fuck, Ariah, what are *you* doing here?"

"I'm here for...I, uh, I'm here for..."

He laughed again, and cupped my cheek. "Ah, don't worry, you can tell me later. You know why I'm here. Remember? Came with a crew to play the houses here."

"You've been here all this time?"

"Yeah. Hey, what're you doing in this spot, though? This is Kelli's place. My pa's best mate Kel, this is his place."

"Vathorem..."

His eyes went wide. "Vathorem?"

"Yes?"

"Right-hand Vathorem? That Vathorem?"

"Yes."

He narrowed his eyes at me. He nodded, frowned slightly, and stood up. "Ah. Ah, I see. I see. This is another thing 'tween you and him, eh? I don't understand you. You're your own man, Ariah. You're not Lor. You don't have to follow in his footsteps."

"You don't...Sorcha, you don't know what you're talking about," I said quietly.

"The hell I don't!"

"You don't. Look, I'm here for me. He's in Rabatha, and I'm here for me." I pulled myself up and sat on the couch. I took a breath. "I'm a shaper. I'm here for training. That's why I'm here, because I'm a shaper," I said quickly. I stared down at my boots as I said it.

Sorcha sat down next to me. "More than just a little, eh?"

"More than just a little."

"Huh. How long are you gonna be here?"

"As long as it takes I guess." I peeked over at him. "Probably a long time."

Sorcha grinned down at his hands. The air was full of warmth and peace, but that sharp, confusing want of mine still remained. He fingered the lapel of my vest. "Look at these togs. Looking sharp, Ariah. Looking fine." His voice was husky, a half-step deeper than usual.

I burned a deep, bright red. I laughed. My hand hovered in the air for a second, uncertain, and landed on his. I held his hand against my heart. I stared down at it, his hand in mine. "I have missed you."

"I knew you would."

"I really have."

Sorcha kissed me on the cheek. "Same."

* * *

Sorcha walked me to the palace the next morning. He was bright and unfettered, talking a mile a minute. I lingered close to him. He felt like home. I let his words wash over me, but it was his tone and the timbre of his voice that sunk in. Vathorem sat on the steps of the palace, smoking a pipe, waiting for me.

"So that's him, eh?" Sorcha said.

"That's him."

"He don't look like much."

Vathorem whistled. He pointed at both of us, each in turn, and waved us over. I took Sorcha by the elbow and led him over. "What does he want with me?" Sorcha asked under his breath.

"We'll find out." Vathorem wore an odd, quiet smile when we approached. He sat with his knees hunched up, his chin braced in one hand. "Good morning, Vathorem."

"Morning. You sleep well?"

"I did."

Vathorem pointed at Sorcha with his pipe. "Who is this?"

"A friend."

"Not a friend you made here." Vathorem leaned forward and studied Sorcha. "You're the little one, aren't you? The youngest brother."

Sorcha went cold beside me. He drew into himself. "I'm Sorcha. That's who I am." He gave Vathorem a slight bow and stepped away.

Vathorem laughed. He patted the step next to him. "So, that one," he said as I sat down.

"What about him?"

Vathorem shook his head. "You need solitude."

"He's my roots."

Vathorem looked over. "Come again?"

I blushed slightly and stared out at the street. "Sorcha, he's...I think he's my roots."

"Do you think you're his roots?" Vathorem asked. His voice was measured and careful.

"I don't know."

"A word of advice, man to man," he said. "It can be hard when you're bound to someone tighter than they're bound to you. Come on, let's get the day started."

I followed him into the palace. It was a spare place, but well built. It was a building of large rooms paneled in wood. It was a rugged, well-crafted building, utterly practical, and not at all ostentatious. The palace was two stories tall, and had three wings: one served as quarters, one served as kitchens and pantries, and the central wing was where the government functioned. From the entrance, we came into a waiting hall littered with red elves. They nodded to Vathorem, and he muttered greetings. Through the door at the end of the room was the throne room. The throne sat in the center near the back of the room. It was a large wooden chair built on a raised platform. It was forlorn and isolated. A narrow table in one corner of the room was crowded with people. Dor sat at his mother's left hand. He nodded to me when we entered. The queen looked up.

She was a hard-eyed, hard-faced woman. She was built of sinew and unbreakable bone. She was strength incarnate, a forbidding person, a person who dared you to challenge her. She wore her authority easily, and she wore it well. "Good. You didn't get yourself killed," she said.

Vathorem grinned. "You didn't either."

"You brought a stray."

Dor leaned towards the queen. "Ma, he mentioned…"

"You've always got a stray with you," she said. She looked at me, studied me. She gestured for me to come over. I sat in the chair beside her, my heart pounding a terrified rhythm. She caught my eye, and she smiled, and I was gone. "What's your story, lad?"

"I'm a shaper."

"There's a shaper under every loose rock, it seems."

"Oh, no, not really. We stick together." There was a slight pause. "No, Dor isn't one."

The room grew quiet. The queen leaned forward.

"He is very smart. Very, very smart," I said.

Dor left the room. Distantly, I heard Vathorem start to speak, but the queen held out her hand. She smiled wider. "But he's quiet. Do you think he's too quiet? Do you think they'll follow someone so quiet? He is…"

Vathorem read me fast and deep. He read me with such force that I cried out, that I was left shaken and nauseous in the wake of it. He jerked me out of the seat. "Nali, you're not fighting a war no more," he whispered. He pulled me out of the room through a side door. Dor sat on a bench in the hall. His hands gripped its underside so tight his knuckles were white. He was rigid, and he was wounded. "Ariah, take off," Vathorem said. "Give us a moment alone."

A cold, remote smile cracked across Dor's face. "Ah, no, he can stay. I'm sure he feels it. What is it you always told Dirva? You lot owe the rest of us an illusion of privacy? Well, hell, Falo, I know it's just an illusion. He can stay."

Vathorem sighed. He sat down beside Dor. Slowly he wrapped an arm around the boy's shoulders. Vathorem winced. He drew out the confusion, the anger, like it was poison from a snake bite.

"I'm sorry," I said quietly.

Dor looked over at me. "You got nothing to apologize for."

"Still," I said. "I'm sorry."

He nodded.

Vathorem walked me back to the Pickled Bear later that afternoon. "So," he said. "Now you've seen the queen."

"She is...regal."

"She is ruthless. And she's good at what she does. And she's never trusted anyone but herself, not really. Not even her consorts. Not even her boys. She's a soldier through and through. And the thing is, Dor's never been a soldier. She plucked him up as her left hand two years ago, and he's done so well sorting trade, getting roads built. Dor's got a knack for peacetime. But Nali, Nali don't know what this place is when there's a peace. She named him heir because I told her I'd leave court if she didn't. He don't know that. He don't know why she named him, and it cuts him to the quick for her to have named him and for her to keep questioning him like she does. Understand?"

"I think so."

Vathorem stopped. He turned me towards him and looked me in the eye. "Secrets is all we are, Ariah, just great tangled nests of stolen secrets. He don't know my role in this, and he's not going to find it out from you, all right? Because what we are is a disruption. Society is built on secrets. We sow chaos, you and I. You saw that today. You can't be blamed for it, but it's a truth about you. The things I'm to teach you, they are the ways I've found to keep from ripping people apart from each other. A lot of it is that you have to learn to let go. Let them live how they live, even if it seems wrong to you. You're judging Nali hard. I feel it in you. You have to get to a point where you see it and you have your thoughts about it, but they are locked down, understand?"

I didn't understand. Or rather, I understood but I deeply disagreed. And I had a sense that he disagreed with what he'd said, too. "If that's true, why force her to name Dor?"

Vathorem dropped his face down. A curtain of steel-gray hair swung between us. His walls flew up. I knew I'd touched a nerve, but what nerve, and why? "Ariah, I'm only telling you this once, so listen close. That boy is far more mine than hers by now. And this damned country, I fought for it as long and as hard as she did. I got my loyalty to Rethnali, I most certainly do, but a man has many loyalties. In me, there is Dor and Pekka, there is Dirva and Yohanni and one day there might even be you. There is Vilahna, and then there is Rethnali. Roots, Ariah. Think on your roots. Think on the choices you'll make, the things you'll do to keep them growing."

CHAPTER 19

SORCHA AND I fell easily back into old habits. We shared a bed. When I was not with Vathorem at court, I was with him. But the time I spent with Vathorem preoccupied me. The training was not so much a set of practical instructions as it was an effort to force me to face myself. Vathorem pushed me to lay myself bare, to inspect the nooks and crannies of my heart. He said it took remarkable self-awareness to be a shaper and live among those who weren't. He was right. The hours I spent with Vathorem left me questions to ponder during the hours I spent with Sorcha.

What was I to him? I wanted so badly to know. There were times I felt it was a balanced thing between us. When he'd come to Vilahna, he'd brought the stack of sketches Liro had drawn of him. They were tacked now above the mantle of the fireplace. But among them, directly in the center, was a small painting of me. Liro painted it from one of the sketches he drew of me the day Nuri died. He painted it for Sorcha, and Sorcha carried it across deserts and mountains with him all the way here to Vilahna. Sometimes, when he did not realize I was watching, Sorcha gazed at it. Sometimes, when he didn't think I could see, he gazed at me. The way he felt then, what I was to him, was obvious.

But there were other moments, and there were other people. Life in Alamadour was not like life in the City. There was no ailing parent; there was no terrible well of grief. He had long ago decided he and I were platonic. Several times I'd come home to find him in the throes of someone else or lounging with some red boy or girl, both of them stark naked on the floor. Once or twice he'd come home very late smelling of someone else. Once he did not come home at all. Those nights, the bed felt foreign and large.

I am not a red elf. I wasn't steeped in their flexibilities. I did not know what it meant to be so curious about him in this terrifying way, to need him so much, and to see him so indiscriminately generous with his time and affections. He was my roots. I woke next to him and knew, with unwavering certainty, that I was more myself when he was there beside me. That with him it was not a matter of getting swept away, or lost: he pulled the slippery, shy me-ness to the surface. I didn't know why it was him that did it instead of someone else, and I didn't know how he did it, but I knew he did it. And I knew that being apart from him had taken a toll, and that I didn't want to brave a separation again. But what was this life I led with him? I had no word for it, no understanding of it. More than friendship. Was it love? Yes. What kind of love? I didn't know. I think it seemed simplest to me if sex was involved. There's no understanding of romance without sex for a Semadran, and no conception of romance with a friend. There are just spouses. But the specter of rejection was paralyzing.

Things grew much more complicated when Dor's half-sister, Fallinal, appeared at court. She was related to him through his father, and they had been raised together. They were close; she seemed to understand him more than anyone else but Vathorem. She came to court, arm in arm with Dor, on a bright fall morning thirteen days after I arrived in Vilahna. She grew herb in the mountain compounds in the north and came to Alamadour to bring crops to market for the harvest a few times a year. That's all it took: thirteen days.

I was a mess when she came through that door. I had spent my whole life hiding from this gift, fighting it, and there I was in a different country with a man who demanded I let it out. Not just that I feel it, and know it, but that I admit it was the way I understood the world around me. That this gift was me, and that I had to embrace it in order to wield it with anything approaching competence. I had stopped holding back. I tried to hold my tongue, but I no longer fought the urge to read someone, and I no longer struggled against wherever my instincts wanted me to look. So, there I was, this conduit for the gift, raw and untempered. Confused, and very young yet, with a young man's curiosities.

She came through the door, and I felt her before I even saw her. I felt an invitation. I felt an attraction like a steel cable between us formed in the space of a heartbeat. I saw her, and she was beautiful. I saw her and I felt her see me as beautiful. I saw her and saw in the way she stood, the way she smiled, what she wanted from me. And I lost myself. The gift came alive with a ferocity. It's all I was, suddenly. The story goes that she came through the door, that she looked at me, and that I jerked upright in my seat like I'd been electrified. The story goes that she laughed, and I was across the room in three steps, and then I had her locked in a kiss. That's how the story goes. All I remember is Vathorem. It was a fog, a haze, until he pulled me out of the room. He held my chin and stared into my eyes. "Ariah. Ariah!"

"Yes, yes, I'm here. What happened?"

"You know why back in the Empire ones like us don't marry, right?"

"Mercy. I...mercy."

"No harm, not this time. But desire is one thing and wanting it is another. You understand? This is a thing you've got to control. You cannot do that, take someone like that. It's not right. It's not fair to them. Do you understand?"

"I didn't mean to," I said. I clutched at his forearms. I felt very small, very weak, and very young.

"Ariah, it don't matter if you meant to if the other person does not want it. You cannot take what is not offered to you. You cannot. No excuses. Understand?"

"But it just happens, doesn't it?"

"Only to those with no respect for anyone but themselves. No. It's a hard thing, I know it is, but I will have nothing to do with you if you think the inconveniences of your gift outweigh the damage you could do to someone with this."

"I understand."

"You sure?"

"I do. I am. I understand. What do I do?"

"You train yourself, you train your body to wait. You stay put. When you feel your grip slipping, you will yourself to stay where you are. You stay with someone who can watch you until you've got it under control. You tell a person who links you like that you're willing, if you are, but you will wait for them to decide when and where and how." He sighed. He grew softer with me. "And Ariah, you...you have to remember you owe it to no one, all right? No matter how much they want you, you never owe them a thing, link or not."

Vathorem sent me home early. He spoke to Fallinal about it. She knew him, and she had a rough understanding of what shaping was, and apparently she'd heard rumors about what shapers can do. And apparently that made her curious. Dor must have told her where I lived. I am certain Vathorem never would have. In the late afternoon, there was a knock on my door. Sorcha went to answer it. As soon as the door opened, I felt the force of that link. It drilled into me, inexorable, inescapable. "Afternoon," she said. "Does Ariah live here?"

Sorcha turned towards me, surprised, but I was already past him. I don't remember moving. I don't know how I got from the couch to the door, but there I was, and there she was, and then my mouth was on hers, and my hands were already working at her clothes. What I remember most is the pattern of her breath as it caught or deepened. I remember the rhythm of her body as mine moved against it. I don't know how we wound up on the floor. I have no idea how long it was. All I know was there was pleasure, her pleasure and my need to give it to her. I was a slave to it, enraptured by it, and I must have felt some myself, but I can't remember what she did to me.

My first clear memory afterwards is her laugh, and the feeling of her fingers in my hair. "A shaper," she said, and she laughed again.

She was sated, and her mind had wandered elsewhere, away from my face and hands and body, and I was left to my own mind again. "I am so sorry," I said. It came out a whisper.

"For what?"

"I am so very sorry."

"What's there to be sorry for?" she asked.

I sat up. I blushed at the sight of my own naked body. "Where's Sorcha?"

"Who's Sorcha?"

"He was here."

"Oh, the other tinker?"

I looked at her. "What?"

"The tink who was here with you? Red hair?"

"Don't call us that."

She sat up and pulled her hair over her shoulder. "That's what you are, though, right?"

"No, I'm Semadran. Don't call me that. And he's from the City. Is he still here?"

"I don't know. I think he left." She bit her lip and leaned forward. "That was something else. Let's go again."

"You should go," I said. I stood up and found my pants on the other side of the room.

"Really?"

"Yes."

"It was so good, though!"

I looked at her over my shoulder. Her wants reached out to me, poured into me, threatened to pull me over. "You called me a tinker. Please, go," I said. I kept my eyes pinned to the floor and went into the bedroom. I leaned against the door, barricading it, hiding from her. A few minutes later, I heard the front door creak open and slam shut.

Sorcha came home an hour or two later. He eased the door open slowly, silently, and peeked through. "Ah, you're done," he said. He came in and dropped his violin case on the couch. He shot me a grin. "You know, I never made you for the exhibitionist type."

I crumpled into a ball. I hugged my knees to my chest and hid my face in my arms. Sorcha was next to me in a second. "Hey," he said. "Hey, what's going on?"

"I hate this."

"Hate what?"

"Hate being a shaper. I hate this."

"Oh." He stroked my hair. "I just thought, you know, it's been over a year...I just thought you'd broken out of your shell."

"I can't control this. Who could control this? Why am I like this?"

"Hey, hey." He coaxed me out. He held me by the shoulders. "Ain't nothing wrong with what you are. It's not easy being anyone, right? You'll be all right. You will. I'll help. If I can, I'll help. Can I help?"

"Next time, stay," I said. "And pull me off. I can't do that again. I woke up from it so hollow."

"Yeah, all right," he said. "Sure, I can do that."

* * *

Word about Fallinal and I spread like wildfire. In the Empire, it would have isolated me. People would have crossed the street and taken pains to keep from looking me in the eye. But Vilahna was not the Empire. The story spread, and it kicked up the old rumors and curiosities about shapers. Within three days everyone in Alamadour knew that the new tinker at court was the best lay in town if you could charm him, and anyone could charm him.

Vathorem tried to protect me at court, but there were times the queen needed him, and I was left alone. Sorcha took to walking me to the palace and walking me home again, but there were times he was out playing sets and we needed fruit, and I braved the markets alone. Within a month of my arrival in Alamadour, I woke up in the beds of seven separate strangers. Two of them were men. I remembered virtually nothing about the sex itself, which disturbed me profoundly.

Afterward, when I was myself again, I forced out questions. Where was I? What time was it? Who were they? How had it happened? Had I made the first move? Sometimes I had started it, sometimes I had frozen and they had started it for me. I could divine no rhyme or reason to the times I showed restraint and the times I didn't. I was never brave enough to ask if it was an intrusion. Or worse, a violation. I am still ashamed I never asked.

I begged Vathorem to let me smoke. "I need it. It's too much."

"What, you think I don't have to weather those storms? No. The herb's a crutch."

I was on the brink of tears. I hid my face in my hands. "I don't remember anything. There's nothing in it. I feel used, Vathorem. I feel empty and scared and…"

"And when you're scared, the gift comes out screaming, which makes it that much more likely to happen," he said. He sighed. He pulled my head to his shoulder with a thoughtless and gentle caress to the back of my head. I fought it, I fought it as hard as I could, but I wept into his shirt nonetheless. "Ah, Ariah. You are so open, and the world is so large. Do you know anything about dancers?"

I pulled away. As discreetly as I could, I wiped my eyes. "No, I don't."

"All right. Well, that's a shame, but given you're Imperial, I can't say it's a surprise. Dancers. The thing with dancers, the thing that lets them keep their balance when they are whipping so fast the world is a blur, is they find a spot. Some spot that don't move. A point of stability. And that's what you need: a thing that centers you and keeps you upright. And yours is the little brother. That's a dangerous game to play, pinning yourself on someone else."

"I need the herb."

"You want to be tethered to a pipe the rest of your life?

You want to be a man who can't handle the world unless he's caught in a haze of smoke?"

"It is so hard here."

"We'll work more on breaking the charms," he said. He checked his watch, a lovely Semadran-made thing Dirva had given him years before. "I've time now. Break eye contact, get yourself some distance. Find your center."

For three hours Vathorem charmed me. For three hours I struggled with it. When I fought the gift, when I pushed it down with all that focus and determination I'd lived with in the Empire, I could scrape together the presence of mind to break his charms. But I was there in Vilahna because ignoring it had only brought me trouble. I wanted mastery of the gift, I wanted to live with it, in it, instead of against it, but I was still so new to it and so _ntampered that I could not see through it. When he charmed me, I felt the magic faster and deeper than I would have otherwise. The charms obliterated me. The effort of fighting them left me exhausted.

That night something broke within me. The strain of it all—the gift, my helplessness, the shame of constant failure—crushed me. I wound up on the floor of the loaned apartment, the blood roaring in my ears. Breath would not come. I felt I was drowning; I felt I was dying. The noises that came from me were these terrible, animal things: hisses and whines. My vision blurred, narrowed. Sorcha brought me back from the dark edge. He charmed me, and it helped. There are different kinds of charms, you know. The way you charm has a lot to do with how well you know who you're charming and what you want from them. Sorcha knew me as well as he knew himself, maybe better than he knew himself. All he wanted from me was my own safety. A charm born of that is a sweet thing, a tender thing. It is a comfort.

He took my face in his hands. My eyes locked to his, terrified, full of wordless pleading. "Shh, shh. Ariah, hey, Ariah, shh," he said. In minute increments, my throat unlocked. I took a breath. He nodded; he smiled. "Hey, see? Ariah, you're all right. You're all right, Ariah." One by one, my muscles unclenched. My heart slowed. Sorcha studied me, took stock of me. "Ariah, I'm here. You're all right."

I held his forearm, just above the wrist. I took a deep breath. I closed my eyes and leaned my head back against the wall. "Thank you." It came out a wounded croak.

He sighed with relief. His hands drifted to my shoulders, then away from me completely. He sat next to me. "What was that?" he asked.

I took some time to catch my breath. My shirt was plastered to me; my face was slick with sweat. "I don't know. Thank you."

"It's this damned training," he said. "That damned man, he don't know what he's doing."

"No, he's…he's right," I said. "I need it. It's just, it's all a lot to unlearn, and this…this is such a hard place to unlearn it in." My thoughts turned again to the charms, the strange apartments, the awful stinging tension in the throne room between Dor and his mother. I remembered again the irritation Vathorem had, and the way the gift took it and welded it to my heart, the way I felt his irritation and my terror at the same time, doubled and redoubled like an image reflected in mirrors facing one another. It all came unbidden. It all came, and my body tore against itself as if it was trying to smother my thoughts without regard to the fact that doing so smothered my body along with them.

"Ariah! Ariah, hey!"

Hands on my hands.

"I'm here, I got you."

Someone else's smell in my nose.

"I'm here. Ariah, I'm here."

Another's body pressed to mine, arms around my back, and a slow, steady heart beating against my chest. My heart found it, clung to it, and started to slow.

"Ariah. Ariah, shh."

And the relentless panic was dammed up again. Sorcha took my chin in his hand. He looked me over, inspecting me like he could see straight through my skin to the psychic wounds below.

"You all right?"

"For now."

"What happened?"

"I was thinking."

"Well, stop! Don't think no more."

I laughed and rested my head on his shoulder. "I wish I knew how to do that."

He was silent a second. "I know how," he said. He stood up and crossed the room. He returned with a pipe packed with herb.

"I can't."

"The hell you can't. You tell him you're like this?"

"He knows."

Sorcha frowned. He tamped down the herb and fished in his pocket for a match. "Then he's a right bastard. Look, you can. You should. You're all taxed, Ariah, all stretched taut. Give yourself an hour."

I smoked nearly the entire bowl myself. Sorcha took just enough to feel it, but not enough to get really stoned, but I drowned myself in it. And it helped. It was a crutch, and it was an escape, but sometimes you have to run away, and a broken leg is nothing on which to do the running. The first thing I did when the herb took hold was peel off my shirt. The air was cold against my damp skin. I pulled off my boots. I leaned back against the wall, eyes closed, and listened to my own heart. I counted my breaths. I felt the world through my skin. I felt contained in that moment, separate and bounded, and it was a relief. "Sorcha," I said.

"Yeah?"

"Thank you."

"Stop thanking me. Nothing to thank me for."

I found his hand with my eyes yet closed. I gave it a squeeze. "Thank you. I am so glad you're here. I'd be lost if you weren't here."

"Oh, Ariah, no. You were fine in Rabatha."

I looked over at him. He was fiddling with the pipe. He wore half a grin, a kind of giddiness. "No, I was a mess there. It was hard. I don't know who I am when I'm not with you."

He laughed. He wouldn't look at me. He beamed, bursting with life. "You're so dramatic. You're you when you're not with me. Same as when you are with me."

"No," I said. "It's different." I watched him spin the pipe in his hands, around and around and around. I watched the rise and fall of his chest. I wanted to preserve the ease of that moment, the security of him. I wanted to forget the terror of the panic. I wanted my body worn out so thoroughly it didn't have the capacity to rebel again. I wanted something corporeal, something good, and I wanted a lasting memory of it. I wanted him wedded to me, as bound to me as I was to him. My heart pounded in my chest, a deep *boom boom boom* that drowned out every other noise. My skin came alive, every nerve alert and full of anticipation. I forgot to breathe. Slowly, I took the pipe from his hand and set it on the floor beside him. He looked over at me, curious and slightly worried. I turned toward him, my left arm crossing his body. I leaned into my arm, and cupped the back of his neck with my other hand. I pulled him to me, and I kissed him. Without regret or hesitation, I kissed him. Man to man without any shadow of shame, I kissed him. And I still remember it with startling clarity, that kiss. It was the first kiss I'd ever had I can remember, the first one with no charms and no shaping wedged between it and my memory.

He tasted of smoke and oranges and slightly of ale. His mouth was hot, and grew hotter as we kissed. His tongue slipped along mine, and the muscles of my back tightened. When our mouths closed, I felt the soft dryness of his lips. He let out a sigh, hot against my jaw. He started to say my name, but my mouth found his a second time. I leaned into him, and we fell against the wall, my body stretched along the length of his. He laughed very softly, pulled just far enough away just long enough to say my name. "Ariah."

My face hovered just in front of his. I breathed his breath in; he breathed in mine. "Yes?" I felt safer, more alive, more complete than I ever had before. It was intoxicating.

"Ariah, what is this? What're you doing?"

I grinned at him. I spoke in his voice. "I thought we were making it finally."

He blushed. With skin as dark as his it's hard to tell, but I was close, and I could not tear my eyes from him, and it was a deep, burning blush. He laughed again, but there was a tension in the laugh. His eyebrows knitted together, and he pushed me gently away from him. "Ah, you're stoned."

"I want to remember it."

He rubbed a hand through his hair and moved slightly away from me. He stared down at his feet. "Ariah, I can't."

"We can."

He shook his head. "You're not listening. Ariah, I can't, not with you, not like this. Look, I just...I know myself. This thing 'tween us, it's all deep down in me. When you left, there were all these memories of you, and I couldn't...I couldn't sleep right. I had to get out. That's why I'm here, right, that's why I've stayed. Fresh start. And I'm nahsiyya, but I'm pretty red when it comes to this. But the thing is, even reds fall hard. It hurts reds, too, when it's one-sided. You and me, what we are, that's all right with me. I'll take it, I want it. But if we fuck, it's over for me. I'm trapped in it. I'll never get out from under it." He swallowed. A muscle in his jaw twitched. "I don't know what this is, what you're doing here right now, but if it's not all I want it to be, it'll hit me hard. So just...Ariah, just don't. Not unless you've thought it through. Really thought it through. Just don't."

"I want you," I said.

He looked at me. His face was the strangest mix of hardness and softness, of cynicism and hope. "Right now you do. But c'mon, how do you know what you really want? These are uncharted waters for you, right, you could bail halfway through, and I'd not fault you for it 'cause you only learn by doing, but you'd leave me all sprung. I love you, I do, and you know it, and what I'm saying is I can't be the one you try on. What you need from me right now, I can't give it to you." He sighed. He ran his hands over his face. He looked over at me, stroked my cheek, and smiled, but the smile was a little sad. "I'm gonna take a walk, clear my head. I'll see you later."

CHAPTER 20

VATHOREM SAT ACROSS from me in a small room in the palace. Somewhere down the hall, a pair of violins played a desperately sad song. Guards in the next room conversed loudly about the recent influx of satyrs into town. "It's not working," he said, half to himself. He peered at me, read me, and shook his head. "Maybe you aren't built to build walls."

"What?"

He shook his head again. "It's not working. Can't force it. We'll have to try something else."

"What else is there to try?" I said. My heart rushed to a sprint.

"Ariah, shh."

My heart slowed down again. "Vathorem, shapers build walls. That's what we do. That's how we manage."

"That's how some of us manage," he said. "But not you."

"But in Moshel Atoosa'Avvah's book..."

"Moshel made guesses. Good guesses, but they were guesses. He didn't know everything about every shaper, just a whole lot about most of them. I've been thinking on this. I know you can't charm none, but there's a trick to charming that might work for you." He held his hand up. "I know you can't charm. I know. It's a technique, Ariah, that charmers use, but that's not to say it might not be a technique shapers could use, too."

No walls. What is a shaper without walls? Lost. Mad. A hermit.

"Ariah. Stop ruminating."

"When you tell me to stop, it just makes it worse."

He sighed. "Ah, it's the same for me. Let me tell you the trick. There is a thing in red magic called a litany, which I think is some convoluted mishmash of charming and shaping. It's complicated, but the gist is you charm someone so much, so deep, that you make a lasting mark. It's a charm that lingers. It's a charm that takes something of yours and puts it in someone else. Not like other charms, where you coax something in them to the surface. You understand what I'm saying? And you have to maintain a litany. And the way you do it is you have to feel yourself and you have to feel them at the same time. It's like you've got two hearts inside you: yours and theirs. To learn a litany, you have to learn to be yourself and not yourself at the same time. Ariah, if you could do that, you might make some progress."

"There's not enough space in a person for more than one heart."

He frowned slightly. "Well, no, not literally."

"I know you didn't mean it literally," I said. "When it happens, I get...pushed out. There's nothing in me but them, what they want, what they feel."

"You're not pushed out," he said. He spoke fast, with a

smile playing around the edges of his mouth. His palpable excitement was contagious. I started to wonder whether this would work. "You're pushed to the side. You're still in there. It's your brain, Ariah! Where else would you be? So, what we have to do is we have to let them wrap around you. You stay right there, right in the center, and they fill up all the rest of the space on the edges. You see?"

"No, not really."

He sighed. "Six months and we're still stuck in place. It was so much faster with Dirva."

"He can build walls. And he can charm. And he..."

"Ariah, you're not him, but that don't mean you're hopeless."

I nodded, even though I didn't really believe him. After a moment or two, I looked over. "How would I do it? How does it work?"

Vathorem pulled his long gray hair off his shoulder. He sighed. "You got to care less."

"Care less? Care less about what?"

"Everything. Anything."

"I don't understand."

"Of course you don't," he said. "What I mean to say is you need to learn to just see the world how it is. You're so wrapped up in the future, in the what-ifs and might-bes. And when you're not running the possibilities, you're stuck in the past. Ariah, you don't really live. You got no sense of the present, the moment to moment. And you need it. You need to learn to feel what you feel—just feel it as it unfolds—and feel what someone else feels, too, without trying to fit it in to some future life or make it make sense with some past thing."

"Actions have consequences."

"I'm not saying they don't. I'm saying you spend a whole lot of time and effort trying to force yourself to feel and think and be one way instead of another. It eats up your energy. Ariah, you've gotten nowhere with this. Maybe you don't know who you are in some grand, total way. Maybe you're not a person like that. Maybe who you are changes moment to moment. That's all right. That's fine. But if that's the case, let yourself change moment to moment."

The words sunk in. They felt true. Later that night I tried to write Dirva about it. I wrote him about everything, partly for him, and mostly for me. It helped me to process the things Vathorem said, which often seemed simple at first and grew increasingly complex as I tried to implement his advice. I was curled up on the couch scratching away at a pad of paper when Sorcha came home. "Writing to Lor?"

"Yeah."

"That old bastard do something awful again today?"

"No, he did something good, maybe." I put down the half-written letter and looked at him. There was a confused pang of something, some unnamable want, some line waiting to be crossed between us. I looked away again, at Liro's painting above the mantle. "Do you think I live in the present?"

There was a slight pause. "Fuck, Ariah, are you a seer? I swear, every other day you've got some new talent."

"No! No. It's something Vathorem said. He thinks I dwell

too much on the past. And the future."

"Yeah, that sounds like you."

"He thinks I should change that."

"Well, maybe. You're fine the way you are," he said, "but you might be wound less tight."

He dropped his violin case in a chair and sat down next to me. He held my feet in his hands to warm them up. "It's getting on to winter. It gets cold here, you silly bastard. Why don't you ever build a fire?"

"It's a lot of work."

He shook his head at me. "So, what're you supposed to do?"

"I don't know. He said something about two hearts. I'm supposed to be myself and not myself at the same time. Or something."

"That man, he just strings words together."

"No, I think he's right. I just don't know how to do it."

"Well," Sorcha said, "you're not about to figure it out tonight. Want to smoke?"

"I shouldn't."

He grinned. "Ah, you want to."

I grinned back. "I do."

"You're supposed to be all in the present, yeah? Sounds like you ought to smoke a bit to me."

We smoked. The pipeherb in Vilahna is uniformly good. A man's status can be derived by the quality of the herb he smokes there, and we were nobodies, but it was still the best herb I've ever had before or since. City herb, coaxed out of an inhospitable climate by blue elvish magic, is extremely potent but harsh. Mountain herb is a soft thing, a smooth thing, a pure pleasure. We lay together in bed, mostly naked, under piles of thick wool blankets. For hours we'd nestled up close, trading stories. I told him about Ardijan. I told him about the odd rhythms of factory life. I told him about hours spent swimming the river. He told me about the time he spent living at Falynn's house. Falynn had three wives and a husband; between them, they had nine children. Sorcha said he slept under piles of children at night. He told me of the first person he'd slept with. It was a girl who worked at a musician's pub. When I asked him what it was like, all he would say is it was clumsy. But he grinned when he said it. Slowly, the herb wore off. Sobriety crept up, and as my mind began to clear, I could feel the way Sorcha's mind turned. It was like his thoughts and his feelings flowed out of his skin and into mine. I was on my back, one arm tucked behind my head and the other cradling his shoulders. He lay on his side, both arms wrapped around my ribs. He'd woven one leg over and around mine.

The gift tugged at me. I let it out, and I read him, and what I felt was strange. It was like seeing myself through someone else's eyes. Like looking in a particularly flattering mirror. For him, in that moment, there was nothing but the two of us in that bed. The rest of the world did not exist.

"You reading me, Ariah?"

"I'm sorry."

He nestled tighter against me. I could feel him smile against my bare chest. "What did you find out?"

"Nothing. You can't read an empty mind."

"You ass."

"Will you do me a favor?"

"Depends."

"Will you charm me?"

Sorcha pulled away from me. "What?"

"I need practice breaking them."

"Oh." He let out an odd, muted laugh. At the same moment, he closed up. Not walls, perhaps, but screens formed between us. "Ah, yeah. Sure. Just any charm?"

I propped myself up on my elbows. The air outside the blankets was terribly cold. "How did you do that?"

"I didn't do nothing yet," he said.

"No, forget about the charm. How did you pull back like that?"

Sorcha's eyebrows furrowed. "I don't know what you're talking about."

"You just—just then, you just made us...uh, separate? How did you make that distance?"

"I don't know."

"Well, what are you hiding from me?"

He sat up. The curve of his back as his shoulders slumped away from me spoke volumes. I immediately wished I hadn't pressed him. If I had stopped at all to think, if I had taken even a second to myself, I would've known. But I hadn't. Wrapped up as I was in my own anxieties, I forgot that he had some, too.

"Ariah, I thought you'd thought it through and come

around," he said quietly. He glanced at me over his shoulder. "I didn't mean to pull back. Just happened. I don't know how I did it, honest. I'd tell you if I did." He lay down again beside me, this time on his stomach. "Hey, I'm good. You know I'm good. Been meaning to ask you something, though."

"Ask me what?"

"I just don't understand why you're here. Don't get me wrong, I'm glad for it, but this training you're putting yourself through. What's the point of it? You were fine in the City."

"I wasn't fine."

"You were."

"I wasn't. Do you remember the family dinners?"

He was quiet for a moment. "But you weren't like that all the time. You managed all right."

I laughed. It was a harsh thing, a bitter thing. He looked over at me. "I was stoned. After you kissed me, I kept myself as stoned as possible. There's nothing to manage when I'm stoned. And then, after, Sorcha, I...the gift had me twisted. I got detained at the border. I did stupid things. I was constantly on the verge of getting arrested or reassigned to line work or worse in Rabatha. Dirva pulled a lot of strings to keep me safe."

"You got detained?"

I nodded.

"For what?"

"For being a shaper. For wearing your clothes. For being an elf. Not for any good reason."

"What happened?"

"Nothing good."

He reached over and took my hand. "You'll be all right. This training, though. You sure it's worth it?"

"I think so."

* * *

Dor charmed me without a word. We sat in the library of the palace, just him and I. He had been translating letters of asylum from Athenorkos to Semadran, and I was there to check and double-check his grammar and vocabulary. He had, in particular, problems switching tenses. "This conjugation here is wrong," I said. I looked up to see if he was paying attention. Dor's chin was lifted slightly. He stared down the length of his nose at me. One corner of his mouth turned up.

I felt the pull of it. I think he was bored, or perhaps he was stuck on someone. He may have been curious about me, like Fallinal all over again. Maybe he just wanted me to stop correcting his grammar. In any case, he wanted me. He wanted me there in a room with no locks.

I felt the pull of it, and my body moved towards him of its own accord. Dor smiled just a hair wider. The way he sat, the way he breathed a silent laugh, sent his amusement pouring into my mind. The shift in him was slight, fleeting, but the shift was a thing I sensed. *I* sensed it; my mind found it and tracked it. There was a startling moment of clarity there, an awareness that I was still there, that my mind still turned. I froze in place. I shut my eyes. And the charm broke.

"Did you just break that?" Dor asked.

"I...I think so," I said. My eyes stayed close. I laughed. "I think I did."

"I'll go get Vathorem," Dor said, and then he was out of the room.

Vathorem rushed in with Dor close at his heels. "You broke a charm?"

"I did!" I laughed, giddy, drunk on pride. "I did."

Vathorem laughed. He clapped his hands together. "Grand news. Grand news. It'll get easier from here, I'm sure of it." He looked over his shoulder at Dor. "You know better than to charm him."

"Falo, he broke it. If I'd not charmed him, he'd not have anything to break."

"Dor."

After approximately two seconds of defiance, Dor apologized. I accepted it. "What now?" I asked. "What's next?"

"Now, Ariah," Vathorem said, "now we work."

Endless drills. Regimented schedules. Ruthless discipline. Vathorem had a work ethic that could have been forged in an Imperial elvish ghetto. First, he ran me through charm after charm after charm to hone this trick on which I'd stumbled. It was nearly a week before I managed it again, and then four days before I managed it a third time. Then, it happened again after just one more day. After that, I managed to break charms with something approaching consistency. It was like learning a language: once I had the grammar of it, once that elemental pattern emerged, everything else about shaping, about charms, began to make sense. I felt immensely accomplished for about two hours, and then he pushed me into hard, uncharted territory again. He had everyone and anyone charm me. Everyone charms a little differently. If you are sensitive enough, you can tell who is charming you or shaping you by the feel of it alone. It took a little while to get the hang of breaking anyone's charms, but not as long as I expected. I found it simplest to break charms by people I knew, even though those charms tended to be deepest. I think it's because with someone I know it's easier to distinguish between my heart and theirs when both are inside me.

I made progress quickly, but that's not to say it was easy work. I learned to break charms and mirrors, and I learned what it meant to use my gift. I had always thought mastery meant you kept the gift walled up within, doling it out in the right dose at the right time. That's largely how it is with mimicry. But shaping is a completely different animal. It's a gift that permeates everything you do, everything you are. It is a way of living more than it is a talent. After a lifetime of trying to separate it and me, this was a hard lesson to learn.

In his writings, Moshel Atoosa'Avvah talks about walls and anchors. His techniques are built on separation, a stability of self, which I have always lacked. It felt strange to abandon his techniques, which were steeped deeply in the traditions and gathered knowledge of Semadran magic. Abandoning them felt like yet another wedge between the life I lived and the life I was expected to live. Vathorem and I drew on anything and everything we could find to build a new framework for me. We found different tools to reach the same end. Vathorem taught me much about the litanies. I learned Old Athenorkos for it, and he was thrilled to teach someone even a little bit about it. "Litanies, they're rare," he said one day. He sat next to me and blew the dust off the cover of a large, leather-bound book. It was hundreds of years old, the pages made of vellum instead of paper. "It would be a shame for them to die out with me."

"You're the only one?" I asked.

Vathorem shrugged. "Perhaps. Perhaps not. They're rare. The woman who taught them to me, who gave me this book, she's long gone." He ran his hands over the cover and smiled.

"There are coppers in the City."

"Coppers?"

"Half Semadran, half Athenorkos. I bet some of them could do it."

"Huh. I bet that's so. If I'm ever allowed to retire, maybe I'll make my way to the City, seek some out. That's enough talk; let's get to work."

To perform a litany, you catch attention first with a charm. Then, you sync your mind with the receiver's. Chants in Old Athenorkos are used for this. The chants function as a way to keep yourself focused, to keep hold of yourself, while also letting someone else into you. The mantras worked well for me. It was easier to track myself when I allowed my mind only one train of thought. Vathorem taught me everything there is to know about litanies and the kind of shaping they use. They give you a measure of control over someone else. They let you guide someone's feelings, and when you guide their emotions, you have a good chance at guiding their thoughts, too. It is a powerful and dangerous thing. He made me a true shaper before he taught me restraint, or how to catch just bare glimpses, or how to pull back my instincts. In school, they teach us that mastery is shown through restraint of a gift rather than its use. It was years before I could claim mastery, but there with Vathorem, I can say I began to understand the shape of my gift, the things it could do, the way it functioned.

The progress was intoxicating. With each new skill, it seemed the world was a little different, a little less mysterious. I had an urge to revisit things. I dug out my notebooks of Droma songs, read and reread them. I spent nights poring over them. It was a search, but for what was not clear to me until I found it. Phrases began to jump out at me: "A shared skin between vim and I," or "the thoughts were mine and vis and ours at once," or "in the grass, there is no you or me but only an us."

There is not much that can be gleaned from a handful of stolen songs, but these phrases haunted me. They felt like truth. They felt like hope. But I didn't understand them. I translated some of them and brought them to the palace once. Vathorem read them, then gave me the oddest look. "Ariah, why did you give these to me?"

"I think they could help?"

"Help with what?"

"With my training."

Vathorem read me. It was a hot flash; he could have charmed me, but it took time to make me comfortable that he did not always want to waste. "Ariah, these are just poems."

"Well…yes."

"This is not a technique."

"Well, no, not outright," I said. I took the sheaf of papers from him and thumbed through the pages. "It's not what they say, it's what they're about. There's some technique they have that could help, I think. I can tell from the poems."

Vathorem sighed. "If reading them helps, keep reading them, but all they are to me are strings of pretty words."

CHAPTER 21

THE LONGER I stayed in Vilahna, the less likely it seemed I would ever return to the Empire. The longer I stayed in Vilahna, the less I wanted to return to the Empire. I had Sorcha in Alamadour. I had Vathorem to keep me sane. I had a clumsy but firm grip on the shaping. When I had honed my ability to break charms and mirrors, sex became more fascinating than terrifying, and in Alamadour I had the space to explore it. Fallinal came again to the markets, and again she sought me out. This time, though, I was trained and stoned when she appeared at my door. I remember it all. I didn't like her, but I wanted her, and I wanted a memory built on my own terms. She came to my door, and I answered, and she smiled. When I didn't come barreling across the threshold at her, she frowned. "Come in," I said, holding the door wide for her.

"You sick or something?" she asked.

I caught Sorcha's eye and nodded to the door. His eyebrows leapt up, but he gave me the space to do it. "No, I'm not sick. You can come in. Have you eaten?"

She lingered near the door. "You sure you're all right?"

"I'm fine. Charm me."

She stepped close to me. She smiled and said my name. The charm held for two, three seconds, and then I shook it off. I grinned at her, triumphant, with some play at dominance. She smirked in response. "I see you've done some learning since I saw you last."

"I have."

"It's a shame."

I wanted to lash out at her. I wanted to scream at her and tell her how terrifying it had been to realize what had happened when she'd ambushed me months before. I wanted control of the situation this time. I wanted to take it without asking the way she'd taken it from me, and that scared me. I took a step away from her. "You can go if you don't want to." I said it careful, measured, reading her just a little to make sure she saw it as an offer and not as a challenge or a threat. "You can go any time you like."

She shook the hair out of her face. She grinned. "But I can stay, too, eh?"

"Yes, Fallinal, you can stay."

She chose to stay. I chose to let her. It was a slow, drawn-out thing. It was an exploration of my body as much as it was an exploration of hers. I let her tell me what to do, when to do it, and where. I took her direction well. I reveled in taking her direction. I was well and thoroughly stoned when she'd arrived, but some residue of the gift must have been coaxed out during the act itself. The longer we stayed locked together, the more I fell into the rhythms of her body and lost sight of the rhythms of my own. But I remember it. I remember every caught breath, every shudder. I remember the way her hands felt against me and the way her sweat tasted. When we lay side by side on the floor afterward, both naked, both slick and panting, I laughed. I couldn't stop laughing. I pressed my hands against my face, but it did no good.

"What the hell?" she asked.

I was too spent too care. I was too boneless to have any dignity left. "Well, that was something," I said. The laughter grew softer, more sporadic.

"Not bad," she said. "Not like it was before, but not bad. You're new at this?"

"I am."

"Aye, you seem it. Now, you seem it. Seemed an old hand before."

"That wasn't me. That was the magic."

"You are your magic." She rolled her eyes as she said it.

I studied her profile. She stared up at the ceiling, one arm tucked beneath her head. Her red hair—a bright, golden red—was pooled around her, looped over an arm here, tucked under a shoulder there. Her nose was sharp. Beads of sweat dotted her forehead, glinting in the fickle light of oil lamps strewn throughout the room. "I am, and I'm not."

She frowned slightly. "You lot, you always talk in riddles."

I sat up and ran a hand through my hair. My limbs felt loose and long. "Don't."

"Don't what?"

"Don't talk about Semadrans like you know anything

about us. Are you hungry?"

"I don't know. What have you got?"

"Eggs. Bread. Apples."

"Bacon?" she asked.

"I don't eat meat."

"That's to do with…"

"Yes," I said. I stood up and went towards the pantry. "That's to do with being Semadran. I'll make you eggs."

She was gone by the time Sorcha returned. I was curled up in bed by then, still naked. A laziness came over me after sex, a willful luxuriance of my own skin. There are times I still get that way. He shook my shoulder until I woke up. I sat up, blinking at him, wincing in the light of the lamp he'd lit. "Hey, you all right?" he asked.

"I'm fine. Have to get up tomorrow. Douse the lamp."

"I will in a second. Ariah, you all right? Really all right?"

I fell back into the bed and pulled a blanket up over my eyes. "I'm fine."

"Last time you weren't."

"This time was different. I remember it."

He was quiet for a long time. The room grew dark, and I felt him slide into the bed next to me. His arm wound around my ribs, and my hand patted his forearm. His face tucked into the space between my shoulder blades. "Nice to see you not scared for once," he said softly. "That girl's a terror."

I laughed. "She is. You know, she really is. I made her eggs, and she complained about them the whole time she ate them."

Sorcha laughed and held me a little tighter. "Ariah, you silly git, you didn't have to cook for her. Could've just sent her on her way."

"Well, I was hungry. It only seemed fair to offer her some food, too."

Sorcha laughed again. "You got your memory, you said?"

"I did."

"Well. That's something. I'm glad you got it."

* * *

There were others after Fallinal. There was the bartender from the bar downstairs. There was a guard at court. There was a musician friend of Sorcha's, a guitarist with perfect hands. They were each so utterly unique, each woman a private little world, but it always happened the same as it had with Fallinal. They came to me. They coaxed me through it. I gave, and they took, and I delighted in the giving. Afterward, invariably, I offered to cook for them. I don't mean to imply that this was a frequent thing, because it wasn't, but it did happen. And each time it happened, I felt that much more settled outside the Empire. I felt that much more comfortable in the life in which I'd landed. And I always returned to Sorcha. No matter how late it was, I always made the walk home to him. It felt like the day hadn't really ended until we were tucked against each other in the shared bed. Those nights I wondered about him and me, about what we were, about if I wanted from him what he wanted from me. I never found an answer. I could feel myself approach one, make slow inexorable progress towards it, but life intervened before I reached it. Life has a way of doing that.

Given the single entrance to the apartment, I passed through the bar every morning. This had its perks, as sometimes the bartender would pass me a slice of bread on my way out if I looked harried and ill-slept and generally like I might have skipped breakfast. One morning in high summer, about two years into my stay there, Sorcha and I passed the bar. Pannali was already there. She grinned at me, and I blushed. I shot her a shy, hopeful smile. Sorcha laughed and pushed me past the bar. "You'll be late, you silly git!"

"Wait!" Pan called after us.

"He ate," Sorcha said.

"No, there's this…well, shit, I don't know what it is, but it looks Semadran."

I half-turned and glanced over my shoulder. Sorcha crashed into me. "What do you mean?"

She waved me over. "I mean this," she said. She placed a small, lifeless clockwork bird on the bar. "Came in the back window. Hit the kitchen wall and just stopped flying. I don't what it is or what it's here for, but I bet it's to do with you."

"That's a messenger bird," I said. I glanced at Sorcha; he shrugged. I picked it up and found the pressure plate on its belly. It was bent slightly from the crash, and I had to pry it off with a butter knife. I felt terrible about it; I've never been any good with clockworks, and I knew I'd never be able to repair it. It seemed an untoward fate for the thing. The message was rolled tight and slipped into a waterproof sleeve. It took me some time to peel it off. My heart pounded when I had the tube of paper freed from it, waiting to be read. I knew it was bad news. I knew it. A dead parent. An arrested mentor. Revocation of citizenship rights. Something somehow worse than any of those things.

"What is it?" Pan asked.

"It's...it's a message. News, probably."

"Oh." She laughed. "That bird, it looked alive. You send notes in birds?"

"Only important notes."

"Read it," Sorcha said.

"I..." I frowned.

"Ariah, just read it," he said.

So I did. It was a short letter, but carefully written. I could tell in the sweep of Dirva's handwriting how much thought had been put into it, how exacting the choice of words was.

Nisa is pregnant. Will you be the child's falo? Please consider it.

My eyes went wide. Sorcha and Pan pestered me, demanded to know what was in the letter. "I have to go back," I said.

"To where?" Pan asked.

"To the Empire. To Rabatha."

Sorcha plucked the letter out of my hand. He frowned. "I can't read this. Is this Semadran?"

"Yes."

"What does it say? Are you in trouble?" he asked.

"It, uh...I'm not in trouble. It's good news. Thank you, Pan."

"My pleasure."

I dragged Sorcha out to the street. "What is it?" he asked. "Why do you have to go?"

"Dirva's wife is having a baby. He wants me to be the godfather."

It is a rare moment when Sorcha is at a loss for words. He gaped at me, at the street, at the door of the tavern for what felt like an endless stretch of time. He jammed his hands in his pockets and stared down at his boots. "He married," he said. It came out quiet, private, only half a question.

"You...you didn't know that?" Sorcha shook his head. "I thought he told Cadlah. He got her to get papers forged for me before the wedding. I thought...I thought he told her, and I thought she told the rest of you."

"Maybe she did. Maybe she didn't," he said. "Caddie can keep a secret. They might all know. I told you I been down here since you left."

"They would have written to you."

He gave me a hard look. "You know I'm not a good reader. I get news from merchants about them now and again. I'm not like you. I don't write letters. They never sent word to me."

"Oh."

"He married."

"That's why Vathorem was in the Empire. I came back

with Vathorem after the wedding."

Sorcha ran a hand through his hair. He drew in a breath and swung his head to the side, away from me. "I wonder if Ro knows."

"He does."

Sorcha looked at me again. "How do you know that?"

"Liro came to the Empire. It was before it was set, but Dirva knew that's where it was going with Nisa, I think, and he told him. I'm sure Liro knows. I'm sure Liro told Amran."

Sorcha threw up his hands. "Fuck! Fuck, Ariah, everyone knows but me? People crossing borders to find out, and I'm in the fucking dark?"

"I'm sorry! I thought you knew!"

"You've been here two years! You couldn't have mentioned it?"

"You don't like to talk about him! I thought you knew!"

"I didn't! I didn't know!" He passed his hands over his face and took a breath. He glanced up at the sky. He did his best to compose himself. "All right. Lor went and got married. Now he's having a kid. A little silver kid with a little silver wife in a little silver house. All right. And he wants you to play falo?"

"He wants me to be falo."

"He wants you to be a red godfather to a silver kid?"

"Yes," I said. "He does."

"And you're going to."

"I am, yes."

Sorcha waved his hand at me, dismissive, imperious. "Go on then. Run on back. In Rabatha you'll just be a glorified babysitter, and no one'll touch you with a ten-foot pole. You want that life, go and take it."

"Sorcha, I…"

"You're a lot like him, you know, with all this leaving."

"Sorcha, you should come, too," I said.

He blinked at me. "What?" he asked softly.

"I think you should come."

"What fucking for? There's nothing there for me."

I frowned. I chewed on the inside of my cheek. "I want you to come for me. You don't have to, of course you don't have to, but I want you to. For me. Rabatha will eat me alive without you there, I know it will. And if you don't come, I'll miss you. And nothing will feel right. And I'll miss your music. And…"

He grinned. He cocked his head to the side and laughed. He raised his eyebrows and laughed again. "Ariah, there is nothing there for me. I'm half ghalio and all nahsiyya and I'm a street musician. What am I gonna do in the Empire? Lor don't want me there. Hell, I didn't even know he was hitched."

"You don't have to go. But I do. The only thing that'll be there for you will be me. That's it. It's selfish to ask, I know that, but I'm…I guess I'm asking anyway."

Sorcha stared at me, hard, penetrating, like he was the shaper. "I'll think on it. I'll consider. Give me a few days?"

"Consider as long as you want."

CHAPTER 22

"HOW MUCH DO we have between us?" Sorcha asked.

"Not much. It's not like Vathorem paid me. All we have is what you got with your violin and what I brought with me."

"So, how much is that, exactly?"

"I have two hundred and thirty marks left. Which is, uh, around three hundred Vilahnan leaves," I said. "How much do you have?"

"Three fifty."

"Marks?"

"Leaves." He frowned. He kicked at the dirt. Sorcha had been nervous and bad-tempered for weeks. The tension in him ratcheted up as the deadline to leave Alamadour loomed closer and closer. "This fool's errand is going to clean us both out, Ariah."

"Thank you for coming," I said. I had said that a lot in the days since he decided to travel with me.

"You owe me, Ariah."

"I do."

"As long as you know you owe me."

"I do know." It was early afternoon, and the Alamadour markets soaked up the bright sunlight. It was a rare, clear day. The skies in the south are nests of clouds: gray, constantly shadowed. The brightness of the day's naked sun made me think of Rabatha and the City. It seemed a fitting day to arrange transport. I shielded my eyes and studied the crowds.

"There are some tahrqs over there," said Sorcha.

"I will not travel with them."

"All right. All right."

"They would fleece us anyway. We'd end up as slaves."

"I said all right." Sorcha tugged at my sleeve and pointed behind me. "How about them, eh? Semadran to a man."

I glanced over my shoulder, and the sight of her unmanned me. I blushed. My laugh was loud and slightly unhinged. I prayed it was a phantom recognition, that it was not really her, but she heard me. She cocked her head to one side, and then she turned around.

Shayat was still so much herself. It had been two years since I had seen her last, and then I had known her only while she prepared herself to live the life she now led. From across the market she gave me that utterly familiar look of condescending amusement. She said something to a tall man next to her and made her way towards us. She walked with such effortless certainty, gently nudging people out of her way like she owned the entire market district. I tried and failed to gather my bearings. Sorcha pestered me with questions, but I was laughing too hard to give him any answers. By the time she reached me my ribs ached, and my face was covered in tears. I stood braced against Sorcha, my sense of balance long lost.

Shayat stood in front of me, smirking, arms crossed. "Hello, professor."

I managed, finally, to get control of myself. I wiped my face, grinning so wide it hurt. I had missed her. I hadn't known until she appeared in front of me that I had, or how much. "You cut your hair," I said.

"You stopped cutting yours," she said. "You look ridiculous."

I laughed again and rubbed my jaw to relieve some of the soreness from having laughed so much already. Sorcha ran a hand through my hair. Shayat's eyebrows raised just the slightest bit. I felt in her a spark of curiosity. "It suits him," Sorcha said. He spoke Semadran with a pronounced City flair.

Shayat pointed at him. "Who is this?"

"Sorcha. This is Sorcha," I said. "He is my...we are..."

Sorcha held out his hand. "We're brotherly."

"You're brothers?" she asked.

"No," Sorcha said. "We're brotherly. Who are you?"

"This is Shayat Bachel'Parvi," I said. "I taught her Modern Athenorkos and Coastal Lothic back in Rabatha. Shayat! Shayat, what are you doing here?"

"Caravanning," she said. "I come through here every six months or so." She grinned; pride poured out of her. "I have the lead mercantile license. I have an all-elvish caravan."

"Really?"

"First one in Rabatha. You have no idea the hoops they made me jump through to get it."

"Shayat, that's…how did you manage that?"

"Compromises," she said. "Any Qin official can confiscate up to one-eighth of my goods, no questions asked, as a tariff."

"They'll take your goods one eighth at a time," I said.

"They haven't yet. They won't. I'm smarter than they are. My route has one single border check. One. I lose an eighth there, and that's it. I sell to the ghetto out of Papa's shop. The Qin in the Rabathan markets never even see the goods."

"Speaking of routes," Sorcha said, "we're looking for one."

Shayat looked at me, and laughter again bubbled up my throat. I turned a deep red.

"Me and him, we've got to get to Rabatha. Are you heading back there soon?" Sorcha asked.

One corner of Shayat's mouth hitched up. She looked me right in the eyes. "You're going back to Rabatha?"

"I am."

"And he is going with you?"

"Sorcha is, yes."

"May I ask why you're going back?"

"Personal reasons."

"Personal reasons," she said. "Personal reasons are the only reasons you ever have for anything, professor."

"So, can we tag along with you or not?" Sorcha asked.

"How soon?"

Sorcha elbowed me in the ribs. "Soon," I said.

Shayat looked over her shoulder at her crew. There were

five of them, all men but her. They were expressive, free with laughter. One leaned against the caravan's single wagon and flirted with a Vilahnan girl half his age. "The crew gets two months here."

"Shayat, you've come to Alamadour two, three times? And every time you've stayed for months?"

"Yes."

"I've been here this whole time!"

"Well," she said. She dropped her hands to her hips and smiled. It was a guileless, unadorned smile. My heart skipped a beat. "I did think about tracking you down."

"Why didn't you?"

"Personal reasons."

* * *

Three days later, Shayat appeared at my door. It was quite late; had we already been back in Rabatha, it would have been well after curfew. I was stoned and shirtless, already half-asleep. Sorcha was deep into a bottle of Vilahnan wine all by himself. He sat against the side of the fireplace, idly poking at the burning log. The summer night was warm, but he had built the fire anyway. I answered the door thinking, perhaps, it was the bartender. But it wasn't.

Shayat grinned like a cat when I opened the door. She drank in the sight of me, bold, unfazed by my half-naked state. "Is this a bad time, professor?"

I leapt behind the door. "Oh! Oh, I...no, I just, uh...I'll

find a shirt." I let her in and ducked into the bedroom.

"If you insist," she said.

I stuck my head through the door. "I'm sorry, what?"

Shayat, still grinning, still self-possessed, shrugged. Sorcha caught my eye and shot me a curious look. I stumbled around ineptly until I found one of his shirts. When I came back into the room, I found Shayat and Sorcha eyeing each other like territorial predators. There was an odd tension in the air, one that pulled at me, but I'd smoked the gift into submission, and I couldn't parse it. "How did you know where to find me?"

"It didn't take much," she said. "You two are the only silver-skinned men who live anywhere but the markets."

"Why are you here?"

"I have a proposition for you. Have you secured transport back yet?"

"We haven't, no."

Shayat nodded and sat down. I sat across from her, eager and compliant. "Then, I have a proposition," she said. "I spoke with my crew. For a reasonable price my cartographer and I would be open to considering loaning you two camels and taking you to Rabatha using our very fast route. Ariah, I know you have valid papers, but does he?"

"He doesn't," Sorcha said. He drank more wine straight out of the bottle.

"Well," Shayat said. "Well, well. For a reasonable price I might be able to secure you some papers. For a price."

"Shayat, you know a forger?"

She answered with an unreadable smile. "Let me tell you

about the route. It is all camelback, up through a mountain pass and then north through the Mother Desert. We don't hit border guards until we ride through Iyairo. Can you ride camels?"

"No trains?" I asked.

"Stationmasters can take an eighth. Police can take an eighth. All camelback."

I frowned. "I hate camels."

"But you can ride?"

"Yes," I said. "I can ride."

"Can he?"

"He can," said Sorcha. "He rides well, actually."

I looked over. "I didn't know that."

He grinned. A flash of better humor brightened the room, and I grinned back. "Ah, you know, you give them a lump of sugar, you coo, and they're putty in your hands."

"They scare me."

Sorcha shook his head. He came and sat next to me on the couch. The half-empty bottle of wine stood abandoned and forlorn next to the fireplace. "Ariah, they're not scary. Sanctuary is scary. Inalans are scary. Camels are just...camels."

Shayat cleared her throat. "Let's talk reasonable prices. With lost time, with the extra feed for the camels, with papers for him, I think twelve hundred marks would be a fair ask."

"We have five hundred," I said. "I don't want to bargain. I don't want to negotiate. I don't want to be cleaned out. Together, Sorcha and I have five hundred marks."

"That's it?" she asked.

"That's it."

She frowned slightly. "I don't believe you."

I pulled all our cash out of a box on the mantle and handed it to her. She counted it and sighed. "So, this is a favor to you."

"Well, yes. I guess so. Though you don't have to take me."

She handed me the cash back and sighed. "You know I love haggling. That's the best part."

"I know. But we've only got five hundred. There's not really anything to haggle over."

Shayat sat with her arms crossed. She glanced around the apartment, considering, taking stock, writing ledgers in her mind. "You have nothing to sell."

"We don't."

She scratched her nose and looked at me. "I will call in a favor and get his papers for free. Three hundred will cover the feed for the camels, water for you, and nothing more." She smiled. "My father will be glad to see you."

PART FIVE:

THE MOTHER DESERT

CHAPTER 23

THE TRAVEL WAS hard. Travel was miserable. My camel was bad tempered, and Sorcha had to charm her and me both in order to get me on her in the mornings. Once in the saddle, I took to smoking more or less constantly to keep the panic at bay. I missed a lot of what was going on around me. In those first few days while we traveled the northern plains of Vilahna, Shayat and her cartographer rode ahead, steeped in private conversation. Shayat's cartographer, a man named Tamir, was the forger. He was a forger, and therefore a criminal in the eyes of the Exalted, but he regarded Sorcha and me with obvious mistrust and distaste. The day we left, he handed Sorcha a set of forged papers without a word, mounted his camel, and rode off at a gallop ahead of us. His brusqueness left me shaken; it left Sorcha curious.

Tamir was middle-aged and hardened, with skin pale enough silver that it looked like the sun had bleached it. He was on the tall side and gaunt. A series of ragged scars raked across a milky, useless eye; the other eye was an endless black ringed in glowing violet that seemed like it did enough seeing for the both of them. He wore Chalir-style robes that hid the rest of his face from view and cut a very striking figure on camelback.

Tamir was the desert incarnate: remote, spare, and uncaring. It was strange to see him in his desert robes on his desert animal among the lush green of Vilahna's fields. He alone of Shayat's crew had been eager to return to the Empire.

We rode north for a week. Farms thinned out and the grass went from green to gold. We traveled a main road, one that passed by compounds and small towns, but the farther north we went, the more insular the red elves became. We rode north right up into the mountains. They loomed huge and gray for days before we made it to their base. I am born of flatness, of space; I come from places with few trees, where the horizon stretches endlessly out. I had seen these mountains before, but they had not lost their novelty. They stretched up, imperious, unassailable. The mountain face was sheer and proud, totally unadorned. The camels grunted in passive protest as the land grew steep. The mountain pass was a narrow, winding path cut through the stone by a long-dead river.

When we entered the mountains, Sorcha picked up his pace. He caught up with Shayat and rode beside her. They were less than a foot from each other, pressed into an odd intimacy by the pass. "Hey, are we going through a mountain compound? Looks like we are."

"Yes, we are," she said.

"Which one? It's not Lachandour, is it?"

"No, it's Bardondour. Why?"

Sorcha slowed his camel to let her ahead. He shrugged.

Shayat peered at him over her shoulder. "Why Lachandour?"

"My pa's from there."

"Does he have people there still?"

"Don't know," Sorcha said. "Thought it might be interesting to find out." The growing distance broke the tenuous thread of their conversation. My camel made slow, bitter progress up the mountain. When I caught up to him, I asked if she had said it was Bardondour we were heading through. He said it was. "Why? What's in Bardondour?"

"I don't know," I said. "But it's strange. Bardondour comes up sometimes at court. It's like a little country of its own. It's not really Vilahnan. Dor's been there a few times. The queen thinks he's wasting his time on the mountain compounds. She says they're still mired in a war no one's fighting, and that Bardondour is the worst of them." I laughed. I lit a match and took another draw from my perpetually packed pipe. "She is such a hypocrite."

"Well, Ariah, don't be shy now. Tell me how you really feel about her."

I shrugged and took another hit. "It's true. Bardondour. You know, Fallinal said they won't even trade goods with the plains towns."

"But they're gonna let a bunch of silvers through?"

I looked up ahead, shielding my eyes to track Shayat's camel. She swayed with its movement. She was a graceful and effortless rider. The black skin of her arms stood out against the mountains. Her cropped hair blew around her. She looked wild. She looked fearless. "Like they could stop her. Shayat could get through anywhere."

"That girl. Hey, I been meaning to ask you something."

"Ask." My camel spat on the ground. I tucked my legs further underneath me.

"Why would she cut us this deal?"

"What do you mean?"

Sorcha shifted in his saddle. He wiped the sweat from his forehead with the back of his hand. "Look, it's not like I know her none, but that one, she strikes me as anything but generous. Why would she break up her route and ferry us up there for no profit?"

"Well, her father is in Rabatha. I think she worries about him."

Sorcha was quiet for a beat. He nudged his camel forward so we could see eye to eye. He gave me a hard look, a challenging look. It was a look of wounded pride. It caught me off guard. "Ariah, just come clean with me. What's with you and her? What happened back in Rabatha?"

"I taught her languages."

"And?"

"And…her father made me clothes."

He sighed. He rubbed his forehead with the palm of his hand and stared at Shayat's back. He sighed again, and he took the pipe from my hands. "All right. Look. I'm all right. Wish you'd've let me know, but I'm all right. But you've got to get your shit together, Ariah. Might make sense for you to scale back, let your talents out a little more."

"What? Why?"

"Ariah, maybe nothing happened back in Rabatha, but

you are damn near swooning over her any time she talks to you. And that one, she's leading you back for no good reason? There's an open door there just waiting for you to walk through it."

* * *

Bardondour was a hard place, a community carved out of the mountains and surviving through sheer force of will. The elves there are clannish and isolate. The compounders spotted us when the mountain pass turned into a valley. We rode past a field of grain. There was a sharp whistle, and a half-dozen elves stood tall in the fields, turned to us in unison. I could make out the silhouette of bows held at the ready. Shayat whistled back: three long calls followed by a short, high note. After a tense moment, the compounders slung the bows back across their shoulders and returned to their fieldwork.

We rode up to the lodge, which was a huge, sprawling building of rough stone with a thatched roof. The windows were placed high on the walls, with ample room for snowdrifts. In a semicircle behind it sat huts of varying sizes: one was a smokehouse, one was an outhouse, one held grain, one was a small stable, and so on. In the center was a well, and next to that was a fire pit. A clutch of elves sat around the fire, each with one or two small children in arm's reach. An older woman stood as we approached and dusted dirt off her thighs. "Shayat," she said. She said it slow, and she dawdled on the last syllable, softening the hard *t* with the shadow of a vowel. "You return already? And with a new crew." The woman spoke Mountain Lothic, which I had never heard before. It is a hard-bitten dialect, a prickly burr with its own, unhurried cadence.

"We come seeking hospitality," Shayat said.

The old woman peered at her. "Hospitality was given a month past, Shayat."

"We come seeking it again."

"Vanniah's reclaimed brother, this debt you have stretched far, Tamir," the old woman said.

Tamir slipped off his camel. He rifled through his packs and pulled out a machete. The polished metal glinted in the light. The people around the fire paused in unison. "The debt is mine for your hospitality," he said. His voice was deep and flat, maddeningly inexpressive. "A gift for you and yours."

The old woman raised her eyebrows. "Quite the gift."

"For your generosity."

She took the machete and ran her finger along the blade. "And these men behind you, these new ones gray as the mountains, we should invite them into our homes, Tamir?"

Tamir glanced at Sorcha and I over his shoulder. "Shayat vouches for them."

"Do you?"

He hesitated. "I vouch for Shayat," he said.

The red elves laughed. Some of the tension broke, but they insisted on searching Sorcha and I before they would agree to let us stay there. They searched our bags, and they patted us down. Sorcha grinned the entire time, trading quips with the younger, more curious compounders. For my part, I clamped my jaw shut and let it pass over me. It reminded me a great deal of the border detainment the last time I'd tried to return to Rabatha. They took our camels, fed and watered them and nestled them into a small stable, which was empty but for a mule. They brought us into the lodge to eat and rest and smoke.

The lodge held one long, long room full of tables. Three fireplaces were built into the west wall at equal intervals, dividing the room in stripes of heat and cold during the night. The other wall was peppered with doors, which led to the large kitchen, closets, a loom room, a woodworker's shop, and two or three storerooms. Ladders between the doors led up to lofts where the compounders slept. The lofts were tucked underneath the slanting roof. No walls divided one sleeping space from another. It was one long stretch of blankets and pillows dotted here and there with parcels of discarded clothing and stuffed toys. The children slept wedged into the narrow eaves with the adults on the interior to keep them from rolling down into the main hall. When we came in, clutches of very young children who had been napping popped up from nests of blankets. Sorcha smiled. "It's like Falynn's house, only bigger," he said.

"Claim a bower for yourselves," the old woman said, "but sleep not yet. A guest works, too, when there is work to be done."

"Just bed down anywhere?" Sorcha asked.

"Anywhere what will have you, lad, aye."

Sorcha handed me his pack and climbed up a ladder.

When he was in the loft, I tossed him his pack and my own and climbed up after him. It wasn't until we'd found a spot for ourselves that I noticed Shayat and Tamir had stayed below in the hall. They watched us, her face intrigued and his perturbed, as they pulled bedding out of their own packs and made pallets on the hall's floor. We were put to work after that: hauling water from the well to the livestock troughs across the field, washing the oils from fragrant newly-sheared wool, weeding the herb garden, that sort of thing. Sorcha drifted to the shepherds and helped them corral the sheep into the pens for the night. It involved a lot of running and a lot of yelling. He grinned while he did it and came back with an arm slung around a compounder girl's shoulders, the pair of them sweaty and slightly out-of-breath.

Shayat and I hauled the water. She wore a Qin robe for travel, but pulled it off for the work. Beneath it she wore a loose Semadran shirt and a pair of leather leggings, expertly tailored. It was the first day since we'd left Alamadour that I had not smoked my mind into oblivion, and Sorcha's words—admonitions? Advice? I couldn't tell exactly what they were—ran through my mind as I watched her haul the buckets up out of the well. She was stronger than me, and I watched the muscles of her forearms twist and bunch as she worked. She stood with one foot planted against the lip of the well and hauled up the heavy buckets, one after another. She pulled up two buckets for her and two for me. We threaded the handles through poles and balanced the weight of them on our shoulders. She already knew the way to the livestock troughs and led me over. She had me pour the buckets into the trough when we got there. "You said you were from Ardijan, professor."

"I am." Pigs ran up to the trough as I poured in the water, jockeying for space, all uniformly disappointed it was nothing more than water.

"Well, your friend Sorcha certainly isn't."

"He's from the City."

"If he's from the City, and you're from Ardijan, how did the pair of you end up in that apartment together in Alamadour?"

"It's a long story." I stood up and straightened my back. "Mercy, that water is heavy."

She laughed. "You would make the worst farmer. You're so delicate."

I looked over at her and found her smiling at me. I laughed and watched the pigs survey the fresh water with haughty indifference. "You don't seem to like him much."

"Who? Sorcha?" She piled both poles on one shoulder. "If I didn't like him, I wouldn't have agreed to travel with him. Come on, we have to water the cows, too."

We walked back to the well slowly. I felt her watching me for some time before she spoke again. "You're not so green anymore, professor. You don't seem so young now."

"I wasn't that young before. It's only been two years."

"You seem older."

"Funny, you seem younger. Caravanning suits you."

She grinned. I blushed, and she grinned wider. "You

think so?"

"Yes. You seem...loose now? More comfortable."

"I am." She nodded, mostly to herself. "I am. May I ask you a personal question, Ariah?"

My head swung over. My heart pounded against my ribs. "Yes?"

She laughed. She clucked her tongue at me, and I stumbled on a patch of grass in my haste to look away again. She caught me by the arm and steadied me. "You came to Vilahna for training, right?"

"I did, yes."

"Was it worth it?"

"It was. I shouldn't have avoided it so long."

"Is your plan still the same?" she asked. "You've got your training, and now you'll slip back into the ghettos and no one will be the wiser? A secret shaper?"

I realized I hadn't thought that far ahead. I had assumed for some time I wouldn't return to the Empire. I left for Rabatha without ever having considered what a return really meant, what it would ask of me and how I would have to adjust. "I...yes, I guess so. I think so."

There was a twinge of something in her when I spoke, a nascent pull between us that made me look over. She smiled and sped up her pace. "Well, your secret's safe with me."

When the work was done, the compounders flocked to the lodge to eat and drink and sleep. Shayat, Tamir, Sorcha, and I sat together, surrounded on all sides by red elves. Sorcha's shepherd friend sat with us, along with the man who had the mysterious debt to Tamir and a handful of curious children and young men and women. They served us ale, which only Sorcha drank. They served us a meat stew, which only Sorcha ate. Tamir, Shayat, and I made do with bread and boiled potatoes. They passed a pipe, which I smoked right in front of Shayat. Tamir looked on in barely-concealed disgust, but Shayat seemed at first surprised, and then curious. The herb was freshly prepared. It was the best I've ever had. I would have been a fool to pass it up. I was thoroughly, irredeemably stoned three hits into it.

Sorcha fit right in there in Bardondour. He captivated attention and held it. He was warm enough, red enough, that the suspicions the compounders held towards the rest of us seemed not to apply to him. He was simply exotic. The shepherd girl offered to marry him that night, only half in jest. Sorcha managed to turn her offer into an opportunity to score us enough Bardondour herb to last the rest of the journey. As the pair of us grew steadily more stoned, we drifted together until I was nestled in the crook of his arm. It was an odd comfort, seeing him in his element like that. It was an odd pleasure to just watch him live his life so fully at that moment, and I felt lucky to be floating around his periphery. With us locked together like that, the ardent attentions of the young and curious compounders began to wane until the night grew very late, and one by one all the compounders climbed to their bowers to turn in. Our bower had been taken. We slept that night wedged amongst piles of red elvish children who seemed utterly unfazed at the strangers sleeping next to them.

CHAPTER 24

BETWEEN THE MOUNTAINS and the Mother Desert lie the Inalan badlands. We picked our way down the mountain pass, and the air changed. It is hard to explain, but the air seemed stale. Lifeless. The view when the mountains opened up to the badlands, with the Mother Desert beyond, was breathtaking. The entire world stretched out before us. It looked pristine, untouched. We had gone far enough that Bardondour was hidden again in its valley, and I could not shake the feeling that the four of us were completely alone in the wide world, that it was just us and immense space. It was a terrible, intoxicating feeling. We camped on a ledge of stone overlooking the badlands. Sorcha and I slept together in a tent—that we struggled to set up night after night—borrowed from one of Shayat's crew who had opted to stay behind in Alamadour. Tamir usually watched us from the edge of camp, snickering to himself.

Shayat put rations on the fire to cook. I sat beside her, and Sorcha sat on my other side. "You two should wear robes from here on out. What you've got is not desert wear."

"The City's in the desert," Sorcha said.

"The City is a desert city. This is desert travel. I have a spare set of robes, and we can cut down a set of Tamir's to fit you."

"We can?" Tamir said.

"My father will make you a new set on the house when we get to Rabatha."

I laughed. Shayat looked over at me, already annoyed. "What?"

"You still do that?"

"Do what?"

"Bargain your father's services without asking him?"

She rolled her eyes and turned back to the rations. "Anyway, that's my advice. Robes, not City wear. This part of the trip is the hardest. This route is ideal in many ways, but this section is...less than ideal. We will be in the badlands for at least a week, likely longer. Have either of you been in the badlands that long?"

"No. Just a day or two on the way to Vilahna," I said.

"Me either," said Sorcha.

Behind us, Tamir let out a sharp, derisive laugh. Shayat watched us closely for a second. She sighed. "You vouched for them, Shayat," Tamir said. "You're the one who wanted two city-soft dandies on this route."

"I know."

"You remember what I said." Tamir's voice had a coldness in it. I glanced over my shoulder, and I read him. I have a peculiar way of doing it—given it's so steeped in red war magic—that eliminates most of the expected burn. I think it's a matter of drawing the other person into me rather than invading their minds with mine. I drew him in and felt the utter disdain in which he held me. I felt nothing that suggested he realized I was there with him, that I was a shaper and using my gifts. There was a deep, prickly fear eating at him, a thing that cast the world in shadows and danger. I blinked and turned away.

"Ariah?" Shayat frowned at me.

"Yes?"

"Answer my question!"

"What question?" Beside me, Sorcha laughed.

"Professor, honestly, you'd think you'd listen. This is not an easy trip," Shayat said. She pulled the pan off the fire and cut an acidic glance my way. "The drain, professor. Do you know about the drain?"

"I don't." I looked over at Sorcha. He sat stretched out, languid. He smelled of Bardondour herb. He shrugged.

Shayat sighed again. "There is no magic in the badlands. None at all. It is...unpleasant to be in a place so lacking in magic," she said.

"It's just land," Sorcha said.

"You'll see what I mean. Take it slow, and stay careful. The drain eats at you and makes you careless. There are things out here—rahksa, the brambles. Bandits are out there. I know the route well, but past Bardondour it becomes dangerous. So, you have to know that going forward. It's dangerous, and there is the drain, and you need to know that going in." She glanced over at the pipe I held in my hands. "You may want to stop smoking that until we're out of the badlands. Best to keep your wits about you."

"If what you're saying about the drain is true," Sorcha said, "and I believe that it is, it sounds right awful. Best to have something on hand to dull it down, eh?"

I felt, rather than saw, the way Tamir stiffened. He let out a noise, which was half growl and half laugh, and slipped into his tent. "Shayat," I said quietly. "Can I ask you something?"

"It better be about the trip, Ariah."

"It is, I think. Or might have been once." She gave me an exasperated, irritated look. I stood up and walked to the ledge, far away from Tamir's tent. I waved at her until she came over, and Sorcha followed quickly on her heels. I stood staring out at the empty badlands while they walked over. It was strange to me that a place so empty, so open, could hold a thousand dangers. I felt with the openness of the land I should be able to see them coming. I am a man prone to such false senses of security. Sorcha appeared on one side of me, and Shayat on the other. I looked over my shoulder at the mouth of Tamir's tent. The tent swayed slightly with his movements within. I dropped my voice to a whisper. "Shayat, you know I have the gift."

"Yes, I do." She cast a wary look at Sorcha.

"For fuck's sake, I know he's a shaper. I live with him. He reads me all the damn time."

"Shayat, Tamir...he seems to have..."

She frowned at me. "You read my cartographer."

"...some, uh, well...Tamir has an apprehensiveness about the journey, I think. And I was wondering what is out there that is bringing that on?"

She was cold and haughty. She gave me the look a Semadran gives a shaper who has stepped out of bounds: a look of disgust, of impatience, of carefully tended walls. "If it was any business of yours, professor, you wouldn't have had to eavesdrop for it," she said.

She turned and started back towards camp, but I caught her by the elbow. Her face swung towards mine, surprised. There was a heavy pause, one where I tried to decide whether to let her go and she tried to decide whether to stay. "Shayat, I only ask so I don't stumble into something awful."

She chewed her lip. She cast a quick look at Sorcha. I shoved him back towards the camp. He grumbled but left us there alone. She watched him walk back to the fire. "Did you know all crews that go through the badlands have a shaper? There's a reason for it. Ariah, can you count?"

"Peripheral counting?"

She nodded.

"I...I don't know. I haven't trained for it. Bandits?"

"And rahksa. Tamir lost an eye to rahksa. He was training with a cartographer whose crew lost their shaper at the border and pressed on anyway. Half the crew died, and he was left half-blind. He refused to come with me until I told him you were a shaper. He won't cross the badlands without one."

"You...Shayat, you didn't."

She looked at me, and her face was absolutely open and perfectly calm. "You need a route, I need him to take you, and he needs a shaper."

I hid my face in my hands. "He does not trust me."

"Well, no. You're a shaper. Can you count?"

"I suppose we'll find out together."

I tried to brush past her, but she grabbed my arm. She pulled me towards her, pulled me close. She had in her an inescapable authority. "You can't count if you're high. In the badlands, we're never safe. Not when we're on the camels and not when we're camped. Be Semadran just for a little while."

"I will feel everything."

"You have been trained."

I sighed. I looked out at the badlands. "All right. You have my word."

I made a move to leave, but she held me in place. Her free hand drifted to my other arm. She caught my eye and smiled. "I trust you."

"You trust me? Trust me to do what?"

"I trust you not to get us killed." She grinned. "Don't crack under the pressure, professor."

* * *

We picked our way through the badlands very slowly. The tension rattled the air and shattered any sense of direction I might have had. I have no clear memory of what the badlands looked like, just what they felt like to me. There was the drain: an appalling emptiness, a vicious, needling lack. It sunk into my bones and crouched there, eating me from the inside. The drain makes magic unstable. With no ambient magic to draw from, something goes wrong with our minds. The control I'd worked so hard to develop in Alamadour leeched away into the mundane sands.

What I remember most is Tamir. He was a raw nerve; every sound, every shadow, opened old wounds. He rode ahead of us, slow, careful, and terrified. His one good eye searched the landscape for a path, and it saw death at every turn. I lived inside his anxiety, drinking it in, drowning in it. I could not see past it. I could not shake the feeling that if I could count—and I wasn't sure I could—that I was useless, as trapped as I was in Tamir's mind. We traveled in the high summer heat. We forced the camels onward through the wretched noon sun. Sorcha and I were grateful for the robes and head scarves, but that kind of heat claws at you, crawls into your lungs and burns you from the inside. Travel would have been easier on us and the camels at dawn or twilight or during the night, but Tamir refused to travel when he could not see the horizon. I remember the taste of my sweat, the way the salt of it never left my mouth, and how it tainted every precious sip of water. I remember the sound of my teeth grinding in rhythm with Tamir's. I do not remember much else.

Sorcha kept a close watch on me in the badlands. He took to charming me to bring me back to myself enough to eat. He slept curled around me, protective, like a living shell of trust and empathy. He gave me some respite from the horrors lurking out there in the dead lands beyond the tent.

There were times Sorcha pulled me out of the fog of Tamir's moods, and I found Shayat studying me from across the campfire. Tamir himself did not understand what was going on. He, I think, thought me childish and weak. When he looked at me, there was no sympathy or concern, no hint that he realized we were in this together, just disdain. And anger. There was anger in him directed to me, and I can't say for sure why I sparked it, but I suspect he saw me struggle and thought it meant I had fallen prey to the heat and stress of travel.

There was a day when Tamir saw something in the rocks that sent him reeling. He was a nest of old fears and new worries. Something to the east of us, I think, but I can't tell you what it was that touched him off. He pushed us hard that day; we covered a lot of ground, and he kept us going until after dusk, driven forward until he felt safe enough to stop. He spoke only once, to tell Shayat he was adjusting the route. Sorcha says the only reason he knew Tamir was in a state was because I was crumbling. I rode the camel hunched over, doubled up. The sun was too bright, the air too thick. For hours I felt like I could not catch my breath. I was constantly on the verge of that same panic that had plagued me in the early days of my training with Vathorem. That night, I smoked.

Tamir ate and retreated to his tent. Shayat lingered with Sorcha and I, vaguely curious at first, and then with a honed and pointed attention when Sorcha brought out the pipe. "What are you doing?" she hissed.

"I need it." She moved to grab the pipe from me; I darted away. "Without it I will be useless tomorrow. He wouldn't have stopped if he wasn't sure we were safe here. He doesn't trust me to count, Shayat. I won't be able to tomorrow without it."

My frankness embarrassed her. She opened her mouth and closed it again. She peered at Tamir's tent. "The shaper in my crew does not smoke," she said quietly.

"Not in front of you," I said. Sorcha laughed.

"What?"

"Shayat, if it's not herb, then it's alcohol. If it's not drink, it's sex. Or rahna. Or violence. We have to cope. It's overwhelming. It's a secret of the gift: you use what you can to take your life back sometimes. I am telling you I am stretched thin. I am telling you he has run me ragged. I will be no use tomorrow without tonight to myself."

She stared at me open-mouthed for a second. She blinked. She was deeply, deeply unsettled. I felt it crawling beneath her skin, this revulsion, this fundamental wince at all the taboos I'd just flouted. All the things I'd just admitted. "Ariah," she said finally, "you are careless with honesty."

I laughed. "Well, yes. I am. I suppose that's true."

And she laughed. Her hand flew to her face as if to trap the laugh before it snuck out into the night. The quality of the air changed. I felt her eyes slide over the planes of my face; I felt a knot form between us. Emboldened by the careless honesty I'd already indulged in, I grinned and I caught her eye. Sorcha placed the pipe in my hand, kissed me on the cheek, and took his leave. Shayat tried and failed to look away from me. I felt...I believe in that moment I felt something like a pure shaper's instinct, a desire and a will to draw her to me. A confidence that I could. It scared me. I broke the eye contact and lit the pipe.

She watched me draw on the pipe. Smoke curled up and

blended with the sparks from the campfire. Shayat sat down next to me. "Can I ask you something personal?"

I nodded. I could feel her looking at me.

"The City, Vilahna. Are you running from the gift?"

Now, there are times when a shock knocks the gift back, just like there are times where a shock forces the gift into play. Her question was so direct, so incredibly personal, that I lost the thread of everyone else's moods. Suddenly I was very much alone in my own mind. I looked over at her, eyebrows raised. "I don't know," I said.

"You don't know?" She was skeptical. She looked at me like I was leading her into a trap.

"I don't. Yes? Well, no, I didn't...the City was different. And Vilahna, it was for training, so no? I wasn't running from it, not in that sense, I..." I laughed. I felt my face burn, and I laughed again. "I can't believe you asked that."

"Well, you don't have to answer."

"I want to, though. The way you ask makes me want to answer." I felt that knot again, and it scared me. I didn't know what it meant, what it entailed, if I knew something to which she had not yet admitted and might never. I smoked the pipe. I smoked until I was well and truly stoned; I smoked the magic into a deep slumber so I would not be able to eavesdrop. "It's late," I said. "We should sleep."

"I don't sleep well out here," Shayat said. "The drain."

"This is a terrible place."

"It is," she said. The firelight played across her face. She smiled. "It is a terrible place, but I still like the route. I like that it's part of the route. It keeps me honest, having to manage this place. It makes me think. Rabatha is not that different than here. It's empty there, too. We're always a heartbeat away from death there, too. It's just dressed up in nicer clothes there, and that's dangerous. Losing sight of that is dangerous. Growing comfortable is dangerous." She leaned her chin into her palm and looked over at me. "You're comfortable with Sorcha. You never looked comfortable in Rabatha, but you do with him."

I felt the question. I didn't need to be a shaper to hear it unasked: *Is he why you run? Is he why you don't belong in Rabatha?* "I never was comfortable in Rabatha."

"But you're going back."

"I have obligations."

"Don't we all," she said. After a moment, she sighed. "When I recruited for the crew, I was looking for people like you. The kind with a foot in each place. The kind who is Semadran and not at the same time. I think caravaners need to be that way; I think if you're not like that, the life eats you alive. I worry about Tam sometimes because of that. I wound up with him, and he's a cartographer who hates the travel, hates leaving his wife and striking out, and the rest are men who just hate the Qin. Which I understand. But there's no adventure in them."

"You think there's adventure in me?"

"There's nothing but adventure in you. You live up to your name, Ariah. You're wild."

I stared at her for a long time. She stared into the fire. The image of her profile silhouetted against the flickering orange light is burned into my mind, a fixed point in time. It's one of those indelible memories that serves to organize a remembered life. "Shayat?"

"Hmm?"

What little grace I ever had with such things had been stolen by the herb. Clumsily, and I suspected ineptly, I nudged a door open. "Remember, I am just a quarter red."

Shayat looked at me. The light caught the shape of her mouth, the sweep of her eyebrows. "Well, I spend half my time outside the Empire. A quarter red is all right by me."

The night air had grown cold. The fire kept off some of the chill, but not all of it. I tapped out the ashes of the pipe. I wanted to reach for her, do something, but all I could do was tap out the ashes of the pipe. My tongue was loosed by the herb, and I was, at least, able to speak. "Shayat, may I tell you something?"

"Sure."

Had I been sober, I never would have said anything that came out of my mouth that night. It was not appropriate, neither the time nor the place. It was presumptuous. It was a stupid thing to do, but I was stoned, and she was magnetic. "The thing about me, Shayat, is that you could do better than me. I have not held to Semadran standards well at all, especially in Vilahna. I mean to say, I am not marriageable. But," and here I laughed, and I looked at her, "but if I were marriageable, I'd court you, I think. You knew how I felt in Rabatha. I'm sure you did. And I feel more strongly now. You are…incomparable."

Shayat turned to face me. She wore a strange smile, something like surprise and victory and humor all threaded together. "You are very stoned," she said.

"Well, yes. But you were right when you said I was carelessly honest. It's all true."

She raised her eyebrows. "That was an out, Ariah. That was me giving you the chance to pretend you never said any of that."

"I know what it was," I said. I inched closer to her. "I don't want an out."

"What do you want?"

"I want you." She gave me a surprised, intrigued look. I think she thought I would pull back, that I would come to my senses. I didn't. I laughed instead, giddy, high now in an altogether different way.

She held her place. She didn't back away from me, and she didn't close the distance between us. She held fast. "Why are you going back?"

"I'm to be godfather to Dirva's baby. His wife is pregnant."

"Godfather?"

"It's a red elf thing."

"He's not red."

"He is and he isn't. It's complicated, and it's not mine to discuss. What about you, Shayat? What do you want?"

She was silent for a long time. She turned to face the fire, her hand hiding her mouth. Her eyes—large, dark eyes with long, dark lashes—creased at the corners, the shadow of a smile. "Well," she said slowly, "I have all the time in the world to decide that. It's not one thing, it's never one thing, and it's not always the same thing. Are you cold, Ariah?"

"A little."

"It will be warm in my tent," she said, and then she doused the campfire.

Her tent was identical to the borrowed tent I shared with Sorcha. It was small, made of camel skins, with a floor of layered, thin, wool blankets. She had a clockwork lamp, which she lit when we crept inside. Yellow light pooled in a corner of her tent. The air was cool in the tent, but it was still and kept out the sandy desert night winds. The tent was small, and the heat from two bodies would warm the air inside it in only a few minutes.

Shayat pulled off her robe and unwound her head scarf. She looked at me, smirking, clear-eyed, utterly self-possessed. "You're sure about this?"

"I'm not sure what you're asking," I said. I thought it was clear how sure I was.

She ran a hand through her hair. It caught the yellow lamplight and shone gold. "You're attached to me. I'm curious about you. That's not even."

"Oh." I smiled at her. "I know that. That's all right."

"You're sure?"

"I'm sure."

"All right," she said. "If you're sure." She leaned into me, kissed me, and I kissed her back.

Her skin was warm and smooth as silk. Her breath was hot, enveloping. Her pointed tongue darted along mine, sure and confident. She pushed me down onto my back, and I felt the press of her body along mine. I held her face gently in my hands, and she slipped a hand beneath my shirt. Her fingers scratched lightly at my ribs, inching higher and higher. She came up for air. She sat back and pulled off her shirt. She let me look; there was a hot, heavy moment of looking where I drank her in. Her arms were long, toned. Her shoulders were broad, set with proud collarbones that flared out like wings. She held her chin up slightly, and the length of her neck called to me. The curve of her breasts caught my eye and would not let it go again. The hard point of her black nipples in the cold desert air cut through civility, politeness, pretension. I waited, trapped, at her mercy, waited for what she wanted next. I wanted to be taken. I wanted to be used in her service.

"Take off your clothes."

I did as she asked. I scrambled out of them, shucking them with more fervor than grace. I did not feel the coldness of the air. All I felt was anticipation. Shayat leaned over me, and ran her hands across my chest. She smiled, and she tucked her face into my neck, peppering my throat with bites. Each one sent a shock wave through me, this delicate dance of pain and pleasure, of her careful control rising and lowering like a tide. I ran a hand along her, jaw to neck to shoulder and down her arm. She caught my hand and held it, tight, and pinned it against the blankets. She took my other hand and moved it to her breast. I rolled the hard knot of her nipple in my fingers, and she sighed. She took me inside her when she wanted. She took me at her pace, and I moved with her, for her, locked in her rhythms. I touched her when and where she wanted; she moved my hands to her hips, her back, pinned them again on the floor. She touched herself, she touched me, and she did it with an intoxicating sureness and right to her own pleasure. She crested a shuddering wave of pleasure, her muscles taut, hard, and then suddenly lax. I would have stopped then and been grateful, but she turned her attentions then to me, and I could not understand my luck.

She brought me to the edge of it and over with her hands. When it was done, she handed me a canteen and a ripped rag. She stretched out beside me, catching her breath, watching me while I cleaned myself. She ran a finger down my spine. I lay down beside her. I laughed, ebullient, knowing I had these memories for the rest of my life. "What?" she asked.

"Nothing."

She tucked an arm behind her head. The fine hair of her armpit brushed against me, light as a moth's wing. She lay with one leg drawn up, one knee jutting into the dark. The light illuminated the hollows and swells of her torso, but her face and legs were beyond it, merging into the darkness. I could see the flash of her white hair and white teeth. "Not bad, professor."

"Oh, don't call me that."

"Not bad, Ariah." She stretched out and rolled onto her side facing me. She grinned, and I basked in her attentions. "It's rare to find a man who knows when to be led," she said.

I grinned back. "Your route," I said, "your rules."

I sat up and felt around for my clothes. She asked me where I was going, and I told her back to my own tent. "That's probably a good idea," she said. She watched me as I dressed, contorting myself this way and that in the cramped space. She traced strange designs on my bare skin with her fingertips until the skin was hidden by clothes. At the mouth of the tent, just as I was leaving, a thought came to me. I turned towards her. "Shayat, do you think this will happen again?"

She shrugged. Her body was strewn out across the floor of the tent, languid and supple as a giant cat. She smiled. "Maybe. If you're lucky."

I grinned. I blushed. "I have to be stoned for it," I said.

"What?"

"I want to be stoned for it if it happens again. It's to do with the gift."

"Oh." She sat up, studying me with her head cocked slightly to the side. "Good to know."

CHAPTER 25

WHEN I WOKE the next morning, Sorcha was already awake and dressed. He grinned at me. "You and our fearless leader, eh?"

"How did you know?"

"I can smell her on you," he said.

"Oh."

Sorcha laughed. "Good on you, Ariah. I mean it. Let's get breakfast."

We fell out of the tent one after the other. Sorcha left me there to wrestle the tent into submission on my own while he secured us rations. Shayat was already saddling her camel, her back turned to me. A grin spread across my face at the sight of her. Sorcha laughed and clapped me on the shoulder.

Tamir crouched by a pack of rations. He looked over at the sound of Sorcha's laugh. His good eye fixed on me, and I fell into him. His anxiety poured over me like scalding oil. "Hey!" Sorcha waved at Tamir to get his attention. "Hey, Tamir, how long until we hit the desert?"

Tamir stood to his full height and peered down at Sorcha. He popped a dried date in his mouth. He chewed for a second, then turned and walked to his camel. Shayat answered without turning around. "Not long," she said. "Three, four days. We're making good progress."

"And then what?" Sorcha asked.

"Then it's the Mother Desert," Shayat said.

"Then it's the Mother Desert," Tamir said, "and with her a set of new dangers. No comfort there."

"What's in the desert?" Sorcha asked.

"Death," Tamir said. He coaxed his camel down to the ground and threw his saddle over its back. His voice when he spoke that single word conjured a thousand gruesome ends. His voice was always gruff, always dry and scratching as a desert wind on the dunes, but there in the badlands it was cold, too. Tamir's voice was a wasteland. He drove us through the heat, and I felt nothing but his maddening fear. He drove us in a stop-start-stop-start stutter as the drain interfered with his gifts. Paths became sinuous, circuitous, elusive. At least twice we had to double back and lost a day of travel. Around the evening campfires, none of us managed to choke down much food. We had been in the badlands for a solid week by then, and it had taken its toll on everyone. Sorcha could not sleep and took to slumping only half-conscious in his saddle. Shayat carried herself with a tall, unforgiving stiffness, a holistic resistance, like she could will the land to turn magical. Tamir pulled into himself, taunted by memories, teased by the instability of his gift. And I, I felt the damned drain twice over: I felt it as myself, and I felt it as Tamir. By a week into the badlands, I had lost my ability to marshal the gift. It flared and flickered, grafting onto the lean and quietly terrified cartographer at odd moments, with a fury that blotted me out of my own mind. Shayat had told Sorcha it would be three or four days, but we spent another full week in that terrible place, making less progress each day that passed.

And then we tasted magic on the wind. Shayat spurred her camel to a gallop and caught up with Tamir, who rode well ahead of us. He had taken to avoiding me in those last few days in the badlands. I don't know if he did it consciously, if he was aware of my gift, but he put as much space between us as he could, and for that I was grateful. "What's all that, you think?" Sorcha asked.

"I don't know. Do you feel different? I feel like my head has cleared for the first time since Bardondour."

"Yeah, I do. I feel good," he said. We watched them talk. Their camels stepped this way and that, they pointed north and sometimes east. Shayat whistled; she waved at us to follow, and then she and Tamir set off at a gallop together. Sorcha took the reins of my camel. He swatted his and mine, driving them to follow before Shayat and Tamir slipped out of sight. They rode up a rise of stone jutting from the dead earth, over a ledge, and disappeared. We followed them over. We rode up the ledge, our camels struggling for footing on the loose scree, and the world opened up before us. The sands came up and swallowed the boulders of the badlands whole. Dunes swept out in elegant arcs; the land ahead was dappled with shadows. It was midmorning when we got to the desert. I remember because you can track the time of day there by the color of the sand. The angles of light as the sun makes its way across the sky turn the sands pink, then orange, then gold, then a ruddy brown, and at sunset the sands glow as red as the sky. The sky was a pristine, cloudless blue. The sun was a hot, vicious yellow. And the sands were moving from orange to gold.

Sorcha turned our camels east. He'd spotted Shayat and Tamir in the shadow of one of the last boulders of the badlands, a huge shelf of stone jutting out into the Mother Desert like a tired sentry. They had dismounted. Tamir unbuckled his camel's saddle while Shayat rooted through her pack. "We're stopping?" Sorcha asked. I waited for the crush of Tamir's endless anxiety, but nothing came. I was yet myself. I laughed. All eyes turned to me. Sorcha filled the silence. "Seems early to stop."

"We need to recover," Shayat said. "Shake off the drain. And we need to stop traveling in the day, stick to traveling through the nights. It's only going to get hotter from here on out. Give your camels some water. We're camping here two days and finding the Lost River tomorrow night. It'll take us up to Rabatha."

"The Lost River?" I asked.

Shayat coaxed my camel down and helped me dismount. I blushed like a school girl. Shayat seemed exactly the same as she always was: I know because Sorcha watched her like a hawk and reported this to me later.

"It used to be a tributary of the Exalted Sea. It dried up hundreds of years ago; no one knows why. It should have been swallowed up, but the Mother Desert keeps it clear. It's a natural highway up to Rabatha. It winds past the oasis at Iyairo,

and then straight up to the market factory district. Good travel."
She smirked and caught my eye. "Good travel for those who
can chart a path through the badlands and get through
Bardondour."

"Which few besides you and your crew can pass
through."

"Which none besides me and my crew can pass through.
The compounders post sentries, and they've shot down bandits
and tahrq caravaners two, three times since I started the crew. I
had to register the route with the trade offices, and it has drawn
some curiosity."

Sorcha gave her a deferent nod. "Well played."

"Yes, I thought so." She retreated to the shadow of the
stone ledge and unwound her head scarf. She poured some
water from her canteen onto her scarf and wrapped it around
her neck. Sorcha and I sat next to her. Tamir began the long and
punishing climb up the stone shelf, the better to survey the land
and plot the next leg of the journey. Shayat settled herself
against the stone, eyes closed. "Welcome, Sorcha, to the edge of
the Qin Empire," she said.

"We're in it now?"

"We are."

"Thought there'd be a wall or something. Isn't there a
wall east of the City?"

"There is," she said. She smiled. "There's a need for it up there.
The desert is passable up there. If it weren't for the Lost River,
this might as well be an ocean. This is the deep desert, the
Mother's Womb; the land is border enough already."

* * *

Shayat looked at me when Sorcha pulled out his pipe, her face an open question. The day was slow, unhurried. The day had space in it for distractions: herb was mine, and I was hers. I smoked and watched her set up her tent in the hard heat of the day. Sorcha watched me watching her. I knew he had curiosities about her, but he kept them to himself. When I was thoroughly stoned, he took his leave. He had questions for Tamir, he said. I told him Tamir would not answer. Sorcha shrugged and stared off into the desert. "No harm in asking, though, eh?" He took Tamir by the elbow and dragged him away from camp. The look on Tamir's face when he did it—an expression of shock and irritation, and confusion—was priceless.

I watched them go. Tamir cast one last look over his shoulder, a failed attempt to catch Shayat's attention. "Do you need a hand with your tent?" I asked.

She didn't. The tent was already set up; she was pounding the stakes into the hard, packed sand of the badlands. She looked up and smiled. "All I need is company."

I blushed. I grinned. I was chaotically taken with her, the burgeoning love and desire all tangled in strange configurations, spilling out and overwhelming me at odd times. She was more herself there in the desert than she had been as my student. She was at peace in her own skin there in the wilderness. I found in her the same halting struggle to fit in the confines of Semadran society I myself struggled with. She was better at contorting herself to fit than I was, but the toll it took on her was the same as the toll it took on me. It was a comfort.

Sex with her the second time, in the hot, dark confines of her tent, was as revelatory as the first time. It was, somehow, sweeter and rougher at once. She left marks: scratches on my shoulder, the fading bruise of teethmarks along the long, pointed lobe of my left ear. I wore them like badges of honor. I wore them like they were proof of something, though I couldn't have said what. Afterward, we lay side by side in the dark retreat of her tent. I lay on my side, facing her, and she lay on her back staring at the roof of the tent while a satisfied smile played around her lips. For some time, we listened to Sorcha pester Tamir. He asked endless questions—Where had Tamir been born? How had he lost the eye? Did he have children? Had he ever been to the City? What was the debt the Bardondour compounder owed him, and how long did he think he could milk it? How much of his life, on average, did he think he'd spent on camelback? Tamir answered rarely, and when he did it was a gruff yes or no, unadorned and not illuminating. But Sorcha asked anyway. I could hear the humor in his voice. I knew him well enough to know that whatever legitimate questions he'd started with had long fallen by the wayside. It was a game to him now.

Sorcha asked Tamir a particularly invasive question, something about whether Tamir and his wife had any sort of "arrangement" since they were separated so long and so often. Shayat laughed and threw her hands over her mouth to stifle it. Sorcha's brashness startled her out of her post-coital serenity. She looked over at me. "Has he always been like that, your friend?" she asked.

"Yes, always."

She smiled and ran her finger along the ridge of my hipbone. "Strange that you two fell in together. You're so protective of your privacy."

"I'm not with him."

"Why not?"

I had no ready answer. There were never any ready answers to explain whatever it was between myself and Sorcha. I coiled a lock of her hair around my finger and tried to gather my thoughts. "Well, he...he is my roots," was the best I could do.

Shayat batted my hand away. "Roots?"

"Yes."

"What do you mean?"

"Sorcha is...he keeps me grounded in myself. There is no need for privacy with him. There is no judgment, no expectations, just solace. Is any of this making sense?"

Shayat propped herself up on her elbows. She gave me a long look. "No wonder you ended up in Vilahna. You know, I always thought people were one way or the other, normal or deviants. I didn't know someone could move back and forth from one to the other like you do."

I was shocked into silence. I wanted to tell her how wrong she was, but I could not bring myself to say I was what she had decided was normal. The truth was a slippery thing that, perhaps, did indeed slide between categories. I sat up, rigid, unnerved. I threaded my legs through my pants in jerky, uneven movements.

"You're going?" she asked.

"Yes."

"Can I ask why?"

I turned to face her. I pointed at her, then me, then back at her. "What is this, Shayat?"

"I don't know what you're asking."

"I'm asking what this is, what we're doing. Is this normal? Is this deviant? Does it matter?"

She sat up and pulled on her shirt, a frown already breaking across her face. "This is just sex, professor."

"All right. Fine. But who back home would see 'just sex' between you and I as a harmless thing? And we both know which of us—if people found out about this—would get shunned. Who the landlords would refuse to rent to. A sullied woman brings bad luck."

She sat tall, the long line of her spine rigid and steely. Her face was a mask. "Get out of my tent."

"It isn't right that you should be punished more than me. It's not fair. If normal means you are shamed for something we both want, for something we both did, something that hurts no one, wouldn't you want to be deviant? Some of these rules we have, that we struggle so hard to live by, sometimes they should be torn apart. I know they haven't been, and I know they might never be, but they should be shattered."

She cut a hard, dark look at me. I waited for her to throw me out. There was fire in her eyes. She looked away from me. She let out a mirthless, hostile laugh and looked down at her hands. "You are so strange."

"I'm sorry."

"None of the others has ever understood any of that. I swear the tahrqs are wrong, and we get reincarnated, too, and you must have been a woman in some past life."

Silence settled heavy on the moment. "I will go if you want me to," I said.

"No, no, you can stay." She chewed the ragged edge of a fingernail. She looked over at me, a rare conciliatory expression on her face. "I don't know what to call it besides deviance."

"Does it matter? Do you have to call it anything? It's personal. Let's leave it at that," I said. It came out harsher than I wanted, clipped and sharp. It came out defensive.

Shayat held her hands up. "All right. I guess…I guess it doesn't matter. It's strange, though, I've never…the others were unattached. This is strange." She laughed. "My father wanted me to get married before I started up the crew," she said after a few minutes of silence. "I even hired a matchmaker, but not much came of it. She was trying to match me when you were teaching me languages."

"I'd think you'd be an easy one to match," I said.

"Apparently you're not the only one who isn't marriageable. Caravaners are hard to match. The distance, you know. And some of the suitors told her I was too…willful. And there have been rumors about me. That I will bring bad luck. I spend a lot of time when I'm in Rabatha quashing those rumors. There's always the chance they'll kill the caravan if they are left untended."

"I will not contribute to the rumors."

A grin flashed across her face. "Well, you'll have enough of them to deal with on your own. The way you dress, the time abroad, and now you're coming back with Sorcha. If I had questions, don't you think the rest of the ghetto will have them, too? Honestly, Ariah, I'm not sure anyone would believe you if you told them everything. You're the only one who poses no real danger."

I laughed. "Mercy, you're right."

"Yes, so let's just wait and see who the landlords turn away."

I laughed again. "You should have left me in Vilahna."

"I know," she said. "Tamir tells me that every day."

"I'm glad you didn't."

She rubbed a hand through her hair. She gave me a peculiar look, one that carried in it a newness, like she had never really seen me before. "Well, if the tahrqs are right, I only have this one life to live. Better not to waste it."

CHAPTER 26

TRAVEL ON THE Lost River was easy and full of solitude. The ground there is packed in, cooked by the sun until it shatters itself into a million interlocking polygons. It is banked on either side by huge dunes, unmarred dunes, that crest with edges sharp as knives. The Mother Desert is a windy place, but the height of the dunes on either side of us shielded us from the wind. The dunes cast shadows and blocked some of the beating heat during the day while we did our best to sleep. We traveled from dusk until dawn in the black night beneath a tremendous amount of stars. Each of us had a clockwork lamp on a pole, which hung out over the heads of our camels, lighting the few feet in front of us. When we traveled, we were four small spheres of light gently bobbing through the empty desert.

The Lost River did much of the navigation on this leg of the journey. Tamir was needed to chart a path through the badlands, and then to find the Lost River from there, but he had little to do but travel like the rest of us once we were on it. Every few days when we stopped at dawn, he would venture out into the loose sands, hauling himself to the top of one of the nearby dunes, and survey the land. There was always a chance that the land magic had turned the river and that we were being led off course. It was a slim chance, but it was there. He enjoyed this leg of the trip. He climbed those dunes with a sense of purpose, and when he fiddled with his compass, he did it half-smiling.

The magic embedded in the desert was a familiar thing to me. It feels different than the magic of Vilahna or the magic of the City. It's a smoother, more sinuous thing, something with no rough edges. Magic slides in and out of you easily there. It felt like home. I found it easier to put the skills I'd learned with Vathorem into practice there. I was able to live that dual life—know my heart and someone else's—without much struggle. I was even able to ignore it when the gift pulled me into someone else. Acknowledge it, know it had happened, but I was able to pay little attention to it. It was like letting someone talk at you, yammer on, but not really hearing any of the conversation they have forced on you.

Sorcha and Shayat warmed up to each other there in the desert. The narrowness of the Lost River forced us to ride single file in the black nights. I had to manage my own camel, which was a slow and arduous thing. Tamir led the way; I in my complete incompetence brought up the rear. Shayat and Sorcha always wound up in the middle together. I listened to them talk. "The one good thing about the Empire," Shayat said one night, "is the plumbing."

"You all have proper plumbing there?" Sorcha asked.

"We do, yes."

"I'd thought it was only the City."

"Well, it was only the City until a couple hundred years ago. When the Exalted took it as a protectorate, the first thing he did was send in a bunch of ours to reverse-engineer the running water. All the major Qin cities have running water, heated water, now," Shayat said. "It will be good to be in a real city again."

"Oh, I know!" Sorcha said. "Alamadour, it's little more than a town. And they're so proud of it."

Shayat laughed. "They really are. It's not a city if you can walk from one end to the other in half an hour. It just isn't."

"Ah, they don't know better."

They talked like this often. Sometimes, Sorcha played his violin as we rode. The thread of his music bobbed along with our small lanterns, cutting through the thick silence of the desert night. It was beautiful and haunting. It was pure and unencumbered. Sometimes after he finished Shayat would ask him questions about music and the violin, and about the lives of musicians in the City and Vilahna. She seemed fascinated by it, this idea that he could scrape by on his violin alone, that he had no job, no mark of employment. But, really, she was fascinated by him. Sometimes, in her tent, when we lay together sweating and half-asleep, she asked about him, and about the us that was him and me. Sometimes in the early morning, when we chewed on rations after a long night's travel, she watched us from across the camp. Sorcha and I sat in the cold blue light, nestled close together to shake off the chill, contained in the ease of our relationship. I'd look out at the dunes—lilac mountains slowly turning a pinkish gold—and catch Shayat studying us with a strange and impenetrable expression. Sorcha had warmed to her and thought highly of her, but he seemed to have little reciprocal curiosity about her.

The question of Sorcha came up just once between us. I smoked at dawn and followed her into her tent as soon as we'd made camp. I'd watched her ride all through the night, the light of my lantern catching the silhouette of her body. She'd seen me smoking and smiled. I followed her into her tent, light-headed with anticipation, and leaned in to kiss her as soon as the flaps were tied shut.

Shayat darted back away from me. "Do you smoke with him, too?"

"We don't," I said. I ran my fingers down her forearm.

"Ariah, you can tell me."

"There's nothing to tell," I said, going to kiss her again. "We don't."

She let me kiss her, then took my face in her hands and pushed me back. Just an inch or so, just a little space between us, but enough distance to keep the conversation going. "You share a tent," she said. "You shared a bed in Alamadour."

"I'm telling you, we don't."

"You don't."

"No, we don't."

She laughed. I toyed with the waistband of her leggings. "Ariah, come on. He is handsome."

My hand drifted to the small of her back. "Oh, I know. And he knows it, too, trust me."

"And I see the way he looks at you."

I sighed and dropped my forehead to her shoulder. My hands fell away from her. "Shayat. Why are you asking all this?"

I felt her blush rather than saw it. She burned with embarrassment, like a child caught stealing. She burned all the way down to her shoulders. "I don't know. I'm just talking. We do talk, sometimes, Ariah."

I sat back, giving her space. "We can talk," I said, though it made me blush right along with her. "We can talk about Sorcha if you want."

She bit her lip. She let out a strangled laugh and peered at me from the corner of her eye. "It's just...why wouldn't you? With him, I mean."

I looked away from her. "It's not simple."

"What do you mean?"

"I mean it's not simple. If it were to happen, it would have to be a careful thing, and it would have consequences. The consequences keep us locked in this...I don't know what it is, what Sorcha and I are doing, but there's a line I think we're both scared to cross. Him more than me, I think." My gaze drifted while I spoke, landing on her dusty boots. I looked back over at her. "We don't, Shayat, and it's his preference that we don't more than mine. Why are you so curious about this all of a sudden?"

"I was just curious. About him. And about you and him. Together."

And it came to me all at once what she was curious

about. "Oh. You mean with you. Us with you."

She glanced around her tent. She waved at me. "We don't have to talk anymore."

"If you're curious about him alone, you should talk to him, Shayat."

She looked over at me. It was a searching, slightly suspicious look. "Do you really mean that?"

"I...yes?"

"Hmm." She looked away again.

"What?"

"That would be all right with you? Really, it would?"

"Well, it...I suppose so. You've made it clear you're not attached. You don't owe me anything. And it's him. It's Sorcha, which would, I don't know why, but if it was him, it would make it easier on me for some reason."

Shayat was quiet for a long time. Her eyebrows knitted together. She looked consumed, serious, like she was weighing something in her mind, making calculations. When she looked at me again, it was with a fierce and unassailable certainty. Some decision had been made about something. "This is good," she said. "No reason to change things. Forget I said anything," she said, and then she kissed me.

Afterward, in the late, hot afternoon, I slipped out of her tent and into my own. Sorcha was sleeping; he lay naked on the blankets, sweat beading on his skin, one arm thrown across his eyes to block the light seeping in through the tent flaps. I sat for a long time staring at him. The talk with Shayat had left me unsettled. She'd said he was handsome. Was he? I knew he was.

But, was it a thing I knew, or a thing I saw myself, with my own eyes? I couldn't be sure. It was true that the sweet and stinging ache Shayat stirred in me with a glance was different than when I looked at him, but there was part of me that wondered if it was to do with all those rules I'd tried to abandon. It can be hard to abandon them when they're woven so thick in you, right from the start. Was it a case of admitting to one and not the other? I tried to remember that night in Vilahna when I'd kissed him, how it felt just before, and found the memories were murky. I looked at him, this handsome sleeping naked man who loved me enough to come to Rabatha, and there was at once great confusion and a crystalline clarity in how I felt. I loved him, of course I did, there was little me without him. But the question of want was elusive as a snake lurking in the shadows.

I woke him with a gentle shake of his shoulder. He stretched and blinked, looked over at me and smiled. "What time is it? We're off?"

"No, there's some time yet before nightfall."

"Oh. You been with Shayat?"

"Yeah."

He rolled on to his side and patted the blankets. "Well, curl up. Get some sleep while you can, eh?" When I didn't immediately fall in beside him, he looked over at me. "Something eating you, Ariah?"

"Are we all right?" I asked. I hadn't meant to ask it, or planned on asking it, but it came out anyway. The thing about trust, with Sorcha at least, is that it pulls things to the surface and lets them run wild.

"Sure, yeah. Always are. Been thinking about the Empire, and you know, it won't be so bad given there's working showers. Alamadour had a good music scene, sure, but showers I have missed."

"No," I said. "No, I mean are you all right with me? With us? That we haven't, uh…"

He laughed. "Oh, sure. Told you true back there. I'm red enough to take what I can get. Besides, you wouldn't have the first clue what to do with me if you had the guts to go for it." He took my hand and pulled me into the blankets. "Get some sleep."

* * *

There was a morning in the desert where I woke, startled into consciousness by nothing I could see or hear. I woke with a deep, urgent foreboding. It was a panic brewing in my bones, but one with no obvious source. We were well into the desert; by Tamir's estimation we were perhaps five days of decent travel out from Iyairo. It had been an uneventful morning following an uneventful night of travel. I'd skipped smoking and bedded down as soon as the tent was up. I'd spent the day before at the mercy of Shayat's sharp-sweet attentions, gotten no sleep, and was too tired to see straight when dawn broke. I had fallen into a deep, black sleep as soon as I'd had the chance. And then, all at once, I was awake.

Sorcha slept beside me. I poked my head through the tent

flaps and found an empty, silent camp biding its time through an empty, silent desert day. Tamir and Shayat were in their tents as well, both sleeping. The air was still and crisp. The sky was a span of endless blue. The camels knelt on the sand with their long necks stretched out, their large liquid eyes closed. The only movement anywhere that I could see was the occasional flick of a camel's tail to drive off an insect.

I tried to go back to sleep and failed. The panic drove me out of the tent. I paced the campsite, peering east, always east. I had slipped out without a robe, with no headscarf. The merciless sun beat down on me and turned me red. I did not notice. The sweat poured out of me, the dry heat of the desert air sucking the moisture from me, but I had no thirst. My full attention was turned to the eastern horizon, which was utterly empty. But I felt something lurking, lying in wait. I felt a trap.

I don't know how long I stood there, staring east. At some point, Tamir stumbled out of his tent to relieve himself. He was bleary eyed and bad tempered and grumbled a hello as he passed me. When he was done and returning to his tent, he was surprised to see me still standing there, still staring out east. "Professor, are you all right?" he asked.

I didn't answer. I barely heard him.

Tamir stepped directly in front of me. His gaunt, scarred face filled my vision and blocked the nagging eastern horizon from view. He took my face in one hand and peered at me. "Sunstroke," he said.

"There is something in the east," I said.

"Let's get you in the shade, Professor. How long have

you been standing out here?"

"Something in the east is watching me," I said. All at once my eyes focused on his; Tamir came into sharp focus. I grabbed him, desperate, my fingers digging into his arms. "There is something in the east!"

It was like something had reached through the organs and gristle and taken hold of my spine. The monstrous, invasive pull dragged me to the edge of camp. I shoved Tamir out of the way and went east. Tamir yelled for Shayat to wake, shook her tent to and fro. She stumbled out, blinking in the bright light. "What? What is it?"

"Something's wrong," Tamir said. "Look at him."

Shayat ran to me, barefoot, in just a shirt and leggings. "Ariah!"

I took her hand and pointed to the empty horizon. "The east! There's something watching us. Don't you feel it? The pull?"

She looked me over, her face hard and closed. "Tamir, you don't think..."

"I do think," he said. He tossed her a knife and came up beside me. He held me by the upper arm, rooted in place, no matter how hard I struggled against him. Shayat let out a stream of curses and slipped back into her tent. "Ariah, you are counting," Tamir said. "Where are they?"

"East!" I pointed to the crest of dune, a place that gnawed at my mind, consuming it piece by terrifying piece. "There, something there."

Tamir fished a scope out of the pocket of his robe and

held it up to his good eye. He thrust me behind him, towards my tent. "Wake up your friend," he said, "and both of you stay out of the way. Shayat! Bandits."

The word shocked me back into myself. "Bandits?"

Tamir shoved me. "Wake up your friend. Stay out of the way."

I took two steps towards my tent before that wretched pull tore me east again. There was this compulsion to go east, to meet the bandits where they were. They watched me, and I was tethered to them. It was Shayat who ended up waking Sorcha. Sorcha ran up to me, tried to pull me back, but I wrenched myself free of him, drawn east, drawn to bandits, drawn to death. I saw the flicker of a shadow on the dunes, a mote of black marring the gold landscape. "There! There!" I cried, and broke into a run.

There was a faint whistling, and then sharp, blinding pain.

I heard myself scream before I knew it was me screaming. Shayat knocked me to the ground and slammed her hand over my mouth. The pain killed the draw, broke me mercifully free of the count. "You've been shot. Stay here, stay quiet." I nodded, and she slunk away from me, soundless and agile as a desert cat.

Sorcha cursed, loudly, and ran to me. Shayat caught his arm and pointed at the camels. "What? Fuck the camels! He's got an arrow sticking out of his chest!"

Shayat wore authority, command, effortlessly. She gave him one look—a single glance of muted impatience. Sorcha frowned and sighed and cast worried glances my way, but he coaxed the camels to him, caught their reins, and led them west into a hollow between dunes. Black figures appeared on the dunes, and a volley of arrows struck the ground where the camels had been moments before. Tamir dodged one arrow by mere inches. Shayat and Tamir exchanged glances, a whole conversation without words. Tamir whistled into the east. "Parley!" he shouted. "Parley!"

Shayat crouched low and crept along the dunes. Tamir pulled me upright, and I wailed. As I've said before, I do not handle pain well, and even less so when it is such a traumatic and unexpected thing as that.

A bandit slid down a dune to the south of us. He was a scout; he'd slipped into place some time before. He trained an arrow on Tamir. He was swathed head to toe in red-brown cloth, covered in sand. All that was visible of him were his eyes and his fingers. His skin was a deep brown, his eyes were human. He was a tall man, even by human standards, and lean. His visible skin was windburned and weathered. I cried out in wordless panic, and the bandit scout aimed his arrow at me. "We want the camels," he said in Inalan, "and anything else you have."

Tamir was quiet for a long while. "How long have you been tracking us?"

"Camels, tinker," the bandit said. He drew the bow, the glinting point of the arrow trained right at my throat. I wrenched myself out of Tamir's grasp and ran. I ran blindly, stupidly, my back to the bandit. I heard the thunk of his bowstring. The arrow lodged into my calf, and I crumpled into the sands. "Camels," the bandit said, "or he dies."

Shayat's voice rang out, clear and hard. "Give the elf your bow," she said, "and you might be able to save your brothers." She spoke Qin. The bandit translated her words slowly. First disbelief, then anger, then fear flickered across his face.

And Shayat laughed. It was a cold laugh, a cruel laugh. When I turned to look at her, I found her standing with a graceless, galling ease as she wiped the blood from a knife. There was a promise of violence in her carriage and in the smoothness of her brow.

The bandit pulled up his bow and aimed at her, but it was after two seconds' hesitance and done too late. As soon as the bandit turned, Tamir had a knife at his throat.

"You have this one chance to save them. You can stand here and fight us while they bleed out, or you can leave us be to tend our wounded while you tend yours."

Shayat, bleeding from a gash across her forehead and covered in the blood of someone else, tossed her knife in the air. It spun end over end in a lazy arc. She caught it thoughtlessly, easily, ready to fight. Tamir let the bandit watch her do it. He let the bandit see, and then he let the bandit go. The bandit lowered his bow to the ground, whispered a prayer, and backed out of the camp.

As soon as the bandit disappeared from view, Tamir went to fetch the camels from Sorcha, and Shayat came to me. She stabbed the bloodied knife into the hard earth of the Lost

River and helped me sit up. She inspected my wounds. I took shallow breaths, my hands hovering uselessly around the shaft of the arrow. It was surreal, seeing it there, jutting out of me. Shayat pulled off her belt and handed it to me, pushing it into my palm and closing my fingers around it. "You're going to want to bite down on this, Ariah. This is going to hurt."

"No, no, I…"

She took the belt back and slipped it into my mouth. She closed my jaws around it and looked me in the eye. "This will hurt." She leaned me forward, taking much of my weight on one of her shoulders. She snapped off the fletching; the force of it jostled the wound, and I howled into her belt. She placed one hand carefully on my back and took hold of the arrow with the other. "Breathe," she said. I didn't. I couldn't. "Breathe," she said again, and then she forced the shaft all the way through my shoulder: through muscle and sinew, all the way from one side of me to the other and through. I thrashed with the pain; I let out muffled screams.

Sorcha appeared beside me. He pulled the belt out of my mouth and took my face in his hands. "Ariah! Ariah, shh!" He tried to charm me, but he was scared, too, and the magic wouldn't flow. He stroked my cheek, made me breathe in rhythm with him. "You're all right, you're all right, Ariah."

"He's not all right yet," Shayat said. "We have to get the other one out, too."

"Fuck!"

Shayat inspected my leg. The arrow was not in deep. She told Sorcha to hold me, and I felt her strong, travel-rough hands on my leg, holding it down, holding it steady. Methodically, slowly, she worked out the arrow. Tears streamed down my face and into Sorcha's shirt. I held on to him so tight I left marks.

"Can he smoke?" Sorcha asked.

Shayat studied me for a moment. "Yes. He can't count right now anyway, not in pain like this. Pack him a pipe."

Sorcha cooed at me, stroked my hair, and slipped away. Tamir brought Shayat her pack, and she pulled out a small bottle of red elvish whiskey and clean bandages. She washed my wounds, and stanched the blood flow. She cut off my shirt with her vicious knife and gently, tenderly, wound the bandages around my chest. She was bandaging my leg when Sorcha came back with the pipe. I smoked hungrily, desperately, and I smoked a lot.

Tamir and Sorcha broke down the camp while Shayat looked me over one last time. She saddled my camel and helped me onto it. I nearly toppled off when the camel rose, but she caught me and kept me in the saddle. She whispered to the camel and stroked its neck to calm it. "Shayat," I said. She looked up at me. "You saved my life."

"We're even, then," she said. "We would have been slaughtered had it not been for your gift."

* * *

I was in bad shape when we reached Iyairo. The wound on my shoulder was deep and vengeful, and the meager supplies we had did little to help me heal. I spent days in a fever. The desert, I found, is a terrible place to have a fever. My memories of those days are hazy, but I know at one point, delirious and frightened, I wandered down the River alone while the rest slept. I was found half-naked and badly sunburned. I know one night as we rode I was taken by shakes, my teeth chattering a *clack clack clack* that echoed through the night. I shook so violently I had trouble staying on my camel. Shayat drove us hard, and the last two days we traveled as far into the burning heat of the day as we could before fatigue got the better of us and the camels.

We reached Iyairo soon after dawn, roughly six days after the bandits' attack. The Lost River hides Iyairo from view until the last possible second. Iyairo was a small, dusty desert town, which sprang up on the banks of an oasis. Its fortunes have waxed and waned according to trade routes, and when we passed through, the rails were still only about five years old. They were new enough that Iyairo was not yet the bustling trade stop it is today. We came up via the Lost River, through these impossibly tall dunes. The River turned us sharply to the west, the dunes opened, and there was Iyairo. Qin patrols stopped us before we entered the town.

Sorcha tells me I nearly got us all detained. I remember very little of it, but I am told I refused to let the patrolmen see my papers, and that when I was ordered down off my camel I laughed at them and spat at their feet. I am told I spoke to them in High Qin, and that when I did so, I quoted their scriptures to them, belligerent and mocking. They tried to arrest me, but Shayat intervened and showed them my wounds. She made them feel the burning heat of my skin. Eventually, she bribed them. They took two of our camels.

Tamir knew a healer in the east reaches of town. She was another person with a mysterious debt to Tamir, and she agreed to provide treatment and lodging at no cost. She agreed to it, but it stretched the relationship she had with Tamir to its limit, and in exchange he had to promise not to call on her again. Sorcha tells me he stood there for a long time, minutes ticking by, his face tight and hard before he finally agreed to it. The healer brought the fever down and cleaned my wounds. It took three days for my mind to clear. I woke to the soft slap of a game of djah. Sorcha sat on one side of the narrow bed, and Shayat sat on the other. They threw cards down in the hollow behind my knees.

"Hey, Shayat," Sorcha said. "Hey, he's awake. Ariah, you awake?"

"I'm awake," I said. I moved to sit up. Sorcha took my hand and my shoulder and guided me upright. Shayat moved a pillow behind me to support me. "Are we in Iyairo?"

"Yeah. How're you feeling? Should we get the healer?"

"We should get the healer," Shayat said.

"No, no, I feel all right." My left shoulder felt tight, constricted, but when I moved it the pain was a dull half-forgotten thing.

Sorcha had not released my hand. He stared at me with this openness, a pure transparency of feeling: relief, hope, worry, happiness all right there on his face. It embarrassed me a little, not because Shayat was there but because I could not understand how I was the root of such strong emotions in someone else. It embarrassed me to see how much I mattered.

I squeezed his hand. "I'm all right." I sat up a little more. "I'm hungry."

Sorcha looked across the bed. "Shayat, would you..."

I heard the screech of a chair across the floorboards. "I'll go get the healer," she said.

Sorcha sat on the edge of the bed and ran a hand through my hair. "Gave us a scare, you did."

"I don't remember much."

"You were a mess."

"What happened?"

"Infection, I think."

The healer fed me broth, then bread the next day. When I kept that down, she declared me fit for travel and kicked us out of her house. Shayat sold her camel and scraped together train fare for her, Sorcha, and myself. Tamir refused to part with his camel, refused to speak to me, and set off to make the last leg of the Lost River alone.

PART SIX:

RABATHA: A RETURN

CHAPTER 27

I LEFT SHAYAT at the Rabathan train stage with a handshake. I couldn't even bring myself to thank her. She told me to take care of myself, nodded at Sorcha, and disappeared into the crush of the crowd. "Quite a trip," Sorcha said.

Again, I found no words. I stared out in the direction she'd gone and laughed. Sorcha threaded an arm around my ribs. He shouldered what was left of our things. "All right," he said, "let's go see what we came here to see."

We walked slowly through the streets of Rabatha in the hand-me-down robes of the trip. We were dusty from travel and smelled of the elvish compartments of the train: a mix of sweat and fear and stale food. Sorcha was so obviously nahsiyya, and standing next to him brought out the nahsiyya in me. He held me with incriminating tenderness. We were stared at. We were stopped by Qin agents and asked for papers over and over and over. I had to explain my injuries a half dozen times. Two different policemen wanted to see the wounds for themselves. It took an absurd amount of time to get to Dirva's house. I was tired, worn, hungry, and thirsty when we found his door.

Dirva had moved to a small house deep in the borough. I

laughed when we found it. Sorcha shot me a curious look. "It's a shaper's house," I said. "The way it's built, it's got doors on both sides. It's a shaper's house. And she doesn't even know."

"Who doesn't know?"

"Nisa. His wife. I'm sure she doesn't know." Sorcha took a step towards the house, but I held him in place. "Do you really want to do this?"

"Well, hell, Ariah, it's a bit late for me to back out now."

"That's not an answer."

Sorcha sighed. He shook his head and glanced out at the narrow street. "Fuck, I don't know. But, look, you got a duty. And I'm here. For better or worse, I'm here, right, so let's just get this over and done with."

I grew oddly nervous as we approached his door. I couldn't explain why, but there was something nerve-wracking about seeing Dirva again after two years of separation. I tried to imagine what he would see when he opened the door, how I'd changed, and whether it was for the better. I knocked on the door, and Dirva answered it.

I don't even think he saw Sorcha. I was passed straight from Sorcha's arms to Dirva's. Dirva held me tight and seemed not to hear when I winced. He held me by the shoulders and smiled. He read me in his gentle half-red way. His smile faltered. "Are you all right? Are you in pain?"

"Yes, I ran into some trouble on the trip."

"At the border?"

"No. Bandits. I'm all right."

"You should sit though," Sorcha said quietly. He stood

very close to me, protective and territorial, but he could not look away from Dirva. "You should drink some water."

"Sorcha, I…" Dirva's voice trailed off. He held out his hand to Sorcha. Sorcha hesitated, drenched in wariness. He slowly, carefully, took Dirva's hand. They shook hands like they had never met before. "There is space in the attic," Dirva said.

"You have a shower?" Sorcha asked.

"Yes."

"I'd like to use it."

"Of course." Dirva held open the door. Sorcha asked him where the attic was, and Dirva pointed down a narrow hallway. Sorcha disappeared around the corner with our packs. Dirva smiled again when he was out of sight. He brushed the hair off my forehead. "You've let it grow out."

"Sloth, not fashion," I said.

"And these robes."

"Pragmatism."

He laughed. "You seem well. Vathorem wrote. He said your training was going well. I'm sorry to have interrupted it."

"It was enough, I think. I'm glad to be here. It's an honor, a real honor."

"The honor is mine, Ariah. Come, sit. Let me get you water. Have you eaten? Let me get you food." He sat me down in the armchair he'd transplanted from his bachelor's apartment. The bookcases were the same, as was the kitchen table. The rest of the furniture was worn, broken in, but unfamiliar to me. I guessed they were transplants from Nisa's previous apartment.

The water he gave me was pure and tasted slightly metallic. I laughed. "What?" Dirva asked.

"Piped water."

"Oh, yes," he said. He sat down beside me. "Vilahna has gotten no better, I take it?"

"If they have gotten better I would hate to see where they started. Where's Nisa?"

"Working," Dirva said. "She wants to work right up until the birth."

"How is she doing?"

"Well. Very well. I've never seen an easier pregnancy," he said. "It is good to see you again."

I finished the water and turned the empty glass in my hands. "About Sorcha…"

"I am glad to see him, too."

"Nisa doesn't know who he is, does she?"

Dirva was quiet for a moment. "No."

"And you'd rather keep it that way?"

"Yes."

"Does she know why I'm here?"

"Yes," he said. "I explained falos to her. I told her it was something I learned about while caravanning in Vilahna. She finds it odd, I think, but she is willing."

"I should find an apartment. I should get a work assignment," I said. "Sorcha and his violin will not be welcome in your attic for long."

Dirva blinked at me. "You think you'll stay.

"Falos stay."

* * *

Nisa was glorious in pregnancy. She radiated joy. She and Sorcha got along very well; I think he was a bit taken with her. Sorcha introduced himself to her as my friend, which she accepted, though she looked at me differently from then on. He sat with her in the evenings when she came home from work and talked with her about pregnancy and childbirth. He had seen a lot of both. Dirva likely had, too, but he kept his knowledge to himself. Sorcha asked her what she had planned for the birth, for the newborn. She had few answers.

"I don't know," she said. "There's a healer down the street in case we need her. Do you think we will?"

"Probably not, but it's always good to have a midwife on hand. You got a midwife?"

"Midwife?"

"You know, the one everyone goes to when it's time."

"That's the healer."

"Ah, no, healing and midwifery, those are two different things. Midwifery, it's a lot of care work, you know, keeping you comfortable, keeping you calm, that sort of thing. Tell you what: I'll be your midwife."

Nisa laughed. Dirva cast a wary look at me, then Sorcha. Sorcha seemed not to notice. He smiled and felt Nisa's belly. She let him. "You're a man," she said.

Sorcha looked up in mock surprise. "What? Really?"

She swatted his shoulder. "I am a married woman."

"So I've heard. And I'm a man who's delivered babies."

This was news to me. "You have?" I asked.

Sorcha nodded. "Was a girl back in the squat house. I was on hand for two of Falynn's little ones. Was a time I thought about going into midwifery proper. I had Falynn bring me along when he had pregnant patients." He smiled at Nisa. "Turned out perfect every time. I've good luck with babies."

"I didn't know you wanted to be a midwife," I said.

"I did. Still do a bit. Picked the violin, though. Anyway, Nisa, I'm here and I'm not doing anything else, so if you do want some help when the time comes it would be my pleasure to provide it."

Nisa laughed and cast a curious look at Dirva. "I'll think about it."

Later that night, as we lay together on the bedrolls we'd rolled out side by side, I thought of Shayat. Memories of her body and her voice came to me at odd moments, taunting me. The thoughts of her sometimes got away from me, and I had a tendency to dwell on her. It nagged at me that she was in the city, probably at Parvi's shop only three streets over, but that we lived separate lives once again. I spoke to Sorcha to take my mind off her. "You know I've never spent much time with pregnant women. Or babies."

"Right, you and your small families."

"Do you think it will go all right for her?"

"No reason to think it won't. Though there are things to check sooner rather than later. Position of the kid, that sort of thing. Maybe she's already had all that looked at." Sorcha yawned. He rolled over to face me. "She is a lovely girl."

"She's a Qin apologist," I said.

"Is she really?"

"She is. She really is."

He idly ran his fingers through my hair. "She's got no idea who I am."

"I'm sorry."

"No, it's…it's not bad, exactly. I knew that going in. But it is strange, you know. I keep thinking she'll figure it out. Me and Lor—Dirva—we both look like Ma. What's his story now? He has a Qin pa?"

"Yes. A Qin father and Semadran mother; both were caravaners. He grew up in Mahlez and worked as a translator in a caravan himself before reassignment to the Rabathan Office of Foreign Relations. His Qin father was in a lost caravan and is presumed dead. His mother died three years ago of an injury sustained in a Mahlez factory. He had no brothers and sisters."

"And you're his family now," Sorcha said.

I winced when he said it. "I'm sorry, Sorcha."

"It is what it is, I guess. And, hell, at least he's got you. Don't know why he had to push the rest of us away, but at least he's got you. I don't understand him. All these lies he's wrapped himself up in. I got to get out of this house, though. I'm going to go stir crazy here."

"We should go to the markets."

"We got no money."

"The gold elves are there."

Sorcha gave me an odd look. He sighed and tucked his face into the hollow of my shoulder. "Maybe I could stake out a spot to play. I got to do something, though. I got no clue how to be around Dirva."

"I'm sorry."

"No harm."

Sorcha and I spent a lot of time at the markets in the weeks that followed. I stole poems from the gold elves, but Sorcha never stayed with me very long when I hung around the live goods. There are slaves in the City, but only in the Qin quarter, and even then they're rare. City slaves exist in an ambiguous legal gray area—slaves cannot be bought or sold in the City walls, though they can be transported through it. Slavery was not a thing he was used to. The sight of them troubled him. The fact that we could do nothing for them troubled him more. He disapproved of my fascination with them, the way I lurked on the outskirts of their lives. He left me at the slavers' platforms to play his violin on street corners instead.

Both of us tempted fate. Busking is not illegal in the Empire, for the sole reason that it is not done. Disturbing the peace, though, did get Sorcha hassled. He did a lot of running from lawmen. He never could play more than one song in one place and never did get any coins from passersby. He liked the running, and he liked taunting the policemen, and there were a few sardonic or brave shopkeepers who would harbor him when he needed to drop out of sight. Myself, my constant watching of the slave market got me noticed. The fact that I constantly scribbled notes while I watched the trade of live goods drew questions. An elf among the buyers there is noticeable. When the Qin agents demanded my papers and saw I had no work assignment there were threats to put me on a factory line. I showed them my injuries and pleaded for time to recover. It worked at first, but it was a temporary excuse, and it was clear I needed a permanent position.

Two and a half weeks after my return to Rabatha, Dirva got me an assignment. I served as a secretary to a minor Qin bureaucrat in the Office of Foreign Relations, a former military man who was placed in Rabatha to issue or deny trade permits to merchants looking to strike out for the Droma grasslands in the east. The first rail to Ma-Halad had been built by the Qin Army a year before, ostensibly to open trade, but the reality was that the only merchants he approved were those that served military supply lines. The Qin Army was gearing up to expand the Exalted's borders. My job was to transcribe his interviews with Rabathan merchants into documents for later perusal. I was good at my job, and after a week or so, he seemed to forget I was there. He had a loose tongue. The merchants' tongues were even looser, and none of them noticed me when they came in for their interviews. I might as well have been a piece of furniture. Many of the merchants seeking eastern trade permissions were slavers looking to partner with the Qin rails for easier transport. Some wanted to buy entire cars for transport and were willing to split the profits with the military. It was hard to make a profit, the slavers said, since so many of the live goods died in the trek across the desert. With the rails, more would survive, which would lower prices on slaves generally, and wouldn't it be something, they asked my employer, if your average middle-class Qin household could afford a slave? I was good at my job, but it was not an easy job for me to have.

Despite the fact that I had little choice in the matter, I had qualms about taking the job, chief among them that Sorcha was left to his own devices while the rest of us were out. It didn't matter how many times I told him the Empire was not like the City. It was a thing, clearly, he had to learn on his own, but I didn't want him to have to learn it. I listened to the merchants with disinterest. My mind drifted often to Sorcha—to what he might be doing, where he might be doing it, who he might be doing it with. Sometimes I wondered about Shayat, but that was a placid and docile thing, where the thoughts of Sorcha were terrible and anxious. I must have seen him die a dozen different ways every day. I knew him well enough to know he would not sit patiently waiting in the house for the rest of us to return. And I was right to worry.

I returned home after work to find a yellow notice taped to the front door. My heart dropped from across the street. I didn't need to read it to know what it said, but I read it anyway. The note stated he'd been arrested for indecency and lewd acts, that he was being held at the 23rd precinct house, and that bail was set at two hundred fifty marks. According to the time stamp on the notice, he'd been in there for seven hours, which meant he must have been arrested not long after I left for work.

I had, to my name, thirty-seven marks. Dirva was not home, and I had no idea where he kept his money. The lack of good options and a wide margin of desperation drove me to

Parvi's shop. He opened the front door with a tape measure slung around his neck and a length of linen draped over on arm. He smiled when he saw me. "Ariah! Shayat said you were in town. Come in!"

"Is she here? I need to ask a favor of her."

"Yes, she's here. Come in," he said. He yelled her name at the stairs. "You look well, Ariah." He thumbed the edge of my vest, which he had sewn for me years ago. "I'm glad to see my work has held up."

I stared anxiously at the stairs, willing her to come down. Parvi asked me if I was all right. "I...yes, I am. A friend is in bad straits."

"Shayat!" Parvi yelled again. "She'll come down. Come by again when your friend is in better straits, yes?"

"I will, Parvi. I promise." He clapped me on the shoulder and left me in the hall.

I heard Shayat before I saw her. The door to the attic creaked open and slammed shut. "Papa, I'm in the middle of..." She saw me. She frowned. We stared at each other for a handful of seconds, and then she waved for me to follow her up to the attic. When we were in her room, she closed the door and leaned against it. "What are you doing here?" she asked.

"Sorcha's in trouble. I'm sorry, I am, but I have no money. He's locked up in the 23rd."

Her eyebrows shot up. "The 23rd?"

"I know."

"Really?"

"Yes! Yes, I need money for bail. Shayat, he's been there

for hours."

She chewed her lip. "How much?"

"I need two hundred thirteen marks."

"Lewd acts?"

"And indecency. Will you help? I'm sorry to barge in like this, I am, but he's there, and I have thirty-seven marks. I can't, Shayat, I can't just leave him there. He came here for me, and now he's at the 23rd!"

She held out her hands. "Ariah!"

"I knew this would happen. I knew it. I never should have asked him to come with me."

"Ariah!"

"Mercy knows what they've done to him. I've...I've heard stories about the 23rd, and..."

Shayat took me by the shoulders. "Ariah, we'll get him out. I have it; I have enough for bail. You can have it. You'll get him out. All right?"

I nodded. My heart beat bloody and wild in my chest. "All right. Thank you. Thank you very much."

She unlocked a chest and counted out the coins. She dropped them into my hand and curled my fingers around them. I thanked her again, breathless and pathetic. "Get him out," she said. "Make him be more careful."

"I'll try. Thank you. And I'm...I'm sorry for coming here. I am."

"Just get him out," she said.

"Thank you," I said

I ran to the 23rd precinct with Shayat's coins rattling in

my pockets. I was covered in sweat and panting like a dog when I got there. The stitch in my side made it hard to speak. I stumbled up to the main desk. The Qin clerk sitting at it cast a wary look to the lawmen milling around behind me. I threw the notice and the money on the desk. "Get him out," I said.

The clerk watched me for a second. He smirked and plucked up the coins. I grabbed him by the wrist. The air went very still. I felt the shadows of the lawmen lurch to attention, felt the burn of their eyes as they turned to look at me. "Do not steal from me," I said. It came out a scratchy growl. "Call the keeper before you take it."

The clerk wrenched his had out of my grasp. "Let me see your papers."

I slammed them down on the desk. "Call the keeper, and let him out!"

"Watch it, tinker," one of the lawmen said. "You're a hair's breadth away from landing down there yourself, with a mouth like that."

His was not an empty threat. I swallowed down the defiance as best I could. I held up my hands and stared at the floor. "My apologies to the Exalted."

"Apologize again."

I dropped to my knees and bowed, forehead to the filthy floor. A boot landed on my neck, pressing down just hard enough to suggest what kind of damage could be done to me. "My apologies to the Exalted," I said again.

The lawmen laughed. One of them grabbed me by the collar and jerked me upright. He was a big man, a slab of muscle and fat. His hands were huge and calloused. A cigarette was planted between his teeth, and when he spoke, the words fought their way through clouds of smoke. "You counted it?"

"All there," said the clerk.

"Give me the notice." The keeper read it and handed it back. He shoved me forward.

"Wait!" I said. "Wait, my papers!"

The keeper held out a hand for my papers. The clerk stamped them and handed them to the keeper, who dropped them on the floor and knocked me to the floor a second after to fetch them. I fell hard and split my lip. He grabbed me again by the collar and sent me flying through a doorway and down a flight of stairs to the lock room.

I had been arrested before, but never in the 23rd. I'd been arrested for being an elf in the wrong part of town, for having eyes the wrong color, but not for something I'd actually done. I'd been taken to lockup at the 12th and the 7th, held for two or three hours with a dozen other quietly-seething elves, and released with orders to pay my own fine. The 23rd was different. I stumbled down the stairs into a pitch-dark cellar. The keeper laughed; it was a mocking, vicious laugh that ricocheted off the stone walls. A man began to cry at the sound of it. The keeper lit a torch—an actual torch, a thing of bright, violent flames—and brushed past me. "He's with the other ghalios," the keeper said. "Follow me."

He led me past cells, some of which were occupied, and some of which weren't. They were narrow, small things built of metal wire. They were not wide enough to lay in and not quite tall enough to stand in, even for an elf. I call them cells but really they were cages. Some of the prisoners shook the doors of their cells and pleaded with the keeper for freedom. Some of them slunk into the corners of their cells, away from the light. "Nahsiyya! You're wife's here for you." He whistled. "She's angry. I see why you strayed from such a nagging shrew."

Up ahead, just out of the reach of the torchlight, I heard the sound of a body slam into the metal meshwork. "Ariah?"

"I'm here!"

"Oh, sweet mercy. Trees and streams. Spirits and sanity." The keeper swung the torch at Sorcha's cell. Sorcha cried out in pain. "Let me out, you bastard!" he roared.

The keeper laughed. "That's getting close to disruption of public order, ghalio. You keep on, and I'll leave you in there. And this one, he might play wife to you but he's a man on his papers. Might have to throw him in lockup, too, if you keep on."

Sorcha caught my eye. I gave him a slight, tense shake of my head. He clamped his jaw shut. The keeper laughed his acid laugh again and unlocked the cell door. He grabbed Sorcha by the wrist. Sorcha screamed and fell to his knees. The keeper dragged him out, and Sorcha scrambled upright, drawing shallow breaths. His shirt was torn. His boots were missing. I guided him out onto the street as soon as we were in the lobby, stopping only long enough to retrieve his papers. I didn't get a good look at him until we were a block east of the precinct. I'd been walking as fast as I could without it properly being called a run. I had hold of his arm and pulled him along with me. I heard the unevenness of his breath, but I didn't think much of it. I didn't think much of anything just then besides getting him back to Dirva's.

"Ariah," he said. His voice was razors and tears. "Ariah, hold on," he said.

I turned and found him collapsed against the wall of a shop. He leaned his full weight against it, his cheek pressed to the rough adobe bricks. His eyes were pinched closed. Blood oozed from a ragged hole in his left ear where his earring had once been. His neck bore dark purple bruises, unmistakably the shape of large hands. He cradled the swollen, bruised fingers of his left hand with his right, but his right hand was in bad shape, too. It bore the shiny, blistered burns of the torch. I sucked in a lungful of air. I had no idea what to do or what to say. "I think my hand's broke," he said. "Something's wrong with my knee. Got to go slower than that."

"I'm sorry."

"It's all right," he said. He peeled himself off the wall slowly, one bone at a time. "Just got to go slow."

I did most of the walking for both of us from there on out. I held him up, half-carried him the two miles back to Dirva's house. Dirva and Nisa were home. Sorcha's condition was met with wariness and concern. Dirva pulled him into a silent hug; Sorcha burst into tears. Nisa asked me what had happened under her breath, but I had no answers. Dirva gave me money to bring the healer and helped Sorcha up the stairs to the attic.

CHAPTER 28

SORCHA DELIVERED NISA'S baby about a week after I bailed him out of the 23rd. She went into labor in the prototype workshop, and her fellow engineers bargained with the Qin shop manager for permission to escort her home. Sorcha was there. He delivered the baby while Dirva and I worked, and he did it with a broken hand and a busted knee and completely by himself. The experience bonded them together in a way I could not and likely never will be able to understand. What I mean to say is that the morning I left, Nisa and Sorcha were friends, but when I came home that night, they were family. Neither ever used the word to describe their relationship, but it was obvious. They sniped at each other and laughed together; they were free with physical affection. They knew each other well, and there was an indefinable trust between them.

Dirva came home to a blindingly new life. He knew what he was coming home to—Nisa convinced one of the other engineers to leave him a message at the Office of Foreign Relations—but knowing it and living it are two different things. Sorcha tells me he wept when he came through the door and saw her with the baby. He said it was silent and dignified, but that Dirva wept. No one had thought to leave me a message, though, and I came home to a complete surprise. Sorcha was in the kitchen drinking tea. I put my papers on the shelf next to the door, turned to ask him how his hand was, and heard the baby's cry. Sorcha smiled. I just stared at him, transfixed, my mind a perfect blank. "It's a boy," Sorcha said. "He's a beauty, he's perfect and healthy. Nisa delivered like she'd already had a dozen. She's tired, but she's fine. Didn't even tear."

"Dirva?"

"Just got in."

I laughed. Sorcha laughed with me. He stared into his cup and said very quietly that maybe he'd give up the violin and take up midwifery for good. "Since we're sticking around, you know."

I stared at him. It was another shock. "You want to stay?"

He smiled softly, very softly. "Yeah. If you'll have me, if they'll have me. A man doesn't just bring a child into the world and then skip off, not if there's space for him."

Some hours later, well into the night, Dirva leaned through the bedroom door and beckoned us over. Sorcha and I had stayed awake playing djah and drinking tea; the kitchen table was littered with bent cards and half-empty teacups. Dirva was happier than I'd ever seen him. He carried in him a deep well of emotion, a sense of rightness. Nisa sat propped up with pillows. She looked exhausted, but she stared into the face of her child with a singular enveloping attention. The baby was a wrinkled, tiny thing, all balled fists and squinched features, but he was a treasure. He slept curled against her breast, his face tucked into the hollow of her shoulder.

"It's time to name him," Dirva said. Nisa nodded and handed him the baby. The child fit neatly into the crook of his arm. The baby stirred, and Dirva cooed it back to sleep. Sorcha stood against the wall just behind Dirva, peeking over his shoulder at the baby. All three of them had the same dark-gray skin. When the baby blinked, just before he settled back to sleep, I could see all three of them had the same green eyes. Everyone in the room had green eyes but Nisa. "His name is Nuri," Dirva said. Sorcha's eyes widened; his attention shifted from the infant in Dirva's arms to Dirva himself. Dirva did not notice. "Nuri Nisa'Dirva."

"It's a good name," Nisa said.

"It is," Dirva said. He stroked the baby's face. He looked over at me and asked me to come closer. "Meet the little one," he said.

I took the child in my arms. My heart scrabbled against my ribs; my arms felt awkward and ungainly. I was terrified I'd drop him. "Hello," I whispered.

"A falo's life is twined with the child," Dirva said. He spoke City Lothic, his mother tongue.

"So it is," I said.

"A falo treats a child as his own blood: raises him, protects him, comforts and teaches him."

"So he does."

"Through the child, the falo is bound to the family. You and I and Nisa share a beating heart."

"So we do. I will be his falo," I said.

Dirva ran a hand over the back of my head. He leaned his forehead against mine. "So you shall," he said.

* * *

I was Nuri's falo. It made no sense to Nisa, but she accepted that in my mind and in Dirva's mind I was part of their family. I did my best to live up to the role, but I'd never been around a newborn before. Mostly I helped keep the house neat and orderly. I did all the laundry, all the dishes. I'd never cooked much, but I cooked most of the meals. With Nuri I was at a loss. I was fascinated by him, but I didn't understand him, so mostly I tried to keep myself out of the way. I was part of the family, and technically I was a parent, but the truth of it was I did more caring for Dirva and Nisa than I did the baby.

Sorcha had no clear role. There was no word for what he was in either language. He stayed home with Nisa and Nuri. The 23rd scared him off from the streets for a while, and Nuri was there, and Nisa needed help while she regained her bearings after the birth. She was torn between a deep peace when she was with Nuri and he wasn't crying, and a whirlwind of anxiety when he slept or fretted. When would she work again? Where would she work again? What did he need? How would she know? Sorcha knew some of the answers to some of her questions and was patient enough to steer her back to Nuri when the questions he couldn't answer loomed too large. They were together, the three of them, all day. Sorcha changed diapers, sang to him, cuddled him when Nisa needed a moment to herself. Sometimes the fatigue got the better of them both and they all slept together in the middle of the afternoon on Dirva's bed, Sorcha on one side, Nisa on the other, and the baby between them. Sorcha didn't have a name or a role, but he was part of the family, too, and as much a parent to that child as I was.

It surprised no one but me when Sorcha began to lactate, but it surprised all of us when Nisa let him nurse the baby. I knew in a clinical and removed way that this happened—that when a father is with the child as often as the mother, among elves at least, that father's milk begins to flow. I knew it in the way that I knew the mechanics of birth, but had never seen it and had no feel for it. Sorcha spent hours with that tiny child nestled inside his shirt, keeping Nuri warm with his own flesh. Sorcha was so deeply connected to that child that in the night when Nuri cried it was first Nisa who woke, then Sorcha, then Dirva. Often Sorcha was already down the stairs when Dirva woke.

I was the first to notice when his breasts began to swell. He was so tired, so distracted by the baby that he hadn't noticed until I pointed it out. We were curled up in bed, lying together like nested spoons, him on the inside and me on the outside. I had my arm around him. He reached up to scratch his ear, and in the process my hand brushed over his chest. What had been hard, smooth, and flat in all the years I'd know him was now slightly rounded, the skin taut, his nipple larger than before. The glands had swollen and were beginning to fill with milk. I cupped his right breast, which fit perfectly in the palm of my hand. "Sorcha, are you...is this...Sorcha, I think you have breasts."

"What?" He had only half-heard me. He was drowsy and irritable from lack of sleep.

I sat up and turned on a light. His shirts were loose, but naked they were unmistakable. "Sorcha, I think you're lactating."

"Oh, no, I'm not. Turn out the damn light."

"I think you are."

He patted his chest. His hand froze there, and his eyes popped open. He sat up and stared down at his chest and laughed. "Holy hell." He squeezed one, gently teased at the nipple. "Well, it's not come in yet. Would you look at that." He cupped both and inspected them for some time. He grinned at me. "Not bad, actually. I'd've been quite the girl. Guess I'm sort of a girl now, half a girl."

It fascinated me, how unperturbed he was by this. When I lactated myself much later, it was a profoundly disorienting experience. I was never able to let my children nurse; the strangeness was too much. The shift in my body unnerved me, made me feel off-kilter and unbalanced. But Sorcha was unfazed by it.

It seems inevitable now that he would nurse Nuri, but the day I came home and found the child at his breast felt like a broken taboo. Which taboo was broken, how he had fractured it, I couldn't name. It is rare, given the demands of work assignments, for a Semadran father to nurse, but it is not unheard of. It is common in the boroughs for new mothers hiding from their work assignments to band together for comfort and convenience; when one woman's milk fails, another steps in to help. Father's milk is accepted, wetnursing is encouraged, but a male wetnurse gave me pause.

I found Sorcha reclined on the couch, naked to the waist. He had Nuri propped on a cushion, and the child had nestled into the crook of his arm. Nuri nursed at his left breast, his tiny hands gently kneading Sorcha's flesh. Sorcha's right breast was bare. He stroked Nuri's cheek and hummed him a lullaby. Sorcha smiled at me when I came through the door and held a finger to his lips. He mimed that Nuri was nearly asleep with his free hand.

"You're nursing him?" I whispered. Sorcha nodded. "Does Nisa know?"

He frowned at me. "Hell, Ariah, of course she knows."

Dirva came home just then. He opened the door and called for Nisa. I shushed him. He looked at me and saw Sorcha and his son just behind me. He opened his mouth to say something, narrowed his eyes, and closed it again. "Hmm," he said. He blinked. Sorcha watched him like a hawk, waiting for judgment or scorn or something else entirely. "Hmm," Dirva said again. He placed his citizenship papers on the shelf by the door and went into his bedroom where his wife lay sleeping.

"Do you think he'll ask me to stop?" Sorcha asked quietly.

I came close and sat on the floor next to the couch. I watched Nuri's sleepy, pinched face, watched his tiny fingers curl and uncurl against Sorcha's breast. "I don't know. If Nisa was fine with it, I can't see why he'd want to stop it."

"He's not very good yet, not very able, this little one," Sorcha said. "He bites. It hurts when he bites. Nisa's tits are battered from him." My eyebrows shot up. Sorcha laughed. "She had me look at them since I know a bit about nursing."

"I believe you." I ran a finger along the sole of Nuri's foot. "What does it feel like?"

"It feels...well, like I said, the little bugger bites. Hard. So, it's not pleasant. Not yet. Once he gets the hang of it, and me and Nisa get the hang of it, it might yet be pleasant. But right now it's not. But it feels...it feels good. Feels warm and soft and relaxed like I've had a fine bottle of wine all to myself." He smiled, first at Nuri, then at me. "I like it."

CHAPTER 29

AS NURI NURSED, Sorcha's breasts grew. The smell of Sorcha changed: no longer herb and resin, now milk and musk. As the weeks stretched on and turned to months, Sorcha's features softened. The hard line of his jaw grew rounder. His hair thickened, grew shiny, just like Nisa's. His lips became fuller. He was still himself, his voice was still that same sing-song baritone it had always been, but he nursed long enough that his body hovered in some murky area between man and woman.

He was frank with the changes. The metamorphosis of his body did not drive him to modesty. Nisa nursed in the bedroom, alone or sometimes with Sorcha there for company or commiseration, and even in her privacy she nursed covered to the chin with a shawl. Sorcha nursed anywhere and always uncovered. His nipples grew chapped and tender some days, and he had no qualms about wandering around the house shirtless. Dirva seemed to hardly notice. He had probably seen a male wetnurse. He'd probably seen his own father nurse Sorcha. But I noticed. At first I thought Sorcha drew my attention because of his utter lack of decorum. That is what I told myself, anyway. But that wasn't it. I woke in the morning with my hand around his breast, drawn to it in my sleep. I woke hard, which sometimes Sorcha joked about and sometimes Sorcha ignored. Weeks passed, and I lingered closer to Sorcha than before, touched him more. In idle moments I studied his mouth, his eyes, his hands, and the urgent want I had not felt since Shayat taunted me. I told myself it was coincidence, that I had grown used to having a partner and was readjusting to life without one.

There was a strange dance between Sorcha and myself in those months when I half-knew my own desires. He'd catch me looking, and he'd grin that same grin he'd worn the day I'd met him. At night he drew close, and sometimes he took my hand and placed it on his breast himself, an act of permission, a door nudged slightly ajar. He left the house infrequently, only ever with me or with Nisa to go to the market, and sometimes when we did the shopping together, he'd make jokes about how long he'd "gone without."

There came days when, on my walk home, it was men who drew my eye more than women. A man with his build, his narrow hips. There was no one moment of startling clarity, no frenzied epiphany. I settled into the realization that I wanted him slowly, acclimating inch by inch, like a child easing into a cold bath.

It happened on the night of Nuri's first birthday. We spent the afternoon and early evening doting on him, cheering as Nuri sat up on his own, grinning back when he smiled at us, cooing to him in his own private language. Nisa and Dirva put him down to sleep and must have been caught in his thrall, because they never came out of their room. Sorcha and I waited for a little while, trading stories about Nuri, wading through memory after memory. Sorcha grinned and rifled through the pantry. He pulled out a bottle of good Semadran wine and raised his eyebrows. "Sorcha, no," I said.

"Why not? It's a celebration!"

"For a child."

"Well, the child's gone to bed. Just grown men left awake now." He grabbed two glasses with one hand. He pulled the cork from the bottle with his teeth and spat it out onto the floor. "They're all down for the night. Come on," he said.

I followed him up the stairs. The wine was still a bad idea: I had to work the next morning, and besides that I do not handle it particularly well. I get drunk very fast, and I am prone to wicked hangovers. But…he was right. It was a celebration.

We piled into bed. I turned on the lantern but set it glowing low. Sorcha had brought the glasses, but they sat untouched at the foot of the bed. We passed the bottle back and forth, back and forth. The movements were precise in their sobriety at first, but grew looser as the wine took root. When he passed me the bottle, my hand lingered on his. I stopped listening to the things he said. His voice washed over me, warm and dark and safe and familiar. At first I simply drew close to him. I slipped my arm behind him, and Sorcha leaned into my chest. I sat turned towards him, but he faced out into the dark room. My eyes slid along the planes of his profile, took in his face which one second was so masculine and the next so feminine. I had drunk enough, by then, that the gift was in slumber. I had no idea what he was feeling just then, if he noticed my attentions. The thing with wine, though, is that it makes me reckless. Sorcha said something, he laughed, and he looked over at me with his eyebrows slightly raised, waiting for a reaction. And I kissed him.

It was not a gentle thing, or a timid kiss. It was an expression of hunger and desire. The force of it knocked the wine bottle from his hand. He drew back from me like he'd been shocked. His face froze on the edge of a question. I nodded, wild-eyed, breathing in the smell of him and kissed him again. Sorcha fell into it with an unbridled ferocity. He was a current, a spark. We devoured each other, breaking apart for air in sudden violent movements. We grappled like boys wrestling after school, but our hands lingered, teased, and grasped. He was strong. The sinuous strength of his arms set me on fire. The push-pull push-pull of us hypnotized me. Sorcha shoved my hand to his breast. His nipple was hard, the flesh damp with leaked milk, and my hand slipped along it, frictionless, smooth, electric.

He was right when he'd said in the desert that I wouldn't know what to do with him if I had him. I didn't. My hands drifted to the small of his back, to his hips, but no further. I felt the hardness of him, the heat of him, the slickness against my thigh, and I wanted him, but the mechanics were elusive and terrifying.

He took the lead. He touched and stroked, his face always just above mine, always grinning. When I began to cry out, he kissed me to keep me quiet, to keep the others asleep.

He brought me to the edge but not over—the ache, the need pulsed through me, a fire stoked higher with every heartbeat, every gasped breath. Sorcha toyed with me, brought me to the brink and then a pause, to the brink and then away.

"Tell me what to do." My voice was ragged, parched, desperate. Elated. Enraptured.

"Fuck," he breathed in my ear. He licked my hand and taught me what to do with him. "Like this," he said.

He lay on his back, one leg wound around my back, gripping me like a vice. My face fell against his breast, breathing in this new scent of him. He wound his fingers in my hair. I was artless; I had none of his finesse. I could not tease and taunt for him like he had for me. All I could do was give him release. He laughed when he came, a throaty, full laugh. He lay in the lamplight, laughing, his hands covering his face. I fell on to him, into the stickiness, the sweat, and laughed into his chest with him. He took my face in his hands and pulled me to him, kissed me, smiled. "Your turn," he said. He half-purred it, half-growled it, and then he took me between his thighs. The tightness of his grip, the heat, it was so strangely different from being with a woman. Strange and similar at the same time. The strangeness of it, the singularity of it, intensified everything. Sorcha caressed me, held me with his large, strong hands, whispered in my ear a stream of unheard words in a voice of pure, raw, untempered pleasure. I confess it hardly took any time at all. I collapsed, boneless, onto him, my face in the curve of his throat. I felt the rise and fall of his breath, a steady, calm thing that grounded me.

We lay there together for a long time. We did not speak. The quietness was a simple thing, a consonance, a comfort. Eventually we cleaned ourselves up and found fresh bedding. Eventually, we fell asleep. I held him like I'd held him every night before that one, except that night we lay together naked, and that night the last shreds of mystery between us were torn away. I kissed the nape of his neck as I drifted to sleep. I told him I loved him. He told me he loved me back. The words when I said them felt no different than they had the night before, but their meaning was clearer.

CHAPTER 30

SORCHA AND I lived with Nisa and Dirva for two years more. When Nisa had weaned Nuri and Sorcha's milk had dried up, it felt like time to find space for ourselves. Nuri walked and ran and climbed out of their bed and into ours. He spoke and laughed and threw tantrums. His things—toys, clothes already too small the third time he wore them, picture books—outnumbered my own. The fact was that Semadran homes are not built to house red elvish families, and we had run out of space. When Nuri was three and weaned, Dirva gave up his post at the Office of Foreign Relations. The borough allowed him into the schoolhouse to teach literacy and magical theory to Semadran youngsters. He taught with Nuri at his feet while Nisa returned to the prototype labs. Nuri spent probably three quarters of his childhood in that schoolhouse. So, when Nuri was three and weaned and underfoot in the schoolhouse, there was nothing left for Sorcha in Dirva's home.

Nisa found us a bachelor's apartment two blocks south of their house. The woman who rented it to us was one of the engineers from Nisa's workshop. We would not have found a place on our own. Shayat was right: there were rumors about me. Nisa never believed those rumors, even though they were true, and apologized over and over again because the apartment she found us had only one room.

We went the two blocks north every night and had dinner with Nuri and Nisa and Dirva, and for a time I still worked during the day for that man who wanted the Empire to push east, east, endlessly east into the Droma grasslands. The nights were just mine and Sorcha's. I had wondered—worried—what would happen between us when motherhood left his body. I had worried I would prove fickle and heartless. I didn't.

During the day, Sorcha wandered. He played his violin. Quietly, discreetly, he strayed from me. He wound up in the 23rd again. It was hard for me to get him out; the jealousy was something I did not expect. He took a beating for flirting with a Qin girl. The beating left him with a broken rib and a broken nose. A Qin doctor intervened before it got any worse and took him to the borough's healer. Sorcha flirted with the borough healer, a young woman transplanted to Rabatha from the Chalir foothills for her training. She healed him for free, and she advocated for him in the borough so he could find work as a midwife. Some of the pregnant women refused to see him, but some let him in, trusted him, and paid him for his service in bread and tea. Midwifery was good for him. It gave him focus and kept him out of trouble. More or less.

It was not an easy life: we were warily watched by half the borough and contemptuously ignored by the other half. Few

Semadrans acknowledged me on the street, and fewer still would speak to me. Sorcha was an outsider, and for that he was given a measure of latitude, but I had lived there with them, and left, and returned a man with nothing but a trail of broken rules behind him. I was a pariah, but I was tolerated because Sorcha had proved useful and Nisa and Dirva had carved out respect from their neighbors. Still though, there was no one to advocate for me when Sorcha's run-ins with the law cost me my job. The stamps of contact covered my papers, marking me as a friend of a repeat convict, and despite my skills I was not worth the trouble to the Qin. I ended up on a factory line. I worked in a wool factory, where I fed raw fiber into the spinners, great metal gears that turned as fast as the wheels of a train. The factory was full of us: disposable people, forgotten people, desperate people. Some were Semadran, but many more were nahsiyya or displaced Chalir. Some bore the brands of the slaveborn on their cheeks. There were accidents, and the accidents were grisly, but I was lucky. The worst I got were burns.

The factory was a terrible place, but still, I was happy. I had Sorcha. I had nothing but Sorcha, but having him was enough. I was happy, and I was settled, and I expected life to stretch on like that forever. But of course it didn't. Life never settles. It slows sometimes, and it grows smooth sometimes, but it never settles.

A woman knocked on the door of our place one afternoon in the brief window between when I got home from my shift on the factory line and when I'd cleaned up enough to go to Dirva's to see my godson. She was young. She was a shaper just starting her training. She had no control, no decorum, nothing but burning curiosity. I winced when she looked at me. She made me nervous; there was a chance she'd see me for what I was and add another rumor about me to the pile. What little reputation I had could not have survived the blow, and there was the chance that Nisa's friend's patience would finally run out. I was afraid I'd land us on the street. I never could build walls, and I never could block, but by then I knew shapers. I knew we are an arrogant bunch, and that resistance of our gifts draws attention. It was painful and nerve-wracking, but the smart thing to do was let her read me.

"You are nervous," she said.

"You are a shaper," I said.

She smiled. She handed me a slip of paper. "My mentor requests your presence." I waited until she left to read the note. All that was written was an address, a familiar one: Shayma Hepzah'Brahim's house.

I pulled Dirva aside after dinner. "This is your matchmaker's address, yes?"

He looked at the address and frowned. He switched to Vahnan. Sorcha heard the switch and looked over, eyebrows slightly raised. Dirva often spoke Vahnan in front of him. Even three years after the move to Rabatha, even while raising a child together, Sorcha and Dirva rarely spoke directly to one another. Neither spoke to me about the other. The weight of Dirva's secrets, the fact that Sorcha himself was one of those secrets, pushed them apart. "Did something happen?" he asked.

"I don't know. Have you heard anything about me on the street?"

"Nothing new. Nothing good."

"Nothing about the gift? Or why I was in Alamadour?"

"Word on the street is you were in Alamadour for him," he said, nodding discreetly at Sorcha.

"Then why does a shaper want to see me?"

Dirva shrugged. He sighed and rubbed a hand through his beard. "She's met you. She knows what you are. They all know what you are, and what I am. They keep the secrets."

"Then why does she want to see me?"

"I don't know. They won't tell me any more than they would tell you. I'm passing, too."

"What do I do?" Dirva gave my shoulder a gentle squeeze. He let me feel his worry for me, his steadfast concern for me, without showing any of it on his face. "Be careful. Go after curfew or before curfew lifts. It's a risk, but not as big a risk as it would be to go during the day when the borough can see you. You can count; count the curfew enforcers."

* * *

I went to Shayma Hepzah'Brahim's house very early. Dawn was little more than a hazy gray creeping across a black sky. The Pet was close; I relied on it to help with the count. I'm not sure I needed magic, though. The night was desolate, the streets were empty, and you could hear echoes of the Qin enforcers' boots a street away. I crouched in the shadows of her doorway and knocked: two sharp raps loud in the night. Her student answered the door wrapped in a shawl. When she saw me, she drew the shawl tight around herself, protective, and leapt back from the door. "It is after curfew," she hissed.

"My presence was requested." I slipped inside and pulled the door shut behind me. The girl yelled, her eyes wide. I indulged in a shaper's instinct that nudged her into calm again.

She blinked at me. "How did you do that?"

Shayma Hepzah'Brahim came down the hallway. "He has nothing to teach you, Biral. Go to bed."

The girl, Biral, cut one last look at me and slipped away. Shayma Hepzah'Brahim turned down the hallway, and I followed. She wound up a lantern, and her eyes flicked up to mine. I burned. She read me deep, and she read me with no gentleness. It was suffocating. "This is not a time for visitors," she said.

"Why am I here? What do you want?"

She laughed. It was a flat laugh, a brittle laugh.

"What is it?"

"It is not I who wants something from you."

"Then who? Then why did you call me here?"

She smirked. She stared down at the nails of one hand, and I could breathe again. "I am a matchmaker. I have been asked to deal with you in that capacity."

"You...what?"

"I have been asked to match you, Mr. Lirat'Mochai."

"Is this a joke?"

"Would that it were."

I stared at her. I confess I tried to read her, but she had walls of pure granite. "You have a match for me?" The idea of it was absurd.

"Perhaps. Perhaps not. I have been asked to match you," she said. She slid along the edges of the truth, halving it and halving it again.

"I don't understand."

"You will," she said, "in time."

"Asked by whom?"

Shayma Hepzah'Brahim stared down at the lantern for a long, long moment. She smirked. "Shayat Bachel'Parvi has expressed an interest in you. Go back to your man, Ariah Lirat'Mochai. You have things to discuss with him. I'll send Biral for you when it's time to speak again."

I crept back home. There were still some four hours yet before my shift at the factory began. I crawled into bed and sat beside Sorcha. I watched him sleep for a little while. I nudged him awake. He rolled onto his back and blinked up at me. He glanced out the window, and back at me. "Why're you dressed? They change your shift?"

"I've been out."

He propped himself up on his elbows. "You've been out? It's well past curfew."

"That girl who came by this afternoon..."

"Are you in trouble? Did I get you in trouble?"

"Do you know her?"

"No," he said. "Should I?" I sighed. He rolled his eyes and took refuge under a blanket. "Not again."

It was, by then, an old argument. Why did he need someone else when I was right there? What did they give him that I didn't? The familiar questions lodged in my throat, held in place by the specter of this match.

Sorcha pulled down the blanket. He gave me a curious look. I curled up around him, still fully dressed, and he nestled against me. He took my hand and kissed it. "Shayat is back," I said.

"Is she?"

"She's hired a matchmaker."

Sorcha squeezed my hand. "Well, she don't know what she's missing."

I tucked my face into the nape of his neck and breathed in the smell of him. It was a test of sorts: did I still want him, this? I did. I very much did. But, still, the teasing possibility of Shayat lingered. "She...she might know. She expressed an interest in me."

Sorcha rolled over onto his back and turned to face me. "She did?"

"She did."

"She's been gone for years, and she rolls into town and hires a matchmaker?"

"Apparently."

"But why? You'd have her if she came calling, I'm sure you would. Why the formality?"

"Well, I...you know, all I can do is speculate. I am likely far off base. I can't say for sure. She said once Parvi wanted her to get married, and it might make sense for her to marry to quash certain rumors about her."

"Married?" he asked.

"Well, that's what matchmakers do: broker marriage. They don't do anything else, really. So, it might make sense for her to marry. Just...uh, just...it might make sense, but it wouldn't make any sense at all for her to marry me."

"Unless she wants to marry you for you," he said.

I laughed. I held him closer, half out of some misplaced excitement and half to remind myself what I already had and how little else I needed. "Maybe we should leave town. Go back to Alamadour. Or the City."

Sorcha took my face in his hands. "You're his falo. Falos stay, remember? What's this about?"

I held his hand against my cheek. I laughed again. "I don't know."

"You want this to happen with her, you think?"

"I don't know." I burned with it, this half-confession. Anything other than a resolute, immediate denial felt to me like a betrayal.

Sorcha searched my face, but I wore an old mask. He pulled me against him, my face in the hollow of his shoulder. He stroked my hair, and he felt calm, but I'd seen the trace of a frown cross his face. The guilt I felt was overwhelming. "Matchmaking with you all, it's not a fast thing."

"No, it isn't. Even when you express an interest it's not a fast thing."

"Then you've got plenty of time yet to decide what you want. Grab a couple hours' sleep before you have to go to that damned factory, yeah? No reason to fret over anything."

He'd said it with unruffled patience, but there had been that frown. I edged just far enough away to get a good look at his face, catch his eye, and then I read him for all I was worth. "You don't think I can split attentions."

Sorcha sat up and turned his back to me. "Oh, come on, don't read me."

"A man needs his privacy?"

"Ariah, stop."

"I love you."

He looked at me over his shoulder.

I laughed. The magic fell away. "I don't know," I said. "I'm not sure if it was you or me that felt that. Probably both of us. But it is true. I do love you."

"I know." He rubbed his face. He leaned against the wall and lit a candle. Our sole clockwork lantern had broken weeks before and neither of us had managed to scrape together enough to replace it. The light flickered a harsh orange. "I guess I'm up," he said.

"I'm sorry."

"Ah, hell, worse things have happened."

"I never expected this."

Sorcha smiled. He held out his arm, and I nestled in against him. "You know," he said slowly, "I didn't expect it, can't claim that, no, but I won't say I'm surprised either."

* * *

It took a little over a month before Biral appeared again at my door. It took long enough that I had begun to suspect, with some relief, that Shayat had been warned off or lost interest, and the courtship had died before it began. Sorcha was tender with me in those weeks. He was careful, and he was sweet, but he threw up the highest, most formidable walls he could manage. The walls were broken in places, the walls had chinks, but they did give him some measure of privacy. The walls terrified me. They made me feel I was walking in a minefield, always one step away from a violent end. I mentioned it once—I was a little drunk, I drank now and again when I had a rare day off—and Sorcha grinned at me. "What?"

"Look, there are more of us than there are of you."

"More of you?"

"Yeah," he said. "Most of us don't got your talents. Most of us aren't shapers. We got to just fend for ourselves without dropping all those eaves everywhere."

Until Biral knocked on the door, that was as close as either of us could seem to get to talking about the match. She came, smirked, and handed me a note. The matchmaker requested a meeting in two days' time after my shift was over. Sorcha leaned against the wall. "That was that shaper girl again?"

I held up the paper. "The matchmaker wants to see me."

"When?"

"The day after tomorrow."

Sorcha raised his eyebrows. "Hmm," he said, and then crossed the room.

I followed him. He half-turned, began to say something, but I didn't give him the chance. I pulled him to me, and I kissed him. The gift poured out of me, and I lost myself. I gave him everything he wanted effortlessly. It was a heartfelt, willing submission. I came to myself again in stages. It was dark; after curfew, and Sorcha lay half-asleep beside me. He was naked, and he was beautiful. I stretched, and he felt the movement and looked over. He fingered my chest hair, a lazy smile on his face. "You shapers," he said. He whistled.

I blushed and hid my face in my hands. He asked me if I was all right. "I am. I'm fine."

"Should we not have?"

"No, no. No, I wanted to. I did."

"Been awhile since you let your gift out like that," he said. And it had been. Even with Sorcha, sex sober was rare for me. Even with him the aftermath was disorienting. The lack of clear memories never became less disturbing, but with him, at least I always felt safe. With him it did not feel dangerous. He sat up and pulled me up with him. He kissed me and held my face in his hands. "You don't got to convince me to stick around, you fool."

I dropped my forehead to his shoulder. "Can I ask you something?"

"Yeah, course."

"There's no going back to how it was before, is there?"

He was silent for a long time. I stayed pressed against him, soaking up his warmth, counting his heartbeats to keep the gift at bay. A man needs his privacy. "Hell," he said. "That's how you see this falling out?"

"I don't know."

He edged away from me. He ran his fingers through my hair as he passed by, but still, he was on one side of the room, and I was on the other. I had landed on a mine. "Look, Ariah, I told you back in Alamadour how it was with me. We been at this now for years, living like we're the ones married for two years. Yeah. There's no going back. I'll not begrudge you what you want, I'll not try and trap you, but yeah, I can't go back to sharing a blanket and hoping, not when we've been living like this."

"Even though you're so red?" I asked.

He laughed. He crossed his arms against his chest and stared down at his feet. "I mean, yeah. Sharing is one thing, and rejection's another." He sighed. He looked over and caught my eye. He had a hardness to him in that moment, an untouchable strength. I'd seen him look at Dirva that way, and it shook me when he looked at me that way. "Can I ask you something, Ariah?"

"Yes."

"What's this been to you? You been treading water with me? Am I a placeholder?"

"No," I said. I stood up and made it to the middle of the room before I froze again. "No. No, this is…No, Sorcha, I love you. I'm…" I blushed, and I lost my nerve, and I turned away. "I'm in love with you. I don't say it enough, I know that. I'm sorry. You're not a placeholder. Everything leading up to you was the placeholder."

"Yeah?"

"Yes. I swear. Yes."

"Then why are you so fucking convinced all that's just going to evaporate as soon as you're in the same room with Shayat?"

"Because...because I'm not red."

He laughed. It was a genuine laugh, a warm laugh. It helped clear the air between us. "You know, you always say that, but from where I'm standing you just get redder every day. Whatever you are now, you sure as hell aren't silver."

"Only skin deep, I guess."

"Like Da," he said.

I laughed. "Mercy, you're right. Sorcha, I leave this room, and so little makes sense. Everything is so complicated, so hard. But you make sense; being with you is easy. I don't want to lose you. And I don't know what it means that I want to let her court me. And I don't know what it means for us."

Sorcha pulled on a pair of pants. He sat cross-legged on the sleeping mat and leaned against the wall. "Fuck, I'd give my arm for some herb right now."

I wrapped a blanket around my waist and sat down next to him. "Me, too."

"All right. Well, the way I see it, her courting you, you wanting her to, that don't really have to mean anything for us. Us is you and me; it's a separate thing. If it don't change the way you are with me, what I am to you, then it's a separate thing. Which I think it is. I think you're overthinking it."

"You think so?"

He unlatched his violin case. "Ariah, you overthink everything. We're fine. We'll stay fine," he said, and then he tuned his violin.

CHAPTER 31

I FULLY EXPECTED every meeting with the matchmaker to be the last one. Certainly, Shayat would come to her senses, or Parvi would put a stop to things, or the matchmaker would refuse to broker the match. But Biral appeared week after week, and I ended up in that house with that matchmaker who had nothing but contempt for me. She read me mercilessly; she poked and prodded me. She asked me invasive questions and permitted herself small noises of disgust when I answered them.

I met with her the customary four times. Biral came to me with a date and a time for the fifth session, traditionally the session where the matched pair meets together. Something snapped in me. Something came loose. Sorcha went to Dirva's house alone. I drank just enough to drown the gift and went to Parvi's shop. I slipped around the back and pelted Shayat's windows with pebbles until she stuck her head through her curtains. She stared at me in shock. She frowned and slammed the window shut. I pelted her window with pebbles again until she opened it once more. She glared at me and pointed into the alley.

She stormed through the alleyway wrapped in Qin robes

worn all wrong. She took me by the elbow and dragged me behind a broken fence in the next yard. Emotions flickered across her face: irritation, then impatience, then amusement. She pinned me against the adobe wall of her neighbor's house and leaned in to kiss me. I slid away, out of her grasp. "Shayat, what the hell is this?"

"It's a courtship," she said. She smirked.

"I'm with Sorcha," I said.

"I heard he was still here. Is he staying out of trouble?"

"No, Shayat, I am *with* him. We're...we're lovers." The word felt strange. Before that moment, I hadn't named it.

Shayat blinked at me. She let out a strangled laugh and stole a glance out at the street. "I'd heard rumors."

"The rumors are true."

"Oh." She frowned. "Ariah, what the hell? You're fucking Sorcha, and you come here asking me what I'm doing? Why have you allowed the match to go on like this if you're with him?"

"No, you answer me first," I said. "It's been years, and you just turn up in town and want to marry me, just like that? It makes no sense."

"Well, it does to me," she said.

"I will marry you, Shayat, if you need me to. Maybe in Iyairo or at the embassies in Vilahna a marriage mark on your papers will help you move easier. But marrying me? I'm on a factory line, Shayat, a fucking factory line. Everyone in the borough knows it. Marrying me will sink you here. Marry someone else—anyone else—unless you're thinking about unloading your goods in Shangri or Tarquintia or someplace else. But you owe me an explanation."

She leaned back away from me like she'd been slapped. "You think this is about the route?"

"What else would it be about?"

"It's about you!"

"What?"

She gestured at me, flustered, irritated. "You! It's easy with you. It's not easy with anyone else. I thought...this is stupid. Fine. I'm refusing the match. Fine."

I caught her arm as she shoved past me. "Wait."

"For what?"

"I just don't understand. A matchmaker? You could have just come to see me."

She shrugged herself out of my grasp. "I wanted it official."

"But why?"

"Because I'm done looking. I'm done. You're the only one who has not been more trouble than he was worth, and even then you dragged me through the desert for no profit and got my camel confiscated right out from under me. I have long nights, and I think about you. I'm with another man, and I think about you. Everything gets measured against you. I'm done measuring." She sighed and glanced at me from the corner of her eye. "I hate this. This is ridiculous. And that damned shaper. I hate her."

"Oh, me too."

Shayat grinned. "She is so..."

"Judgmental," I said.

Shayat laughed. "Yes. Exactly." She leaned against the decrepit fence. She sighed again. "So, you and Sorcha finally crossed that line?"

"We did."

"You're happy?"

"With him, yes. With everything else, less so. I'm on a factory line, Shayat."

She took my hand and turned it palm up. "You've got a line worker's hands, now. They were soft before. How long have you been on it?"

"A year."

She whistled. "Why not leave?"

"Nuri. Dirva's son." I took her hand. She looked over at me. "This match is a farce. But we're not. You should come to my place. We should...we should think this through, see where this can go."

She let go of my hand. She shook her head. "This was a mistake," she said, and then she left.

She said it was a mistake, but she came to my place anyway three days later. I was changing out of my work clothes, and it was Sorcha who opened the door. Our apartment was just that single room and a cramped bathroom crammed in a refurbished closet. He opened the door; I was half-naked and in her line of sight, but my back was turned. "Shayat," he said. I stood up very straight, but I was not brave enough to turn around.

"Sorcha, you look well," she said. "I brought you this."

The door closed. The deadbolt slid into place. "Where did you get this?" he asked. His voice was hushed, half-whisper.

I looked over my shoulder. It was a jar of herb. Sorcha unscrewed the top, and its fragrance poured out. "Bardondour. That's mountain herb," I said. I looked at Sorcha; he grinned. I looked at Shayat, and she grinned an identical grin.

"Let's smoke," Sorcha said.

I put a hand on his arm. "Shayat, what are you here for?"

She leaned against the door. She drank us in, the two of us standing there together. "Well, you know I love to negotiate. I thought the three of us could come up with an, uh…Sorcha, how did you put it that day in the desert?" She snapped her fingers, and her grin turned hopeful and wicked. "An arrangement. Let's make an arrangement."

"I can't smoke," I said, though I very much wanted to. "I'm on the line right after curfew lifts tomorrow morning."

Sorcha breathed in the smell of the herb. The smell alone seemed to get him high: he was only half-present, distracted, with a lazy grin on his face. Shayat glanced around. "You don't have a chair?"

"Nah," Sorcha said.

"Not a single one?"

"Nah."

She slipped off her boots and sat on the edge of our sleeping mats. My eyebrows shot up. Sorcha sat down next to her. "You smoking?"

She smiled. She cut a glance at me. "Yes. I am."

"Since when?" I asked.

"The compounders don't trust elves who don't smoke," she said. "Unless your name is Tamir and they owe you a debt, you have to learn to smoke."

"You didn't smoke when we were there with you."

"Not that you saw," she said. Sorcha laughed. He rifled through his things, looking for his pipe.

"I can't smoke! The line!"

They looked up at me in unison, the same exact impatient look on their faces. Shayat sighed. "Fuck the line. The caravan is doing well. Too well. I keep making this much and the mercantile office will renegotiate my license and take half my profits. It's good for both of us if you let me slip you my surplus."

"What? No."

"Yes," Sorcha said. "We say yes. Ariah, sit down."

"No! You can't just come in here, bribe him with herb and me with money. No, you said this was a mistake."

"Well, I reconsidered," Shayat said.

"I have a life, Shayat! You can't just play with it like this."

Sorcha leaned forward. "We have a life with no chairs. Sit down. Smoke the woman's herb. She wants to negotiate? Let's negotiate."

I stared at him. "Sorcha, I would like to speak with you. Alone."

"What? Why?"

"Please."

He frowned. He set down the herb like it physically

pained him to do it. He slunk across the floor and glared at me when I grabbed his arm and thrust him through the door. "This is a bad idea," I said.

"Why?"

"It just is."

He reached out to touch me, but I backed away for fear the landlady would wander by and glance up the stairs. He dropped his hand and rolled his eyes. "Ariah, for fuck's sake, she…"

"She has plausible deniability, and that's the only thing keeping a roof over our heads," I whispered. I had come to understand in those days after I crossed the line why Dirva had turned to Nisa instead of Liro. The work it took to stay in the borough living like I did was a constant grind, and it took a toll. "She came here with…with that, she came here with promises of money. We have nothing to negotiate with, Sorcha. As soon as you hold that pipe you'll agree to anything. The second she said she'd get me off the line I wanted to marry her, right there. She can make us dance like we're puppets."

"Ariah, she wants you. You've got you to negotiate with."

"No, I don't! I'm a…Sorcha, I will get lost. I forget who I am. I give myself away to anyone who looks at me." Sorcha frowned. I dropped my face into my hands. "No. That's not what happened with you. I swear that's not what happened."

"Guess I'll have to take your word for it."

"You know that's not what I meant! Why would I hesitate with her if it wasn't real with you? You and me, it's both of us."

Sorcha looked me over, his eyes flicked up and down. He stepped to the door. "We're going to have to deal with her at some point. She's not one to be turned out. No reason not to deal with her now." He opened the door and held it wide until I walked through it.

Shayat grinned. She had the pipe packed. The herb sat rich and green in the bowl, tantalizing, seductive. It was by far the most expensive thing in the apartment.

"Ariah's got qualms," Sorcha said. He stood next to me, very close.

"Who among us doesn't?" Shayat said. "Let's just talk, the three of us. Let's just see what our options are."

"We talk first," Sorcha said, "and then we smoke." He sat down on the floor and pulled me down with him. He waved Shayat over.

A sly smile crept across Shayat's face. She set the pipe down and sat down in front of us. She caught my eye, staring down the length of her nose at me, her neck long and taut. I noticed a scar on her forehead. "Is that from the bandits?" I asked.

She touched the scar. "It is. Did they leave you with scars, too?"

"Yes."

Her smile turned tricky. "Can I see them?"

I felt the pull of her, the draw of what she wanted and what I could be for her. I did not realize I had moved toward her until Sorcha pulled me back. "Go smoke," he said.

"I have…"

"You got to keep your wits about you," he said. "Go smoke."

So I did. I took two, three hits by myself while they watched. I swear I could taste the wooded wetland in which the herb had grown. It was earthy and familiar and it took hold immediately. I peeked over at them. They sat there watching, Sorcha with his dogged ease with the world around him, and Shayat with her haughty defiance. They were both, in their own ways, magnificent creatures, and they sat there watching me. It seemed absurd. I was incredibly flattered. I grinned, and I blushed, and I didn't even bother trying to hide it. Sorcha grinned back and held out his arm. I fell in beside him, tucked in close. He played with my hair and kissed me on the cheek. "Good herb?"

"Good herb."

"You all set?"

"I'm set."

"Then let's negotiate."

I looked over at Shayat. She stared at us with a blank mask. She stared at us with an intensity, but what kind of intensity was shielded. What she felt right then, confronted by the facts of my life, could have been disgust as easily as it could have been fascination. "All right," I said. "I am a falo, and falos stay. I stay in Rabatha. I stay with Sorcha."

She leaned forward. Her mask slowly fell away. "Is there space for me?"

I had not expected such a vulnerable question. I expected

her to trick me or trap me, to edge me into a corner. It caught
me off guard. I had to think, fight my through the haze of herb
and really think. "It depends on what you want. What do you
want?"

She chewed on her fingernail. She looked down at the
floor. "I want someone who has given up on these damned
ghettos."

"I didn't give up on the borough, Shayat, the borough
gave up on me."

"In the end, it's the same thing if you're smart. And you
are." She sighed. "I want...I want you. I'm glad you've got
Sorcha. He's lucky, and he knows it. I want to be lucky like that,
too. I see the red elves do it, these threes and fours, and it
works. And I just...I watch them when I'm on the route, in
Alamadour or in Bardondour. I see the way the burden is
shared, the way all those feelings stretch and fit. If they can do
it, I can, too."

"Are you sure?" I asked.

She laughed. "Are you serious?"

"Well, things are different now."

"No, they aren't. You two were practically married back
on the trip. You think I couldn't tell? You think I didn't think
about it? Of course I did. I knew no matter what happened that
there was you, and there was him, and then there was the rest
of the world. I'm not trying to steal you, Ariah. I just want
whatever you've got left over to give to me. And when you
think about it, doesn't that make the most sense for someone
like me? A caravaner? I never wanted to marry. I didn't want to

leave a husband behind for months and months at a time, pining, worrying. And you wouldn't. You have him. I can come and go from this. And if you have him, I could have others, yes? No reason to keep to myself on the routes. This is a thing that makes sense. Don't you see that? And I—look, I have thought this through. There's no one else for me but you, not really, not in a deep way. You understand. The reds, they're good and all, but they don't understand what it's like here. Men here have expectations, restrictions. They are inflexible. I don't know how you did it, how you managed to turn into who you are, but you did, and we fit."

She'd grown animated as she spoke. She spoke with confidence, with a sureness. When she was done, she stared at me hard, willing me to speak. Sorcha stared at her, his eyebrows slightly raised. "I..."

"Yes?" she asked—demanded. She demanded an answer. I was drawn to her entitlement, the way she knew she was worthy of an answer.

I looked at Sorcha. He still stared at her, his head slightly cocked to the side, deep in thought. I wished I could have read him just then, but I couldn't. I tried to speak again and found I had no words. It felt like the world had opened up, that there were endless possibilities, and all of them good. I tried to look anywhere but at Sorcha and couldn't tear my eyes away. And so I watched while he took the decision I'd made but couldn't voice and put it into action. I watched while he leaned forward, leaned onto his hands and knees, and closed the distance between him and Shayat. I watched, transfixed, while she stared at him wide-eyed and curious, and I saw the happy shock on her face when he kissed her. She kissed him back, but looked at me while she did it, a question in her eyes. How much was too much? Where were the lines? Sorcha pulled back and smiled. "One like you," he said, "we got all the space in the world for. Right, Ariah?"

All I could do was nod. All I could do was let them draw me over, draw me in, and follow where they led. I was the center, the heart, the thing keeping the three of us together. Shayat spent the night there, and the next day. I abandoned my place on the line. I drowned myself in their attentions, and I was a conduit for their attentions to each other. Love in a triad is a strange thing: there are times when a pair breaks off and the third is left behind. There are times a pair starts and a third is brought in, but how and when are sometimes clumsy. I had expected, I think, for it to be two pairs: me and Sorcha, and me and Shayat. I had not expected Sorcha to pull us all together, to forge something himself with her. I think if it had occurred to me as a possibility it would have terrified me. I don't think I would have let it happen. I would have pushed her away simply to have him all to myself. But it did happen, and it worked, and somehow the sharing made it sweeter between him and me. I don't know how, I can't explain it, but the three of us fit together: a puzzle solved.

* * *

I helped Shayat gather her things, and Sorcha walked her to the door. She had routes to plan. She had a father to talk out of worry. She promised to come back soon. Sorcha gave her a peck on the cheek and sent her out into the world grinning. I packed away and hid the remaining herb. We'd decided to ration it. "Hey, can we talk?" Sorcha asked.

I looked over my shoulder at him. He frowned and stared down at his feet. I reeled the gift back in. "It's to do with Shayat."

"Prying eyes."

"You know I can't help it. What about her?"

He leaned against the door. He drummed his fingers on the doorknob. "You should've said."

"Said what?"

"How you like it. You should've said."

I caught glimpses of his mind as it turned and looked away to give him privacy. "I don't know what you mean."

He sighed. I wanted him to come to me, but he stayed where he was. "She is rough with you, Ariah."

"Oh." I hugged my knees to my chest. "Well...yes. She is."

"I didn't know."

"Back in the desert you must have noticed. She left marks."

He shook his head. "I didn't. You should've said. Years now I been doing it wrong for you."

I looked up. His face was still, his brows furrowed and mouth tight. "No. No, you haven't. It's different with you, but that's all right."

"You sure?"

"Of course I'm sure."

He crossed the room and sat beside me. "I hope so. Truth be told, I'm not so good at that. Had a girl once who wanted it rough. I did it, but I felt right awful the whole time."

I laughed. I blushed. Even then, even in that wild configuration, I still was not adept at such a discussion. My own body still embarrassed me deeply. "It's good with you. It really is."

He looked at me for a long time. He nodded and crawled under a blanket. He kicked at me until I curled up next to him. "What're you going to do now that you've forsaken the line?"

"I don't know. Lie low, I guess."

"I got a girl I got to see later. Just checking in with her. She's a nervous one. Want to come with?"

"It'll raise questions," I said. "Better to lie low."

"If you're lying low," he said, "you got to do it proper. Don't go skulking around the slave traders stealing songs."

That was exactly what I had planned to do. I hadn't been able to go with the line work; I lacked the time. I sighed and pulled the blanket closer. The songs had a draw on me as tangible and inevitable as Sorcha did, as Shayat did, but he was right. In the days that followed, I spent my time in my apartment or in Dirva's house. I told Dirva everything—Shayat, skipping out on my work assignment, all of it. We sat on his back stoop speaking Vahnan for hours while Sorcha taught Nuri chess and djah. The boy was a wonder with games. Dirva told me I was playing with fire. He told me I had been for a long time. He told me I was reckless. He told me he worried about me. And I had nothing to tell him to assuage his fears.

One evening, he took me outside to talk. We sat close to each other, shoulder to shoulder. Any man sitting close to me, by then, drew looks, and the neighbors took note. Dirva let them. I could feel it bothered him, that it woke a long-buried wariness, but he let them. "I think you should go back to Alamadour. Vathorem says he can find you work. He says Dor is on the lookout for a shaper to take as his right hand."

"Dor will take Vathorem as his right hand."

"Vathorem will not let him. Go to Alamadour. No one will put you in a factory there. No one will care about you and Sorcha and this woman."

"Dirva, no, I'm his falo."

He looked at me and sighed. He let me feel him, then. He pulled all his walls down and let his mind pour into mine. There was worry. There was gratitude. There was a great well of fondness and love. There was no blame. "The thing about red parents is they come and go. Sometimes one has to strike out. Sometimes they just want to strike out. He is safe here, and we can care for him, and you can't care for anyone the way you're living."

I shook my head. "I belong here, with you. With Nuri."

He sighed again. "I shouldn't have asked you to come back. It was selfish."

"You didn't know I would end up like this. No one did."

"It was selfish. I do not always see past myself. Ariah, I am telling you that Rabatha will bring you nothing but struggle and heartache. Like the City brings me nothing but struggle and heartache."

I shook my head again. A thread of anger wound through me. "Sorcha won't leave Nuri."

"He won't want to, no," Dirva said, "but he is smart enough to flee a sinking ship."

"How do you know? You never talk to him!"

Dirva's walls flew back up. He stood up to leave. "I eavesdrop," he said quietly, "and I watch."

I didn't tell Sorcha what Dirva and I had spoken about. I didn't float the idea of leaving. I buried myself in Sorcha and Shayat, in the both of them together. I borrowed armfuls of books from Dirva's house and read voraciously. I must have reread my notebooks full of Droma songs a dozen times as the days slid by. A week passed, and then a month, and then Shayat said her crew was restless and the route beckoned. That night she took me while Sorcha watched. She was rougher than usual, and I cried out in strange blendings of pain and pleasure. In her hands there was no separating one from the other. I felt a trust in her bone deep, and sex with her left me with a sense of purpose. I stayed on the border of stoned and sober: just high enough to keep the gift from taking over, and just sober enough that I felt Sorcha's fascination, his excitement, while he watched. Afterward, Shayat offered to take us with her. "You can count," she said to me, "and the compounders love you," she said to Sorcha.

Sorcha smiled and shook his head. "Got the little one to think of."

She accepted his refusal with grace. Sorcha kissed her, stroked her to show there were no hard feelings. Shayat was insistent with him, demanding, but gentle. She kept her claws in with him. It is strange to see the way a lover changes with someone else. Strange and compelling. Sorcha took me by the hand and pulled me into their knot, and I wound up in the center.

Shayat left us a sum of money large enough to pay rent and buy food until she came back to Rabatha. We gave her nothing in return but gratitude. She left, and Sorcha and I fell into old rhythms together, old ways of being with each other. I read everything. I read and reread Amran's poetry and found it tainted with memories of the man himself. Sorcha drifted in and out, to monitor pregnancies and deliver babies and help new mothers, and I stayed curled in the bed, reading. Sometimes I wrote to my parents or to Vathorem, but mostly I read.

I was reading when the Qin Army came for me. They pounded the door with heavy hands that could only be Qin. "It's time to repay the Exalted's grace," a soldier said. I'd read discarded newspapers along with all the borrowed books, and I knew why they were there for me. The military had mobilized in Ma-Halad. They needed translators. My papers said I was fluent in Droma. I had just enough time to write Sorcha a note and slip it into the hollowed-out book where he stored his pipe before they threatened me with arrest if I didn't open the door.

There was no way out. When the Exalted comes calling, no one refuses. Avoidance of impressment is a crime punishable by death. When it happened, it felt inevitable. I opened the door fully dressed: boots on, coat on even though it was hot out. I had a pack ready and a bedroll strapped to it in less than five minutes. The soldiers were pleasantly surprised. The one in charge asked for my papers, marked this new assignment, and manacled me. "A precaution," he said, "since you flirt with convicts." He tucked my papers in my vest pocket and led me away. I walked through the borough flanked by Qin soldiers in full uniform, handcuffed, while the neighbors watched.

PART SEVEN:

THE GRASSLANDS

CHAPTER 32

THE SOLDIERS GOING to the front had their own train. It was huge, it was armed, and it was state of the art. It ran on a whisper. The metal was some alloy, something light. It was powered by steam and clockworks instead of coal, and the interior had a process that converted riders' waste to usable water for the engines. It was a marvel. It was elf-built, but I was the only elf on the train. Each Qin soldier had his own bunk, but I was cuffed to a pipe in the bowels of the train. They tethered me to a pipe that brought the remnants of boiling water from the furnace to the cisterns. I still have burns on my hand and wrist from where I touched it when I slept. I did not sleep well. A pair of soldiers unlocked me once a day to relieve myself and eat. The rail to Ma-Halad is long, but we made good time. We stopped in no towns. We didn't need to stop: we had fuel and provisions enough.

Two of the train's engineers worked the furnace room. I couldn't see them—my chains didn't allow me enough room to peek around the corner—but I could hear them. They spoke about their orders, about the Exalted's plan for the east. The grasslands were fertile, and the Exalted wanted Qin farmers working it so we no longer had to rely on Vilahnan wheat. There were always rumors that since it was elf-grown it was impure. That was the official story, but the engineers speculated that really the push east had more to do with the gold elves. The Empire needed slave labor. Factory lines are hard to fill with full citizens. I listened, and I seethed, and I hatched fruitless plans.

We came into Ma-Halad's station just before midnight on an unseasonably cold spring night. The air swept down the tall, snow-capped Jalah mountains. It did more than bite; it chewed us alive. My thin coat did me little good. My only real protection from the wind was the bodies of the Qin soldiers flanking me on either side. When the train stopped, they shackled my hands and feet together, and I made my way through the station, bound like a criminal. The Qin settlers gawked at me. The displaced, indentured Chalir discreetly looked away. They were tahrqin, too, but they were beaten and corralled just like elves. They stood tall and dark, wrapped head to toe in black linen. All you could ever see of the Chalir were their tahrqin eyes, which were always large and luminous and burning with cold hatred. The only elves I saw were technicians working on a broken train, and even they were transient. The second that train was up and running, they fled back west. I had nursed a hope on the train that Sorcha and Shayat would come for me, that it was possible for them to come for me. But I was so far from home and in a place so carefully guarded that I was out of their reach. None of Sorcha's sweet talking would work this far out. Shayat, as prodigiously mercantile as she was, could not scrape together enough coin to bribe her way to me.

The soldiers took me to the barracks, where they brought

me to General Muladah al Shahjin'Diladdi, the one Qin historians lovingly call the Butcher of the East. He was a young man, then, not yet forty. He was extraordinary. He had a flashing, violent intelligence that shone like a candle in the dark. He was young but had an air of worldliness about him that made him seem timeless, like a war god. He was magnetic, effortlessly charismatic, the type that could and did lead fevered men gladly to their deaths: a siren of sorts. There was a part of me that wanted to let him lead me, too, wherever he wanted to go. He was the kind that makes a man crave to submit, to give, to follow. He had the westernmost room on the top floor of the barracks. The room held a simple cot and tables littered with maps. When I was brought in, he stood staring out at the night, at the moon, peering west like he could see all the way to the Exalted's tower. He was a deeply religious man; when the soldier shoved me across his threshold, he performed a warding to cleanse himself of my very presence. The Butcher of the East held out his hand to my captor. "His papers."

The soldier handed him my papers. The general took one cursory glance and threw them on a table. "Forgeries."

"Sir?"

"Those papers are forgeries," he said. "Cuff him to the chair and leave him with me."

The soldier did as he asked. I suspected I was going to be killed. I suspected it in a removed, academic way, as if it was not really happening to me. The general pulled up a chair and sat down across from me instead. "Forged papers, and even the forgeries have precinct stamps on them. I am not surprised. All elves are criminals one way or another. All elves are trespassers on the Exalted's lands and thieves of the Exalted's goodwill."

I said nothing. I stared out his window, only half-listening. It was, at least, warm in the room.

He picked up my papers again and thumbed through them. "Is your name Ariah Lirat'Mochai?"

"Yes."

"Tell me why you have forged papers."

I looked over and smiled, reckless and stupid, defiant and wallowing in what I saw as foregone conclusions. I am prone to undignified fatalism. "I am an undeclared shaper."

I caught the tic of nerves on the general's face. He performed another warding. "Eyes on the floor," he said. His voice was even, unruffled, but I had felt his hackles rise. I dropped my eyes. "You speak Droma."

"The soldiers had me demonstrate it on a slave in Rabatha."

"I am aware. How did you come to learn it?"

"From the slaves in Rabatha. From their songs."

"Just from songs? No one taught it to you?"

I grinned. I looked at him, then away. "Magic."

The general sighed. "You are not loyal to the Exalted. I need no magic to see that. You will teach my captains Droma, or you will be put to death for your likely countless crimes against the Empire. Understood?"

"Understood."

* * *

The one thing we elves have over the tahrqin, our one greatest asset, is not our magic. It's patience. We can outlive them, so we can afford to be patient. Time is an ally for us and a terrible foe for them. I regret to say I aided the efforts of the Exalted to take the grasslands. I bided my time, and I taught the captains Droma. They were not very good at it; it's a strange language to someone who only knows Qin. I taught them badly, though, in that way they are used to. Lectures, just lectures. The Butcher sent them out into the grasslands on forays, or brought collected gold slaves to test their language acquisition, and grew more and more frustrated when they remained far from fluent. But I taught the way he had been taught, the way they had all always been taught, which works well for maths and spelling and history and very badly for foreign languages. He begrudgingly saw no fault in me. He demoted captains at such a rate and with such a vengeance that promotion to captaincy was met with condolences.

It took me a year and a half to get out. It was not planned, and it was not orchestrated. It was a fluke, and the only reason I got out was through luck and patience. That's it. It was inevitable that if I stayed quiet and obedient and patient long enough that random Qin error would open a door for me.

I deserted the Qin Army on a warm night in early fall. It was the night of a day of meaning, and a number of the soldiers in Ma-Halad who were off duty had taken the opportunity to get extremely drunk. The Butcher demanded religiosity even from those who were not particularly spiritual. Soldiers faced expulsion or court martial for unseemly behavior, which included drunkenness. But wine flows on days of meaning. Wine flows and brawls happen. Wine flowed, and just after dusk a brawl broke out inside the barracks. I'm not sure how it started, but it spread like wildfire. I was chained to a pillar in a closet, which locked from the outside. I was valuable, so I was kept secure. A soldier was locking me to the chains for the night when the drunken brawlers swept through the hallway like a tidal wave, demolishing everything in their path. The soldier was taken down by a chair to the back of the head. He collapsed on top of me, knocked out cold, the key to my manacles still in his hand. The drunken soldiers did not think to check for an errant elf beneath him, and they passed through, the damage done, nothing else in the hallway to destroy. I pried the key out of his hand and unlocked my manacles. I knew the layout of the building well. I knew on the second floor there was a loose window next to a gutter. I fell unmoving on the floor whenever I heard the rumble of more drunk soldiers. Most of them never even noticed me. It was insultingly easy to get out of the barracks.

Ma-Halad, then, was a military outpost. There was not much to it besides the barracks, the train station, and a paltry market. I stayed in the dark alleys and picked my way across town to the markets. I found a tavern's cellar door propped open with a stick, slipped down into it, and managed to steal a sackful of cheese, several loaves of flatbread, and three skins of water without anyone noticing. Under the cover of night, I ran east into the grass.

CHAPTER 33

I WANDERED EAST, endlessly east. At first I considered travelling back west. I'd escaped—surely I could find Sorcha and Shayat. But I travelled east instead, alone, with no company but my thoughts. And the more I thought about it, the less sense it made to travel west and seek them out. They probably thought me dead. I would probably be captured and hung to death if I tried to re-enter the Empire, even with a smuggler's assistance. And if I made it, somehow, back to Rabatha in one piece, to find them and demand quarter would put them in grave danger. They would be faced with harboring a fugitive—a traitor—and the law would be as merciless on them as it would be on me when I was inevitably found out.

I escaped, and I travelled east out of cowardice and pragmatism. I left them behind for their good and my own. It was a terrible, awful thing. It left me hollow and shattered.

After three days of travel, just as my supplies began to run out, I found a river and followed it farther east. I survived mostly on edible water grasses and fish. I felt guilty about the fish until I managed to snare and eat a rabbit. I wept when I killed it and skinned it and wept again when I ate it. It was a struggle to keep the meat down; the wrongness of it was overwhelming. Still, I needed the protein badly. After that first rabbit, I became carnivorous and killed and ate whatever animals I could.

When I was deep enough in the grasslands that it was unlikely a Qin foray would stumble on me, I took to camping for a week or two in a good spot before moving on. I knew almost nothing about the gold elves besides their language, but I knew they were nomads, and I was on a riverbank. It seemed a certainty that one clan or another would stumble across me. I don't know how long I was out there, hopping from one makeshift lean-to to another, feasting on rabbits and burrowing rats and grass snakes like a rabid wolf. I lost count of the days. I know it must have been three or four months because the seasons turned from fall to winter. The days cooled and shortened, and the grass went from gold to a dead brown. It was strange out there, but it wasn't bad living. Unlike the maudlin days and nights in the Qin barracks, I had no time to dwell. There was too much to do—living off the land is a hard thing, a consuming thing. There is no idleness, and so I rarely thought of Sorcha or Nuri or Shayat or Dirva or my parents. I thought of my next meal and the parts of my shelter that needed fixing and how much fresh water I had stored.

I took to singing to keep myself company. It had practical uses, too. The sound carries in the grasslands; there's nothing to block it but a handful of trees here and there, and the songs, I'd found, tended to keep at bay the wildlife who might otherwise have been attracted by the smell of food. I am an artless singer: the mimicry means I'm technically competent, but the best I can hope for is an accurate reproduction of someone else's art. I sang songs Sorcha had sung to me in his voice. I sang songs I'd overheard at the slave markets. I even sang the wordless, senseless melodies the satyrs in the City sang. It was the songs that brought the gold elves to me. I sang one evening in the winter, used to the solitude, while I built a campfire. I'd caught two perch in the river and looked forward to eating them. My qualms about eating the flesh of animals were long gone by then. I sang a Droma song overheard years before at the Rabathan slave markets. It was one about a river. It was cyclical, verses returning again and again to the river in the same summer afternoon year after year. I sang it thoughtlessly. Halfway through the third verse I felt the pull. It was unmistakable. It was a peripheral count.

I looked over my shoulder. Instinct propelled me to keep singing. Maybe it wasn't instinct; maybe it was the gift, the connection. I'm not sure. In any case, I kept singing. The tall grass shifted. I heard the bleat of goats.

"A Hradata walking song this far west?" A half-grown gold elf emerged from the grass. Ve was not quite as tall as me and whip thin. Ve was burnished a mahogany brown from the sun, with a kinky mane of yellow hair. Goats sauntered around vim, chewing at the grass, peering at me in haughty disinterest. The Droma child blinked at me and sucked in a lungful of air, eyes wide, nostrils flared, on the verge of panic.

I held out my hands, watching vim closely like one

watches a wild animal. "It is just me here. There are no others. Just me."

I took a very small, very slow step towards the child. I remembered the strangeness of Droma gender. I tried very hard to ignore all the signs of biological sex, to see the child as a person, as *voe*. If I was to encroach on their lands and ask for their help in survival, I felt the least I could do was get this one basic thing right. The words were easy, but the seeing was hard. It took a very long time before it was natural, and even then it was hard.

Ve stumbled back and fell over a goat. Ve scrambled upright and held vis walking stick up like a weapon. "Stay back, settler!"

I stayed back. "I left the settlers."

"You're silver! You're a settler!"

"I am alone."

"I'm not for sale, settler!"

Fear poured off vim in waves. Ve was petrified, shaking, a heartbeat away from violence. I shaped vim. I did. I saw no way out but to do it, to manipulate this terrified child using magic ve did not understand. I shaped vim with a song, a Droma song, about birds.

Ve lowered vis stick and frowned. "That one wasn't Hradata. Who are you? Where are you from? How do you know Droma?"

"My name is Ariah. I'm from the west. I know Droma because I listened to ones who were sold."

"What are you doing here?"

"Not much," I said. "Surviving. I ran from the settlers."

"You're just out here by yourself?"

"Yes."

The child chewed vis lip. "You need a clan, settler."

"I had one. The Qin took me away from them."

Ve sighed. Ve plucked at vis hair and poked at the goats with vis stick. "You need a clan," ve said again. Ve left; the grass swallowed vim and the goats back up, and I was alone again.

I caught more fish and made more improvements to my shelter. Three days later, on an unseasonably warm day, the Droma child returned again. I was naked and perched on a rock, washing out my one set of clothes. Once again, I'd been singing. I felt vis presence—it was a gentle tug, like a string wrapped around my wrist—and stood up. I looked around but saw nothing but grass. "Are you out there? Are you back?"

I frowned at my naked body and my wet clothes. I had nothing to cover myself with but the remnants of the sack I'd used to steal cheese some four months before, which I used as a paltry blanket at night. I wrapped it around my hips and stared at the grass. I felt the tug again, this time south of me. "Do you want some fish?" I called out.

The grass swayed. A dark-brown hand pushed a clump aside. The Droma child stepped out, followed by a person about my age. The little goatherd watched me with furrowed brows, but the one ve'd brought with vim regarded me with the hint of a smile. Ve had a knife strapped to vis belt. "A settler with no town," the older one said.

"My name is Ariah. I have no more love for the towns that you do. I'm unarmed."

"How is it you speak Droma so well?"

"Magic," I said.

"Are you an echo, settler?"

The sackcloth threatened to fall to the ground and leave me wholly exposed. I wrestled it back in place. The Droma laughed at me, and I smiled in return. A little of the tension in the air cleared. "I don't know what that is."

The older Droma laughed. "You speak Droma, but you don't know about echoes?" I shook my head. Ve came into my camp with the little goatherd trailing behind. Ve surveyed my camp, and ran a hand along the thatchwork roof of my shelter. "Where did you learn to do this?"

"Experimentation," I said.

Ve took my wrist and turned my hand palm up. "You have a weaver's hands. Have you worked a loom?"

I laughed. Ve gave me a curious look. "I worked wool factories in the towns."

"Not the same," ve said.

"Not at all."

Ve dropped my hand. Ve studied my face, and I studied vim. Ve was full-lipped, with a wide, flat nose. Vis eyes were large and almond-shaped, Semadran-shaped, but the pupils were ringed with a ruddy gold instead of violet. Ve was small, about an inch or so shorter than me, and thinner, too, despite the fact that I'd turned to skin and bone in the months since I'd been taken from Rabatha. Vis hair was identical to the goatherd's: a thick, kinky spray of yellow hair in all directions. Ve smiled. "Say something in your settler tongue, and I'll show you an echo."

"Say something?"

"Yes."

"In Semadran or Qin?"

"It doesn't matter."

One hand kept the sackcloth in place. I held out the other. "My name is Ariah," I said in Lothic.

The Droma pointed at my hand. "You want me to do something with your hand, Ariah?" Ve spoke, and it sounded Lothic to my ears, but something was off. I watched vim closely when ve spoke, and it was like the words I heard and the words ve said did not quite match up. I am no lip reader, but the movements of vis mouth seemed disconnected from the words that came out of it.

"Do you know what language this is?" I asked.

Ve smirked. "That depends on who you ask."

"I'm asking you."

"I speak to you in Droma," ve said. "Whatever you hear it as, that I can't say. You speak, I hear Droma. I speak, you hear what-have-you. This is the echo, see?"

The only way I can describe it was as an auditory mirror. The way red elves can use magic to alter what a person sees, gold elves can do it with what a person hears. It seems to me to be rooted in the same process, built on connections, built on something like a charm. I am no magicologist. All I can say is it is a powerful thing, that it gets the Droma hunted and captured by Qin and pirates alike, and that it is incredibly disorienting. I never got used to it, the mismatch between what I heard and what I saw. I never really had to since I spoke Droma. I switched to Vahnan and spoke again. "This is magic?"

Ve nodded. "Magic, yes," and this time it sounded Vahnan. "If you are not an echo, how do you speak Droma?"

"I learned it. From slaves' songs. I learned it with a different kind of magic," I said. I'd switched to Droma to say it, and I caught vim staring at my mouth, looking for the telltale echo's disconnect between what I said and what I spoke.

Ve raised vis eyebrows. "Strange." Ve gestured at my campsite. "How long have you been here?"

"A week."

"Where were you before?"

I pointed west. "Down the river."

"You have no livestock. You have no weapons. You have no clan. And you wander?"

I took a chance. "I would rather wander with a clan."

"Kisi says you have one in the west."

I looked away, out at the swaying grass. It was a simple statement, simple like a knife is simple, and it cut me deep. "I do," I said softly. "I do, but I have no way back to them."

The older Droma looked at me closely. I felt vis curiosity, vis fascination. I felt the way the thought took slow, improbable formation in vis mind. "You were taken. I have siblings who were taken. Lost to us."

"I...yes."

The Droma were silent for some time. The little goatherd

shifted nervously from foot to foot, but the other stood very straight, arms crossed, lost in thought. "Kisi says you sang a Hradata song."

"I didn't know it was Hradata. Is Hradata a clan?" The Droma nodded. "Not your clan?"

"Not our clan, no, but we know them. The Hradata paths take them close to the edge, and they've had many taken. Like us. But they won't change their paths like we have. How did you learn the songs?"

"They sing them. The ones taken sing them when they are sold off. They sing to each other, and I listened."

"Listened," ve said, "and understood."

"Yes."

"Sing me one of your stolen songs."

I blinked at vim. Ve waved at me to get on with it. I picked one of my favorites, something like a love song. As I sang it, both the Droma stared at me, wide-eyed. When I finished, the older Droma swallowed, fighting back emotion. I stared down at my feet to give vim some privacy. "That is...that is a thing Halaavi said," ve said in a quiet, hollow voice.

"It is, yes."

"I am Halaavi." I looked up and found vim crying. Tears glistened in the sunlight. Ve cried stoically, regally, and with no shame. "There's only one I said that to. And ve was taken, and now I know. Ve was sold."

"I'm sorry."

"The grass grows on," ve said. Ve sighed. The little goatherd took vis hand, and Halaavi relaxed a little, grew more substantial. Halaavi laughed. "The grass grows," ve said, "and sometimes it changes colors. You need a clan, Ariah. I will advocate to the Avolayla for you."

CHAPTER 34

HALAAVI AND KISI led me to the Avolayla's camp. It was about two and a half miles from where I'd settled by the river. Halaavi asked me questions about the Empire while we walked. Ve asked me what the slave markets were like. Ve said ve'd been near Ma-Halad before. The permanence of the settlement bothered vim. Ve said it was unnatural and arrogant to demand one stretch of land to support you forever.

"Well, the Empire may settle," I said, "but it keeps growing. It keeps making that demand of new places."

"Greed," Halaavi said.

"Among other things, yes."

The Avolayla's camp sat on carefully cultivated plains south of the river. The grasses in the living area had been laid down flat. The Droma use boards knotted with rope for this; they step the grass stalks down, coax them flat. You can identify a clan by the pattern of its floorwork: the Avolayla draw the Moon and the Pet overlapping on their grass floors. Around thirty yurts of different sizes sat on the floorwork, the walls of each covered in embroidered skins, and the roofs masterfully thatched. In the center of the camp was a covered canopy protecting the fire pits and stoves, and a longer, larger yurt that served as a meeting place. Stray goats, antelope, and yaks roamed through the camp at will. Chickens clustered in a small pen beside the cooking tent. Children ran in loose packs between the yurts. The air was rich with the smell of smoke, dung, boiling tea, and fresh milk.

Kisi and Halaavi sang a walking song as we approached, a sort of code that alerted the camp to our presence and identified them, at least, as clan members. They were met with smiles, warmth, and then the clan spotted me. The songs stopped, the children skidded to a halt. Steely fear bled from one brown face to another to another. It burned into me, sucked in by the gift. Groups are never easy for a shaper, but groups where emotions are so contagious are especially difficult. I lost myself. I became, in a very literal sense, scared of my own self.

Halaavi took me by the arm and brought me forward. "I advocate for vim."

"Ve is a settler," an old person said. Vis hair was gray and thinning, eyes rheumy and joints swollen with arthritis. The clan parted to let vim through. "Halaavi, you sow chaos."

Kisi shot Halaavi an apologetic look and ran to the rest of the clan. Halaavi stood fast, vis dark brown hand on my pale silver arm. "Sing to them what you sang to me," ve said.

The clan's uniform suspicion did not budge when I sang what Halaavi had said to that slave years and years ago, but interest and curiosity seeped into them. In unison, the clan turned to Halaavi. "Vis name is Ariah. I advocate for vim. If ve proves a danger, both of us will take banishment."

The old Droma stepped forward, right up to Halaavi. They locked eyes, and I felt a transference of feeling from one to the other. There was a sense of communion between them not unlike the shadow of magic I'd felt when Dirva or Vathorem read someone in front of me. "This death wish of yours is unbecoming, Halaavi."

"We turn vim away, and the clan will have blood on its hands. We owe a debt to the land, Idok Arvada, and the land gave us vim. What the land gives, we take."

Arvada frowned at me. "The land didn't give us this; the thieves gave us this. This is not a matter of spirituality, Laavi, this is a matter of safety."

"These two things are not so separate."

"This is chaos."

"In chaos, growth."

"In chaos, death."

Halaavi smiled. It was a cold, removed smile, one that hinted at a well of darkness within vim. I realized ve had not denied that accusation of a death wish. "The land shows us that one begets the other. What grows dies. Death breeds space for new growth. There is no life without chaos. The only thing in the world that is not chaotic is death."

"You confuse chaos and change."

"I confuse nothing. There is not one without the other."

Old Arvada's jaw clenched. Arvada stared at me, hard, and I felt a gentle prick of magic. The Droma do not have shapers, not quite the way we think of them, but there is something there that works in parallel. It pricked my attention, and I read vim back.

When a trained Semadran shaper reads another trained Semadran shaper, it is a battle of walls. Our shapers duel sometimes, each lunging at the other, each parrying with a new formidable wall. Mr. Atoosa'Avvah's book describes it as a necessary aspect of training, but the stories go that he was partial to duels because he won them so often. A Semadran shaper does not read another shaper unless it is a duel or for work; the code of privacy rules it out otherwise. When Athenorkos charmers turn their magic on each other, it is a game, a push-pull of friendly skill. Magic for them is a thing of tricks and traps. With the Droma, magic is understood in an altogether different way. I read Arvada, this old suspicious elf, and ve let me. There was no resistance. There was a muted surprise that I could, but my magic swept into vim with no dams and no barriers. Arvada's surprise bled out to others in the clan: picked up by some, amplified by others, soothed and smoothed out by a few. The magic was communal and utterly frank. This was a people who had never heard of walls and, when I later tried to explain them, found this concept—so central to my understanding of my own magic and culture—distasteful at best and woefully impolite at worst.

I read Arvada and met with nothing but this clear and untroubled link with the other one hundred and seventy souls crowding the center of the camp. I felt, for the first time in my life as a man harnessing magic, a peace with it. There is a terrible clarity to an entwined life like this, a nakedness and constant exposure, but it was revelatory, and it was comforting.

It felt right to me. I felt I belonged. And the link spread this feeling of mine to the rest. As a whole, the clan stepped forward. Arvada's face softened. Ve cut a disapproving look at Halaavi, but Arvada nodded approval. "What skills does this one have for us?" Arvada asked.

"I speak Droma," I said. All eyes turned to me, and I laughed nervously. "I can fish. I should be able to learn to weave. I am able."

"We will teach you what we can," Arvada said.

I stuck close to Halaavi. I was fed, and I was given a set of warmer clothes. The children, especially, were fascinated with me. The adults kept to themselves and gave Halaavi and me a wide berth, but the children crowded around me. They touched my hair, my skin. I had a beard then, and they were fascinated by that, too. The gold elves, like the reds, don't have much luck with facial hair. Around dusk, the herders drove the livestock back to the camp, and I had to be advocated for all over again. It was simpler this time since the rest of the clan had allowed me in, but valid suspicions take root quickly and are hard to eradicate.

After the evening meal—a stew of collected roots and nuts served with sharp goat cheese—Halaavi led me to a yurt on the edge of camp. "We sleep here," ve said, holding the door open for me. Inside, a fire burned in a shallow stone bowl. It threw dancing yellow light around the circular wall of the yurt. Four other people my age sat around it in various states of undress. Three I had met already; the fourth seemed wholly uninterested in me. The floor was strewn with unfurled bedrolls and messy blankets, each like separate untidy islands. Open bags gaped next to the beds, full of clothing and trinkets. Next to one bed sat a set of drums not unlike Abira's. The sight of them gave me pangs of nostalgia. As soon as I felt it, everyone in the yurt turned to look at me. The one I hadn't met followed my eyes to the drums. "Do you play?"

"I don't. I knew a drummer."

"Ve sings," Halaavi said.

One of the others cracked a smile. "We all sing," ve said. "Does ve sing well?" Halaavi gave a noncommittal shrug. The other Droma laughed. The one who'd asked scooted over and patted the blanket. "Come, not-settler. Sit."

I sat. I warmed my hands over the fire, and Halaavi squatted next to me. Ve was very close, almost protective. "Where do I sleep?"

"Anywhere there is an open bed," one of them said.

"This yurt is for unpaired Vralas," Halaavi said. Ve said it *triloshilai-shaah*, literally "without a shared skin." *Triloshilai* was an elusive word, one I had a nebulous sense of from the stolen songs, but not a clear understanding of. I had taken it to mean marriage. Certainly, that was as close to its meaning as I could have gotten in isolation.

"Vralas?" I asked.

"Yes; we are Vrala, all of us. Vrala Halaavi," ve said. Ve pointed across the fire. "Vrala Shinnani. Vrala Kishva." Ve pointed at me. "Vrala Ariah."

"You're related?" I scanned their faces: some bore a resemblance, some did not.

"We're siblings. Born together in the same walk." I, with my Semadran raising, struggled to see through this simplified structure to the bloodlines below it. Further probing revealed none of them paid much attention to parentage. Few knew who had fathered them, and many refused to point out their mothers. It was impolite, Halaavi explained later. It broke the bonds. I once raised a concern about incest, but Halaavi didn't understand. As I said, they were all siblings. No differentiations were made. In a Semadran sense, incest was likely somewhat rare due to generational differences and the fluidity of people's movements between clans. In a Droma sense, incest was common, expected, and encouraged.

That first night, when I was told I was in the unpaired's yurt, I took it to mean those in it were unmarried, and I took that to mean they were abstinent. I was wrong. I woke to the thrashing sounds of sex. Two of the unpaired Vralas had drifted together in the night, and they were at it in earnest. It woke another, who joined them. Halaavi woke next to me and crawled over to the pulsing knot of limbs. As the group of them grew—voices crashing like waves, heat pouring off them, the sounds and sights and smells of it unavoidable—more of the sleeping unpaired Vralas woke and joined them until only I was left. I didn't know what to do. Should I leave? Yes. Yes, I should leave. But I stayed frozen in place, watching, listening, captivated, curious, and embarrassed. Wanting it and frightened of it at the same time. It was animalistic, frenzied, and athletic. It was languageless and purely physical. Kishva, who I later learned was an empath groomed by Old Arvada to take the empathic pulse of the clan when decisions loomed large, extricated vimself from the rest and came to me. Ve was flushed with half-sated desire, wild-eyed and incomparably alive. Ve was fine-boned and delicate, something I'd noticed in the calm in the early evening around the fire. Ve took me by the hand and tugged, but I stayed rooted in place. "You want to," Kishva said. "I feel you want to."

"What is this?"

"Sex."

"No, I mean...are you all..." I couldn't find Droma words for it.

"We're all having sex," ve said. "Shinnani sparked it. Come join the fire before it burns itself out."

"I...no. No, I'm all right," I said, and I slipped out of the yurt into the cold night before Kishva could ask me anything else.

It happened every few nights. Sex always ended up that way: raucous, orgiastic. Decidedly lacking the intimacy I'd grown used to with Sorcha and Shayat. There was no shroud of privacy or tight-knit emotional afterglow. They collapsed in friendly heaps and slept hard after. It was a strange and wholly unfamiliar way of living that took me some time to understand. I avoided the orgies at first, choosing on those nights to slip out of the tent and wander through the clutches of warm, bleating goats. They rarely happened in the daylight, when people spread out and worked at keeping the camp going.

Halaavi taught me weaving and embroidery. Ve had me card the downy undercoat of the clan's yaks, then taught me to spin it into yarn. I learned to dye using the plants and berries of the land. When winter bested the older livestock, we killed and ate them. Halaavi showed me how to tan the skins, and I learned leatherwork, too. We were together, ve and I, most of the day and most of the night. Weeks and weeks together, side by side, working and talking. The only time we were apart was during those raucous, orgiastic nights in the unpaired's yurt: Halaavi participated, and I did not. I sat outside, wrapped in blankets in the cool night, and listened. I tracked who from the paired yurts emerged and joined Halaavi and the rest. Sometimes one did, sometimes both, but always the ones who joined were Vralas.

When spring came and the grass grew green, it was time to move camp. The clan's runners spent weeks scouting the next site. The runners were gifted cartographers, and they pored over maps of their previous routes, of places slavers were known to frequent, and of the intersections between their routes and the routes of other clans. A site was selected, and we broke down the yurt, strapped its pieces to yaks, and drove ourselves and our livestock southeast. We landed in the eastern steppes, a place where the grass is tall and rich. I sang the walking songs with them as we traveled. I ate with them and cooked with them. As the days passed, I thought less and less about the Empire and all that I'd left behind, and more and more about life with the Droma, the way their magic made such easy sense to me. Day by day the others' suspicion of me faded until one day in late spring it seemed there was none left at all. The serenity of the clan was unmarred by my presence.

The day I noticed I'd been woven into the fabric of the clan was a good one. I was in high spirits. I talked to Halaavi about it. "Yes, they see you for you now," ve said. "Silver without; gold within."

I laughed. "An alloy."

Halaavi nodded. Ve looked over at me and smiled. Halaavi's smiles were transformative: vis face was angular and in repose looked harsh, and a smile shattered the angles and made vim young and full of humor. "They see you now like I see you, Vrala Ariah."

"Oh, you just like me because you think I'm chaotic."

Halaavi laughed. "Who says I like you?" I pointed at Halaavi, then at the clan, and smiled. The gift was an ever-present thing then. Old Idok Arvada took to bringing me into vis yurt when ve trained Kishva. I was a noted empath among the Avolayla. Halaavi laughed again. "Yes, fine, I like you."

"No secrets in the clan." The Droma word for secret is indistinguishable from the Droma word for lie, and both have roots in the Droma word for chaos. I ran the shuttle back and forth, back and forth through the loom. "Where I come from, we hold the truth to ourselves."

"We all hold truth to ourselves," Halaavi said.

"No, I mean…where I come from, we are all like islands. We're all like our own separate clan, a clan of just one person, and we hold truth just to ourselves, just to that singled-out clan."

Halaavi raised vis eyebrows. It intrigued vim. Ve was not

secretive, not the way you and I think about it, but ve was an oddity among the clan. Halaavi had perfected a way of thinking, a way of feeling that, though shared, was at times impenetrable to the rest. Halaavi was a voice of the Yavinaha, a band of ascetic monks whose spirituality was deeply embedded in the land. Halaavi had been born to the Yavinaha, raised among the faithful, and joined the Avolayla as a sort of spiritual adviser to the clan. Part of vis raising was a deep tradition of meditation; Halaavi could make vis mind absolutely blank, absolutely still, and absolutely empty, which ve did whenever ve was troubled and did not want the rest to know. There was no judgment from me. I knew of Yavinaha teachings only what I could glean, and I'd lived such a bounded life that Halaavi's questioning, restless mind never struck me as a danger. Halaavi could be intrigued by such things in my presence. Ve worked a while embroidering a lefta. "There are times," ve said finally, "that I wonder about the old ways and how useful they are in this new world. The Yavinaha, the root is change. The world changes: the seasons change, the land shifts, and so must we. I worry about those of us who are taken, who can't hold truth to themselves, and who can't ignore the truth of others. I worry how they fare on their side of the plains."

"The ones taken lose luster quickly. They adapt, or they die."

Halaavi nodded. "And yet the cities birthed you, and here you are, accepted by the Avolyala."

"No accounting for taste, I guess." Halaavi elbowed me, and I laughed.

That night, an orgy broke out in the yurt. And I...the day had felt like a new start, a break with what I had been before. I joined it. I let the crush of bodies fold me in, envelop me. The gift poured out, and I lost myself, but it seemed all right this time. It was a pulsing thing, regulated like tides. I lost myself and came back draped in Vrala arms. The urge took someone else and pulled the gift over, and I lost myself again only to wake in the arms of someone else. Kishva and I seemed drawn together by some inexorable magnetism of the magic. Some fury of the gift brought us together over and over again, night after night. It took me some weeks before I realized I never found myself in Halaavi's arms. Sex was a free thing, a wild thing, a rush of desire and acceptance among the Droma. They stuck fairly close to generational lines, but not exclusively. The Droma give themselves over to it, all of them. I had not seen them discriminate between partners. At first I thought them like the red elves—a culture which embraces an inclusive idea of sexuality. The Droma were biologically differentiated, just like everyone else, but like the red elves same-sex pairings were as common as opposite-sex pairings. But it was more than that. I knew that the Droma didn't conceive of gender and gendered differences like I did, but it was only in living among them that I began to grasp how profound a difference this was between them and me. The lack of discrimination was not an indicator of fluid sexuality but of politeness. It wasn't so much a preference for one kind of body over another so much as the idea that to say no to some people was impolite and to say yes to some others was just as impolite. It was a wholly different way of navigating sex. It took me some time to learn it. It took me some time to notice, for instance, that when sex broke out in the unpaired's yurt, never once did I land next to Halaavi.

First it made me curious, and then it began to nag at me, and of course the rest picked up on my anxieties, and of course they gave me a wide berth. Halaavi brought it up, not me. I sat on the edge of camp, distracted, as annoyed that I'd sowed chaos with the rest as I was about this peculiar pattern. Halaavi came and sat next to me. "Vrala Ariah," ve said. "You are troubled."

"Yes."

"Would you tell me why?"

I didn't want to. Such frank discussions of sex still embarrassed me. They embarrass me even now. I blushed, and I stammered, and Halaavi looked on in amusement. "I never wind up with you," I managed, finally, to get out. "Anyone but you."

"I'm right here. We're together now."

"No. Well, yes, we are, but that…no, I mean in there. In the yurt."

"We share the yurt."

"No! I mean—ah, those nights, the…when the fire breaks out, I lay in the ashes with everyone but you."

"Oh." I stared hard at vim, willing vim to answer me, but ve looked off thoughtfully at the grass. Halaavi was quiet for a long time. Halaavi had a way with quietness, a consonance with it. "I thought you were fluent in Droma," ve said.

"I am."

Ve cracked a smile. "You're not." Ve looked at me, head cocked slightly to one side. "This is a simpler thing with us, you know. Had you been gold on the outside, too, we wouldn't need to talk about it. You'd understand, and we'd land in a yurt. I forget, sometimes, how much you don't know. I had wondered why it was taking so long, but it's not a thing to rush."

"What isn't a thing to rush?"

"A shared skin." *Triloshilai,* ve said. About the two of us.

"You think we're a pair?" I asked.

"You think we're not?" Halaavi said. Ve said it with humor, like it was a foregone conclusion. Which, perhaps, it was.

"How does this work, exactly?"

"It doesn't work, it just is. It is a fact. A stability. We just…live together, in rhythm. In balance." Halaavi felt my confusion. "Pairs usually don't have sex, Ariah. It's not done."

"Why not?"

"Sex is chaos, yes? No balance there. The body wants what it wants, and the heart needs what it needs, and rarely the two come together for long. The unpaired, they bring the chaos, and the paired, they bring the harmony, and together the clan stays in balance."

I tried to understand it, but it made no sense. I thought of Sorcha, and Shayat, and how sex and love with them were all bound up together. In the City, in Rabatha, in Alamadour, desires buffeted me one way or another. Thickets of them, mazes of them, all negotiated or hidden, or displayed like fancy plumage. A constant shifting dance of them. I hadn't noticed that in the clan there was none of that. Sex happened when it happened, and little importance or attention was paid to it. The way I was troubled by what I saw as Halaavi's rejection of me was utterly foreign to them. Ve was right: I was not as fluent in Droma as I thought I was. I didn't understand it, but Halaavi and I set up a yurt together anyway. The clan brought us blankets, a firestone, lanterns—gifts like we'd wedded. We slept together, naked and chaste, on a single pallet. The yurt was nestled in the heart of the camp, and children drifted in and out, sometimes piling into bed with us, and sometimes dragging their own bedrolls into the yurt.

I'd missed the feel of another's body next to mine in the night. I'd missed the whispered conversations as one drifted off to sleep. I'd missed the patter of children. Ve didn't want me, and that was all right. There was the unpaired's yurt for that. It didn't occur to vim to want me, just to love me, and it did not take much time before I forgot to want vim.

CHAPTER 35

IT WAS NEARLY six years before I saw anyone but a member of the Avolayla clan. In that time, the clan changed: children were born to the Vralas and some of the oldest Idoks died. Sometimes Halaavi and I slept with babies and little children between us, and sometimes we sat through the night with the bodies of the dead. With every one of these rituals, I was woven a little tighter into the clan. My universe shrank to this single clan out in the wilds, but time enough passed that my universe expanded again. Clan meetings out in the vastness of the eastern grasslands is a rare thing, avoided because of the mechanics of pasture and the way an unknown person can disrupt an entire clan's mood. But there are times when a clan meeting makes sense. When there are goods to trade, or when the unpaired grow restless and forlorn. When they need news. It had been at least ten years since the Avolayla had had outside contact, and the Idoks suggested it was time to seek another clan out. Decisions are slow and careful among the Droma; it took months for the other generations in the clan to agree or disagree with the Idoks' suggestion. Kishva and I spent a lot of nights facilitating discussion amongst the Vralas. Decisions are unhurried; discussion is circuitous. No direct suggestions are made, only stories that imply one view over another. Kishva and I were there to make sure everyone was heard, and that those who had stirrings of doubt were pushed to speak. It was exhausting. I found the inefficiency of it maddening. In the Empire, where we have so little control over our own lives, we are not used to so much drawn-out participatory consideration. Eventually, the clan reached consensus. We decided to seek out the Shallai.

The runners spent weeks consulting maps. There was no rush to get to the Shallai, no urgency. It was a decision of patient pragmatism, not of any particular need. The runners mapped out a route, settlement areas, that brought us on a slow arc towards where we thought the Shallai might be. The runners recruited a few promising Rishnallas, the batch of siblings just reaching maturity. If we were tracking another clan, Halaavi explained to me, we would need more runners. We struck camp, moved west again into the familiar westlands as spring brought the grass, green and tall, once more. The Vrala runners trained the Rishnallas. The retired Idok runners drilled them when the Vrala runners went scouting. Slowly, the young Rishnallas developed stamina and grace and grew to know the limits of their own bodies. When we struck camp again as spring turned to summer, and the land dried out and the rivers withered, the Rishnallas were ready. We moved south instead of farther west this time. The livestock seemed perturbed at the unfamiliar foothills and the slightly different variant of grass that blanketed the land. It turns reddish instead of pure gold there, a sort of copper. The runners sent the Rishnalla recruits further south and west on forays, looking for tracks of the Shallai. They looked for the telltale remnants of old floorwork and kept an eye on the height and quality of the grass. You have to be careful when you change a clan route, especially if it's to find another clan: the other clan has livestock, too, and you run the risk of winding up in places where the pasture is already bald. Starved livestock is death for a Droma clan.

We Avolayla moved with a patient sense of purpose, moving from one settling place to another as the land and weather shifted us to and fro. The runners ran, the weavers wove, the herders cajoled the goats along. Children grew, and some old folks died. Kishva and I kept an eye on the Vralas, feeling them out and making sure we stayed in harmony. One of the Rishnalla, a lanky youth named Raiwari who Idok Sikelat was trying to train as a healer, found a wounded kestrel in the chicken pen. Ve used the few skills Sikelat managed to teach vim to nurse it back to health, and the bird stayed with us, circling and circling the camp day after day. Sikelat frowned and sighed, hemmed and hawed to the point that the rest of us left vim alone, and then declared that Raiwari had a way with animals but not with elves. But a way with animals is still useful to the clan.

"Maybe," Sikelat said at dinner one night, "if we find the Shallai, they'll have a spare healer we can switch for." Raiwari's kestrel cawed in response.

The runners found remnants of a Shallai camp while they were scouting for a good autumn settlement. It was an old camp, they said. New grass broke through the rotting floorwork, but what could be seen showed the coiled grass snakes of the Shallai clan. Idok Nardu, the oldest and most experienced runner in the clan, had the runners lead vim to the abandoned camp. It took nearly a week for Nardu to get there and back: ve was old; ve walked with a pronounced limp. Sikelat said all those years of running destroyed Nardu's knees. But still, when it came to cartography and land reading, there was no one better among the Avolayla than Nardu. Ve still had a runner's mind. When Nardu returned, ve and the runners called a meeting in the long house. "The camp's been dead four, five walks," Nardu said. Ve had a rasping voice, dry as gold grass in the droughts. "We found rich dirt and bones where dead had been buried. Many dead, but only elves. No livestock."

"Dead how?" Sikelat asked.

Nardu shrugged. "Disease? Famine? Slavers? Who can tell. The land's taken them. The Shallai likely limped off to nurse their wounds, but they did it too long ago for us to follow. There was a time once, when I was young and still an unpaired in the Trilvanda clan, that we Trilvanda thought to find another clan. We found only a few left—maybe twenty. Pirates, you know. This clan had ventured too far south and the pirates took so many. We found these twenty survivors, scarred people, people who thrummed with fear and worry. Who could not sleep nights. We found them, and land save us, we braved the chaos bred in their souls. We took them in. Some stayed with us, and some left in the night, left to wander the land alone and clanless."

Some nodded. Some frowned. Kishva caught my eye from across the house and glanced at Shinnani, who was dark and distracted. I gestured at Moura, a Vrala calmer, to sit next to vim. Moura sidled up close, shoulder to shoulder, and Shinnani grew harmonious again.

Murmurs rippled through the clan. "Such a story," someone said.

"Clans come and go," said another.

Halaavi cleared vis throat. "When I was young and still wandered with the Yavinaha, we saw many things. It is a stranger life than we live, the wanderings of the Yavinaha. No livestock, you know. With no yaks, no goats, you get rooted to the land. Pasture does not matter so much. Think on it, a life where pasture does not matter so much. The Yavinaha wander, but their wanderings are dictated by the ebb and flow of clan routes, and not the growth of grass. The Yavinaha wanderers are at the mercy of the clans they find. No milk without kindness; no furs without generosity. The Avolayla found a Yavinaha band, and they saw in that band a child: ragged, hungry, and calm. And the Avolayla took me in. That Yavinaha band still wanders, but not to the Avolayla."

The clan was quiet for some time. A Rishnalla youth fidgeted. "I am just a goatherd, and I am young. Very young. And boring, so you may ask me to stop telling this story anytime you want. I am sure an Idok has a much more interesting story." Ve cleared vis throat and seemed to run out of steam. A Vrala next to vim patted vis back and gave vim an encouraging nod. The Rishnalla goatherd continued. "I am a goatherd. I've been one not so long as many of you, but long enough to have this story. Some of you might remember when this happened. There was a time a few walks before this one where the rainy season came hard and vengeful. Storms came up suddenly; the land was chaos and danger. It was hard to find good pasture; the rains lingered too long in the soil, and the grass rotted on its stalks. Some of the goats got sick. It was a hard time, and it got harder. A day came where we found decent pasture for the goats and sent them out. I and three others took our herd to pasture. A storm came. A terrible storm. The rain came down in sheets, dark sheets, like night fell early. We drove the herd back towards camp, but one of us counted them and saw we'd lost a few, which was bad since we'd already lost so many to bad pastures. Two of my comrades went off to find them. I and Vrala Savanli drove the goats we had back to camp. The rain eventually stopped, but our comrades didn't come back. At first we thought they'd taken shelter to ride out the storm, but a day passed, and then another, and it was clear something had happened. The runners found them. They'd been washed up in a flood. The runners said their bodies were smashed, splintered. A violent thing, the runners said. All because they could not bear to lose three or four half-dead goats."

The clan chewed over this story. The hour was late, and we dispersed to our yurts. The decision spread slowly, like a disease, from one person to another. No one made a proclamation; no formal decision was made. The runners simply returned to their maps one day, first to see if the Shallai might have crossed paths with some other clan in the region, and then to map a route to connect with the Allunga who roamed in particularly good pasture land northwest of where we were. No one spoke of the Shallai again.

* * *

We crossed paths with the Allunga in high summer. We found them in a region of the grasslands the Droma know as the Slide, a plain that slopes gently downward over miles and miles. Unnamed streams split from the Vanna River to the north and thread through the basin. Rich grass grows on the Slide, and fresh water is abundant even in the dry summer months. There is, on the Slide, enough to pasture livestock from more than one clan, and its consistent richness meant it was likely the Allunga returned there every summer.

We saw their livestock first. Their yaks, like ours, had already shed their downy undercoat. They are sleek animals in the summer, not the shaggy shambling creatures they are in the winter. The Allunga yaks were larger than ours and darker. Not so different, but different enough to the practiced eye. Our runners ran out to meet the Allunga herders, singing walking songs bred by things Halaavi had said to the clan when we first reached the Slide. Halaavi was deeply taken with that part of the land. Ve spoke of harmony and cycles, of the lack of time there. I felt it, what Halaavi spoke of. It felt to me like a shift in the magic. The Slide was a place where the land magic was smooth and pristine, a place where the magic blended with the abundance of the mundane parts of the land instead of fighting with it.

The runners ran, and their voices slipped from earshot. Three days later, the runners returned singing an Allunga running song with Allunga runners in tow. The Allunga runners wore their hair cropped close to their scalps and sported beaded bracelets and anklets made of painted yak bones, which clattered when they moved. They ran into camp swathed in a slight sheen of sweat, grinning, and our runners led them up to our fire tent for food and drink. Avolayla children crowded around them, fingering the beads, asking questions. The Allunga were perfectly at ease until they spotted me. One froze, blinking, ash-faced. Another leapt to vis feet and demanded explanations. Ve called me a settler, a slaver, things I had not been called in years. Halaavi ran over and tried to explain, but the Allunga would not listen until an Idok calmer brought the mood back down.

Kishva came and stood next to me, arms crossed. "Nardu said this might happen."

"Said what might happen?"

Kishva glanced at me. "You might happen, Vrala Ariah. We know you. We trust you. But all they see is someone from the west."

I sighed and pulled my hair over one shoulder. It was a hot day, and I was naked to the waist. My hair by then hung almost to the waistband of my pants, a smooth sheet of white that glinted in the bright summer sunlight. Kishva ran a hand through it. Kishva loved my hair, loved the smoothness of it. I cracked a smile, felt what ve wanted, and knew we'd meet in the unpaired's yurt that night. I had, the second before, wished I looked as Droma as I felt. When Kishva looked at me like that, I didn't mind my Semadran body so much. "What should I do?"

"Nothing," Kishva said. "Know that you've disrupted the harmony a little, but you should just keep doing what you do. Weave. Mind the children. Stick close to Laavi. They'll come around."

"What if they don't?"

Kishva shrugged. "Time is endless. We'll cross with another clan. Just don't startle them. You know, like when we send the little ones to learn the herds."

I laughed. "Kishva, the Allunga are not goats."

"Goats, elves, there's not much difference if you ask me," ve said, still playing with the ends of my hair. Kishva smiled at me and left me to weave on my own while the Allunga stared at me in suspicion. It had been a long time since I'd been the cause of discord. I'd forgotten how to build walls. I found that out when I tried to shield myself from their tempers and worries and couldn't. I practiced Yavinaha meditation to let their emotions pass over me. I had a small measure of success with it. The Allunga left that night with no promise to return. I could not help but feel guilty, though no one seemed to care much, and then I couldn't help but feel guilty for feeling guilty. Kishva did, at least, take my mind off of it when dark fell.

As I have said before, the Droma do not rush into decisions. There was no reason for us to resettle until we needed to, and there was enough grass to sustain both herds. The proximity to the Allunga made life a little more difficult for our herders, who had to make sure they were herding just our livestock and that they had not inadvertently stolen any goats or yaks or antelope from the Allunga, but otherwise there was not much for us to do but wait. Our patience did, eventually, pay off: it took a few weeks, but the Allunga discussed it and traded stories and thought on it and came to the conclusion that I was not a threat. One morning just as high summer peaked and the days began to cool, young Allunga runners clattered into our camp. They were greeted warmly, and they returned the warmth. We fed them, and they told stories to the children, and the unpaired Rishnallas welcomed them into their yurt for the night. At dinner, one of the runners came and sat next to me. Ve cleared vis throat, and conversation died around the table. "Avolayla Vrala Ariah," ve said, "our clan requests your presence in our camp."

I stole a glance at Halaavi. Laavi nodded at me. "I am glad to accept. May I ask why?"

The Allunga runner smiled and ran a hand over vis shorn scalp. "Well, some of us are curious. Some of us are afraid and don't want to be. But we ask your presence because we may have news for you."

"For me?"

"Maybe. We'll find out when you come back with us." Halaavi drifted over. The Allunga runner pointed at us each in turn. "Shared skin?"

"Yes," I said.

"Ve is welcome, too, of course," the Allunga runner said.

"When do we leave?" Halaavi asked.

The runner shrugged and ate a bit of goat cheese. "Tomorrow, the day after. Whenever seems a good time. Can you run?"

"Yes," Halaavi said.

"No," I said. Halaavi glanced over at me and laughed.

The Allunga runner shrugged. "We can go slow. Time is endless."

We left the Avolayla camp two days later just before dawn. The Allunga runners went slowly for me; I walked the entire way. The Allunga runners were a rowdy, young, half-grown bunch. They ran around us while Halaavi and I walked. They struck off on odd little forays, tackled and wrestled each other in the high grass. One challenged Halaavi to a race, and Halaavi grinned and sprinted off. The Allunga won, but not by as wide a margin as ve expected. Halaavi earned the grudging respect of the Allunga runners, and some of that respect bled over to me by association.

The Allunga clan was nearly twice as big as the Avolayla. The old of the Allunga were older, the babies more numerous. The clan's route was a good one, and their herds were large. They stayed in the eastern interior, far away from slavers. Halaavi sang one of vis walking songs as we approached camp. The runners ran ahead. Brown faces peeked out of yurts and around the sheltered sides of the cooking tents. A clutch of elves a generation older than myself and Halaavi—the Nalunghai—snapped to attention. Some of the Allunga sang back to Halaavi. Others stared at me. That clutch of four Nalunghai were the only ones to approach us. The person leading the way was tall and sharp-jawed. Ve had skin like polished wood and an untamed fierceness around the eyes. "Avolayla Vrala Ariah."

"Yes?" Laavi's walking song petered out. The Allunga drank in the silence.

"I am Allunga Nalunghai Koro."

Halaavi looked over. "Koro the Echo?" Koro nodded. Laavi frowned slightly. "You are the one with news for Ariah?"

"I am."

"Are you sure this is news for me?" I asked. I didn't want it to be. I wanted it to be a mistake. Who would have news for me but the Exalted's Army? Who besides the Butcher of the East was out looking for me? I felt my fear rise and rise and overflow, pouring out of me and into Halaavi and the nearby Allunga. I had visions of the Avolayla in chains and their livestock slaughtered and left rotting on the plains, all because they'd had the kindness to take in a stray.

"It may not be for you," Koro said, "but we have not yet met another this news might belong to. You will know, once you hear it, if this is news for you or not. You must be hungry. Are you thirsty?"

"I..." I stole a glance at Halaavi. "If you would not mind, I would like to hear the news first."

Koro blinked at me in surprise but gestured for me to follow vim. Ve led Halaavi and I to vis yurt. Strings of painted beads hung on the door and clacked when ve let us in. Ve left the door open for light, but it was cool in the yurt. Koro rifled through first one bag, then another, before ve found what ve was looking for. Ve pulled out a folded slip of paper. The Droma, who have no written language beside what I stole and transliterated into Semadran characters, have little use for paper. Whatever they want to set down for future generations is woven in a lefta, knotted in a door string, or embroidered on the skins of a yurt. They depict, they don't write—and they certainly don't depict with something as flimsy as paper. Koro held the paper in vis hands and looked over at me. "We were far west when we got this. It was very strange. We were far enough west that we could smell the settler's air. That drought two or three walkings back, did you Avolayla feel it? Yes? That's the one that pushed us west. We followed the Vanna River, which was narrow as a grass snake, because we were afraid that our fall pasture was dead and dry. We have a big herd, you know, we need a lot of pasture. And the westlands, there is much pasture there. We fled the famine into slavers' lands." Koro frowned and turned the paper in vis hands. "Anyway, there was a day a solitary settler rode out to us. The settler didn't know the land, didn't see us close in until it was too late. We roped vis horse and brought it down. The settler ran. That settler could run like a scout, even in settler clothes, even in high, dry grass. The settler ran, and the settler spoke Droma. Not much; not well. Just a string of words, but not words a slaver would know. *Triloshilai, fliyya.*" Shared skin, friend. "I felt it before the others. I was out running, training some of the young ones. I felt how the settler wanted to communicate. I was the one who approached vim. I sang a walking song, and the settler sang back. Not a walking song, not a Droma song, but ve sang back."

Koro came and sat before me at the mouth of the tent. Both ve and I stared down at the paper in vis hands. "I was able to echo because of the song. 'Have you come to take us?' I asked. 'No, I've come to find someone,' ve said. 'Who is out here in the grass for you to find?' I asked vim. Ve went dark, troubled. I'm an echo, not an empath, but even I could feel it without amplification. 'My roots,' ve said. 'My roots, ve is out here.' The settler asked if I'd seen a silver elf, not a slaver. A person who ran east, a person with silver skin and white hair and green eyes. Thin, with large hands. Black birthmark on the ribs."

My breath came shallow. Halaavi sat up tall, alert, like a rabbit a half-second before it bolts. "Did the settler you spoke to—did this person, did ve have red hair?" Koro nodded. "Dark skin?" Koro nodded again. "You say you found vim far west?"

Koro nodded once more. Ve handed me the slip of paper. "The settler said if I found this person, this green-eyed silver elf, to give vim this." Koro tapped the paper, nodded to Halaavi, and left us there in the borrowed privacy of vis yurt.

My hands trembled as I unfolded the paper. The creases were worn through in places; the paper had gone from stiff and structured to soft and cloth-like. The note had been written in pencil, which the years had smudged and worn away. I held the letter up to the light.

I love you. We keep on look out. Me and Shayat going

southways.

"What does it say?" Halaavi asked.

"My…my people are looking for me. Laavi, they're looking for me." I read and reread the note three or four times in quick succession. I stopped when tears slipped down onto the fragile paper. I hadn't realized I was crying, but I was not ashamed by it. Perhaps for the first time in my life, I was not ashamed by it. I folded the paper and tucked it in my lefta. I looked over at Halaavi. Ve took my face in vis hands, careful, worried, asking a thousand questions with a glance. "With you I have a shared skin. I have a…a shared heart with two others. And, Laavi, they're looking for me. All these years and they're looking. Together! Together, they're looking for me! I have to go south!"

Halaavi's grip on me tightened. Vis mouth turned to a hard line. "South?"

I held onto vis forearms and nodded. "Yes. South. I have to go south."

"How far south?"

"I don't know."

"What do you mean, shared heart?"

"Like *triloshilai,* but with sex."

Laavi pulled back; vis hands dropped to my shoulders. "Three *triloshilai?*"

"Yes. Sort of." I wiped the tears off my cheeks with the back of my hand. "I thought I'd lost them. I thought I'd lost them forever. But they're looking."

Halaavi gently coaxed me upright, and gently coaxed me

to a shady spot in the shadow of a cook tent. Ve brought me stew and water and nudged me into eating it. But ve was dark and distracted, and I could not bring myself to care.

CHAPTER 36

GOODS WERE TRADED back and forth between the Avolayla and the Allunga. Some of our unpaired drifted over to the other clan, and some of their unpaired drifted over to us. The mood in the clan—both clans—was buoyant, hopeful. Eventually, neither camp was really Avolayla or Allunga, but some thorough mix of both. All of us Avolayla were siblings, but the Allunga were our cousins. Family is family; among the Droma, family, like time, is endless. They traded stories, lore, news of other clans. Sikelat got a very young healer for training. But fall crept up, and in fall even the abundance of the Slide grows too thin to support two clans' herds. Soon enough, it was time for the clans to part.

The Avolayla were to head east, into the familiar scrubby steppes. The Allunga's route took them south. Halaavi and I didn't discuss it. I didn't discuss it with anyone. No one was surprised when I spent more and more time in the Allunga camp. Halaavi followed me over, and on the day the Allunga broke down their yurts, Nalunghai Koro advocated for us. We became Allunga Boonu Ariah and Allunga Boonu Halaavi. There is always room for those with skills.

The Allunga are a big clan, and harmony is harder to keep the more people you have around. Before we joined, they had three Yavinaha wanderers, one in each of the three oldest sibling groups. Halaavi made a fourth. The Yavinaha wanderers kept council together, not in any official way, but when they spoke together, they were awarded authority. They were together most of the time; Halaavi was the only one of them who had paired. The rest were oddly isolate. They welcomed Halaavi. Halaavi came back from conversations with them a little dazed. "It brings back my childhood," ve said one night as we lay together. "We wanderers, we're a different breed than the clansfolk. Just a little different, not so different you notice if there's just one of us. But with four of us...you can see it plain." And ve was right: the Yavinaha kept their elaborate, unofficial council, and the Allunga waited to do anything until they had Yavinaha guidance. Like the Avolayla, they built consensus slowly, inch by creeping inch, but it was a more directed thing. The Allunga had a clearer sense of hierarchy, and the Yavinaha were at the top. Halaavi very quickly became the voice of the Yavinaha. The other wanderers saw something in vim. The Avolayla had seen it, too, I think, but with less clarity. The Yavinaha wanderers of the Allunga clan regarded Halaavi with a sort of reverence I had not realized the Droma were capable of. One night, at dinner, I happened to wind up next to a Nalunghai wanderer. It was deep winter, and some of the antelope were struggling. A group of emergent leaders were trading stories, circling around and around the question of whether to cull the herd. Each time one told a story, everyone in the group looked at Halaavi. The Nalunghai wanderer pointed at Laavi. "Your pair, ve is only half elf. Halaavi is one with the land; ve feels its beating heart, its pulsing blood. I am a wanderer, yes, but Halaavi is a voice. Rare as a flower in winter." The wanderer took a long look at me. "Someone so Droma, and ve paired with you, Boonu Ariah. The world twists like a grass snake."

"You say what Laavi does is rare?"

"Oh, yes."

"Then it's not so strange we've paired. I know a thing or two about gifts others don't understand. I know what it is to be odd. I know what it is to want someone who does not understand that you're odd."

The Nalunghai wanderer made a noncommittal noise, half-snort, half-laugh, and glanced me over. Ve raised vis eyebrows and shrugged. Let the world twist, vis shoulders said. Let it twist into knots only to unwind again.

I say all this to say Laavi was happy with the Allunga. Ve was happy with the Allunga, but there was a seed of chaos in our yurt. We were all right, I don't mean to say we weren't. Halaavi came with me to the Allunga of vis own accord, and I was grateful for that. The love was still there, the easy intimacy always was there, but there was a sadness in vim that neither of us could ignore. Ve asked me many times what Sorcha was to me, what Shayat was to me, what they were together to me. I explained it as best I could, but Laavi could not quite understand. To vim, skin did not stretch that far. To vim, the only way it made sense was if I split myself apart, shredded my

skin to ribbons, and handed out the bloody pieces. It nagged at vim, and it nagged at me that I could give vim no comfort, but Laavi was Yavinaha, and Laavi had long ago perfected a submission to the present moment, and Laavi did not want to prematurely confront something with that much chaos wound up inside it. And I, I was a coward. There is no other word for it, no better way to explain it. I knew what would happen, and I drank Laavi in anyway, held vim close, shared a bed and a life like the days weren't limited. There were nights as we traveled farther and farther south when I listened to vim sleep and thought of Liro. I thought of how Liro took Dirva in, coaxed him back to the living, and I remembered that desperate pain he carried across borders when Dirva left. At the time I'd thought Dirva heartless, callous. I knew I'd never do that to anyone. But night after night I lay there with Laavi, doing it to vim.

* * *

The Allunga took us far south, but not far enough. *Southways*, Sorcha had written. For him, for Shayat and myself, the only thing that could mean was all the way south, to the southern coasts and beyond to the Pirate Isles. The Allunga was a large enough clan to be brave, but certainly too large to be stupid. They took us south, and lingered long enough to pass me off to the Kivvni before they turned north to safer plains again. The Kivvni were a small, spare clan, hard-eyed and haunted, a group of people who seemed to only find harmony in grave suspicion. They didn't want to meet with the Allunga at first.

They were a small clan pushed farther and farther south because the larger clans needed more pasture for their larger herds. It wasn't malevolent or forced, but the Kivvni had learned to be as wary of other Droma as they were of everyone else.

When the Kivvni crossed paths with the Allunga, the Kivvni sent many of their youths and children over to the other clan. It was a bleak thing. They accepted no one in return; the flow of people from clan to clan was unidirectional. "This clan is dying," Halaavi said. A glance at the Kivvni camp showed it was true: the yurts were threadbare and paltry. There were no chickens, and the goats were thin. They had more yaks than they could herd effectively, and the lactating yaks cried mournfully when the Kivvni could not manage to milk them all. The Kivvni themselves were gaunt and underfed. A dark knot of mistrust was woven deep in them, each and every one, to the point that scarcity and stress and bad luck made them mistrust each other. They knew the Kivvni were done for. They passed off the children to better clans and resigned themselves to hard, bitter lives. This was a clan pushed to the frayed edges of the Droma world. But they were going south. It was not by choice: every turning of the seasons they lost more livestock to the desolate southern stretches near the coast. They went south because they had to. The other clans shoved them out, shoved them down, until at last only the southern stretches were left. When I asked if they were going south, a Kivvni person leaned on vis walking stick and laughed. Ve was a herder, but then again, all the Kivvni were herders. There were not enough people in the clan to differentiate the work. Ve laughed a hard laugh and nodded. "Yes, Allunga settler, we go south."

"Far south?" asked Halaavi.

"We go so far south the rivers turn brackish." Halaavi frowned at that. The Kivvni person's chin jutted up. "We go so far south I can speak patois. And I am no echo."

Halaavi and I were not offered a place to sleep at the Kivvni camp, and we didn't ask for one. We trudged back to the Allunga camp, which was only there that far south, that far into the turning, for me. That night, neither of us got any sleep. Laavi lit a fire in the firestone and sat next to me. I draped an arm around vis naked waist, and ve leaned vis cheek against my shoulder. We watched the dancing flames together. We sat in silence for a very long time. I felt hollowed out, like half a man. Finally, Laavi spoke. "I can't. I can't join the Kivvni."

I had known it was coming, this gentle refusal, but it still hurt. Sometimes, I think, it hurts more when you know an injury is coming than when it sneaks up on you. I cried and tried to hide it. Like a fool, I tried to hide it. "Laavi, I..." But I found nothing to say. What was I going to do, ask vim to come with me? Risk capture by pirates? Demand that if ve was somehow not captured, but instead by some miracle allowed to accompany me to whatever pirate port Sorcha and Shayat had landed in, that ve live a settled life in a settled town where ve would be confronted by the slavery of vis cousins day after day? Time is endless; this would be nothing but an endless torture.

The loss of Halaavi was a thing that swallowed me

whole. It was a black thing, a terrible hungry thing. I tried again to speak. "Laavi, right now, in this moment, I wish I'd never gotten that note."

"But you did get it." Ve pulled vimself upright and looked at me. "And that's all right. That is…that's all right. I am happy for you."

I dropped my face into my hands. "I'm sorry, Laavi."

"I am, too. I keep trying to let the moment pass, to slip deep into the land, but it's hard. It will get easy again, I know, but for now it's hard." Laavi laughed. "Maybe I should go with the Kivvni. I am in their harmony right now."

"I'm sorry."

Ve put a hand on my back. "Ariah. Vrala Ariah. You know, Kishva had things to say to me about the pairing. 'Laavi, always a risk? Of everyone, you are drawn to vim, who has one foot here and one foot there? What happens if ve ends up with both feet there?' And I said, 'What happens if ve ends up with both feet here?' and Kishva said to me 'Laavi, if ve was one to end up with both feet here, you would not be drawn over.' And you know Kishva. Kishva is always right."

"What are you saying? You knew this was going to happen?" Laavi stared into the fire. "That's absurd! I…Laavi, I would not have paired with you if I thought I would ever leave. I swear. Mercy, I wish…I wish there was a way to live two lives at once."

"I wish there were no slavers. I wish there was no winter, only spring. I wish you could live two lives, too."

"I'm sorry."

Laavi tucked vis face back against my shoulder and sighed. "Me, too. I will carry you with me when you go. I'll tell others things you have said."

"No one will listen. You'll lose your reputation. I've never said anything worth repeating."

Laavi smiled. "No," ve said. "I guess you haven't. I guess I'll just tell myself things you've said. Ariah, I hope you remember things I've said. Will you?"

I held vim close, wrapped up tight against me, my face in vis hair. I held vim for a long time while the obstinate fire cracked and popped and would not die. "I have remembered things you said long before I ever met you. Yes, I will remember. I'll remember every single word."

CHAPTER 37

THE KIVVNI DID not like me much, but they were short-handed, so they accepted me anyway. I was put to work as soon as I stepped into their camp. I learned to herd goats, which is not as easy as one would think. I milked yaks until my knuckles ached. Life with the Kivvni was different from with the Avolayla or the Allunga. The clan had around fifty people in it, the youngest of whom was around forty. They did not bother to give me a sibling name because there were only six or so others my age. There were a handful of pairs, but most were unpaired, and likely waiting until the clan dissolved for good before looking for a pair in earnest. There was more work than could get done, which led alternately to days of frenzied exertion followed by dull, meandering days where nothing seemed to happen.

I could see the Kivvni had been a flourishing, grand clan long ago. Some of their older yurt skins bore intricate, beautiful needlework. Some of the firestones were large and made of stone from the far northeast. I asked a Kivvni person about it once. We sat side-by-side milking an endless stream of yaks. Ve was a few years younger than me, and ve shrugged when I asked. "We've always been this way ever since I can remember. Bad luck. This clan is only bad luck, settler. We had good luck once, but all luck turns just like the seasons."

The Kivvni moved camps frequently. The pasture in the south is thin, and it drives you to keep moving. It felt like we only had days between setting up our yurts and tearing them down again. The further south we went, the faster the herds ate what little pasture there was. The soil grew sandy and thin. The water did, indeed, turn brackish. Near the southern coasts, a finger of the Mother Desert slides along the far edge of the grasslands. I had thought that they would take me to the edge of the desert and no farther, but the Kivvni pressed on, farther and farther south, and they moved then with a sense of strange purpose. We walked with camp strapped to our thin yaks for several days, and then we hit a pirate outpost.

Buildings loomed large and stagnant. I had not been in a place with such steadfast permanence since I'd escaped the Ma-Halad barracks over seven years before. I thought it was a mistake; I thought we'd slink back into the dunes and try somewhere else. "There's a town up ahead," I said.

"Yes, that's Zaghir," the person next to me said. "We have an arrangement with the settlers there."

"What? What do you mean you have an arrangement?"

"We have an arrangement," ve said, and then ve picked up vis pace and left me behind. That night, we set up our yurts just a few feet away from the gates of Zaghir. The next morning, the pirates manning the watchtowers let us in. The gates were set on cables and pulleys; shirtless pirates at the eastern watchtower pulled a rope, and the gates swung open like the jaws of some great vicious animal. The Kivvni sang no walking song when we marched through the gate. The silence was damning. Pirates milled around us, leaning on the walls of buildings. Some approached the Kivvni and laid out prices for yak butter, woven goods, and what few other things we had to offer. I watched the back and forth in what passed for Zaghir's market with a sick fascination. Everything seemed wrong. The other Kivvni felt it, knew it, and ignored me.

We bartered our goods, and one of the Kivvni bartered vimself. A young person, no older than fifty, who had already seen too much death and lived too hard a life, bartered with the pirates for a spot as crew on a ship. Apari was a dark soul, cynicism bred right to vis marrow. The clan breathed a callous sigh of relief when the deal was struck. Ve did not return to the yurts that night. "At least ve isn't cargo," someone said to me.

"How is this any better? Ve'll be separated from the land, from you, from the other clans."

"There are Droma in the ports and on the ships. I am not Yavinaha. Well, I am, and I'm not," ve said. "I am Yavinaha here, but were I to join a ship I'd let that go. It wouldn't make any sense out there on the water. I think sometimes the interior clans get confused. I think sometimes they think you're not Droma if you're not following Yavinaha. Apari is Droma. Apari will always be Droma. What that means out there on the water?" Ve shrugged. "Apari will find out."

"You trust them? The pirates? You trust them not to take Apari as a slave?"

"They gave vim a neck tattoo. Neck for crew, wrist for cargo." I frowned, unconvinced this meant anything at all. Ve let out a mocking laugh. "Settler Ariah, you are strange. You worry so much for Apari, but you're the one seeking out the pirates. You wanted to go to the southern reaches? This is life in the southern reaches."

Ve was right. I had asked to come here. I knew finding Sorcha and Shayat meant dealing with pirates on their terms and in their land. The Kivvni left, and when they did, they left without me. They gave me a yurt and two yaks, each with its own finely made, very old saddle. I struck up uneasy friendships with some of the pirates—all of them fleet agents, exiled here to this forgotten outpost for one reason or another. One of them slept with his captain's tether. One of them sold out a fleet, only to be dumped in Zaghir by the fleet he'd sold them out to. They were a weathered bunch, but not particularly bitter. It was quiet in Zaghir, and safe, which counts for a lot for those in the life. It just wasn't profitable there. Once you were in, there was no way out.

Most of the pirates stuck in Zaghir were Chalir. Some were half-Qin, half-Chalir, and a few were nahsiyya with blood so thoroughly mixed you could only make guesses as to parentage. All of them played djah, and I learned the patois by playing it with them. For hours and hours in the hot desert sun we played djah. At heart, they were gamblers, but we were all so poor that we had nothing to gamble with. We played for pebbles and buttons. I was wary at first, but I got to know them quickly. I wouldn't say I trusted any of them, but there were a few who I liked, and who seemed to like me. One man, Fahmi, was a fleet agent for the Sayiff. He was Chalir by birth, but he'd long ago abandoned the book, and he sat before me in just a shirt and trousers. He'd been forced into factory work in Shangri before he was full-grown. He had worked with Semadrans there, and he made me for a shaper the second or third time we spoke. When we played djah together, he tried to recruit me. "There's always a place on a ship for a shaper," he said.

"I don't want a place on a ship," I said.

"Then why are you here? Zaghir is a piss pot. There's nothing here but a bunch of vultures looking for recruits."

And it seemed as good a time as any to ask about Sorcha. That's what I was there for. "I'm looking for someone. He looks Semadran, but he has red hair. Green eyes. I know he came south, and he might have joined..."

Fahmi looked up from his cards. "Plays a violin? His Qin is shit?"

"You know him?" My heart leapt into my throat.

Fahmi slapped down his cards and took the hand. I lost three buttons. "Sorcha. Yes, I know him. Runs with the, uh..." Fahmi leaned back and yelled to another pirate. "Hey! Hey, Maghrib, what fleet does the tink-mix with the fiddle run with?"

"The Fiddler? Oh, he..." The other pirate snapped in triumph: "Nakash! Yeah, he sails with the tink fleet. Nakash. Is that the one he's looking for? Fits the description."

Fahmi shrugged. "Might be. Our silver Droma here says

he's looking for the Fiddler. Small world, eh?"

"It's Zaghir," Maghrib said. "Everything here is small."

"Eh, speak for yourself," Fahmi said. Ripples of laughter ran through the nearby djah players. Fahmi dealt me another hand. "There you go. Nakash. I tell you, the Nakash runner must like him. He's not been in the life long, and he's already an agent with a leash long enough that he can come trawling out this far looking for you."

"Everyone always likes Sorcha. You like him; I can tell."

"I do. You know, I do. Always brings me a crate of good rum when he comes by."

"How often does he come to Zaghir?"

Fahmi shrugged. "Oh, you never can tell. Demands of the fleet, you know? Or, I guess you wouldn't know. Not yet, anyway. You run with Sorcha, and you're bound to wind up in a fleet one way or another." The thought sat heavy in me and not at all well. Fahmi laughed and played a card. "Oh, my silver nomad, the life is just a life. Look, you did low work back west, right?"

"I did. Wool factory."

"Unless you're cargo or prone to seasickness, you'll get nothing that bad in the life."

* * *

There was nothing to do but wait. I hoped Sorcha would turn up in Zaghir eventually, but I had no idea when. It could be days. It could be decades. It could be hours. There was no way to tell. There was no way to send word to him either: ship pirates came to Zaghir rarely, and when they passed through, they always went north. Zaghir was a stopping place to gather supplies for those striking out to take Droma nomads as cargo. When they found what they wanted, they made for Essala where the ships ported. All I could do was wait, and the waiting was terrible.

I dreamed his death at night thousands of different ways. A fall from the crow's nest. Accidentally knocked over the railing of a ship. Purposefully knocked over the railing of a ship. Adrift in a lifeboat in the middle of the ocean. Knife wounds. Bad water. Garrote. Shipwreck. I woke in the mornings fatalistic and aimless. I woke late, always very late, and milked the yaks. The milk and butter and cheese I sold to the pirates. Fahmi or one of the others always managed to coax me into an endless game of djah by afternoon. Sometimes my mood improved, and sometimes it didn't. At night, by the light of a fire in the firestone the Kivvni had given me, in a Droma yurt planted permanently just outside the pirate outpost, I wrote down every song I'd ever heard Halaavi sing. I fell asleep every night alone, in an empty bed, wondering about vim. I missed vim with a ferocity; I still do. But it was fresh in those days, and I could not help but think perhaps I'd given up what I had with vim for nothing. I could not ignore the chance that Sorcha might never come searching for me.

If Vathorem had been there, he would have scolded me for ruminating too much. I kept a journal. I wrote about Dirva and Nuri. I wrote about the guilt I felt for letting them both down as falo. I wrote about my parents, who surely thought me dead. Dirva probably thought me dead, too; any sensible person would have drawn that conclusion. I wrote unsendable letters to them that were nothing but long, mournful apologies. I'd fall asleep, wake late the next morning, and milk my yaks. The seasons turned and turned and turned again. The yaks grew shaggy and warm, and I spun yarn from the downy undercoat they'd shed in the heat of the spring and summer. I had no loom, so I turned to knitting instead, and to do that, I had to whittle needles from discarded pieces of wood I won playing djah. The pirates chided me for doing woman's work. Fahmi sometimes came to my yurt for tea, which I brewed and poured for him. "Sorcha said you were his husband, which..." Fahmi touched his forehead and waved his hand away, palm towards me, a Chalir gesture of good faith and good fortune.

I am certain I blushed; I know I sat up very tall and glanced to where I'd hidden a knife within arm's reach. I did not trust these partially Qin men to do anything good with that particular piece of knowledge. I had hoped Sorcha would've kept that to himself. I don't know why I thought that he would.

"He said husband, but I look around, and it looks more like you're his wife. When he finds you, are you going to do the cooking and cleaning?"

"He's the better cook," I said. It was a thing that would have eaten at me back in the Empire, but years with the Droma had worn away my masculine pride.

Fahmi laughed. He fingered a thick jacket I'd knitted of undyed yak wool. "You'll do the mending, though, eh?"

"Did he tell you about Shayat?"

"Oh, sure."

"Her father is a tailor. She'll do the mending."

"Which makes you what?" Fahmi asked. "Just a pretty face?"

I read him just a little, just to see if there was anything to worry about behind those words. There was nothing there but curiosity, but it made me nervous nonetheless. I drank my tea. "I suppose so. Hand of djah?"

"Always," Fahmi said.

Winter came and went. Spring came and went. That next summer was brutal, and I lost one of the yaks. I wept. I was morose. I had grown very attached to that yak. I sold the saddle to Fahmi for a pittance. The Droma are a people who see omens everywhere, and I must have spent enough time with them to pick up the habit, because my dead yak struck me as a bad sign. Three weeks after the yak died, Sorcha rode into Zaghir. So much for omens.

He came at dawn. He rode the three hundred miles from Essala on that horse, as fast as he could. His horse was half-dead when he got to Zaghir, and none of the pirates were surprised he'd treated it like he had. They'd seen him do it before. He came to Zaghir in the early morning, just after dawn, and knocked on Fahmi's door for water and a place to sleep. Fahmi sent him to me.

He knocked on the door of my yurt. I woke slowly, disgruntled. I opened the door, bad-tempered, half-convinced it was my yak rubbing against the yurt to shake loose the last bits of her undercoat. And there he was. He stood before me as close to shy as I've ever seen him. He looked sheepish and boyish and uncertain. He grinned wide, though, and I could feel the happiness bursting from him. He was there, in one piece. He'd found me, and I'd found him. I threw myself at him, pulled him tight against me. I breathed in his smell and felt his hair against my cheek. I never wanted to let him go. Sorcha took my face in his hands and kissed me. It was soft at first, but grew hungry. Unbridled and desperate. I lost myself in half a second and came to again next to him in the yurt, naked, deliriously happy. He studied me when I came to; there was a trace of worry about him. "You all right? Was that all right?" he asked.

"I'm all right."

"I should've held back, though. Should've checked."

"I'm all right." I drew him over to me, and he tucked his face into my neck. He breathed a long sigh into me, and said my name, and I laughed at the pleasure of hearing my name in his voice again. "I love you," I said.

"I love you, too." He laughed and held me tighter. "Oh, how I've missed you."

I played with his hair. Bright red hair, now with streaks of silver at the temples. "I can't believe you looked for me."

"I did more than that. They locked me in jail for three months in Ma-Halad when I went searching for you. They thought I was an accomplice for your breakout." He laughed. "You deserted the Qin Army. That general, the Butcher? Oh, that got right under his skin."

"They threw you in jail?"

"Shayat got me out."

"She was with you?"

Sorcha pulled away just a little and propped himself up on an elbow. He ran a hand through his hair and sighed. "Right. Ah, you've missed so much. She and I, uh...me and Shayat, we're...we're, uh, hitched."

"Married?"

"Yeah. Got hitched in Iyairo. Easier travel to come get you. Helped to get me out of jail, too. And then, we...well, we stayed hitched. Been together all this time. Is that all right with you? It just happened, you know, me and her." He sighed and looked me in the eye. "When I say we're hitched, I mean I love her. A lot. Deep and true, like with you. That sit all right with you?"

I confess, it took me by surprise. "I...how long?"

"Well, like I said, we hitched pretty soon after the army took you. So, nine years. Getting on ten." He stole a glance at me, then turned his attention to the weave of the blanket we lay on. "As for the rest, me and her...well, you know, I won't speak for her. Just me. As for me, that didn't take all that long. Been sprung on her now for six, seven years." He looked back up at me, searching me. "But, you know, I been looking for you all this time. A dozen years I been looking for you, Ariah. I hope that says something about us."

"It does." I ran a hand down the length of his arm. I looked down the length of him and drank in the sight of him. "I was all right with it in Rabatha."

"Well, it was different in Rabatha," Sorcha said. "It was

sex and friendship, me and her, but it wasn't love. And sometimes, you know, the shift from one to the other can be tricky for other folks involved."

I lay close to him. I moved so we were pressed together, forehead to forehead, toe to toe. I had him there. In that moment, it felt like nothing could go wrong anywhere in the world. "I'm fine with it if she is."

"She is." He kissed me, and then stared at me hard.

"There's more."

"A bit, yeah," he said. He sighed. He drummed his fingers on my arm. I noticed, for the first time, the pirate tattoo on his neck and the fleet mark on his chest. With skin as dark as his, you can barely see them. With skin as black as Shayat's, you don't see them at all. You only know they're there if you run your fingers over her skin. I thought he was going to tell me he was a pirate. He didn't. "Me and Shayat, it's not just me and her. We got twins."

I leaned back away from him. "Twins?"

"Yeah. Little girls, just over four now. Mayim and Ishkallion. Got my hair, her eyes. Beauties."

"You have children?"

"Yeah."

I rolled onto my back. "She was always very careful with me." Sorcha didn't say anything. I found his hand and held it. "Tell me about your girls."

"Our girls. Yours, mine, and hers. Ah, they're...they're troublemakers, you can already tell. Sneaky little buggers. They've hidey-holes all over the house. They got their own language, just a private tongue 'tween the two of them. Smart as whips. Maya's the brave one. Ishie watches everything."

"You have children together. And a house."

"We do, yeah."

I burned with questions, and the questions bred doubt. Sorcha and Shayat had built a life in exile, a full life with toddlers and jobs and doors with hinges that needed to be oiled and windows that stuck in the frames. And I was in a yurt with a yak. It seemed such a perfect thing on its own, their life. Something fragile. A balance I wanted very much not to upset.

Sorcha curled up around me. I felt the slow rhythm of his heart against my chest. "Come home with me," he said.

"Are you sure?"

"I been searching high and low for you. I joined a pirate fleet to find you, and so did Shayat. Come home with me."

And I did.

HOME: AN EPILOGUE

SORCHA AND I made the trip to Essala as soon as his horse was ready. He rode his horse, and rather than sell my yak to Fahmi, I rode the poor thing all the way there. It was slow going, but the trip gave Sorcha and I time to talk, time to relearn each other, time to figure out what was still the same and what the years had changed. He loved my hair; it reminded him of his da's. He made me promise night after night not to cut it. I've kept that promise. A Nakash ship waited in the Essala harbor for us. We were in and out of the city in the blink of an eye. I barely had time to say goodbye to the yak, much less get captured by the Qin police.

The Nakash clipper was manned by a crew of full elves, many of whom were mostly silver. Some were born in Essala and had joined the ships rather that stand in a factory line. The captain of the ship was a friend of Sorcha's; they'd started as crew at the same time and helped each other up the ranks. She gave me passage on her ship without demanding affiliation and let us stay together in the vacant tether's cabin next to her own. I didn't realize at the time how generous this was of her. I was still wary of the pirates then, even though Sorcha was so thoroughly one of them, and I rarely left that cabin. He rarely left it, either. There's not much for a fleet recruiter to do on a ship full of fleet members. He told me about his time on the ships. He traced over the scars I'd gotten in the desert, and I told him about the Avolayla and the Allunga and the Kivvni. I told him about Halaavi. Laavi and I made as little sense to him as Sorcha, Shayat and I made to Laavi. Every conversation ended in sex. Sometimes I stayed shaper, and Sorcha wondered why. Sometimes I drank pirate rum and remembered everything. I was grateful for every second of it.

We ported in Alassah. The Nakash mostly sail the southern swells, and they do not have much of a hold that close to the coast. In Alassah, Sorcha and Shayat are the Nakash fleet, and they are respected. Sorcha led me along the maze of floating piers, which make up the docks. I wore a lefta and no shoes, a Droma transplant through and through. The island is narrow, long and winding like a sea snake, and the buildings are built tall along skinny streets. After years in the open grasslands, it felt horrifically claustrophobic. Sorcha held my hand in plain sight in the street, and no one batted an eye. He walked tall, nahsiyya at a glance, and was not remarkable. I trailed behind him, fighting an urge to sing a walking song to these arrogant buildings. I knew it was absurd, but it seemed rude to enter the city without one.

We turned down an alley, and then another. A pack of children chased a chicken our way, shoving by single file to get past us when it ran through Sorcha's legs. Sorcha frowned at them. "Hey, whose chicken is that?"

"Not yours, Fiddler, promise!" one of the children yelled back.

Sorcha shook his head. He counted his chickens later that night to make sure it wasn't one of his. His grip on my hand tightened as we walked down that narrow street. I felt his heartbeat ratchet up through his palm. We came to a bright blue house with a white door. In the window hung a length of muslin with the twined Nakash serpents twined painted in black. Sorcha fished a key out of his pocket and led me inside.

Shayat stood in a doorway across the room with her back to us. Her short, white hair shone in the light. Her hips had a regal sweep to them. I gripped Sorcha's hand tight. He smiled at me and laid his other hand against my arm. "Shayat," he said. It came out low and lilting, half song.

She started. Toys clattered in the next room. She turned, already smiling, and froze. "Ariah," she whispered.

"I found him."

Shayat slammed into me with enough force that I fell against the door. "You're here," she said, "you're really here."

"I'm here." She turned and looked at Sorcha. Her face in profile brought everything rushing back. "You look lovely, Shayat."

She turned to me again and laughed. She plucked at my hair. "You look ridiculous! This hair? The beard? What are you wearing? You look like you've wandered the wilds."

"I did."

"I know!" she said, grinning, her hands on my cheeks.

"You look it."

I kissed her. She let it be soft, gentle. She let it be sweet. For me, she let it be sweet. When we broke apart, she looked over at Sorcha. "Did you tell him?"

"I did. Of course I did."

"Do you want to meet them?" she asked. "The twins know all about you. We've told them all about you every day. They want to meet you."

"Yes," I said. "I want to meet them, too."

ABOUT THE AUTHOR

B R Sanders is a genderqueer writer who lives and works in Denver, CO, with their family and two cats. Outside of writing, B's two great loves are coffee and sleep. Alas, managing these loves is an eternal struggle. B has published another novel set in the Aerdh universe, *Resistance,* and has published several fantasy and science fiction short stories. B blogs about reading and writing fiction at brsanderswrites.com and tweets @B_R_Sanders.

Made in the USA
Columbia, SC
23 August 2017